THE
STORIES
OF
FRANK
O'CONNOR

THE

STORIES

OF

FRANK

O'CONNOR

HAMISH HAMILTON
LONDON

First Published in Great Britain, 1953
by Hamish Hamilton Ltd.,
90 Great Russell St., London, W.C.1

Second Impression December 1953
Third Impression December 1954
Fourth Impression March 1957
Fifth Impression May 1959
Sixth Impression November 1961
Seventh Impression May 1963
Eighth Impression November 1965
Ninth Impression December 1967
Tenth Impression January 1970

SBN 241 90623 7

Printed by Lowe and Brydone (Printers) Ltd., London, N.W.10

AUTHOR! AUTHOR!

When a writer is asked to gather his best stories for a book like this he feels a glow which he had felt only once before, when, say, the *Atlantic Monthly* published his first good story. It is not only that some devoted publisher feels he has justified some of the energy and talent that has gone into the prosaic business of making him known. It is something for which he has secretly always longed—the Perfect Book; the book he does not feel he really must apologize for before giving it to a friend; the book which sums up all that he has ever wished to be or do from the days when he was a penniless dreamy youngster wandering the streets of a provincial town.

It is for that reason I have included nothing from my first book, *Guests of the Nation*. It is for that reason I have included five new stories, "My Œdipus Complex," "The Pretender," "My Da," "First Love," and "Freedom." Many of the other stories I have rewritten, in part or entirely. In one's Perfect Book could one include anything that was less than perfect?

Besides, some of the stories had already been rewritten twenty, thirty, even fifty times. Not all, of course. As my friend, James Bridie, used to say: "There are two sorts of plays: the sort that takes three days and the sort that takes ten years." "My Œdipus Complex" and "Bridal Night" are more or less what they were when first they came into my head; it is the stories which are not the same that justify one in accepting these bonuses of the Muse. "In the Train" was in type when the drunken man who had just parted his best friend, Michael O'Leary, opened the compartment door, and the editor, my oldest literary friend, L. A. G. Strong, scrapped the type to let him in. "First Confession" has appeared in three quite different forms from the first day when *Lovat Dickson's Magazine* printed it, so I may now hope its ghost has ceased to haunt me. But "The Luceys" is a story I have struggled savagely with over twenty years, and even now I am not certain that this tussle is our last.

Our last? The very words fill me with gloom. Great cracks suddenly begin to appear across the smooth façade of my proofs. Those new stories, for instance? "The Pretender" seems to me as good as it seemed when I wrote it down in a hotel room in Avignon on Christmas Day, but "My Da," which had, I swear, been written fifty times before I sent off the first halting draft to *The New Yorker*, seems to say nothing—nothing at all—of the passion with which I wrote it, and my Perfect Book begins to dwindle to the proportions of Just Another Book. . . . *Encore un livre, O nostalgie!*

> *Gods and men, we are all deluded thus,*
> *It breaks within us, and then we bleed.*

FRANK O'CONNOR

NOTE. Of the stories in this book, the following were printed—some of them in somewhat different form—in earlier collections of Frank O'Connor's stories : "Peasants," "In the Train," "The Majesty of the Law" in *Bones of Contention*; "Old Fellows," "The Long Road to Ummera," "The Bridal Night," "Song without Words," "Uprooted," "The Miser," "The House That Johnny Built," "The Cheapjack" (as "The New Teacher"), and "The Luceys" in *Crab Apple Jelly*; "News for the Church," "Don Juan's Temptation," "The Babes in the Wood," and "The Holy Door" in *The Common Chord*; "The Drunkard" "The Idealist," "First Confession," "Legal Aid," and "The Masculine Principle" in *Traveller's Samples*.

IN MEMORY OF
MARY O'DONOVAN
1865-1952

CONTENTS

CONTENTS

THE
STORIES
OF
FRANK
O'CONNOR

MY ŒDIPUS COMPLEX

FATHER was in the army all through the war—the first war, I mean—so, up to the age of five, I never saw much of him, and what I saw did not worry me. Sometimes I woke and there was a big figure in khaki peering down at me in the candlelight. Sometimes in the early morning I heard the slamming of the front door and the clatter of nailed boots down the cobbles of the lane. These were Father's entrances and exits. Like Santa Claus he came and went mysteriously.

In fact, I rather liked his visits, though it was an uncomfortable squeeze between Mother and him when I got into the big bed in the early morning. He smoked, which gave him a pleasant musty smell, and shaved, an operation of astounding interest. Each time he left a trail of souvenirs—model tanks and Gurkha knives with handles made of bullet cases, and German helmets and cap badges and button-sticks, and all sorts of military equipment—carefully stowed away in a long box on top of the wardrobe, in case they ever came in handy. There was a bit of the magpie about Father; he expected everything to come in handy. When his back was turned, Mother let me get a chair and rummage through his treasures. She didn't seem to think so highly of them as he did.

The war was the most peaceful period of my life. The window of my attic faced southeast. My mother had curtained it, but that had small effect. I always woke with the first light and, with all the responsibilities of the previous day melted, feeling myself rather like the sun, ready to illumine and rejoice. Life never

3

seemed so simple and clear and full of possibilities as then. I put my feet out from under the clothes—I called them Mrs. Left and Mrs. Right—and invented dramatic situations for them in which they discussed the problems of the day. At least Mrs. Right did; she was very demonstrative, but I hadn't the same control of Mrs. Left, so she mostly contented herself with nodding agreement.

They discussed what Mother and I should do during the day, what Santa Claus should give a fellow for Christmas, and what steps should be taken to brighten the home. There was that little matter of the baby, for instance. Mother and I could never agree about that. Ours was the only house in the terrace without a new baby, and Mother said we couldn't afford one till Father came back from the war because they cost seventeen and six. That showed how simple she was. The Geneys up the road had a baby, and everyone knew they couldn't afford seventeen and six. It was probably a cheap baby, and Mother wanted something really good, but I felt she was too exclusive. The Geneys' baby would have done us fine.

Having settled my plans for the day, I got up, put a chair under the attic window, and lifted the frame high enough to stick out my head. The window overlooked the front gardens of the terrace behind ours, and beyond these it looked over a deep valley to the tall, red-brick houses terraced up the opposite hillside, which were all still in shadow, while those at our side of the valley were all lit up, though with long strange shadows that made them seem unfamiliar; rigid and painted.

After that I went into Mother's room and climbed into the big bed. She woke and I began to tell her of my schemes. By this time, though I never seem to have noticed it, I was petrified in my nightshirt, and I thawed as I talked until, the last frost melted, I fell asleep beside her and woke again only when I heard her below in the kitchen, making the breakfast.

After breakfast we went into town; heard Mass at St. Augustine's and said a prayer for Father, and did the shopping. If the afternoon was fine we either went for a walk in the country or a visit to Mother's great friend in the convent, Mother St. Dominic. Mother had them all praying for Father, and every night, going to bed, I asked God to send him back safe from the war to us. Little, indeed, did I know what I was praying for!

One morning, I got into the big bed, and there, sure enough, was Father in his usual Santa Claus manner, but later, instead of uniform, he put on his best blue suit, and Mother was as pleased as anything. I saw nothing to be pleased about, because, out of uniform, Father was altogether less interesting, but she only beamed, and explained that our prayers had been answered, and off we went to Mass to thank God for having brought Father safely home.

The irony of it! That very day when he came in to dinner he took off his boots and put on his slippers, donned the dirty old cap he wore about the house to save him from colds, crossed his legs, and began to talk gravely to Mother, who looked anxious. Naturally, I disliked her looking anxious, because it destroyed her good looks, so I interrupted him.

"Just a moment, Larry!" she said gently.

This was only what she said when we had boring visitors, so I attached no importance to it and went on talking.

"Do be quiet, Larry!" she said impatiently. "Don't you hear me talking to Daddy?"

This was the first time I had heard those ominous words, "talking to Daddy," and I couldn't help feeling that if this was how God answered prayers, he couldn't listen to them very attentively.

"Why are you talking to Daddy?" I asked with as great a show of indifference as I could muster.

"Because Daddy and I have business to discuss. Now, don't interrupt again!"

In the afternoon, at Mother's request, Father took me for a walk. This time we went into town instead of out the country, and I thought at first, in my usual optimistic way, that it might be an improvement. It was nothing of the sort. Father and I had quite different notions of a walk in town. He had no proper interest in trams, ships, and horses, and the only thing that seemed to divert him was talking to fellows as old as himself. When I wanted to stop he simply went on, dragging me behind him by the hand; when he wanted to stop I had no alternative but to do the same. I noticed that it seemed to be a sign that he wanted to stop for a long time whenever he leaned against a wall. The second time I saw him do it I got wild. He seemed to be settling himself forever. I pulled him by the coat and trousers, but, unlike Mother who, if you were too persistent, got into a wax and said: "Larry, if you don't behave yourself, I'll give you a good slap," Father had an extraordinary capacity for amiable inattention. I sized him up and wondered would I cry, but he seemed to be too remote to be annoyed even by that. Really, it was like going for a walk with a mountain! He either ignored the wrenching and pummeling entirely, or else glanced down with a grin of amusement from his peak. I had never met anyone so absorbed in himself as he seemed.

At teatime, "talking to Daddy" began again, complicated this time by the fact that he had an evening paper, and every few minutes he put it down and told Mother something new out of it. I felt this was foul play. Man for man, I was prepared to compete with him any time for Mother's attention, but when he had it all made up for him by other people it left me no chance. Several times I tried to change the subject without success.

"You must be quiet while Daddy is reading, Larry," Mother said impatiently.

It was clear that she either genuinely liked talking to Father better than talking to me, or else that he had some terrible hold on her which made her afraid to admit the truth.

"Mummy," I said that night when she was tucking me up, "do you think if I prayed hard God would send Daddy back to the war?"

She seemed to think about that for a moment.

"No, dear," she said with a smile. "I don't think he would."

"Why wouldn't he, Mummy?"

"Because there isn't a war any longer, dear."

"But, Mummy, couldn't God make another war, if He liked?"

"He wouldn't like to, dear. It's not God who makes wars, but bad people."

"Oh!" I said.

I was disappointed about that. I began to think that God wasn't quite what he was cracked up to be.

Next morning I woke at my usual hour, feeling like a bottle of champagne. I put out my feet and invented a long conversation in which Mrs. Right talked of the trouble she had with her own father till she put him in the Home. I didn't quite know what the Home was but it sounded the right place for Father. Then I got my chair and stuck my head out of the attic window. Dawn was just breaking, with a guilty air that made me feel I had caught it in the act. My head bursting with stories and schemes, I stumbled in next door, and in the half-darkness scrambled into the big bed. There was no room at Mother's side so I had to get between her and Father. For the time being I had forgotten about him, and for several minutes I sat bolt upright, racking my brains to know what I could do with him. He was taking up more than his fair share of the bed, and I couldn't get comfortable, so I gave him several kicks that made him grunt and stretch. He made room all right, though. Mother waked and felt for me. I settled back comfortably in the warmth of the bed with my thumb in my mouth.

"Mummy!" I hummed, loudly and contentedly.

"Sssh! dear," she whispered. "Don't wake Daddy!"

This was a new development, which threatened to be even more serious than "talking to Daddy." Life without my early-morning conferences was unthinkable.

"Why?" I asked severely.

"Because poor Daddy is tired."

This seemed to me a quite inadequate reason, and I was sickened by the sentimentality of her "poor Daddy." I never liked that sort of gush; it always struck me as insincere.

"Oh!" I said lightly. Then in my most winning tone: "Do you know where I want to go with you today, Mummy?"

"No, dear," she sighed.

"I want to go down the Glen and fish for thornybacks with my new net, and then I want to go out to the Fox and Hounds, and—"

"Don't-wake-Daddy!" she hissed angrily, clapping her hand across my mouth.

But it was too late. He was awake, or nearly so. He grunted

and reached for the matches. Then he stared incredulously at his watch.

"Like a cup of tea, dear?" asked Mother in a meek, hushed voice I had never heard her use before. It sounded almost as though she were afraid.

"Tea?" he exclaimed indignantly. "Do you know what the time is?"

"And after that I want to go up the Rathcooney Road," I said loudly, afraid I'd forget something in all those interruptions.

"Go to sleep at once, Larry!" she said sharply.

I began to snivel. I couldn't concentrate, the way that pair went on, and smothering my early-morning schemes was like burying a family from the cradle.

Father said nothing, but lit his pipe and sucked it, looking out into the shadows without minding Mother or me. I knew he was mad. Every time I made a remark Mother hushed me irritably. I was mortified. I felt it wasn't fair; there was even something sinister in it. Every time I had pointed out to her the waste of making two beds when we could both sleep in one, she had told me it was healthier like that, and now here was this man, this stranger, sleeping with her without the least regard for her health!

He got up early and made tea, but though he brought Mother a cup he brought none for me.

"Mummy," I shouted, "I want a cup of tea, too."

"Yes, dear," she said patiently. "You can drink from Mummy's saucer."

That settled it. Either Father or I would have to leave the house. I didn't want to drink from Mother's saucer; I wanted to be treated as an equal in my own home, so, just to spite her, I drank it all and left none for her. She took that quietly, too.

But that night when she was putting me to bed she said gently:

"Larry, I want you to promise me something."

"What is it?" I asked.

"Not to come in and disturb poor Daddy in the morning. Promise?"

"Poor Daddy" again! I was becoming suspicious of everything involving that quite impossible man.

"Why?" I asked.

"Because poor Daddy is worried and tired and he doesn't sleep well."

"Why doesn't he, Mummy?"

"Well, you know, don't you, that while he was at the war Mummy got the pennies from the Post Office?"

"From Miss MacCarthy?"

"That's right. But now, you see, Miss MacCarthy hasn't any more pennies, so Daddy must go out and find us some. You know what would happen if he couldn't?"

"No," I said, "tell us."

"Well, I think we might have to go out and beg for them like the poor old woman on Fridays. We wouldn't like that, would we?"

"No," I agreed. "We wouldn't."

"So you'll promise not to come in and wake him?"

"Promise."

Mind you, I meant that. I knew pennies were a serious matter, and I was all against having to go out and beg like the old woman on Fridays. Mother laid out all my toys in a complete ring round the bed so that, whatever way I got out, I was bound to fall over one of them.

When I woke I remembered my promise all right. I got up and sat on the floor and played—for hours, it seemed to me. Then I got my chair and looked out the attic window for more hours. I wished it was time for Father to wake; I wished someone would make me a cup of tea. I didn't feel in the least like the sun; instead, I was bored and so very, very cold! I simply longed for the warmth and depth of the big featherbed.

At last I could stand it no longer. I went into the next room. As there was still no room at Mother's side I climbed over her and she woke with a start.

"Larry," she whispered, gripping my arm very tightly, "what did you promise?"

"But I did, Mummy," I wailed, caught in the very act. "I was quiet for ever so long."

"Oh, dear, and you're perished!" she said sadly, feeling me all over. "Now, if I let you stay will you promise not to talk?"

"But I want to talk, Mummy," I wailed.

"That has nothing to do with it," she said with a firmness that was new to me. "Daddy wants to sleep. Now, do you understand that?"

I understood it only too well. I wanted to talk, he wanted to sleep—whose house was it, anyway?

"Mummy," I said with equal firmness, "I think it would be healthier for Daddy to sleep in his own bed."

That seemed to stagger her, because she said nothing for a while.

"Now, once for all," she went on, "you're to be perfectly quiet or go back to your own bed. Which is it to be?"

The injustice of it got me down. I had convicted her out of her own mouth of inconsistency and unreasonableness, and she hadn't even attempted to reply. Full of spite, I gave Father a kick, which she didn't notice but which made him grunt and open his eyes in alarm.

"What time is it?" he asked in a panic-stricken voice, not looking at Mother but at the door, as if he saw someone there.

"It's early yet," she replied soothingly. "It's only the child. Go to sleep again. . . . Now, Larry," she added, getting out of bed, "you've wakened Daddy and you must go back."

This time, for all her quiet air, I knew she meant it, and knew that my principal rights and privileges were as good as lost unless I asserted them at once. As she lifted me, I gave a screech, enough to wake the dead, not to mind Father. He groaned.

"That damn child! Doesn't he ever sleep?"

"It's only a habit, dear," she said quietly, though I could see she was vexed.

"Well, it's time he got out of it," shouted Father, beginning to heave in the bed. He suddenly gathered all the bedclothes about him, turned to the wall, and then looked back over his shoulder with nothing showing only two small, spiteful, dark eyes. The man looked very wicked.

To open the bedroom door, Mother had to let me down, and I broke free and dashed for the farthest corner, screeching. Father sat bolt upright in bed.

"Shut up, you little puppy!" he said in a choking voice.

I was so astonished that I stopped screeching. Never, never had anyone spoken to me in that tone before. I looked at him incredulously and saw his face convulsed with rage. It was only then that I fully realized how God had codded me, listening to my prayers for the safe return of this monster.

"Shut up, you!" I bawled, beside myself.

"What's that you said?" shouted Father, making a wild leap out of the bed.

"Mick, Mick!" cried Mother. "Don't you see the child isn't used to you?"

"I see he's better fed than taught," snarled Father, waving his arms wildly. "He wants his bottom smacked."

All his previous shouting was as nothing to these obscene words referring to my person. They really made my blood boil.

"Smack your own!" I screamed hysterically. "Smack your own! Shut up! Shut up!"

At this he lost his patience and let fly at me. He did it with the lack of conviction you'd expect of a man under Mother's horrified eyes, and it ended up as a mere tap, but the sheer indignity of being struck at all by a stranger, a total stranger who had cajoled his way back from the war into our big bed as a result of my innocent intercession, made me completely dotty. I shrieked and shrieked, and danced in my bare feet, and Father, looking awkward and hairy in nothing but a short grey army shirt, glared down at me like a mountain out for murder. I think it must have been then that I realized he was jealous too. And there stood Mother in her nightdress, looking as if her heart was broken between us. I hoped she felt as she looked. It seemed to me that she deserved it all.

From that morning out my life was a hell. Father and I were enemies, open and avowed. We conducted a series of skirmishes against one another, he trying to steal my time with Mother and I his. When she was sitting on my bed, telling me a story, he took to looking for some pair of old boots which he alleged he had left behind him at the beginning of the war. While he talked to Mother I played loudly with my toys to show my total lack of concern. He created a terrible scene one evening when he came in from work and found me at his box, playing with his regimental badges, Gurkha knives and button-sticks. Mother got up and took the box from me.

"You mustn't play with Daddy's toys unless he lets you, Larry," she said severely. "Daddy doesn't play with yours."

For some reason Father looked at her as if she had struck him and then turned away with a scowl.

"Those are not toys," he growled, taking down the box again to see had I lifted anything. "Some of those curios are very rare and valuable."

But as time went on I saw more and more how he managed to alienate Mother and me. What made it worse was that I couldn't grasp his method or see what attraction he had for Mother. In every possible way he was less winning than I. He had a common accent and made noises at his tea. I thought for a while that it might be the newspapers she was interested in, so I made up bits of news of my own to read to her. Then I thought it might be the smoking, which I personally thought attractive, and took his pipes and went round the house dribbling into them till he caught me. I even made noises at my tea, but Mother only told me I was disgusting. It all seemed to hinge round that unhealthy habit of sleeping together, so I made a point of dropping into their bedroom and nosing round, talking to myself, so that they wouldn't know I was watching them, but they were never up to anything that I could see. In the end it beat me. It seemed to depend on being grown-up and giving people rings, and I realized I'd have to wait.

But at the same time I wanted him to see that I was only waiting, not giving up the fight. One evening when he was being particularly obnoxious, chattering away well above my head, I let him have it.

"Mummy," I said, "do you know what I'm going to do when I grow up?"

"No, dear," she replied. "What?"

"I'm going to marry you," I said quietly.

Father gave a great guffaw out of him, but he didn't take me in. I knew it must only be pretence. And Mother, in spite of everything, was pleased. I felt she was probably relieved to know that one day Father's hold on her would be broken.

"Won't that be nice?" she said with a smile.

"It'll be very nice," I said confidently. "Because we're going to have lots and lots of babies."

"That's right, dear," she said placidly. "I think we'll have one soon, and then you'll have plenty of company."

I was no end pleased about that because it showed that in spite of the way she gave in to Father she still considered my wishes. Besides, it would put the Geneys in their place.

It didn't turn out like that, though. To begin with, she was very preoccupied—I supposed about where she would get the seventeen and six—and though Father took to staying out late in the evenings it did me no particular good. She stopped taking me for walks, became as touchy as blazes, and smacked me for nothing at all. Sometimes I wished I'd never mentioned the confounded baby—I seemed to have a genius for bringing calamity on myself.

And calamity it was! Sonny arrived in the most appalling hullabaloo—even that much he couldn't do without a fuss—and from the first moment I disliked him. He was a difficult child—so far as I was concerned he was always difficult—and demanded far too much attention. Mother was simply silly about him, and couldn't see when he was only showing off. As company he was worse than useless. He slept all day, and I had to go round the house on tiptoe to avoid waking him. It wasn't any longer a question of not waking Father. The slogan now was "Don't-wake-Sonny!" I couldn't understand why the child wouldn't sleep at the proper time, so whenever Mother's back was turned I woke him. Sometimes to keep him awake I pinched him as well. Mother caught me at it one day and gave me a most unmerciful flaking.

One evening, when Father was coming in from work, I was playing trains in the front garden. I let on not to notice him; instead, I pretended to be talking to myself, and said in a loud voice: "If another bloody baby comes into this house, I'm going out."

Father stopped dead and looked at me over his shoulder.

"What's that you said?" he asked sternly.

"I was only talking to myself," I replied, trying to conceal my panic. "It's private."

He turned and went in without a word. Mind you, I intended it as a solemn warning, but its effect was quite different. Father started being quite nice to me. I could understand that, of course. Mother was quite sickening about Sonny. Even at mealtimes she'd get up and gawk at him in the cradle with an idiotic smile, and tell Father to do the same. He was always polite about it, but he looked so puzzled you could see he didn't know what she was talking about. He complained of the way Sonny cried at night, but she only got cross and said that Sonny never cried except when there was something up with him—which was a flaming lie, because Sonny never had anything up with him, and only cried for attention. It was really painful to see how simple-minded she was. Father wasn't attractive, but he had a fine intelligence. He saw through Sonny, and now he knew that I saw through him as well.

One night I woke with a start. There was someone beside me in the bed. For one wild moment I felt sure it must be Mother, having come to her senses and left Father for good, but then I heard Sonny in convulsions in the next room, and Mother saying: "There! There! There!" and I knew it wasn't she. It was Father. He was lying beside me, wide awake, breathing hard and apparently as mad as hell.

After a while it came to me what he was mad about. It was his turn now. After turning me out of the big bed, he had been turned out himself. Mother had no consideration now for anyone but that poisonous pup, Sonny. I couldn't help feeling sorry for Father. I had been through it all myself, and even at that age I was magnanimous. I began to stroke him down and say: "There! There!" He wasn't exactly responsive.

"Aren't you asleep either?" he snarled.

"Ah, come on and put your arm around us, can't you?" I said, and he did, in a sort of way. Gingerly, I suppose, is how you'd describe it. He was very bony but better than nothing.

At Christmas he went out of his way to buy me a really nice model railway.

OLD FELLOWS

IF THERE was one thing I could not stand as a kid it was being taken out for the day by Father. My mature view is that he couldn't stand it either but did it to keep Mother quiet. Mother did it to keep him out of harm's way; I was supposed to act as a brake on him.

He always took me to the same place—Crosshaven—on the paddle-boat. He raved about Cork Harbour, its wonderful scenery and sea air. I was never one for scenery myself, and as for air, a little went a long way with me. With a man as unobservant as Father, buttons like mine, and strange boats and public-houses which I couldn't find my way about, I lived in mortal fear of an accident.

One day in particular is always in my memory; a Sunday morning with the bells ringing for Mass and the usual scramble on to get Father out of the house. He was standing before the mirrow which hung over the mantelpiece, dragging madly at his dickey, and Mother on a low stool in front of him, trying to fasten the studs.

"Ah, go easy!" she said impatiently. "Go easy, can't you?"

Father couldn't go easy. He lowered his head all right, but he shivered and reared like a bucking bronco.

"God Almighty give me patience!" he hissed between his teeth. "Give me patience, sweet God, before I tear the bloody house down!"

It was never what you'd call a good beginning to the day. And to see him later, going down to Pope's Quay to Mass, you'd swear butter wouldn't melt in the old devil's mouth.

After Mass, as we were standing on the quay, J. J. came along. J. J. and father were lifelong friends. He was a melancholy, reedy man with a long sallow face and big hollows under his cheeks. Whenever he was thinking deeply he sucked in the cheeks till his face caved in suddenly like a sandpit. We sauntered down a side street from the quay. I knew well where we were bound for, but with the incurable optimism of childhood I hoped again that this time we might be going somewhere else. We weren't. J. J. stopped by a door at a streetcorner and knocked softly. He had one ear cocked to the door and the other eye cocked at Father. A voice spoke within, a soft voice as in a confessional, and J. J. bowed his head reverently to the keyhole and whispered something back. Father raised his head with a smile and held up two fingers.

"Two minutes now!" he said, and then took a penny from his trousers pocket.

"There's a penny for you," he said benignly. "Mind now and be a good boy."

The door opened and shut almost silently behind Father and J. J. I stood and looked round. The streets were almost deserted, and so silent you could hear the footsteps of people you couldn't see in the laneways high up the hill. The only living thing near me was a girl standing a little up from the streetcorner. She was wearing a frilly white hat and a white satiny dress. As it happened, I was wearing a sailor suit for the first time that day. It gave me a slightly raffish feeling. I went up to where she was standing, partly to see what she was looking at, partly to study her closer. She was a beautiful child—upon my word, a beautiful child! And, whatever way it happened, I smiled at her. Mind you, I didn't mean any harm. It was pure good-nature. To this day, that is the sort I am, wanting to be friends with everybody.

The little girl looked at me. She looked at me for a long time; long enough at any rate for the smile to wither off me, and then drew herself up with her head in the air and walked past me down the pavement. Looking back on it, I suppose she was upset because her own father was inside the pub, and a thing like that would mean more to a girl than a boy. But it wasn't only that. By nature she was haughty and cold. It was the first time I had come face to face with the heartlessness of real beauty, and her contemptuous stare knocked me flat. I was a sensitive child. I didn't know where to look, and I wished myself back at home with my mother.

After about ten minutes Father came out with his face all shiny and I ran up to him and took his hand. Unobservant and all as he was, he must have noticed I was upset, because he was suddenly full of palaver about the grand day we were going to have by the seaside. Of course it was all propaganda, because before we reached the boat at all, he had another call.

"Two minutes now!" he said with his two fingers raised and a roguish grin on his face. "Definitely not more than two minutes! Be a good boy!"

At last we did get aboard the paddle-steamer, and, as we moved off down the river, people stood and waved from the road at Tivoli and from under the trees on the Marina walk, while the band played on deck. It was quite exciting, really. And then, all of a sudden, I saw coming up the deck towards us the little girl who had snubbed me outside the public-house. Her father was along with her, a small, fat, red-faced man with a big black beard and a bowler hat. He walked with a sort of roll, and under his arm he carried a model ship with masts and sails—a really superior-looking ship which took my eye at once.

When my father saw him he gave a loud triumphant crow.

"We'll meet in heaven," he said.

"I'd be surprised," said the fat man none too pleasantly.

"Back to the old ship, I see?" said Father, giving J. J. a wink to show he could now expect some sport.

"What exactly do you mean by that?" asked the fat man, giving his moustache a twirl.

"My goodness," said Father, letting on to be surprised, "didn't you tell me 'twas aboard the paddle-boat in Cork Harbour you did your sailoring? Didn't you tell me yourself about the terrible storm that nearly wrecked ye between Aghada and Queenstown?"

"If I mentioned such a thing," said the fat man, "it was only in dread you mightn't have heard of any other place. You were never in Odessa, I suppose?"

"I had a cousin there," said Father gravely. "Cold, I believe. He was telling me they had to chop off the drinks with a hatchet."

"You hadn't a cousin in Valparaiso, by any chance?"

"Well, no, now," said Father regretfully, "that cousin died young of a Maltese fever he contracted while he was with Nansen at the North Pole."

"Maltese fever!" snorted the fat man. "I suppose you couldn't even tell me where Malta is."

By this time there was no holding the pair of them. The fat man was a sailor, and whatever the reason was, my father couldn't see a sailor without wanting to be at his throat. They went into the saloon, and all the way down the river they never as much as stuck their noses out. When I looked in, half the bar had already joined in the argument, some in favour of going to sea and some, like Father, dead against it.

"It broadens the mind, I tell you," said the sailor. "Sailors see the world."

"Do they, indeed?" said Father sarcastically.

"Malta," said the sailor. "You were talking about Malta. Now, there's a beautiful place. The heat of the day drives off the cold of the night."

"Do it?" asked Father in a far-away voice, gazing out the door as though he expected someone to walk in. "Anything else?"

"San Francisco," said the sailor dreamily, "and the scent of the orange blossoms in the moonlight."

"Anything else?" Father asked remorselessly. He was like a priest in the confessional.

"As much more as you fancy," said the sailor.

"But do they see what's under their very noses?" asked Father, rising with his eyes aglow. "Do they see their own country? Do they see that river outside that people come thousands of miles to see? What old nonsense you have!"

I looked round and saw the little girl at my elbow.

"They're at it still," I said.

" 'Tis all your fault," she said coldly.

"How is it my fault?"

"You and your old fellow," she said contemptuously. "Ye have my day ruined on me."

And away she walked again with her head in the air.

I didn't see her again until we landed, and by that time her father and mine had to be separated. They were on to politics, and J. J. thought it safer to get Father away. Father was all for William O'Brien, and he got very savage when he was contradicted. I watched the sailor and the little girl go off along the sea-road while we went in the opposite direction. Father was still simmering about things the sailor had said in favour of John Redmond, a politician he couldn't like. He suddenly stopped and raised his fists in the air.

"I declare to my God if there's one class of men I can't stand, 'tis sailors," he said.

"They're all old blow," agreed J. J. peaceably.

"I wouldn't mind the blooming blow," Father said venomously. " 'Tis all the lies they tell you. San Francisco? That fellow was never near San Francisco. Now, I'm going back," he went on, beginning to stamp from one foot to the other, "and *I'm* going to tell *him* a few lies for a change."

"I wouldn't be bothered," said J. J., and, leaning his head over Father's shoulder, he began to whisper in his ear the way you'd whisper to a restive young horse, and with the same sort of result, for Father gradually ceased his stamping and rearing and looked doubtfully at J. J. out of the corner of his eye. A moment later up went the two fingers.

"Two minutes," he said with a smile that was only put on. "Not more. Be a good boy now."

He slipped me another copper and I sat on the sea-wall, watching the crowds and wondering if we'd ever get out of the village that day. Beyond the village were the cliffs, and pathways wound over them, in and out of groups of thatched cottages. The band would be playing up there, and people would be dancing. There would be stalls for lemonade and sweets. If only I could get up there I should at least have something to look at. My heart gave a jump and then sank. I saw, coming through the crowd, the sailor and the little girl. She was swinging out of his arm, and in her own free arm she carried the model ship. They stopped before the pub.

"Daddy," I heard her say in that precise, ladylike little voice of hers, "you promised to sail my boat for me."

"In one second now," said her father. "I have a certain thing to say to a man in here."

Then in with him to the pub. The little girl had tears in her eyes. I was sorry for her—that's the sort I am, very soft-hearted.

"All right," I said. "I'll go in and try to get my da out."

But when I went in I saw it was no good. Her father was sitting on the windowsill, and behind him the blue bay and the white yachts showed like a newspaper photo through the mesh of the window screen. Father was walking up and down, his head bent, like a caged tiger.

"Capwell?" I heard him say in a low voice.

"Capwell I said," replied the sailor.

"Evergreen?" said Father.

"Evergreen," nodded the sailor.

"The oldest stock in Cork, you said?" whispered Father.

"Fifteenth century," said the sailor.

Father looked at him with a gathering smile as though he thought it was all one of the sailor's jokes. Then he shook his head good-humouredly, and walked to the other side of the bar as though to say it was too much for him. Madness had outranged itself.

"The north side of the city," said the sailor, growing heated at such disbelief, "what is it only foreigners? People that came in from beyond the lamps a generation ago. Tramps and fiddlers and pipers."

"They had the intellect," Father said quietly.

"Intellect?" exclaimed the sailor. "The north side?"

" 'Twas always given up to them," said Father firmly.

"That's the first I heard of it," said the sailor.

Father began to scribble with a couple of fingers on the palm of his left hand.

"Now," he said gravely, "I'll give you fair odds. I'll go back a hundred years with you. Tell me the name of a single outstanding man—now I said an *outstanding* man, mind you—that was born on the south side of the city in that time."

"Daddy," I said, pulling him by the coattails, "you promised to take me up the cliffs."

"In two minutes now," he replied with a brief laugh, and, almost by second nature, handed me another penny.

That was four I had. J. J., a thoughtful poor soul, followed me out with two bottles of lemonade and a couple of packets of biscuits. The little girl and I ate and drank, sitting on the low wall outside the pub. Then we went down to the water's edge and tried to sail the boat, but, whatever was wrong with it, it would only float on its side; its sails got wringing wet, and we left them to dry while we listened to the organ of the merry-go-rounds from the other side of the bay.

It wasn't until late afternoon that the sailor and Father came out, and by this time there seemed to be no more than the breath of life between them. It was astonishing to me how friendly they were. Father had the sailor by the lapel of the jacket and was begging him to wait for the boat, but the sailor explained that he had given his solemn word to his wife to have the little girl home in time for bed and insisted that he'd have to go by the train. After he had departed, my father threw a long, lingering look at the sky, and seeing it was so late, slipped me another penny and retired to the bar till the siren went for the boat. They were hauling up the gangway when J. J. got him down.

It was late when we landed, and the full moon was riding over the river; a lovely, nippy September night; but I was tired and hungry and blown up with wind. We went up the hill in the moonlight and every few yards Father stopped to lay down the law. By this time he was ready to argue with anyone about anything. We came to the cathedral, and there were three old women sitting on the steps gossiping, their black shawls trailing like shadows on the pavement. It made me sick for home, a cup of hot cocoa, and my own warm bed.

Then suddenly under a gas lamp at the streetcorner I saw a small figure in white. It was like an apparition. I was struck with terror and despair. I don't know if J. J. saw the same thing, but all at once he began to direct Father's attention to the cathedral and away from the figure in white.

"That's a beautiful tower," he said in a husky voice.

Father stopped and screwed up his eyes to study it.

"What's beautiful about it?" he asked. "I don't see anything very remarkable about that."

"Ah, 'tis, man," said J. J. reverently. "That's a great tower."

"Now, I'm not much in favour of towers," said Father, tossing his head cantankerously. "I don't see what use are towers. I'd sooner a nice plain limestone front with pillars like the Sand Quay."

At the time I wasn't very concerned about the merits of Gothic and Renaissance, so I tried to help J. J. by tugging Father's hand. It was no good. One glance round and his eye took in the white figure at the other side of the road. He chuckled ominously and put his hand over his eyes, like a sailor on deck.

"Hard aport, mate!" he said. "What do I see on my starboard bow?"

"Ah, nothing," said J. J.

"Nothing?" echoed Father joyously. "What sort of lookout man are you? . . . Ahoy, shipmate!" he bawled across the road. "Didn't your old skipper go home yet?"

"He did not," cried the little girl—it was she of course—"and let you leave him alone!"

"The thundering ruffian!" said my father in delight, and away he went across the road. "What do he mean? A sailorman from the south side, drinking in my diocese! I'll have him ejected."

"Daddy," I wailed, with my heart in my boots. "Come home, can't you?"

"Two minutes," he said with a chuckle, and handed me another copper, the sixth.

The little girl was frantic. She scrawled and beat him about the legs with her fist, but he only laughed at her, and when the door opened he forced his way in with a shout: "Anyone here from Valparaiso?"

J. J. sucked in his cheeks till he looked like a skeleton in the moonlight, and then nodded sadly and followed Father in. The door was bolted behind them and the little girl and I were left together on the pavement. The three old women on the cathedral steps got up and shuffled off down a cobbled laneway. The pair of us sat on the curb and snivelled.

"What bad luck was on me this morning to meet you?" said the little girl.

" 'Twas on me the bad luck was," I said, "and your old fellow keeping my old fellow out."

"Your old fellow is only a common labouring man," said the little girl contemptuously, "and my daddy says he's ignorant and conceited."

"And your old fellow is only a sailor," I retorted indignantly, "and my father says all sailors are liars."

"How dare you!" she said. "My daddy is not a liar, and I hope he keeps your old fellow inside all night, just to piece you out for your impudence."

"I don't care," I said with mock bravado. "I can go home when I like and you can't—bah!"

"You'll have to wait till your father comes out."

"I needn't. I can go home myself."

"I dare you! You and your sailor suit!"

I could have let it pass but for her gibe at my suit; but that insult had to be avenged. I got up and took a few steps, just to show her. I thought she'd be afraid to stay behind alone, but she wasn't. She was too bitter. Of course, I had no intention of going home by myself at that hour of night. I stopped.

"Coward!" she said venomously. "You're afraid."

"I'll show you whether I'm afraid or not," I said sulkily, and went off down Shandon Street—I who had never before been out alone after dark. I was terrified. It's no use swanking about it. I was simply terrified. I stopped every few yards, hoping she'd call out or that Father would come running after me. Neither happened, and at each dark laneway I shut my eyes. There was no sound but feet climbing this flight of steps or descending that. When I reached the foot of Shandon Street by the old graveyard, and saw the long, dark, winding hill before me, my courage gave out. I was afraid to go on and afraid to turn back.

Then I saw a friendly sign; a little huxter shop with a long flight of steps to the door, flanked by iron railings. High over the basement I could see the narrow window decorated in crinkly red paper, with sweet bottles and a few toys on view. Then I saw one toy that raised my courage. I counted my coppers again. There were six. I climbed the steps, went in the dark hallway, and turned right into the front room, which was used as the shop. A little old Mother Hubbard of a woman came out, rubbing her hands in her apron.

"Well, little boy?" she asked briskly.

"I want a dog, ma'am."

"Sixpence apiece the dogs," she said doubtfully. "Have you sixpence?"

"I have, ma'am," said I, and I counted out my coppers. She gave me the dog, a black, woolly dog with two beads for eyes. I ran down the steps and up the road with my head high, whistling. I only wished that the little girl could see me now; she wouldn't say I was a coward. To show my contempt for the terrors of night I stood at the mouth of each laneway and looked down. I stroked the dog's fur, and when some shadow loomed up more frightening than the others I turned his head at it.

"Ssss!" I said. "At him, boy! At him!"

When Mother opened the door I caught him and held him back.

"Down, Towser, down!" I said commandingly. "It's only Mummy."

THE DRUNKARD

It was a terrible blow to Father when Mr. Dooley on the terrace died. Mr. Dooley was a commercial traveller with two sons in the Dominicans and a car of his own, so socially he was miles

ahead of us, but he had no false pride. Mr. Dooley was an intellectual, and, like all intellectuals the thing he loved best was
conversation, and in his own limited way Father was a well-read
man and could appreciate an intelligent talker. Mr. Dooley was
remarkably intelligent. Between business acquaintances and
clerical contacts, there was very little he didn't know about what
went on in town, and evening after evening he crossed the road
to our gate to explain to Father the news behind the news. He had
a low, palavering voice and a knowing smile, and Father would
listen in astonishment, giving him a conversational lead now and
again, and then stump triumphantly in to Mother with his face
aglow and ask: "Do you know what Mr. Dooley is after telling
me?" Ever since, when somebody has given me some bit of information off the record I have found myself on the point of
asking: "Was it Mr. Dooley told you that?"

Till I actually saw him laid out in his brown shroud with the
rosary beads entwined between his waxy fingers I did not take the
report of his death seriously. Even then I felt there must be a
catch and that some summer evening Mr. Dooley must reappear
at our gate to give us the lowdown on the next world. But Father
was very upset, partly because Mr. Dooley was about one age
with himself, a thing that always gives a distinctly personal turn
to another man's demise; partly because now he would have no
one to tell him what dirty work was behind the latest scene at the
Corporation. You could count on your fingers the number of
men in Blarney Lane who read the papers as Mr. Dooley did, and
none of these would have overlooked the fact that Father was
only a labouring man. Even Sullivan, the carpenter, a mere nobody, thought he was a cut above Father. It was certainly a
solemn event.

"Half past two to the Curragh," Father said meditatively, putting down the paper.

"But you're not thinking of going to the funeral?" Mother
asked in alarm.

" 'Twould be expected," Father said, scenting opposition. "I
wouldn't give it to say to them."

"I think," said Mother with suppressed emotion, "it will be as
much as anyone will expect if you go to the chapel with him."

("Going to the chapel," of course, was one thing, because the body was removed after work, but going to a funeral meant the loss of a half-day's pay.)

"The people hardly know us," she added.

"God between us and all harm," Father replied with dignity, "we'd be glad if it was our own turn."

To give Father his due, he was always ready to lose a half day for the sake of an old neighbour. It wasn't so much that he liked funerals as that he was a conscientious man who did as he would be done by; and nothing could have consoled him so much for the prospect of his own death as the assurance of a worthy funeral. And, to give Mother her due, it wasn't the half-day's pay she begrudged, badly as we could afford it.

Drink, you see, was Father's great weakness. He could keep steady for months, even for years, at a stretch, and while he did he was as good as gold. He was first up in the morning and brought the mother a cup of tea in bed, stayed at home in the evenings and read the paper; saved money and brought himself a new blue serge suit and bowler hat. He laughed at the folly of men who, week in week out, left their hard-earned money with the publicans; and sometimes, to pass an idle hour, he took pencil and paper and calculated precisely how much he saved each week through being a teetotaller. Being a natural optimist he sometimes continued this calculation through the whole span of his prospective existence and the total was breathtaking. He would die worth hundreds.

If I had only known it, this was a bad sign; a sign he was becoming stuffed up with spiritual pride and imagining himself better than his neighbours. Sooner or later, the spiritual pride grew till it called for some form of celebration. Then he took a drink—not whisky, of course; nothing like that—just a glass of some harmless drink like lager beer. That was the end of Father. By the time he had taken the first he already realized that he had made a fool of himself, took a second to forget it and a third to forget that he couldn't forget, and at last came home reeling drunk. From this on it was "The Drunkard's Progress," as in the moral prints. Next day he stayed in from work with a sick head while Mother went off to make his excuses at the works, and inside a fortnight he was poor and savage and despondent again. Once he began he drank steadily through everything down to the kitchen clock. Mother and I knew all the phases and dreaded all the dangers. Funerals were one.

"I have to go to Dunphy's to do a half-day's work," said Mother in distress. "Who's to look after Larry?"

"I'll look after Larry," Father said graciously. "The little walk will do him good."

There was no more to be said, though we all knew I didn't need anyone to look after me, and that I could quite well have stayed at home and looked after Sonny, but I was being attached to the party to act as a brake on Father. As a brake I had never achieved anything, but Mother still had great faith in me.

Next day, when I got home from school, Father was there before me and made a cup of tea for both of us. He was very good at tea, but too heavy in the hand for anything else; the way he cut bread was shocking. Afterwards, we went down the hill to the church, Father wearing his best blue serge and a bowler cocked to one side of his head with the least suggestion of the masher. To his great joy he discovered Peter Crowley among the mourners. Peter was another danger signal, as I knew well from certain experiences after Mass on Sunday morning: a mean man, as Mother said, who only went to funerals for the free drinks he could get at them. It turned out that he hadn't even known Mr. Dooley! But Father had a sort of contemptuous regard for him as one of the foolish people who wasted their good money in public-houses when they could be saving it. Very little of his own money Peter Crowley wasted!

It was an excellent funeral from Father's point of view. He had it all well studied before we set off after the hearse in the afternoon sunlight.

"Five carriages!" he exclaimed. "Five carriages and sixteen covered cars!" There's one alderman, two councillors and 'tis unknown how many priests. I didn't see a funeral like this from the road since Willie Mack, the publican, died.

"Ah, he was well liked," said Crowley in his husky voice.

"My goodness, don't I know that?" snapped Father. "Wasn't

the man my best friend? Two nights before he died—only two nights—he was over telling me the goings-on about the housing contract. Them fellows in the Corporation are night and day robbers. But even I never imagined he was as well connected as that."

Father was stepping out like a boy, pleased with everything: the other mourners, and the fine houses along Sunday's Well. I knew the danger signals were there in full force: a sunny day, a fine funeral, and a distinguished company of clerics and public men were bringing out all the natural vanity and flightiness of Father's character. It was with something like genuine pleasure that he saw his old friend lowered into the grave; with the sense of having performed a duty and the pleasant awareness that however much he would miss poor Mr. Dooley in the long summer evenings, it was he and not poor Mr. Dooley who would do the missing.

"We'll be making tracks before they break up," he whispered to Crowley as the gravediggers tossed in the first shovelfuls of clay, and away he went, hopping like a goat from grassy hump to hump. The drivers, who were probably in the same state as himself, though without months of abstinence to put an edge on it, looked up hopefully.

"Are they nearly finished, Mick?" bawled one.

"All over now bar the last prayers," trumpeted Father in the tone of one who brings news of great rejoicing.

The carriages passed us in a lather of dust several hundred yards from the public-house, and Father, whose feet gave him trouble in hot weather, quickened his pace, looking nervously over his shoulder for any sign of the main body of mourners crossing the hill. In a crowd like that a man might be kept waiting.

When we did reach the pub the carriages were drawn up outside, and solemn men in black ties were cautiously bringing out consolation to mysterious females whose hands reached out modestly from behind the drawn blinds of the coaches. Inside the pub there were only the drivers and a couple of shawly women. I felt if I was to act as a brake at all, this was the time, so I pulled Father by the coattails.

"Dadda, can't we go home now?" I asked.

"Two minutes now," he said, beaming affectionately. "Just a bottle of lemonade and we'll go home."

This was a bribe, and I knew it, but I was always a child of weak character. Father ordered lemonade and two pints. I was thirsty and swallowed my drink at once. But that wasn't Father's way. He had long months of abstinence behind him and an eternity of pleasure before. He took out his pipe, blew through it, filled it, and then lit it with loud pops, his eyes bulging above it. After that he deliberately turned his back on the pint, leaned one elbow on the counter in the attitude of a man who did not know there was a pint behind him, and deliberately brushed the tobacco from his palms. He had settled down for the evening. He was steadily working through all the important funerals he had ever attended. The carriages departed and the minor mourners drifted in till the pub was half full.

"Dadda," I said, pulling his coat again, "can't we go home now?"

"Ah, your mother won't be in for a long time yet," he said benevolently enough. "Run out in the road and play, can't you?"

It struck me as very cool, the way grown-ups assumed that you could play all by yourself on a strange road. I began to get bored as I had so often been bored before. I knew Father was quite capable of lingering there till nightfall. I knew I might have to bring him home, blind drunk, down Blarney Lane, with all the old women at their doors, saying: "Mick Delaney is on it again." I knew that my mother would be half crazy with anxiety; that next day Father wouldn't go out to work; and before the end of the week she would be running down to the pawn with the clock under her shawl. I could never get over the lonesomeness of the kitchen without a clock.

I was still thirsty. I found if I stood on tiptoe I could just reach Father's glass, and the idea occurred to me that it would be interesting to know what the contents were like. He had his back to it and wouldn't notice. I took down the glass and sipped cautiously. It was a terrible disappointment. I was astonished that he could even drink such stuff. It looked as if he had never tried lemonade.

I should have advised him about lemonade but he was holding

forth himself in great style. I heard him say that bands were a great addition to a funeral. He put his arms in the position of someone holding a rifle in reverse and hummed a few 'bars of Chopin's Funeral March. Crowley nodded reverently. I took a longer drink and began to see that porter might have its advantages. I felt pleasantly elevated and philosophic. Father hummed a few bars of the Dead March in *Saul*. It was a nice pub and a very fine funeral, and I felt sure that poor Mr. Dooley in Heaven must be highly gratified. At the same time I thought they might have given him a band. As Father said, bands were a great addition.

But the wonderful thing about porter was the way it made you stand aside, or rather float aloft like a cherub rolling on a cloud, and watch yourself with your legs crossed, leaning against a bar counter, not worrying about trifles but thinking deep, serious, grown-up thoughts about life and death. Looking at yourself like that, you couldn't help thinking after a while how funny you looked, and suddenly you got embarrassed and wanted to giggle. But by the time I had finished the pint, that phase too had passed; I found it hard to put back the glass, the counter seemed to have grown so high. Melancholia was supervening again.

"Well," Father said reverently, reaching behind him for his drink, "God rest the poor man's soul, wherever he is!" He stopped, looked first at the glass, and then at the people round him. "Hello," he said in a fairly good-humoured tone, as if he were just prepared to consider it a joke, even if it was in bad taste, "who was at this?"

There was silence for a moment while the publican and the old women looked first at Father and then at his glass.

"There was no one at it, my good man," one of the women said with an offended air. "Is it robbers you think we are?"

"Ah, there's no one here would do a thing like that, Mick," said the publican in a shocked tone.

"Well, someone did it," said Father, his smile beginning to wear off.

"If they did, they were them that were nearer it," said the woman darkly, giving me a dirty look; and at the same moment the truth began to dawn on Father. I suppose I must have looked a bit starry-eyed. He bent and shook me.

"Are you all right, Larry?" he asked in alarm.

Peter Crowley looked down at me and grinned.

"Could you beat that?" he exclaimed in a husky voice.

I could, and without difficulty. I started to get sick. Father jumped back in holy terror that I might spoil his good suit, and hastily opened the back door.

"Run! run! run!" he shouted.

I saw the sunlit wall outside with the ivy overhanging it, and ran. The intention was good but the performance was exaggerated, because I lurched right into the wall, hurting it badly, as it seemed to me. Being always very polite, I said "Pardon" before the second bout came on me. Father, still concerned for his suit, came up behind and cautiously held me while I got sick.

"That's a good boy!" he said encouragingly. "You'll be grand when you get that up."

Begor, I was not grand! Grand was the last thing I was. I gave one unmerciful wail out of me as he steered me back to the pub and put me sitting on the bench near the shawlies. They drew themselves up with an offended air, still sore at the suggestion that they had drunk his pint.

"God help us!" moaned one, looking pityingly at me, "isn't it the likes of them would be fathers?"

"Mick," said the publican in alarm, spraying sawdust on my tracks, "that child isn't supposed to be in here at all. You'd better take him home quick in case a bobby would see him."

"Merciful God!" whimpered Father, raising his eyes to heaven and clapping his hands silently as he only did when distraught, "what misfortune was on me? Or what will his mother say? . . . If women might stop at home and look after their children themselves!" he added in a snarl for the benefit of the shawlies. "Are them carriages all gone, Bill?"

"The carriages are finished long ago, Mick," replied the publican.

"I'll take him home," Father said despairingly. . . . "I'll never bring you out again," he threatened me. "Here," he added, giving me the clean handkerchief from his breast pocket, "put that over your eye."

The blood on the handkerchief was the first indication I got that I was cut, and instantly my temple began to throb and I set up another howl.

"Whisht, whisht, whisht!" Father said testily, steering me out the door. "One'd think you were killed. That's nothing. We'll wash it when we get home."

"Steady now, old scout!" Crowley said, taking the other side of me. "You'll be all right in a minute."

I never met two men who knew less about the effects of drink. The first breath of fresh air and the warmth of the sun made me groggier than ever and I pitched and rolled between wind and tide till Father started to whimper again.

"God Almighty, and the whole road out! What misfortune was on me didn't stop at my work! Can't you walk straight?"

I couldn't. I saw plain enough that, coaxed by the sunlight, every woman old and young in Blarney Lane was leaning over her half-door or sitting on her doorstep. They all stopped gabbling to gape at the strange spectacle of two sober, middle-aged men bringing home a drunken small boy with a cut over his eye. Father, torn between the shamefast desire to get me home as quick as he could, and the neighbourly need to explain that it wasn't his fault, finally halted outside Mrs. Roche's. There was a gang of old women outside a door at the opposite side of the road. I didn't like the look of them from the first. They seemed altogether too interested in me. I leaned against the wall of Mrs. Roche's cottage with my hands in my trousers pockets, thinking mournfully of poor Mr. Dooley in his cold grave on the Curragh, who would never walk down the road again, and, with great feeling, I began to sing a favourite song of Father's.

> *Though lost to Mononia and cold in the grave*
> *He returns to Kincora no more.*

"Wisha, the poor child!" Mrs. Roche said. "Haven't he a lovely voice, God bless him!"

That was what I thought myself, so I was the more surprised when Father said "Whisht!" and raised a threatening finger at me. He didn't seem to realize the appropriateness of the song, so I sang louder than ever.

"Whisht, I tell you!" he snapped, and then tried to work up a smile for Mrs. Roche's benefit. "We're nearly home now. I'll carry you the rest of the way."

But, drunk and all as I was, I knew better than to be carried home ignominiously like that.

"Now," I said severely, "can't you leave me alone? I can walk all right. 'Tis only my head. All I want is a rest."

"But you can rest at home in bed," he said viciously, trying to pick me up, and I knew by the flush on his face that he was very vexed.

"Ah, Jasus," I said crossly, "what do I want to go home for? Why the hell can't you leave me alone?"

For some reason the gang of old women at the other side of the road thought this very funny. They nearly split their sides over it. A gassy fury began to expand in me at the thought that a fellow couldn't have a drop taken without the whole neighbourhood coming out to make game of him.

"Who are ye laughing at?" I shouted, clenching my fists at them. "I'll make ye laugh at the other side of yeer faces if ye don't let me pass."

They seemed to think this funnier still; I had never seen such ill-mannered people.

"Go away, ye bloody bitches!" I said.

"Whisht, whisht, whisht, I tell you!" snarled Father, abandoning all pretence of amusement and dragging me along behind him by the hand. I was maddened by the women's shrieks of laughter. I was maddened by Father's bullying. I tried to dig in my heels but he was too powerful for me, and I could only see the women by looking back over my shoulder.

"Take care or I'll come back and show ye!" I shouted. "I'll teach ye to let decent people pass. Fitter for ye to stop at home and wash yeer dirty faces."

" 'Twill be all over the road," whimpered Father. "Never again, never again, not if I lived to be a thousand!"

To this day I don't know whether he was forswearing me or the drink. By way of a song suitable to my heroic mood I bawled

"The Boys of Wexford," as he dragged me in home. Crowley, knowing he was not safe, made off and Father undressed me and put me to bed. I couldn't sleep because of the whirling in my head. It was very unpleasant, and I got sick again. Father came in with a wet cloth and mopped up after me. I lay in a fever, listening to him chopping sticks to start a fire. After that I heard him lay the table.

Suddenly the front door banged open and Mother stormed in with Sonny in her arms, not her usual gentle, timid self, but a wild, raging woman. It was clear that she had heard it all from the neighbours.

"Mick Delaney," she cried hysterically, "what did you do to my son?"

"Whisht, woman, whisht, whisht!" he hissed, dancing from one foot to the other. "Do you want the whole road to hear?"

"Ah," she said with a horrifying laugh, "the road knows all about it by this time. The road knows the way you filled your unfortunate innocent child with drink to make sport for you and that other rotten, filthy brute."

"But I gave him no drink," he shouted, aghast at the horrifying interpretation the neighbours had chosen to give his misfortune. "He took it while my back was turned. What the hell do you think I am?"

"Ah," she replied bitterly, "everyone knows what you are now. God forgive you, wasting our hard-earned few ha'pence on drink, and bringing up your child to be a drunken corner-boy like yourself."

Then she swept into the bedroom and threw herself on her knees by the bed. She moaned when she saw the gash over my eye. In the kitchen Sonny set up a loud bawl on his own, and a moment later Father appeared in the bedroom door with his cap over his eyes, wearing an expression of the most intense self-pity.

"That's a nice way to talk to me after all I went through," he whined. "That's a nice accusation, that I was drinking. Not one drop of drink crossed my lips the whole day. How could it when he drank it all? I'm the one that ought to be pitied, with my day ruined on me, and I after being made a show for the whole road."

But next morning, when he got up and went out quietly

to work with his dinner-basket, Mother threw herself on me in the bed and kissed me. It seemed it was all my doing, and I was being given a holiday till my eye got better.

"My brave little man!" she said with her eyes shining. "It was God did it you were there. You were his guardian angel."

CHRISTMAS MORNING

I NEVER really liked my brother, Sonny. From the time he was a baby he was always the mother's pet and always chasing her to tell her what mischief I was up to. Mind you, I was usually up to something. Until I was nine or ten I was never much good at school, and I really believe it was to spite me that he was so smart at his books. He seemed to know by instinct that this was what Mother had set her heart on, and you might almost say he spelt himself into her favour.

"Mummy," he'd say, "will I call Larry in to his t-e-a?" or: "Mummy, the k-e-t-e-l is boiling," and, of course, when he was wrong she'd correct him, and next time he'd have it right and there would be no standing him. "Mummy," he'd say, "aren't I a good speller?" Cripes, we could all be good spellers if we went on like that!

Mind you, it wasn't that I was stupid. Far from it. I was just restless and not able to fix my mind for long on any one thing. I'd do the lessons for the year before, or the lessons for the year after: what I couldn't stand were the lessons we were supposed to be doing at the time. In the evenings I used to go out and play with the Doherty gang. Not, again, that I was rough, but I liked the excitement, and for the life of me I couldn't see what attracted Mother about education.

"Can't you do your lessons first and play after?" she'd say, getting white with indignation. "You ought to be ashamed of yourself that your baby brother can read better than you."

She didn't seem to understand that I wasn't, because there didn't seem to me to be anything particularly praiseworthy about reading, and it struck me as an occupation better suited to a sissy kid like Sonny.

"The dear knows what will become of you," she'd say. "If only you'd stick to your books you might be something good like a clerk or an engineer."

"I'll be a clerk, Mummy," Sonny would say smugly.

"Who wants to be an old clerk?" I'd say, just to annoy him. "I'm going to be a soldier."

"The dear knows, I'm afraid that's all you'll ever be fit for," she would add with a sigh.

I couldn't help feeling at times that she wasn't all there. As if there was anything better a fellow could be!

Coming on to Christmas, with the days getting shorter and the shopping crowds bigger, I began to think of all the things I might get from Santa Claus. The Dohertys said there was no Santa Claus, only what your father and mother gave you, but the Dohertys were a rough class of children you wouldn't expect Santa to come to anyway. I was rooting round for whatever information I could pick up about him, but there didn't seem to be much. I was no hand with a pen, but if a letter would do any good I was ready to chance writing to him. I had plenty of initiative and was always writing off for free samples and prospectuses.

"Ah, I don't know will he come at all this year," Mother said with a worried air. "He has enough to do looking after steady boys who mind their lessons without bothering about the rest."

"He only comes to good spellers, Mummy," said Sonny. "Isn't that right?"

"He comes to any little boy who does his best, whether he's a good speller or not," Mother said firmly.

Well, I did my best. God knows I did! It wasn't my fault if, four days before the holidays, Flogger Dawley gave us sums we couldn't do, and Peter Doherty and myself had to go on the lang. It wasn't for love of it, for, take it from me, December is no month for mitching, and we spent most of our time sheltering from the rain in a store on the quays. The only mistake we made was imagining we could keep it up till the holidays without being spotted. That showed real lack of foresight.

Of course, Flogger Dawley noticed and sent home word to know what was keeping me. When I came in on the third day the mother gave me a look I'll never forget, and said: "Your dinner is there." She was too full to talk. When I tried to explain to her about Flogger Dawley and the sums she brushed it aside and said: "You have no word." I saw then it wasn't the langing she minded but the lies, though I still didn't see how you could lang without lying. She didn't speak to me for days. And even then I couldn't make out what she saw in education, or why she wouldn't let me grow up naturally like anyone else.

To make things worse, it stuffed Sonny up more than ever. He had the air of one saying: "I don't know what they'd do without me in this blooming house." He stood at the front door, leaning against the jamb with his hands in his trouser pockets, trying to make himself look like Father, and shouted to the other kids so that he could be heard all over the road.

"Larry isn't left go out. He went on the lang with Peter Doherty and me mother isn't talking to him."

And at night, when we were in bed, he kept it up.

"Santa Claus won't bring you anything this year, aha!"

"Of course he will," I said.

"How do you know?"

"Why wouldn't he?"

"Because you went on the lang with Doherty. I wouldn't play with them Doherty fellows."

"You wouldn't be left."

"I wouldn't play with them. They're no class. They had the bobbies up to the house."

"And how would Santa know I was on the lang with Peter Doherty?" I growled, losing patience with the little prig.

"Of course he'd know. Mummy would tell him."

"And how could Mummy tell him and he up at the North Pole? Poor Ireland, she's rearing them yet! 'Tis easy seen you're only an old baby."

"I'm not a baby, and I can spell better than you, and Santa won't bring you anything."

"We'll see whether he will or not," I said sarcastically, doing the old man on him.

But, to tell the God's truth, the old man was only bluff. You could never tell what powers these superhuman chaps would have of knowing what you were up to. And I had a bad conscience about the langing because I'd never before seen the mother like that.

That was the night I decided that the only sensible thing to do was to see Santa myself and explain to him. Being a man, he'd probably understand. In those days I was a good-looking kid and had a way with me when I liked. I had only to smile nicely at one old gent on the North Mall to get a penny from him, and I felt if only I could get Santa by himself I could do the same with him and maybe get something worth while from him. I wanted a model railway: I was sick of Ludo and Snakes-and-Ladders.

I started to practise lying awake, counting five hundred and then a thousand, and trying to hear first eleven, then midnight, from Shandon. I felt sure Santa would be round by midnight, seeing that he'd be coming from the north, and would have the whole of the South Side to do afterwards. In some ways I was very farsighted. The only trouble was the things I was farsighted about.

I was so wrapped up in my own calculations that I had little attention to spare for Mother's difficulties. Sonny and I used to go to town with her, and while she was shopping we stood outside a toyshop in the North Main Street, arguing about what we'd like for Christmas.

On Christmas Eve when Father came home from work and gave her the housekeeping money, she stood looking at it doubtfully while her face grew white.

"Well?" he snapped, getting angry. "What's wrong with that?"

"What's wrong with it?" she muttered. "On Christmas Eve!"

"Well," he asked truculently, sticking his hands in his trouser pockets as though to guard what was left, "do you think I get more because it's Christmas?"

"Lord God," she muttered distractedly. "And not a bit of cake in the house, nor a candle, nor anything!"

"All right," he shouted, beginning to stamp. "How much will the candle be?"

"Ah, for pity's sake," she cried, "will you give me the money and not argue like that before the children? Do you think I'll leave them with nothing on the one day of the year?"

"Bad luck to you and your children!" he snarled. "Am I to be slaving from one year's end to another for you to be throwing it away on toys? Here," he added, tossing two half-crowns on the table, "that's all you're going to get, so make the most of it."

"I suppose the publicans will get the rest," she said bitterly.

Later she went into town, but did not bring us with her, and returned with a lot of parcels, including the Christmas candle. We waited for Father to come home to his tea, but he didn't, so we had our own tea and a slice of Christmas cake each, and then Mother put Sonny on a chair with the holy-water stoup to sprinkle the candle, and when he lit it she said: "The light of heaven to our souls." I could see she was upset because Father wasn't in—it should be the oldest and youngest. When we hung up our stockings at bedtime he was still out.

Then began the hardest couple of hours I ever put in. I was mad with sleep but afraid of losing the model railway, so I lay for a while, making up things to say to Santa when he came. They varied in tone from frivolous to grave, for some old gents like kids to be modest and well-spoken, while others prefer them with spirit. When I had rehearsed them all I tried to wake Sonny to keep me company, but that kid slept like the dead.

Eleven struck from Shandon, and soon after I heard the latch, but it was only Father coming home.

"Hello, little girl," he said, letting on to be surprised at finding Mother waiting up for him, and then broke into a self-conscious giggle. "What have you up so late?"

"Do you want your supper?" she asked shortly.

"Ah, no, no," he replied. "I had a bit of pig's cheek at Daneen's on my way up (Daneen was my uncle). I'm very fond of a bit of pig's cheek. . . . My goodness, is it that late?" he exclaimed, letting on to be astonished. "If I knew that I'd have gone to the North Chapel for midnight Mass. I'd like to hear the *Adeste* again. That's a hymn I'm very fond of—a most touching hymn."

Then he began to hum it falsetto.

> *Adeste fideles*
> *Solus domus dagus.*

Father was very fond of Latin hymns, particularly when he had a drop in, but as he had no notion of the words he made them up as he went along, and this always drove Mother mad.

"Ah, you disgust me!" she said in a scalded voice, and closed the room door behind her. Father laughed as if he thought it a great joke; and he struck a match to light his pipe and for a while puffed at it noisily. The light under the door dimmed and went out but he continued to sing emotionally.

> *Dixie medearo*
> *Tutum tonum tantum*
> *Venite adoremus.*

He had it all wrong but the effect was the same on me. To save my life I couldn't keep awake.

Coming on to dawn, I woke with the feeling that something dreadful had happened. The whole house was quiet, and the little bedroom that looked out on the foot and a half of back yard was pitch-dark. It was only when I glanced at the window that I saw how all the silver had drained out of the sky. I jumped out of bed to feel my stocking, well knowing that the worst had happened. Santa had come while I was asleep, and gone away with an entirely false impression of me, because all he had left me was some sort of book, folded up, a pen and pencil, and a tuppenny bag of sweets. Not even Snakes-and-Ladders! For a while I was too stunned even to think. A fellow who was able to drive over rooftops and climb down chimneys without getting stuck—God, wouldn't you think he'd know better?

Then I began to wonder what that foxy boy, Sonny, had. I went to his side of the bed and felt his stocking. For all his spelling and sucking-up he hadn't done so much better, because, apart from a bag of sweets like mine, all Santa had left him was a pop-gun, one that fired a cork on a piece of string and which you could get in any huxter's shop for sixpence.

All the same, the fact remained that it was a gun, and a gun was better than a book any day of the week. The Dohertys had a gang, and the gang fought the Strawberry Lane kids who tried to play football on our road. That gun would be very useful to me in many ways, while it would be lost on Sonny who wouldn't be let play with the gang, even if he wanted to.

Then I got the inspiration, as it seemed to me, direct from heaven. Suppose I took the gun and gave Sonny the book! Sonny would never be any good in the gang: he was fond of spelling, and a studious child like him could learn a lot of spellings from a book like mine. As he hadn't seen Santa any more than I had, what he hadn't seen wouldn't grieve him. I was doing no harm to anyone; in fact, if Sonny only knew, I was doing him a good turn which he might have cause to thank me for later. That was one thing I was always keen on; doing good turns. Perhaps this was Santa's intention the whole time and he had merely become confused between us. It was a mistake that might happen to anyone. So I put the book, the pencil, and the pen into Sonny's stocking and the popgun into my own, and returned to bed and slept again. As I say, in those days I had plenty of initiative.

It was Sonny who woke me, shaking me to tell me that Santa had come and left me a gun. I let on to be surprised and rather disappointed in the gun, and to divert his mind from it made him show me his picture book, and cracked it up to the skies.

As I knew, that kid was prepared to believe anything, and nothing would do him then but to take the presents in to show Father and Mother. This was a bad moment for me. After the way she had behaved about the langing, I distrusted Mother, though I had the consolation of believing that the only person who could contradict me was now somewhere up by the North Pole. That gave me a certain confidence, so Sonny and I burst in with our presents, shouting: "Look what Santa Claus brought!"

Father and Mother woke, and Mother smiled, but only for an instant. As she looked at me her face changed. I knew that look;

I knew it only too well. It was the same she had worn the day I came home from langing, when she said I had no word.

"Larry," she said in a low voice, "where did you get that gun?"

"Santa left it in my stocking, Mummy," I said, trying to put on an injured air, though it baffled me how she guessed that he hadn't. "He did, honest."

"You stole it from that poor child's stocking while he was asleep," she said, her voice quivering with indignation. "Larry, Larry, how could you be so mean?"

"Now, now, now," Father said deprecatingly, " 'tis Christmas morning."

"Ah," she said with real passion, "it's easy it comes to you. Do you think I want my son to grow up a liar and a thief?"

"Ah, what thief, woman?" he said testily. "Have sense, can't you?" He was as cross if you interrupted him in his benevolent moods as if they were of the other sort, and this one was probably exacerbated by a feeling of guilt for his behaviour of the night before. "Here, Larry," he said, reaching out for the money on the bedside table, "here's sixpence for you and one for Sonny. Mind you don't lose it now!"

But I looked at Mother and saw what was in her eyes. I burst out crying, threw the popgun on the floor, and ran bawling out of the house before anyone on the road was awake. I rushed up the lane behind the house and threw myself on the wet grass.

I understood it all, and it was almost more than I could bear; that there was no Santa Claus, as the Dohertys said, only Mother trying to scrape together a few coppers from the housekeeping; that Father was mean and common and a drunkard, and that she had been relying on me to raise her out of the misery of the life she was leading. And I knew that the look in her eyes was the fear that, like my father, I should turn out to be mean and common and a drunkard.

THE IDEALIST

I DON'T know how it is about education, but it never seemed to do anything for me but get me into trouble.

Adventure stories weren't so bad, but as a kid I was very serious and preferred realism to romance. School stories were what I liked best, and, judged by our standards, these were romantic enough for anyone. The schools were English, so I suppose you couldn't expect anything else. They were always called "the venerable pile," and there was usually a ghost in them; they were built in a square that was called "the quad," and, according to the pictures, they were all clock-towers, spires, and pinnacles, like the lunatic asylum with us. The fellows in the stories were all good climbers, and got in and out of school at night on ropes made of knotted sheets. They dressed queerly; they wore long trousers, short, black jackets, and top hats. Whenever they did anything wrong they were given "lines" in Latin. When it was a bad case, they were flogged and never showed any sign of pain; only the bad fellows, and they always said: "Ow! Ow!"

Most of them were grand chaps who always stuck together and were great at football and cricket. They never told lies and wouldn't talk to anyone who did. If they were caught out and asked a point-blank question, they always told the truth, unless someone else was with them, and then even if they were to be expelled for it they wouldn't give his name, even if he was a thief, which, as a matter of fact, he frequently was. It was surprising in such good schools, with fathers who never gave less than five quid, the number of thieves there were. The fellows in our school hardly ever stole, though they only got a penny a week, and sometimes not even that, as when their fathers were on the booze and their mothers had to go to the pawn.

I worked hard at the football and cricket, though of course we never had a proper football and the cricket we played was with a hurley stick against a wicket chalked on some wall. The officers in the barrack played proper cricket, and on summer evenings I used to go and watch them, like one of the souls in Purgatory watching the joys of Paradise.

Even so, I couldn't help being disgusted at the bad way things were run in our school. Our "venerable pile" was a red-brick building without tower or pinnacle a fellow could climb, and no ghost at all: we had no team, so a fellow, no matter how hard he worked, could never play for the school, and, instead of giving you "lines," Latin or any other sort, Murderer Moloney either lifted you by the ears or bashed you with a cane. When he got tired of bashing you on the hands he bashed you on the legs.

But these were only superficial things. What was really wrong was ourselves. The fellows sucked up to the masters and told them all that went on. If they were caught out in anything they tried to put the blame on someone else, even if it meant telling lies. When they were caned they snivelled and said it wasn't fair; drew back their hands as if they were terrified, so that the cane caught only the tips of their fingers, and then screamed and stood on one leg, shaking out their fingers in the hope of getting it counted as one. Finally they roared that their wrist was broken and crawled back to their desks with their hands squeezed under their armpits, howling. I mean you couldn't help feeling ashamed, imagining what chaps from a decent school would think if they saw it.

My own way to school led me past the barrack gate. In those peaceful days sentries never minded you going past the guard-room to have a look at the chaps drilling in the barrack square; if you came at dinnertime they even called you in and gave you plumduff and tea. Naturally, with such temptations I was often late. The only excuse, short of a letter from your mother, was to say you were at early Mass. The Murderer would never know whether you were or not, and if he did anything to you you could easily get him into trouble with the parish priest. Even as kids we knew who the real boss of the school was.

But after I started reading those confounded school stories I was never happy about saying I had been to Mass. It was a lie, and I knew that the chaps in the stories would have died sooner than tell it. They were all round me like invisible presences, and I hated to do anything which I felt they might disapprove of.

One morning I came in very late and rather frightened.

"What kept you till this hour, Delaney?" Murderer Moloney asked, looking at the clock.

I wanted to say I had been at Mass, but I couldn't. The invisible presences were all about me.

"I was delayed at the barrack, sir," I replied in panic.

There was a faint titter from the class, and Moloney raised his brows in mild surprise. He was a big powerful man with fair hair and blue eyes and a manner that at times was deceptively mild.

"Oh, indeed," he said, politely enough. "And what delayed you?"

"I was watching the soldiers drilling, sir," I said.

The class tittered again. This was a new line entirely for them.

"Oh," Moloney said casually, "I never knew you were such a military man. Hold out your hand!"

Compared with the laughter the slaps were nothing, and besides, I had the example of the invisible presences to sustain me. I did not flinch. I returned to my desk slowly and quietly without snivelling or squeezing my hands, and the Murderer looked after me, raising his brows again as though to indicate that this was a new line for him, too. But the others gaped and whispered as if I were some strange animal. At playtime they gathered about me, full of curiosity and excitement.

"Delaney, why did you say that about the barrack?"

"Because 'twas true," I replied firmly. "I wasn't going to tell him a lie."

"What lie?"

"That I was at Mass."

"Then couldn't you say you had to go on a message?"

"That would be a lie too."

"Cripes, Delaney," they said, "you'd better mind yourself. The Murderer is in an awful wax. He'll massacre you."

I knew that. I knew only too well that the Murderer's professional pride had been deeply wounded, and for the rest of the day I was on my best behaviour. But my best wasn't enough, for I underrated the Murderer's guile. Though he pretended to be reading, he was watching me the whole time.

"Delaney," he said at last without raising his head from the book, "was that you talking?"

" 'Twas, sir," I replied in consternation.

The whole class laughed. They couldn't believe but that I was deliberately trailing my coat, and, of course, the laugh must have convinced him that I was. I suppose if people do tell you lies all day and every day, it soon becomes a sort of perquisite which you resent being deprived of.

"Oh," he said, throwing down his book, "we'll soon stop that."

This time it was a tougher job, because he was really on his mettle. But so was I. I knew this was the testing-point for me, and if only I could keep my head I should provide a model for the whole class. When I had got through the ordeal without moving a muscle, and returned to my desk with my hands by my sides, the invisible presences gave me a great clap. But the visible ones were nearly as annoyed as the Murderer himself. After school half a dozen of them followed me down the school yard.

"Go on!" they shouted truculently. "Shaping as usual!"

"I was not shaping."

"You were shaping. You're always showing off. Trying to pretend he didn't hurt you—a blooming crybaby like you!"

"I wasn't trying to pretend," I shouted, even then resisting the temptation to nurse my bruised hands. "Only decent fellows don't cry over every little pain like kids."

"Go on!" they bawled after me. "You ould idiot!" And, as I went down the school lane, still trying to keep what the stories called "a stiff upper lip," and consoling myself with the thought that my torment was over until next morning, I heard their mocking voices after me.

"Loony Larry! Yah, Loony Larry!"

I realized that if I was to keep on terms with the invisible presences I should have to watch my step at school.

So I did, all through that year. But one day an awful thing happened. I was coming in from the yard, and in the porch outside our schoolroom I saw a fellow called Gorman taking something from a coat on the rack. I always described Gorman to myself as "the black sheep of the school." He was a fellow I disliked and feared; a handsome, sulky, spoiled, and sneering lout. I paid no attention to him because I had escaped for a few moments into my dream-world in which fathers never gave less than fivers and the honour of the school was always saved by some quiet, unassuming fellow like myself—"a dark horse," as the stories called him.

"Who are you looking at?" Gorman asked threateningly.

"I wasn't looking at anyone," I replied with an indignant start.

"I was only getting a pencil out of my coat," he added, clenching his fists.

"Nobody said you weren't," I replied, thinking that this was a very queer subject to start a row about.

"You'd better not, either," he snarled. "You can mind your own business."

"You mind yours!" I retorted, purely for the purpose of saving face. "I never spoke to you at all."

And that, so far as I was concerned, was the end of it.

But after playtime the Murderer, looking exceptionally serious, stood before the class, balancing a pencil in both hands.

"Everyone who left the classroom this morning, stand out!" he called. Then he lowered his head and looked at us from under his brows. "Mind now, I said everyone!"

I stood out with the others, including Gorman. We were all very puzzled.

"Did you take anything from a coat on the rack this morning?" the Murderer asked, laying a heavy, hairy paw on Gorman's shoulder and staring menacingly into his eyes.

"Me, sir?" Gorman exclaimed innocently. "No, sir."

"Did you see anyone else doing it?"

"No, sir."

"You?" he asked another lad, but even before he reached me

at all I realized why Gorman had told the lie and wondered frantically what I should do.

"You?" he asked me, and his big red face was close to mine, his blue eyes were only a few inches away, and the smell of his toilet soap was in my nostrils. My panic made me say the wrong thing as though I had planned it.

"I didn't take anything, sir," I said in a low voice.

"Did you see someone else do it?" he asked, raising his brows and showing quite plainly that he had noticed my evasion. "Have you a tongue in your head?" he shouted suddenly, and the whole class, electrified, stared at me. "You?" he added curtly to the next boy as though he had lost interest in me.

"No, sir."

"Back to your desks, the rest of you!" he ordered. "Delaney, you stay here."

He waited till everyone was seated again before going on.

"Turn out your pockets."

I did, and a half-stifled giggle rose, which the Murderer quelled with a thunderous glance. Even for a small boy I had pockets that were museums in themselves: the purpose of half the things I brought to light I couldn't have explained myself. They were antiques, prehistoric and unlabelled. Among them was a school story borrowed the previous evening from a queer fellow who chewed paper as if it were gum. The Murderer reached out for it, and holding it at arm's length, shook it out with an expression of deepening disgust as he noticed the nibbled corners and margins.

"Oh," he said disdainfully, "so this is how you waste your time! What do you do with this rubbish—eat it?"

" 'Tisn't mine, sir," I said against the laugh that sprang up. "I borrowed it."

"Is that what you did with the money?" he asked quickly, his fat head on one side.

"Money?" I repeated in confusion. "What money?"

"The shilling that was stolen from Flanagan's overcoat this morning."

(Flanagan was a little hunchback whose people coddled him; no one else in the school would have possessed that much money.)

"I never took Flanagan's shilling," I said, beginning to cry, "and you have no right to say I did."

"I have the right to say you're the most impudent and defiant puppy in the school," he replied, his voice hoarse with rage, "and I wouldn't put it past you. What else can anyone expect and you reading this dirty, rotten, filthy rubbish?" And he tore my school story in halves and flung them to the furthest corner of the classroom. "Dirty, filthy, English rubbish! Now, hold out your hand."

This time the invisible presences deserted me. Hearing themselves described in these contemptuous terms, they fled. The Murderer went mad in the way people do whenever they're up against something they don't understand. Even the other fellows were shocked, and, heaven knows, they had little sympathy with me.

"You should put the police on him," they advised me later in the playground. "He lifted the cane over his shoulder. He could get the gaol for that."

"But why didn't you say you didn't see anyone?" asked the eldest, a fellow called Spillane.

"Because I did," I said, beginning to sob all over again at the memory of my wrongs. "I saw Gorman."

"Gorman?" Spillane echoed incredulously. "Was it Gorman took Flanagan's money? And why didn't you say so?"

"Because it wouldn't be right," I sobbed.

"Why wouldn't it be right?"

"Because Gorman should have told the truth himself," I said. "And if this was a proper school he'd be sent to Coventry."

"He'd be sent where?"

"Coventry. No one would ever speak to him again."

"But why would Gorman tell the truth if he took the money?" Spillane asked as you'd speak to a baby. "Jay, Delaney," he added pityingly, "you're getting madder and madder. Now, look at what you're after bringing on yourself!"

Suddenly Gorman came lumbering up, red and angry.

"Delaney," he shouted threateningly, "did you say I took Flanagan's money?"

Gorman, though I of course didn't realize it, was as much at sea as Moloney and the rest. Seeing me take all that punishment rather than give him away, he concluded that I must be more afraid of him than of Moloney, and that the proper thing to do was to make me more so. He couldn't have come at a time when I cared less for him. I didn't even bother to reply but lashed out with all my strength at his brutal face. This was the last thing he expected. He screamed, and his hand came away from his face, all blood. Then he threw off his satchel and came at me, but at the same moment a door opened behind us and a lame teacher called Murphy emerged. We all ran like mad and the fight was forgotten.

It didn't remain forgotten, though. Next morning after prayers the Murderer scowled at me.

"Delaney, were you fighting in the yard after school yesterday?"

For a second or two I didn't reply. I couldn't help feeling that it wasn't worth it. But before the invisible presences fled forever, I made another effort.

"I was, sir," I said, and this time there wasn't even a titter. I was out of my mind. The whole class knew it and was awe-stricken.

"Who were you fighting?"

"I'd sooner not say, sir," I replied, hysteria beginning to well up in me. It was all very well for the invisible presences, but they hadn't to deal with the Murderer.

"Who was he fighting with?" he asked lightly, resting his hands on the desk and studying the ceiling.

"Gorman, sir," replied three or four voices—as easy as that!

"Did Gorman hit him first?"

"No, sir. He hit Gorman first."

"Stand out," he said, taking up the cane. "Now," he added, going up to Gorman, "you take this and hit him. And make sure you hit him hard," he went on, giving Gorman's arm an encouraging squeeze. "He thinks he's a great fellow. You show him now what we think of him."

Gorman came towards me with a broad grin. He thought it a great joke. The class thought it a great joke. They began to roar with laughter. Even the Murderer permitted himself a modest grin at his own cleverness.

"Hold out your hand," he said to me.

I didn't. I began to feel trapped and a little crazy.

"Hold out your hand, I say," he shouted, beginning to lose his temper.

"I will not," I shouted back, losing all control of myself.

"You what?" he cried incredulously, dashing at me round the classroom with his hand raised as though to strike me. "What's that you said, you dirty little thief?"

"I'm not a thief, I'm not a thief," I screamed. "And if he comes near me I'll kick the shins off him. You have no right to give him that cane, and you have no right to call me a thief either. If you do it again, I'll go down to the police and then we'll see who the thief is."

"You refused to answer my questions," he roared, and if I had been in my right mind I should have known he had suddenly taken fright; probably the word "police" had frightened him.

"No," I said through my sobs, "and I won't answer them now either. I'm not a spy."

"Oh," he retorted with a sarcastic sniff, "so that's what you call a spy, Mr. Delaney?"

"Yes, and that's what they all are, all the fellows here—dirty spies!—but I'm not going to be a spy for you. You can do your own spying."

"That's enough now, that's enough!" he said, raising his fat hand almost beseechingly. "There's no need to lose control of yourself, my dear young fellow, and there's no need whatever to screech like that. 'Tis most unmanly. Go back to your seat now and I'll talk to you another time."

I obeyed, but I did no work. No one else did much either. The hysteria had spread to the class. I alternated between fits of exultation at my own successful defiance of the Murderer, and panic at the prospect of his revenge; and at each change of mood I put my face in my hands and sobbed again. The Murderer didn't even order me to stop. He didn't so much as look at me.

After that I was the hero of the school for the whole afternoon. Gorman tried to resume the fight, but Spillane ordered him away contemptuously—a fellow who had taken the master's cane to another had no status. But that wasn't the sort of hero I wanted to be. I preferred something less sensational.

Next morning I was in such a state of panic that I didn't know how I should face school at all. I dawdled, between two minds as to whether or not I should mitch. The silence of the school lane and yard awed me. I had made myself late as well.

"What kept you, Delaney?" the Murderer asked quietly.

I knew it was no good.

"I was at Mass, sir."

"All right. Take your seat."

He seemed a bit surprised. What I had not realized was the incidental advantage of our system over the English one. By this time half a dozen of his pets had brought the Murderer the true story of Flanagan's shilling, and if he didn't feel a monster he probably felt a fool.

But by that time I didn't care. In my school sack I had another story. Not a school story this time, though. School stories were a washout. "Bang! Bang!"—that was the only way to deal with men like the Murderer. "The only good teacher is a dead teacher."

FIRST CONFESSION

ALL the trouble began when my grandfather died and my grand-mother—my father's mother—came to live with us. Relations in the one house are a strain at the best of times, but, to make matters worse, my grandmother was a real old countrywoman and quite unsuited to the life in town. She had a fat, wrinkled old face, and, to Mother's great indignation, went round the house in bare feet—the boots had her crippled, she said. For dinner she had a jug of porter and a pot of potatoes with—sometimes—a bit of salt fish, and she poured out the potatoes on the table and ate them slowly, with great relish, using her fingers by way of a fork.

Now, girls are supposed to be fastidious, but I was the one who suffered most from this. Nora, my sister, just sucked up to the old woman for the penny she got every Friday out of the old-age pension, a thing I could not do. I was too honest, that was my trouble; and when I was playing with Bill Connell, the sergeant-major's son, and saw my grandmother steering up the path with the jug of porter sticking out from beneath her shawl I was mortified. I made excuses not to let him come into the house, because I could never be sure what she would be up to when we went in.

When Mother was at work and my grandmother made the dinner I wouldn't touch it. Nora once tried to make me, but I hid under the table from her and took the bread-knife with me for protection. Nora let on to be very indignant (she wasn't, of course, but she knew Mother saw through her, so she sided with Gran) and came after me. I lashed out at her with the bread-knife, and after that she left me alone. I stayed there till Mother came in from work and made my dinner, but when Father came in later Nora said in a shocked voice: "Oh, Dadda, do you know what Jackie did at dinnertime?" Then, of course, it all came out; Father gave me a flaking; Mother interfered, and for days after that he didn't speak to me and Mother barely spoke to Nora. And all because of that old woman! God knows, I was heart-scalded.

Then, to crown my misfortunes, I had to make my first confession and communion. It was an old woman called Ryan who prepared us for these. She was about the one age with Gran; she was well-to-do, lived in a big house on Montenotte, wore a black cloak and bonnet, and came every day to school at three o'clock when we should have been going home, and talked to us of hell. She may have mentioned the other place as well, but that could only have been by accident, for hell had the first place in her heart.

She lit a candle, took out a new half-crown, and offered it to the first boy who would hold one finger—only one finger!—in the flame for five minutes by the school clock. Being always very ambitious I was tempted to volunteer, but I thought it might look greedy. Then she asked were we afraid of holding one finger— only one finger!—in a little candle flame for five minutes and not afraid of burning all over in roasting hot furnaces for all eternity. "All eternity! Just think of that! A whole lifetime goes by and it's nothing, not even a drop in the ocean of your sufferings." The woman was really interesting about hell, but my attention was all fixed on the half-crown. At the end of the lesson she put it back in her purse. It was a great disappointment; a religious woman like that, you wouldn't think she'd bother about a thing like a half-crown.

Another day she said she knew a priest who woke one night to find a fellow he didn't recognize leaning over the end of his bed. The priest was a bit frightened—naturally enough—but he asked the fellow what he wanted, and the fellow said in a deep, husky voice that he wanted to go to confession. The priest said it was an awkward time and wouldn't it do in the morning, but the fellow said that last time he went to confession, there was one sin he kept back, being ashamed to mention it, and now it was always on his mind. Then the priest knew it was a bad case, because the fellow was after making a bad confession and committing a mortal sin. He got up to dress, and just then the cock crew in the yard outside, and—lo and behold!—when the priest looked round there was no sign of the fellow, only a smell of burning timber, and when the priest looked at his bed didn't he see the print of two hands burned in it? That was because the fellow had made a bad confession. This story made a shocking impression on me.

But the worst of all was when she showed us how to examine our conscience. Did we take the name of the Lord, our God, in vain? Did we honour our father and our mother? (I asked her did this include grandmothers and she said it did.) Did we love our neighbours as ourselves? Did we covet our neighbour's goods? (I thought of the way I felt about the penny that Nora got every Friday.) I decided that, between one thing and another, I must have broken the whole ten commandments, all on account of that old woman, and so far as I could see, so long as she remained in the house I had no hope of ever doing anything else.

I was scared to death of confession. The day the whole class went I let on to have a toothache, hoping my absence wouldn't be noticed; but at three o'clock, just as I was feeling safe, along comes a chap with a message from Mrs. Ryan that I was to go to confession myself on Saturday and be at the chapel for communion with the rest. To make it worse, Mother couldn't come with me and sent Nora instead.

Now, that girl had ways of tormenting me that Mother never knew of. She held my hand as we went down the hill, smiling sadly and saying how sorry she was for me, as if she were bringing me to the hospital for an operation.

"Oh, God help us!" she moaned. "Isn't it a terrible pity you weren't a good boy? Oh, Jackie, my heart bleeds for you! How will you ever think of all your sins? Don't forget you have to tell him about the time you kicked Gran on the shin."

"Lemme go!" I said, trying to drag myself free of her. "I don't want to go to confession at all."

"But sure, you'll have to go to confession, Jackie," she replied in the same regretful tone. "Sure, if you didn't, the parish priest would be up to the house, looking for you. 'Tisn't, God knows, that I'm not sorry for you. Do you remember the time you tried to kill me with the bread-knife under the table? And the language you used to me? I don't know what he'll do with you at all, Jackie. He might have to send you up to the bishop."

I remember thinking bitterly that she didn't know the half of what I had to tell—if I told it. I knew I couldn't tell it, and understood perfectly why the fellow in Mrs. Ryan's story made a bad confession; it seemed to me a great shame that people wouldn't stop criticizing him. I remember that steep hill down to the church, and the sunlit hillsides beyond the valley of the river, which I saw in the gaps between the houses like Adam's last glimpse of Paradise.

Then, when she had manœuvred me down the long flight of steps to the chapel yard, Nora suddenly changed her tone. She became the raging malicious devil she really was.

"There you are!" she said with a yelp of triumph, hurling me

C

through the church door. "And I hope he'll give you the penitential psalms, you dirty little caffler."

I knew then I was lost, given up to eternal justice. The door
with the coloured-glass panels swung shut behind me, the sunlight went out and gave place to deep shadow, and the wind
whistled outside so that the silence within seemed to crackle like
ice under my feet. Nora sat in front of me by the confession box.
There were a couple of old woman ahead of her, and then a
miserable-looking poor devil came and wedged me in at the
other side, so that I couldn't escape even if I had the courage. He
joined his hands and rolled his eyes in the direction of the roof,
muttering aspirations in an anguished tone, and I wondered had
he a grandmother too. Only a grandmother could account for a
fellow behaving in that heartbroken way, but he was better off
than I, for he at least could go and confess his sins; while I would
make a bad confession and then die in the night and be con-
tinually coming back and burning people's furniture.

Nora's turn came, and I heard the sound of something slamming, and then her voice as if butter wouldn't melt in her mouth,
and then another slam, and out she came. God, the hypocrisy of
women! Her eyes were lowered, her head was bowed, and her
hands were joined very low down on her stomach, and she
walked up the aisle to the side altar looking like a saint. You
never saw such an exhibition of devotion; and I remembered the
devilish malice with which she had tormented me all the way
from our door, and wondered were all religious people like that,
really. It was my turn now. With the fear of damnation in my
soul I went in, and the confessional door closed of itself behind
me.

It was pitch-dark and I couldn't see priest or anything else.
Then I really began to be frightened. In the darkness it was a
matter between God and me, and He had all the odds. He knew
what my intentions were before I even started; I had no chance.
All I had ever been told about confession got mixed up in my
mind, and I knelt to one wall and said: "Bless me, father, for I
have sinned; this is my first confession." I waited for a few
minutes, but nothing happened, so I tried it on the other wall.
Nothing happened there either. He had me spotted all right.

It must have been then that I noticed the shelf at about one height with my head. It was really a place for grown-up people to rest their elbows, but in my distracted state I thought it was probably the place you were supposed to kneel. Of course, it was on the high side and not very deep, but I was always good at climbing and managed to get up all right. Staying up was the trouble. There was room only for my knees, and nothing you could get a grip on but a sort of wooden moulding a bit above it. I held on to the moulding and repeated the words a little louder, and this time something happened all right. A slide was slammed back; a little light entered the box, and a man's voice said: "Who's there?"

" 'Tis me, father," I said for fear he mightn't see me and go away again. I couldn't see him at all. The place the voice came from was under the moulding, about level with my knees, so I took a good grip of the moulding and swung myself down till I saw the astonished face of a young priest looking up at me. He had to put his head on one side to see me, and I had to put mine on one side to see him, so we were more or less talking to one another upside-down. It struck me as a queer way of hearing confessions, but I didn't feel it my place to criticize.

"Bless me, father, for I have sinned; this is my first confession," I rattled off all in one breath, and swung myself down the least shade more to make it easier for him.

"What are you doing up there?" he shouted in an angry voice, and the strain the politeness was putting on my hold of the moulding, and the shock of being addressed in such an uncivil tone, were too much for me. I lost my grip, tumbled, and hit the door an unmerciful wallop before I found myself flat on my back in the middle of the aisle. The people who had been waiting stood up with their mouths open. The priest opened the door of the middle box and came out, pushing his biretta back from his forehead; he looked something terrible. Then Nora came scampering down the aisle.

"Oh, you dirty little caffler!" she said. "I might have known you'd do it. I might have known you'd disgrace me. I can't leave you out of my sight for one minute."

Before I could even get to my feet to defend myself she bent down and gave me a clip across the ear. This reminded me that I was so stunned I had even forgotten to cry, so that people might think I wasn't hurt at all, when in fact I was probably maimed for life. I gave a roar out of me.

"What's all this about?" the priest hissed, getting angrier than ever and pushing Nora off me. "How dare you hit the child like that, you little vixen?"

"But I can't do my penance with him, father," Nora cried, cocking an outraged eye up at him.

"Well, go and do it, or I'll give you some more to do," he said, giving me a hand up. "Was it coming to confession you were, my poor man?" he asked me.

" 'Twas, father," said I with a sob.

"Oh," he said respectfully, "a big hefty fellow like you must have terrible sins. Is this your first?"

" 'Tis, father," said I.

"Worse and worse," he said gloomily. "The crimes of a lifetime. I don't know will I get rid of you at all today. You'd better wait now till I'm finished with these old ones. You can see by the looks of them they haven't much to tell."

"I will, father," I said with something approaching joy.

The relief of it was really enormous. Nora stuck out her tongue at me from behind his back, but I couldn't even be bothered retorting. I knew from the very moment that man opened his mouth that he was intelligent above the ordinary. When I had time to think, I saw how right I was. It only stood to reason that a fellow confessing after seven years would have more to tell than people that went every week. The crimes of a lifetime, exactly as he said. It was only what he expected, and the rest was the cackle of old women and girls with their talk of hell, the bishop, and the penitential psalms. That was all they knew. I started to make my examination of conscience, and barring the one bad business of my grandmother it didn't seem so bad.

The next time, the priest steered me into the confession box himself and left the shutter back the way I could see him get in and sit down at the further side of the grille from me.

"Well, now," he said, "what do they call you?"

"Jackie, father," said I.

"And what's a-trouble to you, Jackie?"

"Father," I said, feeling I might as well get it over while I had him in good humour, "I had it all arranged to kill my grandmother."

He seemed a bit shaken by that, all right, because he said nothing for quite a while.

"My goodness," he said at last, "that'd be a shocking thing to do. What put that into your head?"

"Father," I said, feeling very sorry for myself, "she's an awful woman."

"Is she?" he asked. "What way is she awful?"

"She takes porter, father," I said, knowing well from the way Mother talked of it that this was a mortal sin, and hoping it would make the priest take a more favourable view of my case.

"Oh, my!" he said, and I could see he was impressed.

"And snuff, father," said I.

"That's a bad case, sure enough, Jackie," he said.

"And she goes round in her bare feet, father," I went on in a rush of self-pity, "and she know I don't like her, and she gives pennies to Nora and none to me, and my da sides with her and flakes me, and one night I was so heart-scalded I made up my mind I'd have to kill her."

"And what would you do with the body?" he asked with great interest.

"I was thinking I could chop that up and carry it away in a barrow I have," I said.

"Begor, Jackie," he said, "do you know you're a terrible child?"

"I know, father," I said, for I was just thinking the same thing myself. "I tried to kill Nora too with a bread-knife under the table, only I missed her."

"Is that the little girl that was beating you just now?" he asked.

" 'Tis, father."

"Someone will go for her with a bread-knife one day, and he won't miss her," he said rather cryptically. "You must have great courage. Between ourselves, there's a lot of people I'd like to do the same to but I'd never have the nerve. Hanging is an awful death."

"Is it, father?" I asked with the deepest interest—I was always very keen on hanging. "Did you ever see a fellow hanged?"

"Dozens of them," he said solemnly. "And they all died roaring."

"Jay!" I said.

"Oh, a horrible death!" he said with great satisfaction. "Lots of the fellows I saw killed their grandmothers too, but they all said 'twas never worth it."

He had me there for a full ten minutes talking, and then walked out the chapel yard with me. I was genuinely sorry to part with him, because he was the most entertaining character I'd ever met in the religious line. Outside, after the shadow of the church, the sunlight was like the roaring of waves on a beach; it dazzled me; and when the frozen silence melted and I heard the screech of trams on the road my heart soared. I knew now I wouldn't die in the night and come back, leaving marks on my mother's furniture. It would be a great worry to her, and the poor soul had enough.

Nora was sitting on the railing, waiting for me, and she put on a very sour puss when she saw the priest with me. She was mad jealous because a priest had never come out of the church with her.

"Well," she asked coldly, after he left me, "what did he give you?"

"Three Hail Marys," I said.

"Three Hail Marys," she repeated incredulously. "You mustn't have told him anything."

"I told him everything," I said confidently.

"About Gran and all?"

"About Gran and all."

(All she wanted was to be able to go home and say I'd made a bad confession.)

"Did you tell him you went for me with the bread-knife?" she asked with a frown.

"I did to be sure."

"And he only gave you three Hail Marys?"

"That's all."

She slowly got down from the railing with a baffled air. Clearly, this was beyond her. As we mounted the steps back to the main road she looked at me suspiciously.

"What are you sucking?" she asked.

"Bullseyes."

"Was it the priest gave them to you?"

" 'Twas."

"Lord God," she wailed bitterly, "some people have all the luck! 'Tis no advantage to anybody trying to be good. I might just as well be a sinner like you."

MY DA

IT's funny the influence fathers can have on fellows—I mean without even realizing it. There was a lad called Stevie Leary living next door to us in Blarney Street. His mother and father had separated when he was only a baby, and his father had gone off to America and never been heard of after. His mother had left Stevie behind and followed him there, but of course she had never found him.

Stevie was a real comical artist. We all laughed at him but he didn't seem to mind. My mother had great pity for him because she thought he was a bit touched. She said he was a good poor slob. Even his own mother hadn't much to say for him. "Ah, he'll never be the man his father was, ma'am," she'd say mournfully, over-right the kid himself. He didn't seem to worry about that, either. He was a big overgrown streel of a boy with a fat round idiotic face and a rosy complexion, a walk that was more of a slide, and a shrill scolding old-woman's voice. He wore baggy knickerbockers and a man's cap several sizes too big for him.

Stevie took life with deadly seriousness. It might have been that his mother had told him the life story of some American million-aire, for he was full of enterprise, always in a hurry, and whenever he stopped it was as thought someone were pulling the reins and forcing him to a halt. He slithered and skidded till he stopped, with his big moony face over one shoulder, like some good-na-tured old horse. He collected swill for the Mahonys who kept pigs, and delivered messages for the Delurys of the pub where his mother worked, and for a penny would undertake anything from minding the baby to buying the week's groceries. He had no false pride. He had a little tuppenny notebook he wrote his com-missions in with a bit of puce pencil that he wet with his tongue, trying to look as much like a commercial traveller as he could, and with that queer crabbed air of his he'd rattle away in his shrill voice about what was the cheapest sort of meat to make soup of. "You ought to try Reillys, ma'am. Reillys keeps grand stewing-beef." He suggested modestly to Reillys that they might consider giving him a commission, but they wouldn't. He pre-tended to think we made fun of him only because we were jealous, because we were only kids and didn't know any better. He said no one need be poor! Look at him with a Post Office account; good money accumulating at two per cent! "Aha, boy," he said gloatingly, "that's the way to get on!" The fellow really behaved as though the rest of us were halfwits. You couldn't help feeling he was touched.

There was only one obstacle to Stevie's progress towards a million, and that was his mother, a grand bosomy capacious woman whom my mother was very fond of. Sometimes they'd sit for a whole evening over the fire, taking snuff and connoisseuring about Mrs. Leary's unfortunate marriage. Innocence and experi-ence were nothing to them, with Mrs. Leary saying in her husky voice that a man would never love you till he'd beat you, and that if it was the last breath in her body she'd have to hit back. "That's how I lost my good looks, girl," she would say. "I had great feel-ings, and nothing ages a woman like the feelings."

But she still had plenty of feelings left, and sometimes they got the upper hand of her. Stevie would be sitting outside the cottage of an evening, watching the kids playing with a smile that was both lonesome and superior, as befitted a fellow with a Post Office account, when some little girl would come up the road, bawling out the news.

"Stevie Leary, your old one is on it again."

Stevie's smile would fade, and he would wander off aimlessly down the road, till, getting out of our sight, he put on his businessman's air, and darted briskly into each pub he passed in search of his mother.

"You didn't see my ma today, Miss O.?" he would shout. "She's on it again."

Eventually he would run her to earth in some snug with a couple of cronies. Mrs. Leary was never the lonesome sort of boozer; she liked admirers.

"God help us!" one of the hangers-on would say hypocritically when Stevie tried to detach them from their quarry, "isn't he a lovely little boy, God bless him?"

"Ah, he'll never be the man his father was, ma'am," Mrs. Leary would say with resignation, taking another pinch of snuff.

"But with the help of God he'll be steadier," another crony would add meaningly.

"Ah, what steady?" Mrs. Leary would retort contemptuously. "I wouldn't give a snap of my fingers for a man that wouldn't have a bit of the devil in him. Old mollies!"

It might be nightfall before Stevie manœuvred her home, a mountain of a woman who'd have stunned him if she fell on him.

"Wisha, indeed and indeed, Mrs. Leary," Mother would say as she tried to settle her, "you ought to be ashamed of yourself. Look at the cut of you!"

But before bedtime Mr. Leary would be on the prowl again, with Stevie crying: "Ah, stop in, Ma, and I'll get it for you," and his mother shouting: "Gimme the money, can't you? Gimme the money, I say!"

With the low cunning of the drunkard she knew to a penny how much poor Stevie had, and night after night she shambled down to Miss O.'s with nothing showing under the peak of her shawl but one bleak, bloodshot eye; and tuppence by tuppence Stevie's savings vanished till he started life again with all the bounce gone out of him, as poor as any of us who had never heard the life story of an American millionaire. He tried to get her to regard it as a loan and pay him interest on it at the rate of a penny in the shilling, but a woman of such feelings couldn't be expected to understand the petty notions of finance. To be a proper millionaire you need a settled home life.

Then one night to everyone's astonishment Frankie Leary came home from America. There was nothing you could actually call a homecoming about it. Father and I were at the door when we spotted the strange man coming up the road; a lean, leathery man with a long face, cold eyes, and a hard chin. You wouldn't have been surprised if you heard he came from the North Pole. He went next door, and Father at once turned in to the kitchen to ask Mother who he could be. There were screams and sobs from next door. " 'Tis never Frankie!" said Mother, growing pale. "But the man hadn't as much at a kitbag," said Father. Ten minutes later Mrs. Leary herself came in to tell us. She was delirious with excitement. "The old devil!" she said with her eyes shining. "I wouldn't doubt him. He never lost it." It seems that when she tried to embrace him in a wifely way he merely said coldly that he had a crow to pluck with her, and that when Stevie, who was equal to any social occasion, asked him if he had had a nice journey, he never replied at all. Of course, as Mother said, he might have had a nasty crossing.

For weeks Frankie's arrival kept Stevie in a state bordering on hysteria. In one way Frankie was a disappointment, the first American Stevie had heard of who returned home without a rex. But that was only a trifle beside the real thing. For the first time in his life Stevie had a father of his own like the rest of us, and if he had given birth to him himself he couldn't have had more old swank about it. America was an additional feather in his cap; day in, day out, we heard nothing but the wonders of America, houses and trains, taller and longer. No normal son would ever have behaved like that, but then Stevie wasn't normal. As fathers were generally called in for the sole purpose of flaking hell out of us, Stevie felt it was up to him to go in fear and trembling too; it gave him a sort of delighted satisfaction to refuse good money for going on a message, all because of what his father might say. He turned down the money for the pleasure of calling attention to the fact that he had a father; pure showing off.

Frankie knew as little about being a father as Stevie did about being a son, and compromised on an amateurish imitation of an elder brother. He soon discovered Stevie's passion for America, and talked about it to him in a heavy, informative way, while Stevie, in an appalling imitation of a public-house expert, sat back with his hands in his trouser pockets. When Frankie did check him it was about things like that, and the effect on Stevie was magical. It was as though these were the words of wisdom he'd been waiting for all his life. He began deliberately trying to moderate his shuffle so that he wouldn't have to pull himself up on the rein, and to break his voice of its squeak. Stevie trying to be tough like his old fellow was one of his funniest phases for, undoubtedly, Frankie was the man he'd never be.

Frankie was a queer man, an arid, unnatural man. The first evening my father and he talked at the door, Father described him as "a most superior, well-informed, manly chap," but he changed his views the very next day when Frankie all but cut him at the foot of Blarney Street. Father was a sociable creature; he felt he might have said something wrong; he begged Mother to ask Mrs. Leary if Frankie hadn't misunderstood some remark of his, but Mrs. Leary only laughed and said: "He never lost it." "I wouldn't doubt him," and "he never lost it," two highly ambiguous sayings, were as close as she ever got to defining her husband's character. After that, Father put him down as "moody and contrary" and kept his distance.

But he had good points. He was steady; he didn't drink or smoke. He made Mrs. Leary give up the daily work and wear a hat and coat instead of the shawl; he made Stevie give up the swill and messages and learn to read and write, accomplishments which were apparently omitted from the curriculum of whatever millionaire Stevie was modelling himself on. The change in the cottage was remarkable.

At times of course there were rows when Mrs. Leary came home with the sign of drink on her, but they weren't rows as we understood them. Frankie didn't make smithereens of the furniture or fling his wife and child out of doors in their nightclothes the way other fathers did, but, trifling as they were, they left

Stevie shattered. He burst into tears and begged his parents to agree.

One night about six months later Mrs. Leary rambled in, a bit more expansive than usual. She wasn't drunk, just amiable. Frankie, who had been waiting for his tea, looked up from the paper he was reading.

"What kept you?" he asked in his shrill voice.

"I ran into Lizzie Desmond at the Cross and we started talking," said Mrs. Leary, so snug in her hammock of whisky that she never noticed the vessel begin to roll.

"Ye started drinking, I suppose," said Frankie.

"Wisha, we had a couple of small ones," said Mrs. Leary. "That old Cross is the windiest hole to stand talking in! Have you the kettle boiling, Stevie, boy?"

"You'd better remember what the small ones did for you before," Frankie said grimly.

"And wasn't I well able for it?" she retorted, beginning to raise her voice.

"Whisht, Ma, whisht!" Stevie cried in an agony of fear. "You know my da is only speaking for your good."

"Speaking for my good?" she trumpeted, her feelings overcoming her all at once at the suggestion that she needed such correction. "How dare you!" she added to Frankie, drawing herself up with great dignity and letting the small ones speak for her. "Is that my thanks after all I done for you, crossing the briny ocean after you, you insignificant little gnat?"

"What's that you said?" asked Frankie, throwing down his paper and striding up to her with his fists clenched.

"Gnat!" she repeated scornfully, looking him up and down. "If I might have married a man itself instead of an insignificant little article like you that wouldn't make a bolt for a back door!"

Even before Stevie knew what he was up to, Frankie drew back his fist and gave it to her full in the mouth. Mrs. Leary let one great shriek out of her and fell. Stevie, who was as strange as my mother to the ways of a man in love, let out another shriek and threw himself on his knees beside her.

"Oh, Ma, look at me, look at me!" he bawled distractedly. "I'm Stevie, your own little boy."

That didn't produce whatever it was intended to produce in the way of response, so Stevie cocked an eye up at his father.

"Will I get the priest for her, Dadda?" he asked in languishing tones. "I think she's dying."

"Get to hell out of this," said Frankie shortly. "It's time you were in bed."

It wasn't, but Stevie knew better than to contradict him. A little later Frankie went to bed himself, leaving his wife lying on the floor—dead, no doubt. Mother wanted to go in to her, but Father stopped that at once.

"Now," he said oracularly, "there's a man in the house," and for years afterwards I found myself at intervals trying to analyse the finality of that pronouncement. An hour later, Mrs. Leary got up and made herself a cup of tea. "She can't be so badly hurt," said my mother with relief. I could see she was full of pity for Stevie, having to allow his mother to remain so long like that, without assistance. There was a man in the house all right.

Next morning, the poor kid woke with all the troubles of the world on him. He poured them all out to Mother. Things were desperate in the home. All the light he had on it was one sermon he had heard at a men's retreat which he shouldn't have attended, in which the missioner had said that a child was the great bond between the parents. "Would you say I'd be a bond, Mrs. O.?" squeaked Stevie. Doing his best to be a bond, he gave his mother a pot of tea in bed and made his father's breakfast. After Frankie had gone to work, he begged his mother to stay in bed, and even offered to bring her up the porter, but she wouldn't. Her pride was too hurt. Stevie knew she was much more frightened of Frankie than he was, but her pride wouldn't let her yield.

In the afternoon he found her again in a pub in town and brought her home, shaking his head and cluck-clucking fondly over her. She was a sight, the hood of her shawl pulled down over her face, and a bloodshot eye and a bruised mouth just visible beneath it. Stevie did all he could to make her presentable; brewed her tea, washed her face, combed her hair, and even tried to make her take shelter with us and leave him to deal with his father, but compromise was an expression she didn't understand.

At six Frankie came in like a thundercloud, and Stevie bustled round him eagerly and clumsily, getting his supper. He had everything neat and shining. In his capacity as bond he had reverted to type.

"You'd like a couple of buttered eggs?'" he squeaked cheerfully. "You would to be sure. Dwyers keeps grand eggs."

Neither of his parents addressed one another. After supper Frankie took his cap to go out.

"You won't be late, Dadda?" Stevie asked anxiously, but his father didn't reply. Stevie went to the door after him and watched him down the road.

"I'd be afraid he mightn't come back," he said.

"That he mightn't!" his mother said piously. "We done without him before and we can do without him again. Conceited jackeen!"

Then he came into our house to report his lack of success as a bond. What made it so queer was that he sounded cheerful.

"A father is a great loss, Mr. O." he said to my father. "A house is never the same without a man."

"You ought to see is he in your Uncle John's," said my mother a bit anxiously.

"I wouldn't say so," said Stevie. "The sort my da is, he'd be too proud. He wouldn't give it to say to them."

The child showed real insight. However he'd managed it, Frankie was off on his travels again, with a fresh disillusionment to fly from. Even my mother didn't blame him, though she thought he should have done something for Stevie. Little by little, the old air of fecklessness and neglect came back. Stevie was completely wretched—a fellow who couldn't mind a father when he got one. He lost his bounce entirely, and took to mooning about the chapel, lighting candles for his father's return. Mrs. Leary went back to the shawl and the daily work, Stevie to the swill and the messages, all exactly as though Frankie had never returned, as though it had all been a dream.

But if it had become a dream, the dream had the power of robbing reality of its innocence. Because it was the only thing Frankie had asked of him, the only way in which he could get closer to his father, Stevie took to attending night school and joined the public library. Sometimes I met him coming back over the New Bridge with his books and we exchanged impressions. Clearly he didn't think much of the Wild West stories I loved.

Stevie being intellectual made us laugh, but it was nothing to what followed, because, as a result of something the teacher in the Technical School said to the Canon, the Canon saw Stevie, and Mrs. Leary got regular cleaning-work in the presbytery while Stevie went to the seminary. It seemed he had suddenly discovered a vocation for the priesthood!

This was no laughing matter. It was almost a scandal. Of course, even if he got ordained, it wouldn't be the same thing as Mrs. Delury's son who had been to Maynooth; it could only mean the Foreign Mission, but you'd think that even the Foreign Mission would draw a line. Mother, in spite of her pity for him, was shocked. I was causing her concern enough as it was, for I had just lost my faith for the first time, and, though she never put it in so many words, I fancy she felt that if the Church had to fall back on people like Stevie Leary, I might have some reason.

I remember the first time I saw him in his clerical black I realized that he had heard about my losing my faith, for he behaved as though I had lost the week's wages. It was exactly like our meetings on the way to the library. I could almost hear him say that no one need lose his faith in the same tone in which, as a kid, he used to say that no one need be poor. All you had to do was put it in the Post Office. "Aha, boy, that's the way to get on!" I felt that he might at least have shown some sympathy for me.

Not that anyone showed him much—except Mother. When he said his first Mass in the parish church we all turned up. Mrs. Delury, her two sons and a daughter, were all there, boiling with rage to think of their charwoman's son being a priest like their own Miah, and blaming it all on America. Such a country!

Stevie preached on the Good Shepherd and, whether it was the excitement or the sight of four Delurys in one pew—a sight to daunt the boldest—he got all mixed up between the ninety-nine and the one; though in his maundering, enthusiastic style it didn't make much difference. But you could almost hear the Delurys crowing.

My mother and I went round to the sacristy to get his blessing (by this time I had got back my faith and didn't lose it again for another two years), but as we knelt I could scarcely keep my face straight because, God forgive me, I expected at every moment that Stevie would say: "Wouldn't a few pounds of stewing-beef be better, ma'am?"

The Opposition, headed by Mrs. Delury, was in session outside the church when we left.

"Poor Father Stephen got a bit mixed in his sums," Mrs. Delury said regretfully.

"Ah, the dear knows, wouldn't anybody?" retorted my mother, flushed and angry.

"I don't suppose in America they'll notice much difference," said Mrs. Delury.

"America?" I said. "Is that where he's going?"

And suddenly it struck me with the force of a revelation that fathers had their good points after all. That evening I dropped in on the Learys. I wanted to see Stevie again. I had realized after Mass that, like the Delurys, I had for years been living with a shadow-Stevie, a comic kid who had disappeared ages ago under our eyes without our noticing. I wasn't surprised to meet for the first time an unusually intelligent and sensitive young man.

"Ah, he'll love it in America, Larry," his mother said in her snug, husky voice. "'Twill be new life to him; fine open-handed people instead of the articles we have around here that think they're somebody. The dear knows, I wouldn't mind going back myself."

But we all knew there wasn't much chance of that. If there's one thing a young priest has to deny himself, it's a mother whose feelings become too much for her, and though the whole time he was at home she was irreproachable, the night she saw him off, a good-natured policeman had to bring her home and my mother put her to bed.

"Ah, indeed and indeed, Mrs. Leary," said my mother, quivering with indignation to see a woman so degrade herself, "you ought to be ashamed of yourself. What would Father Stephen say if he saw you now?"

But there was no Father Stephen to see her, then or any other time. Stevie had at last become the man his father was and left us all far behind him.

THE PRETENDER

SUSIE and I should have known well that Denis Corby's coming "to play with us" would mean nothing only trouble. We didn't want anyone new to play with; we had plenty, and they were all good class. But Mother was like that; giddy, open-handed and ready to listen to any tall tale. That wouldn't have been so bad if only she confined her charity to her own things, but she gave away ours as well. You couldn't turn your back in that house but she had something pinched on you, a gansey, an overcoat, or a pair of shoes, and as for the beggars that used to come to the door—! As Susie often said, we had no life.

But we were still mugs enough to swallow the yarn about the lovely lonesome little boy she'd found to play with us up on the hill. Cripes, you never in all your life got such a suck-in! Eleven o'clock one Saturday morning this fellow comes to the door, about the one age with myself only bigger, with a round red face and big green goggle-eyes. I saw at the first glance that he was no class. In fact I took him at first for a messenger boy.

"What do you want?" I asked.

"Me mudder said I was to come and play with you," he said with a scowl, and you could see he liked it about as much as I did.

"Is your name Corby?" I asked in astonishment.

"What's that?" he asked and then he said: "Yes." I didn't honestly know whether he was deaf or an idiot or both.

"Mummy!" I shouted. "Look who's here"—wondering at the

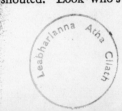

same time if she could have seen him before she asked him to the house.

But she'd seen him all right, because her face lit up and she told him to come in. He took off his cap and, after taking two steps and hearing the clatter he made in the hall with his hobnailed boots, he did the rest of it on tiptoe.

I could have cried. The fellow didn't know a single game, and when we went out playing with the Horgans and the Wrights I simply didn't know how to explain this apparition that hung on to us like some sort of poor relation.

When we sat down to dinner he put his elbows on the table and looked at us, ignoring his plate.

"Don't you like your dinner, Denis?" asked Mother—she never asked us if we liked our dinner.

"What's that?" he said, goggling at her. I was beginning to notice that he said "What's that?" only to give himself time to think up an answer. " 'Tis all right."

"Oh, you ought to eat up," said Father. "A big hefty fellow like you!"

"What does your mummy usually give you?" asked Mother.

"Soup," he said.

"Would you sooner I gave you a spoon so?"

"I would."

"What do you like for your dinner and I'll get it for you?"

"Jelly."

Now, if that had been me, not saying "please" or "thank you," I'd soon have got the back of my father's hand, but it seemed as if he could say what he liked and only eat what suited him. He took only a few mouthfuls of potatoes and gravy.

After dinner we went up to our bedroom so that we could show him our toys. He seemed as frightened of them as he was of a knife and fork.

"Haven't you any toys of your own?" I asked.

"No," he said.

"Where do you live?" asked Susie.

"The Buildings."

"Is that a nice place?"

" 'Tis all right." Everything was "all right" with him.

Now, I knew the Buildings because I passed it every day on the way to school and I knew it was not all right. It was far from it. It was a low-class sort of place where the kids went barefoot and the women sat all day on the doorsteps, talking.

"Haven't you any brothers and sisters?" Susie went on.

"No. Only me mudder. . . . And me Auntie Nellie," he added after a moment.

"Who's your Auntie Nellie?"

"My auntie. She lives down the country. She comes up of an odd time."

"And where's your daddy?" asked Susie.

"What's that?" he said, and again I could have sworn he was thinking up an answer. There was a longer pause than usual. "I tink me daddy is dead," he added.

"How do you mean you think he's dead?" asked Susie. "Don't you know?"

"Me mudder said he was dead," he said doubtfully.

"Well, your mother ought to know," said Susie. "But if your daddy is dead where do ye get the money?"

"From my Auntie Nellie."

"It's because your daddy is dead that you have no toys," Susie said in her usual God-Almighty way. " 'Tis always better if your mummy dies first."

"It is not better, Susie Murphy," I said, horrified at the cold-blooded way that girl always talked about Mummy. "God will kill you stone dead for saying that. You're only saying it because you always suck up to Daddy."

"I do not always suck up to Daddy, Michael Murphy," she replied coldly. "And it's true. Everyone knows it. If Mummy died Daddy could still keep us, but if Daddy died, Mummy wouldn't have anything."

But though I always stuck up for Mummy against Susie, I had to admit that her latest acquisition wasn't up to much.

"Ah, that woman would sicken you," Susie said when we were in bed that night. "Bringing in old beggars and tramps and giving them their dinner in our kitchen, the way you couldn't have a soul in to play, and then giving away our best clothes. You couldn't have a blooming thing in this house."

Every Saturday after that Denis Corby came and tiptoed in the hall in his hobnailed boots and spooned at his dinner. As he said, the only thing he liked was jelly. He stayed on till our bedtime and listened to Mother reading us a story. He liked stories but he couldn't read himself, even comics, so Mother started teaching him and said he was very smart. A fellow who couldn't read at the age of seven, I didn't see how he could be smart. She never said I was smart.

But in other ways he was smart enough, too smart for me. Apparently a low-class boy and a complete outsider could do things I wasn't let do, like playing round the parlour, and if you asked any questions or passed any remarks, you only got into trouble. The old game of wardrobe-raiding had begun again, and I was supposed to admire the way Denis looked in my winter coat, though in secret I shed bitter tears over that coat, which was the only thing I had that went with my yellow tie. And the longer it went on, the deeper the mystery became.

One day Susie was showing off in her usual way about having been born in Dublin. She was very silly about that, because to listen to her you'd think no one had ever been born in Dublin only herself.

"Ah, shut up!" I said. "We all know you were born in Dublin and what about it?"

"Well, you weren't," she said, skipping round, "and Denis wasn't."

"How do you know he wasn't?" I asked. "Where were you born, Denis?"

"What's that?" he asked and gaped. Then, after a moment, he said: "In England."

"Where did you say?" Susie asked, scowling.

"In England."

"How do you know?"

"Me mudder told me."

I was delighted at the turn things had taken. You never in all your life saw anyone so put out as Susie at the idea that a common boy from the Buildings could be born in a place she wasn't born in. What made it worse was that Mummy had worked in England, and it seemed to Susie like a shocking oversight not to have had her in a place she could really brag about. She was leaping.

"When was your mummy in England?" she asked.

"She wasn't in England."

"Then how could you be born there, you big, silly fool?" she stormed.

"My Auntie Nellie was there," he said sulkily.

"You couldn't be born in England just because your Auntie Nellie was there," she said vindictively.

"Why couldn't I?" he asked, getting cross.

That stumped Susie properly. It stumped me as well. Seeing that we both thought Mother had bought us from the nurse, there didn't seem to be any good reason why an aunt couldn't have bought us as well. We argued about that for hours afterwards. Susie maintained with her usual Mrs. Know-all air that if an aunt bought a baby she stopped being his aunt and became his mummy but I wasn't sure of that at all. She said she'd ask Mummy, and I warned her she'd only get her head chewed off, but she said she didn't mind.

She didn't either. That kid was madly inquisitive, and she had ways of getting information out of people that really made me ashamed. One trick of hers was to repeat whatever she'd been told with a supercilious air and then wait for results. That's what she did about Denis Corby.

"Mummy," she said next day, "do you know what that silly kid, Denis, said?"

"No, dear."

"He said he was born in England and his mother was never in England at all," said Susie and went off into an affected laugh.

"The dear knows ye might find something better to talk about," Mother said in disgust. "A lot of difference it makes to the poor child where he was born."

"What did I tell you?" I said to her afterwards. "I told you you'd only put Mummy in a wax. I tell you there's a mystery about that fellow and Mummy knows what it is. I wish he never came here at all."

The Saturday following we were all given pennies and Denis and I were sent off for a walk. I thought it very cool of Mother, knowing quite well that Denis wasn't class enough for the fellows I mixed with, but it was one of those things she didn't seem to understand and I could never explain to her. I had the feeling that it would only make her mad.

It was a nice sunny afternoon, and we stayed at the cross, collecting cigarette pictures from fellows getting off the trams. We hadn't been there long when Bastable and another fellow came down the hill, two proper toffs—I mean they weren't even at my school but went to the Grammar School.

"Hullo, Bastable," I said, "where are ye off to?" and I went a few steps with them.

"We have a boat down the river," he said. "Will you come?"

I slouched along after them, between two minds. I badly wanted to go down the river, and it was jolly decent of Bastable to have asked me, but I was tied to Denis, who wasn't class enough to bring with me even if he was asked.

"I'm with this fellow," I said with a sigh, and Bastable looked back at Denis, who was sitting on the high wall over the church, and realized at the first glance that he wouldn't do.

"Ah, boy, you don't know what you're missing," he said.

I knew that only too well. I looked up and there was Denis, goggling down at us, close enough to remind me of the miserable sort of afternoon I'd have to spend with him if I stayed, but far enough away not to be on my conscience too much.

"Denis," I shouted, "I'm going down a bit of the way with these chaps. You can wait for me if you like."

Then I began to run and the others ran with me. I felt rather ashamed, but at the time I really did intend not to stay long with them. Of course, once I got to the river I forgot all my good resolutions—you know the way it is with boats—and it wasn't until I was coming back up the avenue in the dusk and noticed the gas lamps lit that I realized how late it was and my heart sank. I was really soft-hearted and I felt full of pity for poor old Denis waiting there for me all the time. When I reached the cross and found he wasn't there it only made it worse, because it must have meant he'd given me up and gone home. I was very upset about it, particularly about what I was going to say to the mother.

When I reached home I found the front door open and the

kitchen in darkness. I went in quietly and to my astonishment I saw Mother and Denis sitting together over the fire. I just can't describe the extraordinary impression they made on me. They looked so snug, sitting there together in the firelight, that they made me feel like an outsider. I came in conscience-stricken and intending to bluff, and instead I suddenly found myself wanting to cry, I didn't know for what reason.

"Hullo," Denis said, giving me a grin, "where did you go?"

"Ah, just down the river with Bastable," I said, hanging up my cap and trying to sound casual. "Where did you get to?"

"I came back," he said still grinning.

"And indeed, Michael, you should be thoroughly ashamed of yourself, leaving Denis like that," Mother said sharply.

"But really, Mummy, I didn't," I said weakly. "I only just went down a bit of the way with them, that's all."

I found it difficult enough to get even that much out without blubbing. Denis Corby had turned the tables on me with a vengeance. It was I who was jealous, and it took me weeks to see why. Then I suddenly tumbled to the fact that though he was quite ready to play with Susie and me it wasn't for that he came to the house. It was Mother, not us, he was interested in. He even arranged things so that he didn't have to come with us and could stay behind with her. Even when she didn't want him in the house he was content to sit on the wall outside just to have her to himself if she came to the door or wanted someone to run a message for her. It was only then that my suspicions turned to panic. After that I was afraid of leaving him behind me because of what he might do or say when my back was turned. And of course he knew I knew what was in his mind, and dared me.

One day I had to go on a message to the cross and I asked him to come. He wouldn't; he said he wanted to stay and play with Susie, and she, flattered at what she thought were his attentions, took his part.

"Go on now, Michael Murphy!" she said in her bossy way. "You were sent on the message and you can go by yourself. Denis is stopping here with me."

"It's not you he wants to stop with, you little fool!" I said, losing my patience with her. "It's Mummy."

"It is not," he said, and I saw from the way he reddened that he knew I had him caught.

"It is," I said truculently. "You're always doing it. You'd better let her alone. She's not your mother."

"She's my aunt," he said sullenly.

"That's a lie," I shouted, beside myself with rage. "She's not your aunt."

"She told me to call her that," he said.

"That has nothing to do with it," I said. "She's my mummy, not yours."

He suddenly gave me a queer look.

"How do you know?" he asked in a low voice.

For a moment I was too stunned to speak. It had never struck me before that if his Aunt Nellie could be his mother, Mummy, whom he called Aunt Kate, could be his mother as well. In fact, anyone could be a fellow's mother if only he knew. My only chance was to brazen it out.

"She couldn't be," I said. "Your mother lives up the Buildings."

"She's not me mudder," he said in the same low voice.

"Oh, there's a thing to say!" I cried, though the stupefaction was put on.

"How could she be me mudder?" he went on. "She was never in England."

The mystery was so close I felt I could solve it in a few words if only I knew which. Of course it was possible that Mother, having worked in England, could be his real mother while his own mother couldn't, and this was what had been between them both from the start. The shock of it was almost more than I could bear. I could keep my end up at all only by pretending to be scandalized.

"Oh," I cried, "I'll tell her what you said."

"You can if you like," he replied sullenly.

And of course he knew I couldn't. Whatever strange hold he had over her, you simply daren't ask her a reasonable question about him.

Susie was watching the pair of us curiously. She felt there was something wrong but didn't know what. I tried to enlighten her that night in bed: how it all fitted in, his mother who couldn't be his mother because she'd never been to England, his Aunt Nellie who could but probably wasn't because he saw so little of her, and Mummy who had not only been to England but saw him every week, made a pet of him, and wouldn't let you say a word against him. Susie agreed that this was quite probable, but she was as heartless as usual about it.

"She can be his mummy if she likes," she said with a shrug. "I don't care."

"That's only because you're Daddy's pet," I said.

"It is not, Michael Murphy, but it doesn't make any difference what she is so long as he only comes every Saturday."

"You wait," I whispered threateningly. "You'll see if his mother dies he'll come and live here. Then you'll be sorry."

Susie couldn't see the seriousness of it because she was never Mummy's pet as I was, and didn't see how Denis Corby was gradually replacing us both in Mother's affection, or how day after day she mentioned him only to praise him or compare him with us. I got heart-scalded hearing how good he was. I couldn't be good in that sly, insinuating way, just trying to get inside other people. I tried, but it was no use, and after a while I lost heart and never seemed to be out of mischief. I didn't know what was wrong with me, but I was always breaking, losing, pinching. Mother didn't know either and only got more impatient with me.

"I don't know under God what's come over you," she said angrily. "Every week that passes you're becoming more and more of a savage."

As if I could be anything else, knowing what I knew! It was Denis, Denis, Denis the whole time. Denis was sick and had to be taken to a doctor and the doctor said he was worrying about something. Nothing was said about the way I was worrying, seeing him turn me into a stranger in my own house. By this time I was really desperate.

It came to a head one day when Mother asked me to go on a message. I broke down and said I didn't want to. Mother in her fury couldn't see that it was only because I'd be leaving Denis behind me.

"All right, all right," she snapped. "I'll send Denis. I'm fed up with you."

But this was worse. This was the end of everything, the final proof that I had been replaced.

"No, no, Mummy, I'll go, I'll go," I said, and I took the money and went out sobbing. Denis Corby was sitting on the wall and Susie and two other little girls were playing pickie on the garden path. Susie looked at me in surprise, her left leg still lifted.

"What ails you?" she asked.

"I have to go on a message," I said, bawling like a kid.

"Well, that's nothing to cry about."

"I have to go by myself," I wailed, though I knew well it was a silly complaint, a baby's complaint, and one I'd never have made in my right mind. Susie saw that too, and she was torn between the desire to go on with her game and to come with me to find out what was wrong.

"Can't Denis go with you?" she asked, tossing the hair from her eyes.

"He wouldn't come," I sobbed.

"You never asked me," he said in a loud, surly voice.

"Go on!" I said, blind with misery and rage. "You never come anywhere with me. You're only waiting to go in to my mother."

"I am not," he shouted.

"You are, Denis Corby," Susie said suddenly in a shrill, scolding voice, and I realized that she had at last seen the truth for herself and come down on my side. "You're always doing it. You don't come here to play with us at all."

"I do."

"You don't, you don't," I hissed, losing all control of myself and going up to him with my fists clenched. "You Indian witch!"

It was the most deadly insult I could think of, and it roused him. He got off the wall and faced Susie and me, his hands hanging, his face like a lantern.

"I'm not an Indian witch," he said with smouldering anger.

"You are an Indian witch, you are an Indian witch," I said and gave him the coward's blow, straight in the face. He didn't try to hit back though he was twice my size, a proper little sissy.

"God help us!" one of the little girls bawled. "You ought to be ashamed of yourself, hitting the little boy like that, Michael Murphy."

"Then he ought to let our mummy alone," Susie screeched. Now that she saw the others turn against me she was dancing with rage, a real little virago. "He's always trying to make out that she's his mummy, and she isn't."

"I never said she was my mummy," he said, sulky and frightened.

"You did say it," I said, and I hit him again, in the chest this time. "You're trying to make out that I'm your brother and I'm not."

"And I'm not your sister either," Susie screeched defiantly, doing a war-dance about him. "I'm Michael Murphy's sister, and I'm not your sister, and if you say I am again I'll tell my daddy on you."

"Michael, Michael Murphy! Susie! What are you doing to the little boy?" shouted a wrathful voice, and when I looked up there was an officious neighbour, clapping her hands from the gate at us. There were others out as well. We had been all shouting so loudly that we had gathered an audience. Suddenly Susie and I got two clouts that sent us flying.

"What in God's holy name is the meaning of this?" cried Mother, taking Denis by the hand. "How dare you strike that child, you dirty little corner-boy?"

Then she turned and swept in with Denis, leaving the rest of us flabbergasted.

"Now we'll all be killed," Susie snivelled, between pain and fright. "She'll murder us. And 'twas all your fault, Michael Murphy."

But by then I didn't care what happened. Denis Corby had won at last and even before the neighbours was treated as Mother's pet. In an excited tone Susie began telling the other girls about Denis and all his different mothers and all the troubles they had brought on us.

He was inside a long time, a very long time it seemed to me. Then he came out by himself and it was only afterwards I remembered that he did it on tiptoe. Mother looked like murder all that day. The following Saturday Denis didn't come at all and the Saturday after Mother sent Susie and me up to the Buildings for him.

By that time I didn't really mind and I bore him no grudge for what had happened. Mother had explained to us that she wasn't really his mother, and that, in fact, he hadn't any proper mother. This was what she had told him when she brought him in, and it seems it was a nasty shock to him. You could understand that, of course. If a fellow really did think someone was his mother and then found she wasn't it would be quite a shock. I was full of compassion for him really. The whole week I'd been angelic—even Mummy admitted that.

When we went in he was sitting at the fire with his mother—the one he thought at first was, his mother. She made a fuss of Susie and me and said what lovely children we were. I didn't like her very much myself. I thought her too sweet to be wholesome.

"Go on back with them now, Dinny boy," she said, pawing him on the knee. "Sure you haven't a soul to play with in this old hole."

But he wouldn't come, and nothing we said could make him. He treated us like enemies, almost. Really I suppose he felt a bit of a fool. His mother was a wrinkled old woman; the house was only a labourer's cottage without even an upstairs room; you could see they were no class, and as I said to Susie on the .way home, the fellow had a cool cheek to imagine we were his brother and sister.

FIRST LOVE

PETER met Mick Dowling for the first time when he was sixteen and Mick was eighteen. The age gap between them was wide but it was not the only thing that divided them. Mick was a

university student and Peter an office boy. He called himself a
junior clerk but that was only to save his face. And as well as
that, Peter was moody and contrary, boastful and inclined to
self-pity, unable to concentrate. Now it was a commercial career
he proposed for himself, and he took up accountancy, but by the
following week he had already tired of that and wanted to be a
soldier, a man of action, to travel and see the world. Then he
took up French and smoked French cigarettes. Mick already
stood out among his contemporaries, a grown man, tall, well-
built and extremely sedate. He had an inexpressive face, handsome in a rough-hewn way, which would have been dull but for
the flush which occasionally lit it up and hinted at the depth of
feeling beneath.

Their first meeting threw Peter into a perfect fever. He knew
at once that Mick was the one man in the world he wanted to
be. In the office he tried to imitate Mick's manners and way of
speech; very slow, very serious, even dull except for an almost
imperceptible streak of poker-faced humour. But either it did not
suit the office or it didn't suit Peter, because several of the clerks
looked at him in astonishment and said: "What's wrong with
you, Dwyer? Are you sick?" When they started to ridicule him
he decided to reserve his imitation of Mick for more suitable
company.

Unfortunately, Mick did not seem to like him at all. When they
met he was usually with two friends of his own age, Conway and
Hynes, and Peter had to force his company on them. They treated
him as a kid, and Peter, stung, talked well above his age and
station, bragging and blustering, though at the same time he
knew that he was behaving in a way the very opposite of Mick's.
Sometimes he caught the calm grey eyes fixed searchingly on
him for a moment and then a mask of reserve, like creeping
paralysis, spread down Mick's handsome face.

Peter took his evening walk up the Western Road, and sometimes caught Mick, Conway, and Hynes when they were sitting
on the river wall below the bridge and could not escape him.
Their departure left him giddy and inclined to tears. As his
bluster only roused their mockery he resolved to be profound,
and for weeks spoke only in a deep voice on serious subjects,

while to keep his face from betraying him he adopted the air of a man recovering from a serious illness. He thought he saw Mick give him that furtive puzzled look a little oftener, but then one evening Mick crushed him with a few words and in a way that showed he had found Peter out. Peter walked back by Sunday's Well in the moonlight, wept a little, and resolved not to speak to Mick again till he was a great and famous man and could show Mick how wrong he had been.

This mood lasted a whole day but, with the bottling-down effect of the office, enthusiasm returned towards evening, and it seemed to him that it was rather unjust to Mick to punish him so severely for a moment's ill humour, and his imagination got to work again. In the talk between Mick and his friends he had noticed that Mick was more deeply concerned about religion than they. They only chattered about priests being rich and having cars and being seen with girls—the usual envious talk of young men with salaries too small for their imaginations—but Mick always brought the talk back to fundamentals: Eternity, Hell, Purgatory, Limbo, Sin. Now Peter knew that fundamentals were his own strong point. He had studied them all and decided that they were grossly exaggerated. This, he felt, was the way to attract Mick's attention. He succeeded only too well. As he talked, Mick's face grew blacker and blacker.

"If you knew what you were talking about, Dwyer," he said in a low voice, "you'd want your backside kicked."

Stung to tears, not so much by the rebuke as by the presence of Hynes and Conway, whom he despised, Peter retorted by calling Mick "a crawthumper" and "a bourgeois parasite," and stamped off, in real despair this time. How was he to have known that Mick's intellectual corns were so tender? He felt now that he had succeeded in making Mick his enemy for life and that even becoming a great and famous man would not wipe out the injury.

A week later he ran into the three of them on the Western Road. They were coming up as he was returning and he deliberately looked the other way. He didn't intend Mick to get away with the impression that he couldn't be done without. From the corner of his eye he saw Mick stare and then stop. The others stopped as well.

"Hullo, Peter," he said.

"Oh, hullo, Mick," Peter said with fictitious surprise.

"Come along back with us," Mick said more by way of an order than an invitation.

Peter was so astonished that he was modest and almost silent for a quarter of an hour. He couldn't make it out. He didn't know whether Mick had recognized the justice of his charge about being "a bourgeois parasite" or was so full of pity for his ignorance that he wanted to be kind. To be truthful with himself, he had to admit that he didn't give a damn. The main thing was that Mick had wiped out the injury.

But there were stranger things to come. On the way back Hynes stopped outside a pub and suggested a drink with something like a gangster air. As Peter had only a shilling and didn't know whether or not it would buy a round of drinks he pleaded an appointment. Mick didn't even ask whom the appointment was with. He merely took Peter firmly by the arm and pushed him in, laughing and uneasy. In a furtive whisper Hynes asked each what they'd have, and Peter, copying the others, said in a low voice: "Stout, please."

"Stout, right," said Hynes with a nod.

"He's having ginger beer, Bill," Mick said quietly, and Peter, thrilled at the tone of quiet authority with which he spoke, said at once: "All right. Ginger beer will do."

He watched to see how much Hynes paid, and then stood up and said with a grown-up air: "Same again, lads?" But before the others could reply Mick had chimed in with his poker-faced air.

"There's a bobby in plain clothes at the bar. Children under twelve aren't supposed to be here. I'd hide if I was you."

Peter felt suddenly close to tears. It was not only a recognition that his position was privileged by the fact that he couldn't afford it; it was an admission that he was now, really and truly, one of the group.

Clearly, Hynes and Conway could not understand what Mick

saw in him, and when they got Peter alone they ragged him unmercifully, but even their ragging was now on a different key; it was the ragging of a mascot whose extravagances provided them with entertainment, not the ragging of an outsider who tried to butt in. Even alone he was protected by his friendship with Mick. Mick called for him and Peter suffered endless embarrassment mingled with pride, knowing his visits were talked of. He in turn soon got to know Mick's people, who lived in a small house on a terrace. His father was a builder, his mother a tall, sugary, pious woman who was a sore trial to Mick. She was a hard-working woman but she had no method, was always losing or mislaying money, borrowing to make it up so that her husband wouldn't know, and then taking sips of whisky on the side to nerve her for the ordeal of "telling Dowling." If she worried about her husband and son, this was pure good-nature on her part, because she had cause enough to worry about herself. All the same it riled Mick, particularly when she made novenas for him to pass his examinations. When everyone in the university recognizes your industry and brilliance, it's not pleasant to have all the credit go to the Infant Jesus of Prague or St. Rose of Lima. Mick argued with her and denounced her superstition, but she only looked at him with a pitying, good-natured smile and said: "We're all smart when we're your age." She was a plain woman who looked on heaven as a glorified extension of the County Council, where saints, with the faces of County Councillors, made it their business to look after the interests of relatives and constituents.

Though Mick was rather silent about his parents, he once confessed to Peter that it was largely because of her that he was so touchy about religion. He lived in dread of losing his faith. To Peter, strong on fundamentals, this did not seem such a serious loss, but Mick went on to explain that it was different for him because he was a man of ungovernable passions and religion was the only thing which stood between them and him. When he walked through town he averted his eyes from the shopwindows with their frillies and half-dressed tailors' dummies, and suffered agonies of conscience with Babiche Regan, the girl he walked out with, comparing his own gloomy fantasies of lust with her radiance and innocence. But Peter knew himself to be of coarser stuff altogether; though he had no Babiche Regan to act as a standard for judging himself, he was merely thrilled by the blast of inconsequence and frivolity that came from the nightdresses in shopwindows and explained and humanized the frosty beauties who ignored him in the street; and though he now realized that Mick's quiet manner concealed passions stronger than his own, and continued to admire him as a marvel of self-control, he felt no conflict whatever in himself and thought that, if all he heard was true, sexual experience and losing one's faith were equally interesting and exhilarating.

But his own life continued to be bounded by home and the office, and whenever he met a girl he became impossible. It was just as with Mick only worse; the profound sense of his own inadequacy hit him like a gale of wind, and at once he began to rave about Tolstoy and his views of women. What was worse, he even did it to Babiche and Rosemary. One evening Mick and himself met them in town, and Mick, whose passions were probably giving him trouble, suggested that the four of them go for a walk over the hills to the river. It was an attractive suggestion; too attractive for Peter, because his panic grew to such an extent that within ten minutes his conversation had sent the two girls flying. It was a summer evening and Mick stood in an almost empty street, looking after them, his hands in his trousers pockets and as mad as ever Peter had seen him look.

"What the hell did Tolstoy say about women anyway?" he asked gruffly over his shoulder without even looking at Peter.

"Oh, about clothes," stammered Peter, feeling only too well how unconvincing it sounded. "That women are only interested in a man's clothes."

"Sounds as if Tolstoy wanted his backside kicked too," Mick said gloomily.

Peter's eyes suddenly filled with tears.

"It's only nerves, you know, Mick," he said in a high, squeaky voice.

Mick thought about that for a moment and then gave a faint grin.

"I used to talk to Babiche about building," he said.

D

Babiche was really pretty and attractive and unlike any other girl whom Peter had met. He was really quite satisfied that she escaped from Tolstoy's generalization. She was frank, inconsequent, and startlingly generous. When Mick took Peter to her house she insisted on showing him the bathroom herself, and when they met in town and he had the nerve to ask her to have coffee she wanted to force a ten-shilling note on him. She was the only girl Peter had met who seemed to have any intuition about the agonies of self-consciousness that young fellows went through, and Peter could well believe that she had cured Mick of talking about building technique.

He sometimes felt that if only he had been lucky enough to discover her for himself she could have cured him too, but as Mick's intended she could do nothing for him. For Mick's sake he tried hard to like her, but he couldn't like anyone who took Mick away from him so many nights in the week. When they were going to the theatre he spent a gloomy day in the office because of the lonesome evening which faced him. When they went for a walk he turned deliberately in the opposite direction, trying to say lightly to Hynes or Conway when they asked where Mick was: "Oh, out with the doll as usual." And then when Mick and he met he had to listen to Mick repeating her amusing remarks, all off at a tangent, and all, according to Mick, who seemed to brood over them as though they were oracles, peculiarly and even unnaturally apposite and witty, and pretend to be amused himself while wondering at the blindness of such a brilliant man. He wished to be just but he knew he was jealous.

Mick, who seemed to recognize it, tried bringing Peter with them but Peter talked so much that Babiche never got a chance. Then she took a hand by bringing Rosemary as well. Babiche was convinced that Rosemary was an intellectual, and that, since Peter was intellectual too, they should hit it off. Actually Rosemary, gold to Babiche's black, though quite as pretty, was the silliest girl God ever put into the world. Mick had a very soft spot for her, but then Mick had what Peter lacked, a philosophic interest in the silliness of girls compared with the silliness of fellows. Rosemary attended the School of Art and fooled with amateur theatricals. Naturally Peter could not let her get away with this, and whenever she talked of some dim acquaintance in the School of Art who was supposed to draw well he said firmly that no modern could draw except perhaps Degas, knowing perfectly well that Rosemary would never have heard of Degas or remembered it if she had.

But though Peter could quench the girls' chatter in a way that made Mick sigh, they had ways of getting their own back on him against which he was defenceless. It didn't even have to be a joke; a glance or a smile could be sufficient. There were times after he had been out with them when he felt he had been scratched all over and wondered at Mick's lack of taste. Babiche was better than Rosemary, of course; Babiche at least was human, but all the same she was not good enough for Mick. It was not her fault that she was shallow, uneducated and provincial, but there was more than that in it. Jealousy apart, he felt that she lacked Mick's nobility of character and that sooner or later she would be bound to betray his trust. Peter was too modest to lay claim to nobility himself, but he knew it when he saw it; he felt that Mick's crude passions might be less dangerous to their happiness than Babiche's good-natured commonness, and that the radiance and innocence against which Mick contrasted himself was probably no more than another of his illusions. There was tragedy in the situation. He saw it all coming, but was powerless to intervene. The disparity of ages made it impossible. With a younger man—indeed with anyone else except Mick—he would merely have said: "You know, old man, Babiche is a very attractive girl but she isn't your weight."

Mick left the university and took his first job, in a country town. For the first time Peter really knew what loneliness was. Mick wrote frequently and amusingly, and the whole life of the small town was revealed in his letters, but somehow the life of the city as Peter tried to bottle it in its own letters seemed cruelly dull; without Mick it seemed that it could be nothing but dull. He went down and spent a weekend at Mick's lodgings and this was wonderful, because Mick took him to the hotel and laid on all the characters whose amusing remarks had filled his letters, like the inspector of schools who said that the only thing he really missed in the Irish countryside was a nice dish of Roumanian pie.

They all seemed to drink a good deal, and Mick took bottle for bottle with them, but in the way in which he did everything else, without once losing control of the situation. Even in drink Mick remained himself.

Back in town, Peter's loneliness returned worse than ever. He began to feel that he couldn't continue there much longer. He too would have to break out, and if it was only as a labourer in an English town it would be better than hanging on as a clerk among people whom he despised. He went for walks only with Conway and Hynes, but since Mick's departure they had proved mediocre company. He talked of Mick to them, but they didn't seem to realize that they were talking of a man who was immeasurably their superior. Then he took to calling at Mick's house by way of inquiring if there was anything he could do for Mrs. Dowling, but really to talk of him and get material for his letters. But Mrs. Dowling too seemed to be unaware that there was anything remarkable about her son, and seemed inclined to credit it all to the account of the Infant Jesus of Prague and St. Rose of Lima. Mick's father was an intelligent, excitable man who had no truck with saints, and Peter felt sure that he could tell him a lot about Mick if only he ever happened to think of him while Peter was there, but the visits and the occasions when he thought of Mick never seemed to synchronize, and all Peter got from him were reminiscences of the Civil War—a trifling affair, as Peter thought. There was nothing else for it. Babiche was the only one he could talk to about Mick, and to Babiche he went, Rosemary notwithstanding. With Mick absent and visited by them both only on occasional weekends, he was prepared to call an armistice to jealousy.

Babiche seemed to like it too. At least she always lit up whenever he came, in a way quite different to her old watchful good-humoured air. It even struck Peter that she was probably a bit lonely herself, because even if you are not worthy of a man like Mick, he still leaves a gap in your life. It also seemed to have occurred to her that even if Rosemary was intellectual it was not in quite the same way as he, and whenever he called to bring her for a walk she always put on her hat and coat very firmly without hinting to Rosemary that she might join them. Rosemary giggled at them both with a malicious and knowing air.

"I hope Mick Dowling doesn't get to hear of this," she said.

"I tell Mick about everything we do," Peter said in a crushing tone, but Babiche only laughed and bit her underlip as she glanced in the mirror over the fireplace.

"Anyway, it's his own fault for leaving me in Peter's charge," she said as she pulled on her belt, apparently not in the least put out by Rosemary's ragging.

Peter didn't altogether like her taking that tone with Rosemary; someone, he felt, should really tell the girl that she dragged down everything she touched to the level of her own sordid day-dreaming.

But Babiche was grand. She never seemed to weary talking of Mick. The walks they took were his favourite walks, along the river and up the hills; the things they admired were those that interested him, like the old Georgian houses behind their belts of trees; and, imagining how they would strike Mick, Peter imitated his gravity, his concentration, and his solemn poker-faced humour until Babiche shrieked with laughter, grabbed his arm and shouted: "Stop!" She said he was the funniest thing she'd ever seen, and at home she insisted on his repeating it for her family and their guests. "Go on, Peter!" she would say eagerly. "Do Mick for us—he's a scream!" she would add inconsequently to anyone who happened to be there. And Peter would sit up stiff in his chair with unblinking inexpressive eyes and, apparently struggling for every word, announce that mimicry was more suitable for children than for adults, and Babiche would go into shrieks of laughter again till she had everyone laughing with her. "It's Mick!" she cried. "Mick down to the ground! Do Mick at the races!" For the first time Peter found himself a social success and stopped talking of Tolstoy and Degas.

He was almost too successful. This was not the purpose for which his imitation of Mick was intended at all. He had begun it in the office, in the same way as he had begun imitating Mick's handwriting, because he had at last discovered the person he really wanted to be, and continued it because when he was lonely it was a way of evoking Mick's personality so that he could carry on interesting conversations with himself on his solitary walks; but when he did it like this before strangers—even before Babiche —it was not the same thing at all. It was almost as though characteristics in himself which he didn't even know of were crowding to it as a safety valve, and what emerged was not glorification but ridicule. He always felt uneasy after it, as though he had exposed the more precious part of himself to mockery, and he even resented the way Babiche encouraged him. It only showed her even less worthy of Mick.

But at the same time he could not refuse her, could not even check her. The truth was that as he grew accustomed to being with her and to the chaffing of fellows in the office about her he found himself becoming jealous of Mick as well as of her. His mimicry, which had been a way of aspiring to Mick, was now turning into a way of being superior to him. He wanted to be Mick; he wanted to be well-balanced and serious, and because in some way Mick's seriousness was connected with his love of Babiche, Peter felt he must love her too. While he was with her, though still professing to admire Mick, he found himself trying to shake Babiche's confidence in him. Though he knew he was behaving badly he repeated to her things that Mick had said to him about the trouble he had with his ungovernable passions. Alternatively and contradictorily he stressed Mick's preoccupation with religion and suggested that Mick would never really be happy as anything but a monk—preferably a Trappist. Whichever line he took it was to sympathize with her in having to deal with such an unpredictable man. At the same time he was slightly annoyed because she didn't seem to mind.

One evening as they walked up a dark lane from the river Peter probed her like that—slyly as he thought. This time it was Mick's ungovernable passions that were uppermost.

"I suppose he must have another girl down there," he said sadly.

"You didn't meet her?" she asked with interest.

"No, but you know how secretive Mick is. You wouldn't blame him, of course—a chap as elemental as that."

"I'm not blaming him," she said with a shrug. "I suppose it's only natural. I don't mind."

They emerged onto an open place above the roofs of a terrace. The valley of the river stretched up from them, the meadows flooded, the city in the background, spires peering out of brown mist. It was obvious that Babiche did not care greatly for Mick. What was worse, her standards of fidelity were as low as Peter had always suspected. But he didn't care about that.

"All right," he said in a low voice. "If he picks up with another girl, you take me and then we'll all be happy."

She looked at him in surprise for a moment and shrugged herself again. She seemed more surprised than annoyed.

"Don't be silly!" she said. "You'd never be satisfied with someone like me."

"Don't be too sure of that," he said earnestly, taking her hand. It was so small it almost frightened him into dropping it again, small and living and frightening like a bird the time you take it up. She didn't seem to mind his holding it. She didn't even seem to mind his kissing her, but she was alarmed at the way he did it.

"All right, all right," she said with a grin. "Don't make a show of us. Come in here where we won't be seen."

After that they returned to her house and she made tea. She seemed quietly, snugly happy and without a shadow of guilt, and whenever her eye caught his she grinned and wriggled her shoulders contentedly. Peter, who would have plunged at once into a discussion of the difference the evening had made in the relations of both of them with Mick, felt it might be in bad taste while she continued in this humour.

Then the detestable Rosemary came in and seemed to understand it all at a glance. She stood in the doorway, tapping a theatre program on her knee, and looked knowingly from one to the other.

"Sorry to intrude," she said in a high, giggling, affected voice. "You really should have a red light outside the studio. Babiche, have you been at my rouge again?"

Babiche tucked in her chin, grinned knowingly, and did some-

thing attractive and silly with her back hair. Peter sat and glowered in silence. It was as though Rosemary had been expecting
and prophesying it for months and Babiche was amused at her
shrewdness. She accompanied Peter to the gate and he kissed her
good-night in a tumult of emotion. In his arms she felt real,
but she looked and spoke like something out of a fairy tale. Obviously, Tolstoy hadn't a clue. Peter felt suddenly as though he
had become ten years older, full of power, peace, and self-confi-
dence, never again to be shaken to the heart by some generalization out of a book. He had broken out of the magic circle of
fantasy into the wide world of reality where Mick lived. He was
Mick; he was loved by the girl Mick loved; what better proof
could anyone ask for? The moon was high in the sky over the
valley of the city, where now the mist was white, and he stood
for a few moments in a gateway, looking down at it through the
bars as though he had just given birth to it.

Then his mind reverted to the problem Babiche's nonchalance
had deferred. What was to happen about Mick? He could, of
course, take Babiche from Mick, but when it came to the point
he felt that he needed Mick more than Babiche. His duty to
Mick required him to see that nothing of the sort occurred again.
This would be a strain, but nothing like the strain it would have
continued to be unless it had happened. Since it had, and could
not be denied, he was enabled to bear the thought of the future
with equanimity. He would easily find another girl, since after
Babiche the rest would be child's play. Nothing whatever could
now stop him in a career of conquest. But it occurred to him
that it might be difficult to make Babiche take the same noble
view. As Peter had always suspected, she was an impulsive, sensual girl who always needed a man about her. And again it
astonished him that Mick, years older than he and so much more
brilliant, had not realized it for himself. Babiche was a nice girl,
a really delightful girl, but quite unworthy of his friend.

Unfortunately, this was something that Peter still could not
tell him, even now. Particularly now. It would always have to
remain a secret between Babiche and himself, and this would be
made far more difficult by the malice of Rosemary who, to avenge
the way he had humiliated her on the subject of Degas, would

take any opportunity of injuring him with Mick. This time it was his own blindness that he wondered that. As a realist he should have seen that Rosemary expected what had happened merely because she knew her sister so much better than Mick or himself knew her, and had merely waited cynically for the moment when some man would give her an opportunity. Probably the only thing which had surprised them both was the length of time Peter had taken about it. There were depths of unworthiness in Babiche which even he had not suspected. She wouldn't do; she wouldn't do at all. It was madness to have endangered his friendship with Mick over such a woman.

But it was only in bed that the full madness of his conduct was revealed to him. He had indeed proved Babiche unworthy of Mick, but only at the cost of proving himself unworthy of him. Mick would forgive Babiche because unworthy women had the advantage of being forgiven. He wouldn't be forgiven, and all his ideas of covering it up were only fantasies. He couldn't lie to Mick because Mick was both inside and outside him; he was Mick, and he knew that the Mick within him would not let him rest. His mistake had been in trying to become Mick in the outside world as well, for in that process he had become something which the real Mick would despise.

He knew it was hopeless. He did not go to Babiche's again. She wrote asking him to tea—a cheerful, inconsequent, rattle-pated letter that showed her entirely devoid of any sense of guilt—but he didn't reply. Mick came home on holidays but didn't call to see him. Peter knew he had learned the whole story from herself, or worse, from Rosemary. All lies, he knew, but no lies could be worse than the truth. In sober moments he realized that it was only growing-pains. There would be other friends and other girls but never again anything like this. His treachery had made two parts of him. He had become a man. But the idea gave him singularly little comfort.

FREEDOM

When I was interned during the war with the British I dreamed endlessly of escape. As internment camps go, ours was pretty good. We had a theatre, games, and classes, and some of the classes were first-rate.

It was divided into two areas, North Camp and South, and the layout of the huts was sufficiently varied to give you a feeling of change when you went for a stroll round the wires. The tall wooden watchtowers, protected from the weather by canvas sheets, which commanded the barbed wire at intervals had a sort of ragged functional beauty of their own. You could do a five-mile walk there before breakfast and not feel bored.

But I ached to get away. It is almost impossible to describe how I ached. In the evenings I walked round the camp and always stopped at least once on a little hillock in the North Camp which had the best view of the flat green landscape of Kildare that stretched all round us for miles. It was brilliantly green, and the wide crowded skies had all the incredible atmospheric effects of flat country, with veil after veil of mist or rain even on the finest days, and I thought of the tinker families drifting or resting in the shadow of the hedges while summer lasted. God, I used to think, if only I could escape I'd never stop, summer or winter, but just go on and on, making my fire under a hedge and sleeping in a barn or under an upturned cart. Night and day I'd go on, maybe for years, maybe till I died. If only I could escape!

But there isn't any escape. I saw that even in the camp itself. I became friendly with two prisoners, Matt Deignan and Mick Stewart, both from Cork. They were nice lads; Mick sombre, reserved, and a bit lazy; Matt noisy, emotional, and energetic. They messed together and Matt came in for most of the work. That wasn't all he came in for. When Mick was in one of his violent moods and had to have someone to wrestle with, Matt was the victim. Mick wrestled with him, ground his arms behind his back, made him yelp with pain and plead for mercy. Sometimes he reduced Matt to tears, and for hours Matt wouldn't speak to him. It never went farther than that though. Matt was Caliban to Mick's Prospero and had to obey. He would come to me, a graceless gawk with a moony face, and moan to me about Mick's cruelty and insolence, but this was only because he knew Mick liked me, and he hoped to squelch Mick out of my mouth. If anyone else dared to say a word against Mick he mocked at them. They were jealous!

Matt had a job in the Quartermaster's store, the Quartermaster, one Clancy, being some sort of eminent, distant cousin of whom Matt was enormously proud. Mick and he both dossed in J Hut in the North Camp. Now J was always a rather tony hut, quite different from Q, where I hung out, which was nothing but a municipal slaughterhouse. The tone of J was kept up by about a dozen senior officers and politicians, businessmen and the like. The hut leader, Jim Brennan, a tough little Dublin mason whom I admired, though not class himself, liked class: he liked businessmen and fellows who wore silk pyjamas and university students who could tell him all about God, V. D., and the next world. It broadened a man's mind a lot. These got off lightly; either they had doctor's certificates to prove they couldn't do fatigues or they had nominal jobs, which meant they didn't have to do them. You couldn't blame Jim; it was his hut, and he kept it like a battleship, and to get into it at all was considered a bit of luck. Nor did the other men in the hut object; they might be only poor country lads, but, like Jim, they enjoyed mixing with fellows of a different class and listening to arguments about religion over the stove at night. It might be the only opportunity most of them would ever have of hearing anything except about drains and diseases of cattle, and they were storing it up. It was a thoroughly happy hut, and it rather surprised me that two attempts at tunneling had begun from it; if it wasn't that the occupants wanted to show off their intelligence, you wouldn't know what they wanted to escape for.

But Mick Stewart rather resented the undemocratic tone of the hut and was careful to keep the camp aristocracy at a distance. When someone like Jack Costello, the draper, addressed Mick with what he thought undue familiarity, Mick pretended not to hear. Costello was surprised and Brennan was seriously displeased. He thought it disrespectful. He never noticed Mick except to give him an order. A couple of times he made him go over a job twice, partly to see it was properly done, partly to put Mick in his place.

Now, Mick was one of those blokes who never know they have a place. One day he just struck. While the others continued scrubbing he threw himself on his bed with his hands under his head and told the hut leader to do it himself. He did it with an icy calm which anyone who knew Mick would have known meant danger.

"You mean you call that clean?" Brennan asked, standing at the end of Mick's bed with his hands in his trouser pockets and his old cap over one eye.

"It's not a matter of opinion," Mick said in his rather high-pitched, piping voice.

"Oh, isn't it?" asked Brennan and then called over Jack Costello. "Jack," he continued mildly, "is that what you'd call clean?"

"Ah, come on, Stewart, come on!" Costello said in his best "Arise, Ye Sons of Erin" manner. "Don't be a blooming passenger!"

"I didn't know I asked your advice, Costello," Mick said frostily, "but as you seem to be looking for a job as a deckhand, fire ahead!"

"I certainly will," Costello said gamely. "Just to show I'm not too proud to be a deckhand."

"No, you won't, Jack," Brennan said heavily. "There's going to be no passengers on this boat. Are you going to obey orders, Stewart?"

"If you mean am I going to do every job twice, I'm not," replied Mick with a glare.

"Good enough," Brennan said moodily as he turned away. "We'll see about that."

Now, I should perhaps have explained that the camp duplicated the whole British organization. Each morning we stood to attention at the foot of our beds to be counted, but one of our own officers always accompanied the counting party and ostensibly it was for him and not for the British officer that we paraded. It was the same with everything else; we recognized only our own officers. The Quartermaster drew the stores from the British and we received them from him and signed for them to him. The mail was sorted and delivered by our own post-office staff. We had our cooks, our doctors, our teachers and actors—even our police. Because, if one of our fellows was caught pinching another man's stuff, we had our own police to arrest him and our own military court to try him. In this way, we of the rank and file never came into contact at all with our jailers.

That morning two of the camp police, wearing tricolour armlets, came to march Mick down to the hut where his case was to be tried. One of them was a great galumphing lout called Kenefick, a bit of a simpleton, who cracked heavy jokes with Mick because he felt so self-conscious with his armlet. The case was heard in the camp office. When I passed I saw Matt Deignan outside, looking nervous and lonely. I stopped to talk with him and Brennan passed in, sulky and stubborn, without as much as a glance at either of us. Matt burst into a long invective against him, and I tried to shut him up, because in spite of his boorishness I respected Brennan.

"Ah, well," I said, "you can't put all the blame on Brennan. You know quite well that Mick is headstrong too."

"Headstrong?" yelped Matt, ready to eat me. "And wouldn't he want to be with a dirty lout like that?"

"Brennan is no lout," I said. "He's a fine soldier."

"He is," Matt said bitterly. "He'd want to walk on you."

"That's what soldiers are for," I said, but Matt wasn't in a mood for facetiousness.

The court seemed to be a long time sitting, and it struck me that it might have been indiscreet enough to start an argument with Mick. This would have been a long operation. But at last he came out, a bit red but quite pleased with himself, and I decided that if there had been an argument he had got the better of it. We set off for a brisk walk round the camp. Mick would talk of everything except the case. Mick all out! He knew poor Matt was broken down with anxiety and was determined on toughening him.

"Well," I said at last, "what's the verdict?"

"Oh, that business!" he said contemptuously. "Just what you'd expect."

"And what's the sentence? Death or a five year dip?"

"A week's fatigues."

"That's not so bad," I said.

"Not so bad?" cried Matt, almost in tears. "And for what? Pure spite because Mick wouldn't kowtow to them. 'Tis all that fellow Costello, Mick boy," he went on with a tragic air. "I never liked him. He's the fellow that's poisoning them against you."

"He's welcome," Mick said frostily, deprecating all this vulgar emotionalism of Matt's. "I'm not doing extra fatigues for them."

"And you're right, Mick," exclaimed Matt, halting. "You're right. I'd see them in hell first."

"You don't mean you're going to refuse to obey the staff?" I asked doubtfully.

"What else can I do?" Mick asked in a shrill complaining voice. "Don't you realize what will happen if I let Brennan get away with this? He'll make my life a misery."

"Starting a row with the camp command isn't going to make it exactly a honeymoon," I said.

It didn't, but even I was astonished at the feeling roused by Mick's rebellion. Men who knew that he and I were friendly attacked him to me. No one said a word in his favour. And it wasn't that they were worried by the thing that worried me—that right or wrong, the camp command was the only elected authority in the camp—oh, no. Mick was disloyal to the cause, disloyal to the camp; worst of all, he was putting on airs. You would think that men who were rebels themselves and suffering for their views would have some sympathy for him.

"But the man is only sticking out for what he thinks are his rights," I protested.

"Rights?" one man echoed wonderingly. "What rights has he? Haven't we all to work?"

After a while I gave up arguing. It left me with the feeling that liberty wasn't quite such a clear-cut issue as I had believed it. Clancy, the Quartermaster, though himself one of the staff, was the most reasonable man on the other side. No doubt he felt he had to be because Mick was his cousin's friend. He was a gallant little man, small, fiery, and conscientious, and never really himself till he began to blaspheme. This wasn't yet a subject for blasphemy so he wasn't quite himself. He grasped me firmly by the shoulder, stared at me closely with his bright blue eyes and then looked away into an infinite distance.

"Jack," he said in a low voice, "between friends, tell that boy, Stewart, to have sense. The Commandant is very vexed. He's a severe man. I wouldn't like to be in Stewart's shoes if he crosses him again."

"I suppose ye'd never use your brains and send Stewart and Matt to Q Hut?" I asked. "It's only the way Mick and Brennan don't get on, and two human beings would improve Q Hut enormously."

"Done!" he exclaimed, holding out his hand in a magnificent gesture. "The minute he has his fatigues done. I'll tell the Commandant."

I put that solution up to Mick and he turned it down in the most reasonable way in the world. That was one thing I was learning: your true rebel is nothing if not reasonable; it is only his premises that are dotty. Mick explained patiently that he couldn't agree to a compromise which would still leave him with a stain on his character because if ever we resurrected the army again and the army got down to keeping records it would count as a black mark against him.

"You mean for a pension?" I said, turning nasty, but Mick didn't realize that. He only thought it was rather crude of me to be so materialistic about a matter of principle. I was beginning to wonder if my own premises were quite sound.

Next morning I went over to J Hut to see how things were panning out. They looked pretty bad to me. It was a large, light, airy hut like a theatre with a low wooden partition down the middle and the beds ranged at either side of the partition and along the walls. It was unusually full for that hour of the morning, and there was a peculiar feeling you only get from a mob which is just on the point of getting out of hand. Mick was lying on his own bed, and Matt sitting on the edge of his, talking to him. No one seemed interested in them. The rest were sitting round the stove or fooling with macramé bags, waiting to see what happened. Three beds down from Mick was a handsome young Wexford fellow called Howard, also lying on his bed and ostensibly talking to his buddy. He saw me come in and raised his voice.

"The trouble is," he was saying, "people who won't pull their weight would be better at the other side of the wire."

"Are you referring to me, Howard?" Mick asked harshly.

Howard sat up and turned a beaming adolescent face on him.

"As a matter of fact I am, Stewart," he said.

"We were on the right side before ever ye were heard of, Howard," bawled Matt. "What the hell did ye ever do in Wexford beyond shooting a couple of misfortunate policemen?"

I started talking feverishly to avert the row, but fortunately just then Kenefick and another policeman of the right sort came in. This time they showed no embarrassment and there was nothing in the least matey about their attitude. It gave their tricolour armlets a certain significance. As we followed them out the whole hut began to hiss. Matt turned as though something had struck him but I pushed him out. It was all much worse than I expected.

Again Matt and I had to wait outside the office while the trial went on, but this time I wasn't feeling quite so light-hearted, and as for Matt, I could see it was the most tragic moment of his life. Never before had he thought of himself as a traitor, an enemy of society, but that was what they were trying to make of him.

This time when Mick emerged he had the two policemen with him. He tried to maintain a defiant air, but even he looked depressed.

"What happened, Mick?" bawled Matt, hurling himself on him like a distracted mother of nine.

"You're not supposed to talk to the prisoner," said Kenefick.

"Ah, shut up you, Kenefick!" I snapped. "What's the result, Mick?"

"Oh, I believe I'm going to jail," said Mick, laughing without amusement.

"Going where?" I asked incredulously.

"So I'm told," he replied with a shrug.

"But what jail?"

"Damned if I know," he said, and suddenly began to laugh with genuine amusement.

"You'll know soon enough," growled Kenefick, who seemed to resent the laughter as a slight on his office.

"Cripes, Kenefick," I said, "you missed your vocation."

It really was extraordinary, how everything in that camp became a sort of crazy duplicate of something in the outside world. Nothing but an armlet had turned a good-natured halfwit like Kenefick into a real policeman, exactly like the ones who had terrified me as a kid when I'd been playing football on the road. I had noticed it before; how the post-office clerks became sulky and uncommunicative; how the fellows who played girls in the Sunday-evening shows made scenes and threw up their parts exactly like film stars, and some of the teachers started sending them notes. But now the whole crazy pattern seemed to be falling into place. At any moment I expected to find myself skulking away from Kenefick.

We moved in a group between the huts to the rather unpleasant corner of the camp behind the cookhouse. Then I suddenly saw what Kenefick meant. There was a little hut you wouldn't notice, a small storeroom which might have been a timekeeper's hut in a factory only that its one small window had bars. The pattern was complete at last; as well as store, school, theatre, church, post office, and police court we now had a real jail of our own. Inside it had bedboards, a three-biscuit mattress, and blankets.

They had thought of everything down to the bucket. It amused me so much that I scarcely felt any emotion at saying good-bye to Mick. But Matt was beside himself with rage.

"Where are you off to?" I asked as he tore away across the camp.

"I'm going to hand in my resignation to Clancy," he hissed.

"But what good will that do? It'll only mean you'll have to do fatigues instead and Brennan will get his knife in you too."

"And isn't that what I want?" he cried. "You don't think I'm going to stop outside in freedom and leave poor Mick in there alone?"

I was on the point of asking him his definition of freedom, but I realized in time that he wasn't in a state to discuss the question philosophically, so I thought I had better accompany him. Clancy received us in a fatherly way; his conscience was obviously at him about having sent Mick to jail.

"Now don't do anything in a hurry, boy," he said kindly. "I spoke to the Commandant about it. It seems he admires Stewart a lot, but he has to do it for the sake of discipline."

"Is that what you call discipline?" Matt asked bitterly. "You can tell the Commandant from me that I'm resigning from the army as well. I wouldn't be mixed up with tyrants like ye."

"Tyrants?" spluttered Clancy, getting red. "Who are you calling tyrants?"

"And what the hell else are ye?" cried Matt. "The English were gentlemen to ye."

"Clear out!" cried Clancy. "Clear out or I'll kick the ass off you, you ungrateful little pup!"

"Tyrant!" hissed Matt, turning purple.

"You young curl!" said Clancy. "Wait till I tell your father about you!"

That evening I stood for a long time outside the prison window with Matt, talking to Mick. Mick had to raise himself on the bucket; he held onto the bars with both hands; he had the appearance of a real prisoner. The camp too looked like a place where people were free; in the dusk it looked big and complex and citified. Twenty yards away the prisoners on their evening strolls went round and round, and among them were the camp command, the Commandant, the Adjutant, and Clancy, not even giving a look in our direction. I had the greatest difficulty in keeping Matt from taking a fistful of stones and going round breaking windows to get himself arrested. I knew that wouldn't help. His other idea was that the three of us should resign from the army and conclude a separate peace with the British. That, as I pointed out, would be even worse. The great thing was to put the staff in the wrong by showing ourselves more loyal than they. I proposed to prepare a full statement of the position to be smuggled out to our friends at Brigade Headquarters outside. This idea rather appealed to Mick who, as I say, was very reasonable about most things.

I spent the evening after lock-up and a good part of the following morning on it. In the afternoon I went over to J with it. Brennan was distributing the mail and there were a couple of letters for Matt.

"Isn't there anything for Stewart?" he asked in disappointment.

"Stewart's letters will be sent to the staff hut," growled Brennan.

"You mean you're not going to give the man his letters?" shouted Matt.

"I mean I don't know whether he's entitled to them or not," said Brennan. "That's a matter for the Commandant."

Matt had begun a violent argument before I led him away. In the temper of the hut he could have been lynched. I wondered more than ever at the conservatism of revolutionaries.

"Come to the staff hut and we'll inquire ourselves," I said. "Brennan is probably only doing this out of pique."

I should have gone alone, of course. The Adjutant was there with Clancy. He was a farmer's son from the Midlands, beef to the heels like a Mullingar heifer.

"Brennan says Mick Stewart isn't entitled to letters," Matt squeaked to Clancy. "Is that right?"

"Why wouldn't it be?" Clancy asked, jumping up and giving one truculent tug to his moustache, another to his waistcoat. Obviously he didn't know whether it was or not. With the new jail only just started, precedents were few.

"Whenever the English want to score off us they stop our

letters and parcels," I said. "Surely to God ye could think up something more original."

"Do you know who you're speaking to?" the Adjutant asked.

"No," replied Matt before I could intervene. "Nor don't want to. Ye know what ye can do with the letters."

Mick, on the other hand, took the news coolly. He had apparently been thinking matters over during the night and planned his own campaign.

"I'm on hunger strike now," he said with a bitter smile.

The moment he spoke I knew he had found the answer. It was what we politicals always did when the British tried to make ordinary convicts of us. And it put the staff in an impossible position. Steadily more and more they had allowed themselves to become more tyrannical than the British themselves, and Mick's hunger strike showed it up clearly. If Mick were to die on hunger strike—and I knew him well enough to know that he would, rather than give in—no one would ever take the staff seriously again as suffering Irish patriots. And even if they wished to let him die, they might find it difficult, because without our even having to approach the British directly we involved them as well. As our legal jailers they would hate to see Mick die on anyone else's hands. The British are very jealous of privileges like that.

At the same time I was too fond of Mick to want things to reach such a pass, and I decided to make a final appeal to Clancy. I also decided to do it alone, for I knew Matt was beyond reasonable discussion.

When I went into him at the store, Clancy lowered his head and pulled his moustache at me.

"You know about Mick Stewart?" I began.

"I know everything about him from the moment he was got," shouted Clancy, putting his hand up to stop me. "If you didn't hear of that incident remind me to tell you some time."

This was a most unpromising beginning. The details of Mick's conception seemed to me beside the point.

"What are you going to do about it?" I asked.

"What do you think we're going to do about it?" he retorted, taking three steps back from me. "What do you think we are? Soldiers or old women? Let the bugger starve!"

"That's grand," I said, knowing I had him where I wanted him. "And what happens when we go on hunger strike and the British say: 'Let the buggers starve'?"

"That has nothing at all to do with it."

"Go on!" I said. "By the way, I suppose ye considered forcible feeding?"

Then he said something very nasty, quite uncalled-for, which didn't worry me in the least because it was the way he always talked when he was his natural self, and I got on very well with Clancy's natural self.

"By the way," I said, "don't be too sure the British will let ye starve him. You seem to forget that you're still prisoners yourselves, and Stewart is their prisoner as much as yours. The English mightn't like the persecution of unfortunate Irish prisoners by people like you."

Clancy repeated the uncalled-for remark, and I was suddenly filled with real pity for him. All that decent little man's life he had been suffering for Ireland, sacrificing his time and money and his little business, sleeping on the sofa and giving up his bed, selling raffle tickets, cycling miles in the dark to collect someone's subscription, and here was a young puppy taking the bread and water from his mouth.

That evening Matt and I stayed with Mick till the last whistle. You couldn't shift Matt from the window. He was on the verge of a breakdown. He had no one to coddle or be bullied by. Caliban without Prospero is a miserable spectacle.

But Clancy must have had a sleepless night. Next morning I found that Mick had already had a visit from the Adjutant. The proposal now was that Mick and Matt should come to my hut, and Mick could do his week's fatigues there—a mere formality so far as Q was concerned because anyone in that hut would do them for a sixpenny bit or five cigarettes. But no, Mick wouldn't agree to that either. He would accept nothing less than unconditional release, and even I felt that this was asking a lot of the staff.

But I was wrong. The staff had already given it up as a bad job. That afternoon we were summoned to the dining hall "to make arrangements about our immediate release" as the signaller told us—his idea of a joke. It looked like a company meeting. The staff sat round a table on the stage, Clancy wearing a collar and tie to show the importance of the occasion. The Commandant told us that the camp was faced with an unprecedented crisis. Clancy nodded three times, rapidly. They were the elected representatives of the men, and one man was deliberately defying them. Clancy crossed his legs, folded his arms tightly and looked searchingly through the audience as if looking for the criminal. They had no choice only to come back for fresh instructions.

It was a nice little meeting. Jack Costello, speaking from the hall, did a touching little piece about the hunger strike as the last weapon of free men against tyrants, told us that it should never be brought into disrepute, and said that if the man in question were released his loyal comrades would no doubt show what they thought of his conduct. Matt tried to put in a few words but was at once shouted down by his loyal comrades. Oh, a grand little meeting! Then I got up. I didn't quite know what to say because I didn't quite know what I thought. I had intended to say that within every conception of liberty there was the skeleton of a tyranny; that there were as many conceptions of liberty as there were human beings, and that the sort of liberty one man needed was not that which another might need. But somehow when I looked round me, I couldn't believe it. Instead, I said that there was no crisis, and that the staff were making mountains of principle out of molehills of friction. I wasn't permitted to get far. The Adjutant interrupted to say that what Mick was sentenced for couldn't be discussed by the meeting. Apparently it couldn't be discussed at all except by a Court of Appeal which couldn't be set up until the Republic proclaimed in 1916 was re-established, or some such nonsense. Listening to the Adjutant always gave me the impression of having taken a powerful sleeping-pill; after a while your hold on reality began to weaken and queer dissociated sentences began to run through your mind. I went out, deciding it was better to walk it off. Matt and I met outside the jail and waited till Kenefick came to release the prisoner. He did it in complete silence. Apparently orders were that we were to be sent to Coventry.

That suited me fine. The three of us were now together in Q and I knew from old experience that anyone in Q would sell his old mother for a packet of cigarettes. But all the same I was puzzled and depressed. Puzzled because I couldn't clarify what I had really meant to say when I got up to speak at the meeting, because I couldn't define what I really meant by liberty; depressed because if there was no liberty which I could define then equally there was no escape. I remained awake for hours that night thinking of it. Beyond the restless searchlights which stole in through every window and swept the hut till it was bright as day I could feel the wide fields of Ireland all round me, but even the wide fields of Ireland were not wide enough. Choice was an illusion. Seeing that a man can never really get out of jail, the great thing is to ensure that he gets into the biggest possible one with the largest possible range of modern amenities.

NEWS FOR THE CHURCH

WHEN Father Cassidy drew back the shutter of the confessional he was a little surprised at the appearance of the girl at the other side of the grille. It was dark in the box but he could see she was young, of medium height and build, with a face that was full of animation and charm. What struck him most was the long pale slightly freckled cheeks, pinned high up behind the grey-blue eyes, giving them a curiously oriental slant.

She wasn't a girl from the town, for he knew most of these by sight and many of them by something more, being notoriously an easy-going confessor. The other priests said that one of these days he'd give up hearing confessions altogether on the ground that there was no such thing as sin and that even if there was it didn't matter. This was part and parcel of his exceedingly angular character, for though he was kind enough to individual sinners, his mind was full of obscure abstract hatreds. He hated England; he hated the Irish government, and he particularly hated the middle classes, though so far as anyone knew none of them had ever done him the least bit of harm. He was a heavy-built man, slow-moving and slow-thinking with no neck and a Punchinello chin, a sour wine-coloured face, pouting crimson lips, and small blue hot-tempered eyes.

"Well, my child," he grunted in a slow and mournful voice that sounded for all the world as if he had pebbles in his mouth, "how long is it since your last confession?"

"A week, father," she replied in a clear firm voice. It surprised him a little, for though she didn't look like one of the tough shots, neither did she look like the sort of girl who goes to confession every week. But with women you could never tell. They were all contrary, saints and sinners.

"And what sins did you commit since then?" he asked encouragingly.

"I told lies, father."

"Anything else?"

"I used bad language, father."

"I'm surprised at you," he said with mock seriousness. "An educated girl with the whole of the English language at your disposal! What sort of bad language?"

"I used the Holy Name, father."

"Ach," he said with a frown, "you ought to know better than that. There's no great harm in damning and blasting but blasphemy is a different thing. To tell you the truth," he added, being a man of great natural honesty, "there isn't much harm in using the Holy Name either. Most of the time there's no intentional blasphemy but at the same time it coarsens the character. It's all the little temptations we don't indulge in that give us true refinement. Anything else?"

"I was tight, father."

"Hm," he grunted. This was rather more the sort of girl he

had imagined her to be; plenty of devilment but no real badness. He liked her bold and candid manner. There was no hedging or false modesty about her as about most of his women penitents. "When you say you were 'tight' do you mean you were just merry or what?"

"Well, I mean I passed out," she replied candidly with a shrug.

"I don't call that 'tight,' you know," he said sternly. "I call that beastly drunk. Are you often tight?"

"I'm a teacher in a convent school so I don't get much chance," she replied ruefully.

"In a convent school?" he echoed with new interest. Convent schools and nuns were another of his phobias; he said they were turning the women of the country into imbeciles. "Are you on holidays now?"

"Yes. I'm on my way home."

"You don't live here then?"

"No, down the country."

"And is it the convent that drives you to drink?" he asked with an air of unshakable gravity.

"Well," she replied archly, "you know what nuns are."

"I do," he agreed in a mournful voice while he smiled at her through the grille. "Do you drink with your parents' knowledge?" he added anxiously.

"Oh, yes. Mummy is dead but Daddy doesn't mind. He lets us take a drink with him."

"Does he do that on principle or because he's afraid of you?" the priest asked dryly.

"Ah, I suppose a little of both," she answered gaily, responding to his queer dry humour. It wasn't often that women did, and he began to like this one a lot.

"Is your mother long dead?" he asked sympathetically.

"Seven years," she replied, and he realized that she couldn't have been much more than a child at the time and had grown up without a mother's advice and care. Having worshipped his own mother, he was always sorry for people like that.

"Mind you," he said paternally, his hands joined on his fat belly, "I don't want you to think there's any harm in a drop of drink. I take it myself. But I wouldn't make a habit of it if I were you. You see, it's all very well for old jossers like me that have the worst of their temptations behind them, but yours are all ahead and drink is a thing that grows on you. You need never be afraid of going wrong if you remember that your mother may be watching you from heaven."

"Thanks, father," she said, and he saw at once that his gruff appeal had touched some deep and genuine spring of feeling in her. "I'll cut it out altogether."

"You know, I think I would," he said gravely, letting his eyes rest on her for a moment. "You're an intelligent girl. You can get all the excitement you want out of life without that. What else?"

"I had bad thoughts, father."

"Ach," he said regretfully, "we all have them. Did you indulge them?"

"Yes, father."

"Have you a boy?"

"Not a regular: just a couple of fellows hanging round."

"Ah, that's worse than none at all," he said crossly. "You ought to have a boy of your own. I know there's old cranks that will tell you different, but sure, that's plain foolishness. Those things are only fancies, and the best cure for them is something real. Anything else?"

There was a moment's hesitation before she replied but it was enough to prepare him for what was coming.

"I had carnal intercourse with a man, father," she said quietly and deliberately.

"You what?" he cried, turning on her incredulously. "You had carnal intercourse with a man? At your age?"

"I know," she said with a look of distress. "It's awful."

"It is awful," he replied slowly and solemnly. "And how often did it take place?"

"Once, father—I mean twice, but on the same occasion."

"Was it a married man?" he asked, frowning.

"No, father, single. At least I think he was single," she added with sudden doubt.

"You had carnal intercourse with a man," he said accusingly, "and you don't know if he was married or single!"

"I assumed he was single," she said with real distress. "He was the last time I met him but, of course, that was five years ago."

"Five years ago? But you must have been only a child then."

"That's all, of course," she admitted. "He was courting my sister, Kate, but she wouldn't have him. She was running round with her present husband at the time and she only kept him on a string for amusement. I knew that and I hated her because he was always so nice to me. He was the only one that came to the house who treated me like a grown-up. But I was only fourteen, and I suppose he thought I was too young for him."

"And were you?" Father Cassidy asked ironically. For some reason he had the idea that this young lady had no proper idea of the enormity of her sin and he didn't like it.

"I suppose so," she replied modestly. "But I used to feel awful, being sent up to bed and leaving him downstairs with Kate when I knew she didn't care for him. And then when I met him again the whole thing came back. I sort of went all soft inside. It's never the same with another fellow as it is with the first fellow you fall for. It's exactly as if he had some sort of hold over you."

"If you were fourteen at the time," said Father Cassidy, setting aside the obvious invitation to discuss the power of first love, "you're only nineteen now."

"That's all."

"And do you know," he went on broodingly, "that unless you can break yourself of this terrible vice once for all it'll go on like that till you're fifty?"

"I suppose so," she said doubtfully, but he saw that she didn't suppose anything of the kind.

"You suppose so!" he snorted angrily. "I'm telling you so. And what's more," he went on, speaking with all the earnestness at his command, "it won't be just one man but dozens of men, and it won't be decent men but whatever low-class pups you can find who'll take advantage of you—the same horrible, mortal sin, week in week out till you're an old woman."

"Ah, still, I don't know," she said eagerly, hunching her shoulders ingratiatingly, "I think people do it as much from curiosity as anything else."

"Curiosity?" he repeated in bewilderment.

"Ah, you know what I mean," she said with a touch of impatience. "People make such a mystery of it!"

"And what do you think they should do?" he asked ironically. "Publish it in the papers?"

"Well, God knows, 'twould be better than the way some of them go on," she said in a rush. "Take my sister, Kate, for instance. I admit she's a couple of years older than me and she brought me up and all the rest of it, but in spite of that we were always good friends. She showed me her love letters and I showed her mine. I mean, we discussed things as equals, but ever since that girl got married you'd hardly recognize her. She talks to no one only other married women, and they get in a huddle in a corner and whisper, whisper, whisper, and the moment you come into the room they begin to talk about the weather, exactly as if you were a blooming kid! I mean you can't help feeling 'tis something extraordinary."

"Don't you try and tell me anything about immorality," said Father Cassidy angrily. "I know all about it already. It may begin as curiosity but it ends as debauchery. There's no vice you could think of that gets a grip on you quicker and degrades you worse, and don't you make any mistake about it, young woman! Did this man say anything about marrying you?"

"I don't think so," she replied thoughtfully, "but of course that doesn't mean anything. He's an airy, light-hearted sort of fellow and it mightn't occur to him."

"I never supposed it would," said Father Cassidy grimly. "Is he in a position to marry?"

"I suppose he must be since he wanted to marry Kate," she replied with fading interest.

"And is your father the sort of man that can be trusted to talk to him?"

"Daddy?" she exclaimed aghast. "But I don't want Daddy brought into it."

"What you want, young woman," said Father Cassidy with sudden exasperation, "is beside the point. Are you prepared to talk to this man yourself?"

"I suppose so," she said with a wondering smile. "But about what?"

"About what?" repeated the priest angrily. "About the little matter he so conveniently overlooked, of course."

"You mean ask him to marry me?" she cried incredulously. "But I don't want to marry him."

Father Cassidy paused for a moment and looked at her anxiously through the grille. It was growing dark inside the church, and for one horrible moment he had the feeling that somebody was playing an elaborate and most tasteless joke on him.

"Do you mind telling me," he inquired politely, "am I mad or are you?"

"But I mean it, father," she said eagerly. "It's all over and done with now. It's something I used to dream about, and it was grand, but you can't do a thing like that a second time."

"You can't what?" he asked sternly.

"I mean, I suppose you can, really," she said, waving her piously joined hands at him as if she were handcuffed, "but you can't get back the magic of it. Terry is light-hearted and good-natured, but I couldn't live with him. He's completely irresponsible."

"And what do you think you are?" cried Father Cassidy, at the end of his patience. "Have you thought of all the dangers you're running, girl? If you have a child who'll give you work? If you have to leave this country to earn a living what's going to become of you? I tell you it's your bounden duty to marry this man if he can be got to marry you—which, let me tell you," he added with a toss of his great head, "I very much doubt."

"To tell you the truth I doubt it myself," she replied with a shrug that fully expressed her feelings about Terry and nearly drove Father Cassidy insane. He looked at her for a moment or two and then an incredible idea began to dawn on his bothered old brain. He sighed and covered his face with his hand.

"Tell me," he asked in a far-away voice, "when did this take place?"

"Last night, father," she said gently, almost as if she were glad to see him come to his senses again.

"My God," he thought despairingly, "I was right!"

"In town, was it?" he went on.

"Yes, father. We met on the train coming down."

"And where is he now?"

"He went home this morning, father."

"Why didn't you do the same?"

"I don't know, father," she replied doubtfully as though the question had now only struck herself for the first time.

"Why didn't you go home this morning?" he repeated angrily. "What were you doing round town all day?"

"I suppose I was walking," she replied uncertainly.

"And of course you didn't tell anyone?"

"I hadn't anyone to tell," she said plaintively. "Anyway," she added with a shrug, "it's not the sort of thing you can tell people."

"No, of course," said Father Cassidy. "Only a priest," he added grimly to himself. He saw now how he had been taken in. This little trollop, wandering about town in a daze of bliss, had to tell someone her secret, and he, a good-natured old fool of sixty, had allowed her to use him as a confidant. A philosopher of sixty letting Eve, aged nineteen, tell him all about the apple! He could never live it down.

Then the fighting blood of the Cassidys began to warm in him. Oh, couldn't he, though? He had never tasted the apple himself, but he knew a few things about apples in general and that apple in particular that little Miss Eve wouldn't learn in a whole lifetime of apple-eating. Theory might have its drawbacks but there were times when it was better than practice. "All right, my lass," he thought grimly, "we'll see which of us knows most!"

In a casual tone he began to ask her questions. They were rather intimate questions, such as a doctor or priest may ask, and, feeling broadminded and worldly-wise in her new experience, she answered courageously and straightforwardly, trying to suppress all signs of her embarrassment. It emerged only once or twice, in a brief pause before she replied. He stole a furtive look at her to see how she was taking it, and once more he couldn't withhold his admiration. But she couldn't keep it up. First she grew uncomfortable and then alarmed, frowning and shaking herself in her clothes as if something were biting her. He grew graver and more personal. She didn't see his purpose; she only saw that 'he was stripping off veil after veil of romance, leaving her with nothing but a cold, sordid, cynical adventure like a bit of greasy meat on a plate.

"And what did he do next?" he asked.

"Ah," she said in disgust, "I didn't notice."

"You didn't notice!" he repeated ironically.

"But does it make any difference?" she burst out despairingly, trying to pull the few shreds of illusion she had left more tightly about her.

"I presume you thought so when you came to confess it," he replied sternly.

"But you're making it sound so beastly!" she wailed.

"And wasn't it?" he whispered, bending closer, lips pursed and brows raised. He had her now, he knew.

"Ah, it wasn't, father," she said earnestly. "Honest to God it wasn't. At least at the time I didn't think it was."

"No," he said grimly, "you thought it was a nice little story to run and tell your sister. You won't be in such a hurry to tell her now. Say an Act of Contrition."

She said it.

"And for your penance say three Our Fathers and three Hail Marys."

He knew that was hitting below the belt, but he couldn't resist the parting shot of a penance such as he might have given a child. He knew it would rankle in that fanciful little head of hers when all his other warnings were forgotten. Then he drew the shutter and didn't open the farther one. There was a noisy woman behind, groaning in an excess of contrition. The mere volume of sound told him it was drink. He felt he needed a breath of fresh air.

He went down the aisle creakily on his heavy policeman's-feet and in the dusk walked up and down the path before the presbytery, head bowed, hands behind his back. He saw the girl come out and descend the steps under the massive fluted columns of the portico, a tiny, limp, dejected figure. As she reached the pavement she pulled herself together with a jaunty twitch of her shoulders and then collapsed again. The city lights went on and made globes of coloured light in the mist. As he returned to the church he suddenly began to chuckle, a fat good-natured chuckle, and as he passed the statue of St. Anne, patron of marriageable girls, he almost found himself giving her a wink.

DON JUAN'S TEMPTATION

AGAINST the Gussie Leonards of the world, we poor whores have no defences. Sons of bitches to a man, we can't like them, we can't even believe them, and still we must listen to them because deep down in every man jack of us there is the feeling that our own experience of life is insufficient. Humanly we understand our wives and girls and daughters; we put up with their tantrums and consider what we imagine are their wishes, but then the moment comes and we realize that that fat sleeky rascal understands them at a level where we can never even meet them, as if they put off their ordinary humanity as they put off their clothes, and went wandering through the world invisible except to the men like Gussie whose eyes are trained only to see them that way. The only consolation we have is that they too have their temptations—or so at least they say. The sons of bitches! Even that much you can't believe from them.

Anyhow, Gussie met this girl at a party in the Green and picked her out at once. She was young, tall, dark, good-looking, but it wasn't so much her looks that appealed to Gussie as the naturalness with which she moved among all those wooden dolls in night-dresses. She was a country town girl who had never learned to dress up and pose, and however she moved or whatever she said it always seemed to be natural and right.

They left together and she took Gussie's arm with a boyish camaraderie that delighted him. It was a lovely night with the moon nearly at the full. Gussie's flat was in a Georgian house on the street which ran through the Green; she had a room in Pembroke Road, and as they passed the house Gussie halted and asked her in. She gave a slight start, but Gussie, having a few drinks in, didn't notice that until later.

"For what?" she asked gaily.

"Oh, for the night if you like," Gussie replied in the same tone and felt like biting off his tongue when he heard it. It sounded so awkward, like a schoolboy the first time he goes with a girl.

"No, thanks," she said shortly. "I have a room of my own."

"Oh, please, Helen, please!" he moaned, taking her hand and squeezing it in the way of an old friend of the family. "You're not taking offence at my harmless little joke. Now you'll have to come up and have a drink, just to show there's no ill feeling."

"Some other night," she said, "when it's not so late."

He let it go at that because he knew that anything further he said would only frighten her more. He knew perfectly well what had happened. The Sheehans, mischief-makers and busybodies, had warned her against him, and he had walked straight into the trap. She still held onto his arm, but that was only not to make a fuss. Inside she was as hurt as anything. Hurt and surprised. In spite of the Sheehans' warnings she had taken him at his face value, not believing him to be that sort at all. Or rather, as Gussie, whose eyes were differently focused from ours, phrased it to himself, knowing damn well he was that sort but hoping that he would reveal it gradually so that she wouldn't be compelled to take notice.

She stopped at the canal bridge and leaned over to look at the view. It was beautiful there in the moonlight with the still water, the trees, the banked houses with odd windows caught in the snowy light, but Gussie knew it was not the moonlight she was thinking of. She was getting over her fright and now it was her pride that was hurt.

"Tell us," she said, letting on to be very light-hearted and interested in the subject, as it were, only from the psychological standpoint, "do you ask all the girls you meet the same thing?"

E

"But my goodness, didn't I tell you it was only a joke?" Gussie asked reproachfully.

She rested her head on her arms and looked back at him over her shoulder, the cloche hat shading her face to the chin. It was a natural, beautiful pose but Gussie knew she wasn't aware of it.

"Now you're not being honest," she said.

"Are you?" Gussie asked with a faint smile.

"Am I what?" she replied with a start.

"Can't you admit that you were warned against me?" he said.

"As a matter of fact I was," she replied candidly, "but I didn't pay much attention. I take people as I find them."

"Now you're talking sensibly," said Gussie and thought in a fatherly way: "The girl is nice. She's a bit shocked but she'll have to learn sooner or later and it would be better for her to learn from someone who knows." The awkwardness of Irish husbands was a theme song of Gussie's. The things their wives told you were almost incredible.

"You probably wouldn't believe me if I told you how few women interest me enough for that," he said.

"But the ones you do ask," she went on, sticking to her point, though pretending to be quite detached as though she really were only looking for information, "do they come?"

"Some," he said, smiling at her innocence. "Sometimes you meet a difficult girl who makes a hullabaloo and won't even come and have a drink with you afterwards."

"Married women or girls?" she asked in the tone of an official filling up a form, but the quaver in her voice gave her away.

"Both," said Gussie. If he had been perfectly honest he would have had to admit that at that time there was only one of the former and not exactly a queue of the latter but he had decided, purely in Helen's own interest, that since she needed to have her mind broadened there was no use doing it by halves. It was better to get it over and be done with it, like having a tooth out. "Why?"

"Oh, nothing," she said casually, "but I'm not surprised you have such a poor opinion of women if you can pick them up as easily as that."

This view of the matter came as a real surprise to Gussie, who would never have described his conduct in that way.

"But my dear young lady," he said offering her a cigarette, "whoever said I have a poor opinion of women? What would I be doing with women if I had? On the contrary, I have a very high opinion of women, and the more I see of them the more I like them."

"Have you?" she asked, stooping low over the match-flame so that he shouldn't see her face. He guessed that it was very flushed. "It must be a poor opinion of me so."

"What an extraordinary idea!" said Gussie, still genuinely trying to fathom it. "How can you make out that wanting to see more of you means I have a poor opinion of you. Even if I do want to make love to you. As a matter of fact, if it's any news to you, I do."

"You want it rather easy, don't you?" she asked with a trace of resentment.

"Why?" he asked blandly. "Do you think it should be made difficult?"

"I thought it was the usual thing to ask a girl to go to the pictures with you first," she said with a brassy air that wouldn't have taken in a child.

"I wouldn't know," murmured Gussie in amusement. "Anyway, I suppose I thought you weren't the usual sort of girl."

"But if you get it as easy as that, how do you know if it's the real thing or not?" she asked.

"How do you know anything is the real thing?" he retorted. "As you say yourself, you have to take things as you find them."

"Taking them as you find them doesn't mean swallowing them whole," she said. "It would be rather late in the day to change your mind about a thing like that."

"But what difference does it make?" he asked wonderingly. "It happens every day of the week. You do it yourself with boys you go out walking with. You spoon with them till you find they bore you and then you drop them. There's no difference. You don't suddenly change your character. People don't say when they meet you in the street: 'How different that girl is looking! You can see she has a man.' Of course, if you attach so much importance to the physical side of it—"

"I do," she said quickly. By this time Gussie noticed to his surprise that she was almost laughing. She had got over her fright and hurt and felt that in argument she was more than a match for him. "Isn't it awful?" she added brightly. "But I'm very queer like that."

"Oh, there's nothing queer about it," Gussie said, determined on keeping control of the situation and not letting her away with anything. "It's just ordinary schoolgirl romanticism."

"Is that all?" she asked lightly, and though she pretended not to care he saw she was stung. "You have an answer for everything, haven't you?"

"If you call that everything, my dear child," he replied paternally patting her on the shoulder. "I call it growing-pains. I don't know, with that romantic nature of yours, whether you've noticed that there's a nasty wind coming up the canal."

"No," she said archly, "I hadn't," and then turned to face him, resting her elbows on the coping of the bridge. "Anyhow, I like it. Go on with what you were saying. Being romantic is thinking you ought to stick to someone you're fond of, isn't that it?"

Gussie was amused again. The girl was so transparent. It was clear now that she was in love with some young fellow who couldn't afford to marry her and that they were scarifying one another in the usual adolescent rough-and-tumble without knowing what ailed them.

"No, my dear, it isn't," said Gussie. "Being romantic is thinking you're very fond of someone you really don't give a damn about, and imagining on that account that you're never going to care for anyone else. It goes with your age. Come on now, or you'll be catching something worse."

"You don't mean you were ever like that?" she asked, taking his arm again as they went on down Pembroke Road. Even her tone revealed her mingled fascination and loathing. It didn't worry Gussie. He was used to it.

"Oh," he said sentimentally, "we all go through it."

There were a lot of contradictions in Gussie. Despising youth and its illusions, he could scarcely ever think of his own youth without self-pity. He had been lonely enough; sometimes he felt no one had ever been so lonely. He had woken up from a nice, well-ordered, intelligible world to find eternity stretching all round him and no one, priest or scientist, who could explain it to him. And with that awakening had gone the longing for companionship and love which he had not known how to satisfy, and often he had walked for hours, looking up at the stars and thinking that if only he could meet an understanding girl it would all explain itself naturally. The picture of Gussie's youth seemed to amuse Helen.

"Go on!" she said gaily, her face turned to his, screwed up with mischief. "I could have sworn you must have been born like that. How did you get sense so young?"

"Quite naturally," Gussie said with a grave priestly air. "I saw I was only making trouble for myself, as you're doing now, and as there seemed to be quite enough trouble in the world without that, I gave it up."

"And lived happy ever after?" she said mockingly. "And the women you knock round with? Aren't they romantic either?"

"Not since they were your age," he said mockingly.

"You needn't rub it in about the age," she said without taking umbrage. "It'll cure itself soon enough. Tell us more about your girls—the married ones, for instance."

"That's easy," he said. "There's only one at the moment."

"And her husband? Does he know?"

"I never asked him," Gussie said slyly. "But I dare say he finds it more convenient not to."

"Obliging sort of chap," she said. "I could do with a man like that myself."

Gussie stopped dead. As I say there were contradictions in Gussie, and for some reason her scorn of Francie's husband filled him with indignation. It was so uncalled-for, so unjust!

"Now you are talking like a schoolgirl," he said reproachfully.

"Am I?" she asked doubtfully, noticing the change in him. "How?"

"What business have you talking in that tone about a man you never even met?" Gussie went on, growing quite heated. "He isn't a thief or a blackguard. He's a decent, good-natured man.

It's not his fault if after seventeen or eighteen years of living together his wife and himself can't bear the living sight of one
another. That's a thing that happens everybody. He only does
what he thinks is the best thing for his family. You think, I
suppose, that he should take out a gun to defend his wife's
honour?"

"I wasn't thinking of her honour," she protested quietly.

"His own then?" Gussie cried mockingly. "At the expense of
his wife and children? He's to drag her name in the mud all
because some silly schoolgirl might think his position undignified.
Ah, for goodness' sake, child, have sense! His wife would have
something to say to that. Besides, don't you see that at his age it
would be a very serious thing if she was to leave him?"

"More serious than letting her go to your flat—how often did
you say?"

"Now you're talking like a little cat," he snapped, and went
on. He really was furious. "But as a matter of fact it would," he
went on in a more reasonable tone. "Where she goes in the
evenings is nobody's business. Whether the meals are ready is
another matter. They have two daughters at school—one nearly
the one age with yourself."

"I wonder if he lets them out at night," she said drily. "And
what sort of woman is their mother?"

"You wouldn't believe me if I told you," said Gussie, "but she's
a great sort; a woman who'd give you her heart out."

"I wonder what she'd say if she heard you asking another girl
in to spend the night," she added in the same casual tone. Gussie
was beginning to conceive a considerable respect for her tongue.

"Ah," he said without conviction, "I don't suppose she has
many illusions left," but the girl had scored and she knew it. The
trouble with Francie was that she had far too many illusions left,
even about Gussie. And the greatest illusion of all was that if
only she had married a man whose intelligence she respected as
she respected his, she could have been faithful to him.

"She can't have," said Helen, "but I still have a few."

"Oh, you!" Gussie said with a jolly laugh which had got him
out of many tight corners. "You're walking with them."

"They must be in the family," she said. "Daddy died five years ago and Mum still thinks he was the one really great man that walked the world."

"I dare say," Gussie said wearily. "And they were probably often sick to death of one another."

"They were," she agreed. "They used to fight like mad and not talk for a week, and then Dad would go on the booze and Mum would take it out of me. Cripes, I used to go up to him with my bottom so sore I could hardly sit down and there he'd be sprawled in his big chair with his arms hanging down, looking into the grate as if 'twas the end of the world, and he'd just beckon me to come on his knee. We'd stop like that for hours without opening our gobs, just thinking what a bitch of hell Mum was. . . . But the thing is, young man, they stuck it out, and when 'tis her turn to go, she won't regret it because she's certain the Boss will be waiting for her. She goes to Mass every morning but that's only not to give God any excuse for making distinctions. Do you think he will?"

"Who will?" asked Gussie. In a curious way the story had gripped him. A woman could bawl her heart out on Gussie, and he'd only think her a nuisance, but he was exceedingly vulnerable to indirect sentiment.

"The Boss," she explained. "Meet her, I mean?"

"Well," Gussie said feebly, "there's nothing like optimism." At the same time he knew he was not being altogether truthful, because orthodoxy was one of Gussie's strongest lines.

"I know," the girl said quickly. "That's the lousy part of it. But I suppose she's lucky even to be able to kid herself about it. Death doesn't frighten her the way it frightens me. . . . But that's what I mean by love, Mr. L.," she added light-heartedly.

"I hope you get it, Miss C." replied Gussie in the same tone.

"I don't suppose I'm likely to," she said with resignation. "There doesn't seem to be much of it round. I suppose it's the shortage of optimists."

When they reached her flat, she leaned against the railings with her legs crossed and her hands behind her back—again a boyish attitude which attracted Gussie.

"Well, good night, Miss Romantic," he said ceremoniously, taking her hand and kissing it.

"Good night, Don Juan," she replied to Gussie's infinite delight. Nobody had ever called Gussie that before.

"When do I see you again?"

"Are you sure you want to see me?" she asked with light mockery. "An old-fashioned girl like me!"

"I still have hopes of converting you," said Gussie.

"That's marvellous," she said. "I love being converted. I was nearly converted by a parson once. Give us a ring-up some time."

"I will to be sure," said Gussie, and it was not until he reached the canal bridge that he realized he had really meant: "What a fool you think I am!" He felt sore all over. "The trouble with me is that I'm getting things too easy," he thought. He felt exactly like a man with a thousand a year whom somebody wanted to push back into the thirty-shilling-a-week class. Thirty shillings a week was all right when you had never been accustomed to anything else, but to Gussie it meant only one thing— destitution. He knew exactly what he would be letting himself in for if he took the girl on her own terms; the same thing that some poor devil of a boy was enduring with her now; park benches and canal banks with a sixty-mile-an-hour gale blowing round the corner, and finally she would be detained at the office —by a good-looking chap in uniform. "What a fool I am!" he thought mockingly.

But even to find himself summing up the odds like this was a new experience for Gussie. He was attracted by the girl; he couldn't deny that. Instead of crossing the bridge he turned up the moonlit walk by the canal. This was another new thing and he commented ironically on it to himself. "Now this, Gussie," he said, "is what you'll be letting yourself in for if you're not careful." He suddenly realized what it was that attracted him. It was her resemblance to Joan, a girl who had crossed for a moment his lonely boyhood. He had haunted the roads at night, trying to catch even a glimpse of her as she passed. She was a tall, thin, reedy girl, and, though Gussie did not know it, already far gone with the disease which killed her. On the night before she left for the sanatorium he had met her coming from town, and as they came up the hill she had suddenly slipped her hand into his. So she too, it seemed, had been lonely. He had been too shy to look for more; he hadn't even wished to ask for more. Perfectly happy, he had held her hand the whole way home and neither had spoken a word. It had been something complete and perfect, for in six months' time she was dead. He still dreamt of her sometimes. Once he dreamt that she came into the room where he was sitting with Francie, and sat on the other side of him and spoke to Francie in French, but Francie was too indignant to reply.

And now, here he was fifteen years later feeling the same sort of thing about another girl who merely reminded him of her, and though he knew Helen was talking rubbish he understood perfectly what she wanted; what Joan had wanted that night before she went to the sanatorium; something bigger than life that would last beyond death. He felt himself a brute for trying to deprive her of her illusions. Perhaps people couldn't do without illusions. Walking by the canal in the moonlight, Gussie felt he would give anything to be able to feel like that about a woman again. Even a sixty-mile-an-hour gale would not have put him off.

Then, as he came back up the street from the opposite direction, he noticed how the moonlight fell on the doctors' houses at the other side. His was in darkness. He put his key in the lock and then started, feeling frightened and weak. There was a figure by the door, leaning back against the railings, her hands by her side, her face very white. She stood there as though hoping he would pass without noticing her. "It's Joan" was his first thought, and then: "She's come back," and finally, with a growing feeling of incredulity: "So it does last." He looked again and saw who it really was.

"My goodness, Helen," he said almost petulantly, "what are you doing here?"

"Well," she said in a low voice, doing her best to smile, "you see I was converted after all."

He led her silently up the stairs with a growing feeling of relief, but it wasn't until they were in his own flat that he really knew how overjoyed he was. It was all over now, but he felt he had been through a really terrible temptation, the temptation of a lifetime. Only that people might interpret it wrongly, and he was really a most decorous man, he would have said his guardian angel had been looking after him.

Sons of bitches! That's what they are, to a man.

THE LONG ROAD TO UMMERA

Stay for me there. I will not fail
To meet thee in that hollow vale.

ALWAYS in the evenings you saw her shuffle up the road to Miss O.'s for her little jug of porter, a shapeless lump of an old woman in a plaid shawl, faded to the colour of snuff, that dragged her head down on to her bosom where she clutched its folds in one hand; a canvas apron and a pair of men's boots without laces. Her eyes were puffy and screwed up in tight little buds of flesh and her rosy old face that might have been carved out of a turnip was all crumpled with blindness. The old heart was failing her, and several times she would have to rest, put down the jug, lean against the wall, and lift the weight of the shawl off her head. People passed; she stared at them humbly; they saluted her; she turned her head and peered after them for minutes on end. The rhythm of life had slowed down in her till you could scarcely detect its faint and sluggish beat. Sometimes from some queer instinct of shyness she turned to the wall, took a snuffbox from her bosom, and shook out a pinch on the back of her swollen hand. When she sniffed it it smeared her nose and upper lip and spilled all over her old black blouse. She raised the hand to her eyes and looked at it closely and reproachfully, as though astonished that it no longer served her properly. Then she dusted herself, picked up the old jug again, scratched herself against her clothes, and shuffled along close by the wall, groaning aloud.

When she reached her own house, which was a little cottage in a terrace, she took off her boots, and herself and the old cobbler who lodged with her turned out a pot of potatoes on the table, stripping them with their fingers and dipping them in the little mound of salt while they took turn and turn about with the porter jug. He was a lively and philosophic old man called Johnny Thornton.

After their supper they sat in the firelight, talking about old times in the country and long-dead neighbours, ghosts, fairies, spells, and charms. It always depressed her son, finding them together like that when he called with her monthly allowance. He was a well-to-do businessman with a little grocery shop in the South Main Street and a little house in Sunday's Well, and nothing would have pleased him better than that his mother should share all the grandeur with him, the carpets and the china and the chiming clocks. He sat moodily between them, stroking his long jaw, and wondering why they talked so much about death in the old-fashioned way, as if it was something that made no difference at all.

"Wisha, what pleasure do ye get out of old talk like that?" he asked one night.

"Like what, Pat?" his mother asked with her timid smile.

"My goodness," he said, "ye're always at it. Corpses and graves and people that are dead and gone."

"Arrah, why wouldn't we?" she replied, looking down stiffly as she tried to button the open-necked blouse that revealed her old breast. "Isn't there more of us there than here?"

"Much difference 'twill make to you when you won't know them or see them!" he exclaimed.

"Oye, why wouldn't I know them?" she cried angrily. "Is it the Twomeys of Lackroe and the Driscolls of Ummera?"

"How sure you are we'll take you to Ummera!" he said mockingly.

"Och aye, Pat," she asked, shaking herself against her clothes with her humble stupid wondering smile, "and where else would you take me?"

"Isn't our own plot good enough for you?" he asked. "Your own son and your grandchildren?"

"Musha, indeed, is it in the town you want to bury me?" She shrugged herself and blinked into the fire, her face growing sour and obstinate. "I'll go back to Ummera, the place I came from."

"Back to the hunger and misery we came from," Pat said scornfully.

"Back to your father, boy."

"Ay, to be sure, where else? But my father or grandfather never did for you what I did. Often and often I scoured the streets of Cork for a few ha-pence for you."

"You did, amossa, you did, you did," she admitted, looking into the fire and shaking herself. "You were a good son to me."

"And often I did it and the belly falling out of me with hunger," Pat went on, full of self-pity.

" 'Tis true for you," she mumbled, " 'tis, 'tis, 'tis true. 'Twas often and often you had to go without it. What else could you do and the way we were left?"

"And now our grave isn't good enough for you," he complained. There was real bitterness in his tone. He was an insignificant little man and jealous of the power the dead had over her.

She looked at him with the same abject, half-imbecile smile, the wrinkled old eyes almost shut above the Mongolian cheekbones, while with a swollen old hand, like a pot-stick, it had so little life in it, she smoothed a few locks of yellow-white hair across her temples—a trick she had when troubled.

"Musha, take me back to Ummera, Pat," she whined. "Take me back to my own. I'd never rest among strangers. I'd be rising and drifting."

"Ah, foolishness, woman!" he said with an indignant look. "That sort of thing is gone out of fashion."

"I won't stop here for you," she shouted hoarsely in sudden, impotent fury, and she rose and grasped the mantelpiece for support.

"You won't be asked," he said shortly.

"I'll haunt you," she whispered tensely, holding on to the

mantelpiece and bending down over him with a horrible grin.

"And that's only more of the foolishness," he said with a nod of contempt. "Haunts and fairies and spells."

She took one step towards him and stood, plastering down the two little locks of yellowing hair, the half-dead eyes twitching and blinking in the candlelight, and the swollen crumpled face with the cheeks like cracked enamel.

"Pat," she said, "the day we left Ummera you promised to bring me back. You were only a little gorsoon that time. The neighbours gathered round me and the last word I said to them and I going down the road was: 'Neighbours, my son Pat is after giving me his word and he'll bring me back to ye when my time comes.' . . . That's as true as the Almighty God is over me this night. I have everything ready." She went to the shelf under the stairs and took out two parcels. She seemed to be speaking to herself as she opened them gloatingly, bending down her head in the feeble light of the candle. "There's the two brass candlesticks and the blessed candles alongside them. And there's my shroud aired regular on the line."

"Ah, you're mad, woman," he said angrily. "Forty miles! Forty miles into the heart of the mountains!"

She suddenly shuffled towards him on her bare feet, her hand raised clawing the air, her body like her face blind with age. Her harsh croaking old voice rose to a shout.

"I brought you from it, boy, and you must bring me back. If 'twas the last shilling you had and you and your children to go to the poorhouse after, you must bring me back to Ummera. And not by the short road either! Mind what I say now! The long road! The long road to Ummera round the lake, the way I brought you from it. I lay a heavy curse on you this night if you bring me the short road over the hill. And ye must stop by the ash tree at the foot of the boreen where ye can see my little house and say a prayer for all that were ever old in it and all that played on the floor. And then—Pat! Pat Driscoll! Are you listening? Are you listening to me, I say?"

She shook him by the shoulder, peering down into his long miserable face to see how was he taking it.

"I'm listening," he said with a shrug.

"Then"—her voice dropped to a whisper—"you must stand up overright the neighbours and say—remember now what I'm telling you!—'Neighbours, this is Abby, Batty Heige's daughter, that kept her promise to ye at the end of all.'"

She said it lovingly, smiling to herself, as if it were a bit of an old song, something she went over and over in the long night. All West Cork was in it: the bleak road over the moors to Ummera, the smooth grey pelts of the hills with the long spider's-web of the fences ridging them, drawing the scarecrow fields awry, and the whitewashed cottages, poker-faced between their little scraps of holly bushes looking this way and that out of the wind.

"Well, I'll make a fair bargain with you," said Pat as he rose. Without seeming to listen she screwed up her eyes and studied his weak melancholy face. "This house is a great expense to me. Do what I'm always asking you. Live with me and I'll promise I'll take you back to Ummera."

"Oye, I will not," she replied sullenly, shrugging her shoulders helplessly, an old sack of a woman with all the life gone out of her.

"All right," said Pat. "'Tis your own choice. That's my last word; take it or leave it. Live with me and Ummera for your grave, or stop here and a plot in the Botanics."

She watched him out the door with shoulders hunched about her ears. Then she shrugged herself, took out her snuffbox and took a pinch.

"Arrah, I wouldn't mind what he'd say," said Johnny. "A fellow like that would change his mind tomorrow."

"He might and he mightn't," she said heavily, and opened the back door to go out to the yard. It was a starry night and they could hear the noise of the city below them in the valley. She raised her eyes to the bright sky over the back wall and suddenly broke into a cry of loneliness and helplessness.

"Oh, oh, oh, 'tis far away from me Ummera is tonight above any other night, and I'll die and be buried here, far from all I ever knew and the long roads between us."

Of course old Johnny should have known damn well what she was up to the night she made her way down to the cross, creeping along beside the railings. By the blank wall opposite the lighted pub Dan Regan, the jarvey, was standing by his old box of a covered car with his pipe in his gob. He was the jarvey all the old neighbours went to. Abby beckoned to him and he followed her into the shadow of a gateway overhung with ivy. He listened gravely to what she had to say, sniffing and nodding, wiping his nose in his sleeve, or crossing the pavement to hawk his nose and spit in the channel, while his face with its drooping moustaches never relaxed its discreet and doleful expression.

Johnny should have known what that meant and why old Abby, who had always been so open-handed, sat before an empty grate sooner than light a fire, and came after him on Fridays for the rent, whether he had it or not, and even begrudged him the little drop of porter which had always been give and take between them. He knew himself it was a change before death and that it all went into the wallet in her bosom. At night in her attic she counted it by the light of her candle and when the coins dropped from her lifeless fingers he heard her roaring like an old cow as she crawled along the naked boards, sweeping them blindly with her palms. Then he heard the bed creak as she tossed about in it, and the rosary being taken from the bedhead, and the old voice rising and falling in prayer; and sometimes when a high wind blowing up the river roused him before dawn he could hear her muttering: a mutter and then a yawn; the scrape of a match as she peered at the alarm clock—the endless nights of the old—and then the mutter of prayer again.

But Johnny in some ways was very dense, and he guessed nothing till the night she called him and, going to the foot of the stairs with a candle in his hand, he saw her on the landing in her flour-bag shift, one hand clutching the jamb of the door while the other clawed wildly at her few straggly hairs.

"Johnny!" she screeched down at him, beside herself with excitement. "He was here."

"Who was there?" he snarled back, still cross with sleep.

"Michael Driscoll, Pat's father."

"Ah, you were dreaming, woman," he said in disgust. "Go back to your bed in God's holy name."

"I was not dreaming," she cried. "I was lying broad awake,

saying my beads, when he come in the door, beckoning me. Go down to Dan Regan's for me, Johnny."

"I will not indeed, go down to Dan Regan's for you. Do you know what hour of night it is?"

" 'Tis morning."

" 'Tis. Four o'clock! What a thing I'd do! . . . Is it the way you're feeling bad?" he added with more consideration as he mounted the stairs. "Do you want him to take you to hospital?"

"Oye, I'm going to no hospital," she replied sullenly, turning her back on him and thumping into the room again. She opened an old chest of drawers and began fumbling in it for her best clothes, her bonnet and cloak.

"Then what the blazes do you want Dan Regan for?" he snarled in exasperation.

"What matter to you what I want him for?" she retorted with senile suspicion. "I have a journey to go, never you mind where."

"Ach, you old oinseach, your mind is wandering," he cried. "There's a divil of a wind blowing up the river. The whole house is shaking. That's what you heard. Make your mind easy now and go back to bed."

"My mind is not wandering," she shouted. "Thanks be to the Almighty God I have my senses as good as you. My plans are made. I'm going back now where I came from. Back to Ummera."

"Back to where?" Johnny asked in stupefaction.

"Back to Ummera."

"You're madder than I thought. And do you think or imagine Dan Regan will drive you?"

"He will drive me then," she said, shrugging herself as she held an old petticoat to the light. "He's booked for it any hour of the day or night."

"Then Dan Regan is madder still."

"Leave me alone now," she muttered stubbornly, blinking and shrugging. "I'm going back to Ummera and that was why my old comrade came for me. All night and every night I have my beads wore out, praying the Almighty God and his Blessed Mother not to leave me die among strangers. And now I'll leave my old bones on a high hilltop in Ummera."

Johnny was easily persuaded. It promised to be a fine day's outing and a story that would delight a pub, so he made tea for her and after that went down to Dan Regan's little cottage, and before smoke showed from any chimney on the road they were away. Johnny was hopping about the car in his excitement, leaning out, shouting through the window of the car to Dan and identifying big estates that he hadn't seen for years. When they were well outside the town, himself and Dan went in for a drink, and while they were inside the old woman dozed. Dan Regan roused her to ask if she wouldn't take a drop of something and at first she didn't know who he was and then she asked where they were and peered out at the public-house and the old dog sprawled asleep in the sunlight before the door. But when next they halted she had fallen asleep again, her mouth hanging open and her breath coming in noisy gusts. Dan's face grew gloomier. He looked hard at her and spat. Then he took a few turns about the road, lit his pipe and put on the lid.

"I don't like her looks at all, Johnny," he said gravely. "I done wrong. I see that now. I done wrong."

After that, he halted every couple of miles to see how she was and Johnny, threatened with the loss of his treat, shook her and shouted at her. Each time Dan's face grew graver. He walked gloomily about the road, clearing his nose and spitting in the ditch. "God direct me!" he said solemnly. " 'Twon't be wishing to me. Her son is a powerful man. He'll break me yet. A man should never interfere between families. Blood is thicker than water. The Regans were always unlucky."

When they reached the first town he drove straight to the police barrack and told them the story in his own peculiar way.

"Ye can tell the judge I gave ye every assistance," he said in a reasonable brokenhearted tone. "I was always a friend of the law. I'll keep nothing back—a pound was the price agreed. I suppose if she dies 'twill be manslaughter. I never had hand act or part in politics. Sergeant Daly at the Cross knows me well."

When Abby came to herself she was in a bed in the hospital. She began to fumble for her belongings and her shrieks brought a crowd of unfortunate old women about her.

"Whisht, whisht, whisht!" they said. "They're all in safe-keeping. You'll get them back."

"I want them now," she shouted, struggling to get out of bed while they held her down. "Leave me go, ye robbers of hell! Ye night-walking rogues, leave me go. Oh, murder, murder! Ye're killing me."

At last an old Irish-speaking priest came and comforted her. He left her quietly saying her beads, secure in the promise to see that she was buried in Ummera no matter what anyone said. As darkness fell, the beads dropped from her swollen hands and she began to mutter to herself in Irish. Sitting about the fire, the ragged old women whispered and groaned in sympathy. The Angelus rang out from a near-by church. Suddenly Abby's voice rose to a shout and she tried to lift herself on her elbow.

"Ah, Michael Driscoll, my friend, my kind comrade, you didn't forget me after all the long years. I'm a long time away from you but I'm coming at last. They tried to keep me away, to make me stop among foreigners in the town, but where would I be at all without you and all the old friends? Stay for me, my treasure! Stop and show me the way. . . . Neighbours," she shouted, pointing into the shadows, "that man there is my own husband, Michael Driscoll. Let ye see he won't leave me to find my way alone. Gather round me with yeer lanterns, neighbours, till I see who I have. I know ye all. 'Tis only the sight that's weak on me. Be easy now, my brightness, my own kind loving comrade. I'm coming. After all the long years I'm on the road to you at last. . . ."

It was a spring day full of wandering sunlight when they brought her the long road to Ummera, the way she had come from it forty years before. The lake was like a dazzle of midges; the shafts of the sun revolving like a great millwheel poured their cascades of milky sunlight over the hills and the little whitewashed cottages and the little black mountain-cattle among the scarecrow fields. The hearse stopped at the foot of the lane that led to the roofless cabin just as she had pictured it to herself in the long nights, and Pat, looking more melancholy than ever, turned to the waiting neighbours and said:

"Neighbours, this is Abby, Batty Heige's daughter, that kept her promise to ye at the end of all."

THE BRIDAL NIGHT

It was sunset, and the two great humps of rock made a twilight in the cove where the boats were lying high up the strand. There was one light only in a little whitewashed cottage. Around the headland came a boat and the heavy dipping of its oars was like a heron's flight. The old woman was sitting on the low stone wall outside her cottage.

" 'Tis a lonesome place," said I.

" 'Tis so," she agreed, "a lonesome place, but any place is lonesome without one you'd care for."

"Your own flock are gone from you, I suppose?" I asked.

"I never had but the one," she replied, "the one son only," and I knew because she did not add a prayer for his soul that he was still alive.

"Is it in America he is?" I asked. (It is to America all the boys of the locality go when they leave home.)

"No, then," she replied simply. "It is in the asylum in Cork he is on me these twelve years."

I had no fear of trespassing on her emotions. These lonesome people in wild places, it is their nature to speak; they must cry out their sorrows like the wild birds.

"God help us!" I said. "Far enough!"

"Far enough," she sighed. "Too far for an old woman. There was a nice priest here one time brought me up in his car to see him. All the ways to this wild place he brought it, and he drove me into the city. It is a place I was never used to, but it eased my mind to see poor Denis well-cared-for and well-liked. It was a trouble to me before that, not knowing would they see what a good boy he was before his madness came on him. He knew me; he saluted me, but he said nothing until the superintendent came to tell me the tea was ready for me. Then poor Denis raised his head and says: "Leave ye not forget the toast. She was ever a great one for her bit of toast." It seemed to give him ease and he cried after. A good boy he was and is. It was like him after seven long years to think of his old mother and her little bit of toast."

"God help us," I said for her voice was like the birds', hurrying high, immensely high, in the coloured light, out to sea to the last islands where their nests were.

"Blessed be His holy will," the old woman added, "there is no turning aside what is in store. It was a teacher that was here at the time. Miss Regan her name was. She was a fine big jolly girl from the town. Her father had a shop there. They said she had three hundred pounds to her own cheek the day she set foot in the school, and—'tis hard to believe but 'tis what they all said: I will not belie her—'twasn't banished she was at all, but she came here of her own choice, for the great liking she had for the sea and the mountains. Now, that is the story, and with my own eyes I saw her, day in day out, coming down the little pathway you came yourself from the road and sitting beyond there in a hollow you can hardly see, out of the wind. The neighbours could make nothing of it, and she being a stranger, and with only the book Irish, they left her alone. It never seemed to take a peg out of her, only sitting in that hole in the rocks, as happy as the day is long, reading her little book or writing her letters. Of an odd time she might bring one of the little scholars along with her to be picking posies.

"That was where my Denis saw her. He'd go up to her of an evening and sit on the grass beside her, and off and on he might take her out in the boat with him. And she'd say with that big laugh of hers: 'Denis is my beau.' Those now were her words and she meant no more harm by it than the child unborn, and I knew it and Denis knew it, and it was a little joke we had, the three of us. It was the same way she used to joke about her little hollow. 'Mrs. Sullivan,' she'd say, 'leave no one near it. It is my nest and my cell and my little prayer-house, and maybe I would be like the birds and catch the smell of the stranger and then fly away from ye all.' It did me good to hear her laugh, and whenever I saw Denis moping or idle I would say it to him myself: 'Denis, why wouldn't you go out and pay your attentions to Miss Regan and all saying you are her intended?' It was only a joke. I would say the same thing to her face, for Denis was such a quiet boy, no way rough or accustomed to the girls at all—and how would he in this lonesome place?

"I will not belie her; it was she saw first that poor Denis was after more than company, and it was not to this cove she came at all then but to the little cove beyond the headland, and 'tis hardly she would go there itself without a little scholar along with her. 'Ah,' I says, for I missed her company, 'isn't it the great stranger Miss Regan is becoming?' and Denis would put on his coat and go hunting in the dusk till he came to whatever spot she was. Little ease that was to him, poor boy, for he lost his tongue entirely, and lying on his belly before her, chewing an old bit of grass, is all he would do till she got up and left him. He could not help himself, poor boy. The madness was on him, even then, and it was only when I saw the plunder done that I knew there was no cure for him only to put her out of his mind entirely. For 'twas madness in him and he knew it, and that was what made him lose his tongue—he that was maybe without the price of an ounce of 'baccy—I will not deny it: often enough he had to do without it when the hens would not be laying, and often enough stirabout and praties was all we had for days. And there was she with money to her name in the bank! And that wasn't all, for he was a good boy; a quiet, good-natured boy, and another would take pity on him, knowing he would make her a fine steady husband, but she was not the sort, and well I knew it from the first day I laid eyes on her, that her hand would never rock the cradle. There was the madness out and out.

"So here was I, pulling and hauling, coaxing him to stop at home, and hiding whatever little thing was to be done till evening the way his hands would not be idle. But he had no heart in the work, only listening, always listening, or climbing the cnuceen to see would he catch a glimpse of her coming or going. And, oh, Mary, the heavy sigh he'd give when his bit of supper was over and I bolting the house for the night, and he with the long hours of darkness forninst him—my heart was broken thinking of it. It was the madness, you see. It was on him. He could hardly sleep or eat, and at night I would hear him, turning and groaning as loud as the sea on the rocks.

"It was then when the sleep was a fever to him that he took to walking in the night. I remember well the first night I heard him lift the latch. I put on my few, things and went out after him. It was standing here I heard his feet on the stile. I went back and latched the door and hurried after him. What else could I do, and this place terrible after the fall of night with rocks and hills and water and streams, and he, poor soul, blinded with the dint of sleep. He travelled the road a piece, and then took to the hills, and I followed him with my legs all torn with briars and furze. It was over beyond by the new house that he gave up. He turned to me then the way a little child that is running away turns and clings to your knees; he turned to me and said: 'Mother, we'll go home now. It was the bad day for you ever you brought me into the world.' And as the day was breaking I got him back to bed and covered him up to sleep.

"I was hoping that in time he'd wear himself out, but it was worse he was getting. I was a strong woman then, a mayen-strong woman. I could cart a load of seaweed or dig a field with any man, but the night-walking broke me. I knelt one night before the Blessed Virgin and prayed whatever was to happen, it would happen while the light of life was in me, the way I would not be leaving him lonesome like that in a wild place.

"And it happened the way I prayed. Blessed be God, he woke that night or the next night on me and he roaring. I went in to him but I couldn't hold him. He had the strength of five men. So I went out and locked the door behind me. It was down the hill I faced in the starlight to the little house above the cove. The Donoghues came with me: I will not belie them; they were fine powerful men and good neighbours. The father and the two sons came with me and brought the rope from the boats. It was a hard struggle they had of it and a long time before they got him on the floor, and a longer time before they got the ropes on him. And when they had him tied they put him back into bed for me, and I covered him up, nice and decent, and put a hot stone to his feet to take the chill of the cold floor off him.

"Sean Donoghue spent the night sitting beside the fire with me, and in the morning he sent one of the boys off for the doctor. Then Denis called me in his own voice and I went into him. 'Mother,' says Denis, 'will you leave me this way against the time they come for me?' I hadn't the heart. God knows I hadn't. 'Don't do it, Peg,' says Sean. 'If 'twas a hard job trussing him before, it will be harder the next time, and I won't answer for it.'

" 'You're a kind neighbour, Sean,' says I, 'and I would never make little of you, but he is the only son I ever reared and I'd sooner he'd kill me now than shame him at the last.'

"So I loosened the ropes on him and he lay there very quiet all day without breaking his fast. Coming on to evening he asked me for the sup of tea and he drank it, and soon after the doctor and another man came in the car. They said a few words to Denis but he made them no answer and the doctor gave me the bit of writing. 'It will be tomorrow before they come for him,' says he, 'and 'tisn't right for you to be alone in the house with the man.' But I said I would stop with him and Sean Donoghue said the same.

"When darkness came on there was a little bit of a wind blew up from the sea and Denis began to rave to himself, and it was her name he was calling all the time. 'Winnie,' that was her name, and it was the first time I heard it spoken. 'Who is that he is calling?' says Sean. 'It is the schoolmistress,' says I, 'for though I do not recognize the name, I know 'tis no one else he'd be asking for.' 'That is a bad sign,' says Sean. 'He'll get worse as the night goes on and the wind rises. 'Twould be better for me go down and get the boys to put the ropes on him again while he's quiet.' And it was then something struck me, and I said: 'Maybe if she came to him herself for a minute he would be quiet after.' 'We can try it anyway,' says Sean, 'and if the girl has a kind heart she will come.'

"It was Sean that went up for her. I would not have the courage to ask her. Her little house is there on the edge of the hill; you can see it as you go back the road with the bit of garden before it the new teacher left grow wild. And it was a true word Sean said for 'twas worse, Denis was getting, shouting out against the wind for us to get Winnie for him. Sean was a long time away or maybe I felt it long, and I thought it might be the way she was afeared to come. There are many like that, small blame to them. Then I heard her step that I knew so well on the boreen beside the house and I ran to the door, meaning to say I was sorry for the trouble we were giving her, but when I opened the door Denis called out her name in a loud voice, and the crying fit came on me, thinking how light-hearted we used to be together.

"I couldn't help it, and she pushed in apast me into the bedroom with her face as white as that wall. The candle was lighting on the dresser. He turned to her roaring with the mad look in his eyes, and then went quiet all of a sudden, seeing her like that overright him with her hair all tumbled in the wind. I was coming behind her. I heard it. He put up his two poor hands and the red mark of the ropes on his wrists and whispered to her: 'Winnie, asthore, isn't it the long time you were away from me?'

" 'It is, Denis, it is indeed,' says she, 'but you know I couldn't help it.'

" 'Don't leave me any more now, Winnie,' says he, and then he said no more, only the two eyes lighting out on her as she sat by the bed. And Sean Donoghue brought in the little stooleen for me, and there we were, the three of us, talking, and Denis paying us no attention, only staring at her.

" 'Winnie,' says he, 'lie down here beside me.'

" 'Oye,' says Sean, humouring him, 'don't you know the poor girl is played out after her day's work? She must go home to bed.'

" 'No, no, no,' says Denis and the terrible mad light in his eyes. 'There is a high wind blowing and 'tis no night for one like her to be out. Leave her sleep here beside me. Leave her creep in under the clothes to me the way I'll keep her warm.'

" 'Oh, oh, oh, oh,' says I, 'indeed and indeed, Miss Regan, 'tis I'm sorry for bringing you here. 'Tisn't my son is talking at all but the madness in him. I'll go now,' says I, 'and bring Sean's boys to put the ropes on him again.'

" 'No, Mrs. Sullivan,' says she in a quiet voice. 'Don't do that at all. I'll stop here with him and he'll go fast asleep. Won't you, Denis?'

" 'I will, I will,' says he, 'but come under the clothes to me. There does a terrible draught blow under that door.'

" 'I will indeed, Denis,' says she, 'if you'll promise me to go to sleep.'

" 'Oye, whisht, girl,' says I. ' 'Tis you that's mad. While you're here you're in my charge, and how would I answer to your father if you stopped in here by yourself?'

" 'Never mind about me, Mrs. Sullivan,' she said. 'I'm not a bit in dread of Denis. I promise you there will no harm come to me. You and Mr. Donoghue can sit outside in the kitchen and I'll be all right here.'

"She had a worried look but there was something about her there was no mistaking. I wouldn't take it on myself to cross the girl. We went out to the kitchen, Sean and myself, and we heard every whisper that passed between them. She got into the bed beside him: I heard her. He was whispering into her ear the sort of foolish things boys do be saying at that age, and then we heard no more only the pair of them breathing. I went to the room door and looked in. He was lying with his arm about her and his head on her bosom, sleeping like a child, sleeping like he slept in his good days with no worry at all on his poor face. She did not look at me and I did not speak to her. My heart was too full. God help us, it was an old song of my father's that was going through my head: 'Lonely Rock is the one wife my children will know.'

"Later on, the candle went out and I did not light another. I wasn't a bit afraid for her then. The storm blew up and he slept through it all, breathing nice and even. When it was light I made a cup of tea for her and beckoned her from the room door. She loosened his hold and slipped out of bed. Then he stirred and opened his eyes.

" 'Winnie,' says he, 'where are you going?'

" 'I'm going to work, Denis,' says she. 'Don't you know I must be at school early?'

" 'But you'll come back to me tonight, Winnie?' says he.

" 'I will, Denis,' says she. 'I'll come back, never fear.'

"And he turned on his side and went fast asleep again.

"When she walked into the kitchen I went on my two knees before her and kissed her hands. I did so. There would no words come to me, and we sat there, the three of us, over our tea, and I declare for the time being I felt 'twas worth it all, all the troubles of his birth and rearing and all the lonesome years ahead.

"It was a great ease to us. Poor Denis never stirred, and when the police came he went along with them without commotion or handcuffs or anything that would shame him, and all the words he said to me was: 'Mother, tell Winnie I'll be expecting her.'

"And isn't it a strange and wonderful thing? From that day to the day she left us there did no one speak a bad word about what she did, and the people couldn't do enough for her. Isn't it a strange thing and the world as wicked as it is, that no one would say the bad word about her?"

Darkness had fallen over the Atlantic, blank grey to its farthest reaches.

LEGAL AID

DELIA CARTY came of a very respectable family. It was going as maid to the O'Gradys of Pouladuff that ruined her. That whole family was slightly touched. The old man, a national teacher, was hardly ever at home, and the daughters weren't much better. When they weren't away visiting, they had people visiting them, and it was nothing to Delia to come in late at night and find one of them plastered round some young fellow on the sofa.

That sort of thing isn't good for any young girl. Like mistress like maid; inside six months she was smoking, and within a year she was carrying on with one Tom Flynn, a farmer's son. Her father, a respectable, hard-working man, knew nothing about it, for he would have realized that she was no match for one of the Flynns, and even if Tom's father, Ned, had known, he would never have thought it possible that any labourer's daughter could imagine herself a match for Tom.

Not, God knows, that Tom was any great catch. He was a big uncouth galoot who was certain that lovemaking, like drink, was one of the simple pleasures his father tried to deprive him of, out of spite. He used to call at the house while the O'Gradys were away, and there would be Delia in one of Eileen O'Grady's frocks and with Eileen O'Grady's lipstick and powder on, doing the lady over the tea things in the parlour. Throwing a glance over his shoulder in case anyone might spot him, Tom would heave himself onto the sofa with his boots over the end.

"Begod, I love sofas," he would say with simple pleasure.

"Put a cushion behind you," Delia would say.

"Oh, begod," Tom would say, making himself comfortable, "if ever I have a house of my own 'tis unknown what sofas and cushions I'll have. Them teachers must get great money. What the hell do they go away at all for?"

Delia loved making the tea and handing it out like a real lady, but you couldn't catch Tom out like that.

"Ah, what do I want tay for?" he would say with a doubtful glance at the cup. "Haven't you any whisky? Ould O'Grady must have gallons of it. . . . Leave it there on the table. Why the hell don't they have proper mugs with handles a man could get a grip on? Is that taypot silver? Pity I'm not a teacher!"

It was only natural for Delia to show him the bedrooms and the dressing-tables with the three mirrors, the way you could see yourself from all sides, but Tom, his hands under his head, threw himself with incredulous delight on the low double bed and cried: "Springs! Begod, 'tis like a car!"

What the springs gave rise to was entirely the O'Gradys' fault since no one but themselves would have left a house in a lonesome part to a girl of nineteen to mind. The only surprising thing was that it lasted two years without Delia showing any signs of it. It probably took Tom that time to find the right way.

But when he did he got into a terrible state. It was hardly in him to believe that a harmless poor devil like himself whom no one ever bothered his head about could achieve such unprecedented results on one girl, but when he understood it he knew only too well what the result of it would be. His father would first beat hell out of him and then throw him out and leave the farm to his nephews. There being no hope of conciliating his father, Tom turned his attention to God, who, though supposed to share Ned Flynn's views about fellows and girls, had some nature in Him. Tom stopped seeing Delia, to persuade God that he was reforming and to show that anyway it wasn't his fault. Left alone he could be a decent, good-living young fellow, but the Carty girl was a forward, deceitful hussy who had led him on instead of putting him off the way any well-bred girl would do. Between lipsticks, sofas, and tay in the parlour, Tom put it up to God that it was a great wonder she hadn't got him into worse trouble.

Delia had to tell her mother, and Mrs. Carty went to Father Corcoran to see could he induce Tom to marry her. Father Corcoran was a tall, testy old man who, even at the age of sixty-five, couldn't make out for the life of him what young fellows saw in girls, but if he didn't know much about lovers he knew a lot about farmers.

"Wisha, Mrs. Carty," he said crankily, "how could I get him to marry her? Wouldn't you have a bit of sense? Some little financial arrangement, maybe, so that she could leave the parish and not be a cause of scandal—I might be able to do that."

He interviewed Ned Flynn, who by this time had got Tom's version of the story and knew financial arrangements were going to be the order of the day unless he could put a stop to them. Ned was a man of over six foot with a bald brow and a smooth unlined face as though he never had a care except his general concern for the welfare of humanity which made him look so abnormally thoughtful. Even Tom's conduct hadn't brought a wrinkle to his brow.

"I don't know, father," he said, stroking his bald brow with a dieaway air, "I don't know what you could do at all."

"Wisha, Mr. Flynn," said the priest who, when it came to the pinch, had more nature than twenty Flynns, "wouldn't you do the handsome thing and let him marry her before it goes any farther?"

"I don't see how much farther it could go, father," said Ned.

"It could become a scandal."

"I'm afraid 'tis that already, father."

"And after all," said Father Corcoran, forcing himself to put in a good word for one of the unfortunate sex whose very existence was a mystery to him, "is she any worse than the rest of the girls that are going? Bad is the best of them, from what I see, and Delia is a great deal better than most."

"That's not my information at all, father," said Ned, looking like "The Heart Bowed Down."

"That's a very serious statement, Mr. Flynn," said Father Corcoran, giving him a challenging look.

"It can be proved, father," said Ned gloomily. "Of course I'm not denying the boy was foolish, but the cleverest can be caught."

"You astonish me, Mr. Flynn," said Father Corcoran who was beginning to realize that he wasn't even going to get a subscription. "Of course I can't contradict you, but 'twill cause a terrible scandal."

"I'm as sorry for that as you are, father," said Ned, "but I have my son's future to think of."

Then, of course, the fun began. Foolish to the last, the O'Gradys wanted to keep Delia on till it was pointed out to them that Mr. O'Grady would be bound to get the blame. After this, her father had to be told. Dick Carty knew exactly what became a devoted father, and he beat Delia till he had to be hauled off her by the neighbours. He was a man who loved to sit in his garden reading his paper; now he felt he owed it to himself not to be seen enjoying himself, so instead he sat over the fire and brooded. The more he brooded the angrier he became. But seeing that, with the best will in the world, he could not beat Delia every time he got angry, he turned his attention to the Flynns. Ned Flynn, that contemptible bosthoon, had slighted one of the Cartys in a parish where they had lived for hundreds of years with unblemished reputations; the Flynns, as everyone knew, being mere upstarts and outsiders without a date on their gravestones before 1850—nobodies!

He brought Delia to see Jackie Canty, the solicitor in town. Jackie was a little jenny-ass of a man with thin lips, a pointed nose, and a pince-nez that wouldn't stop in place, and he listened with grave enjoyment to the story of Delia's misconduct. "And what happened then, please?" he asked in his shrill singsong, looking at the floor and trying hard nót to burst out into a giggle of delight. "The devils!" he thought. "The devils!" It was as close as Jackie was ever likely to get to the facts of life, an opportunity not to be missed.

"Anything in writing?" he sang, looking at her over the pince-nez. "Any letters? Any documents?"

"Only a couple of notes I burned," said Delia, who thought him a very queer man, and no wonder.

"Pity!" Jackie said with an admiring smile. "A smart man! Oh, a very smart man!"

"Ah, 'tisn't that at all," said Delia uncomfortably, "only he had no occasion for writing."

"Ah, Miss Carty," cried Jackie in great indignation, looking at her challengingly through the specs while his voice took on a steely ring, "a gentleman in love always finds plenty of occasion for writing. He's a smart man; your father might succeed in an action for seduction, but if 'tis defended 'twill be a dirty case."

"Mr. Canty," said her father solemnly, "I don't mind how dirty it is so long as I get justice." He stood up, a powerful man of six feet, and held up his clenched fist. "Justice is what I want," he said dramatically. "That's the sort I am. I keep myself to myself and mind my own business, but give me a cut, and I'll fight in a bag, tied up."

"Don't forget that Ned Flynn has the money, Dick," wailed Jackie.

"Mr. Canty," said Dick with a dignity verging on pathos, "you know me?"

"I do, Dick, I do."

"I'm living in this neighbourhood, man and boy, fifty years, and I owe nobody a ha-penny. If it took me ten years, breaking stones by the road, I'd pay it back, every penny."

"I know, Dick, I know," moaned Jackie. "But there's other things as well. There's your daughter's reputation. Do you know what they'll do? They'll go into court and swear someone else was the father."

"Tom could never say that," Delia cried despairingly. "The tongue would rot in his mouth."

Jackie had no patience at all with this chit of a girl, telling him his business. He sat back with a weary air, his arm over the back of his chair.

"That statement has no foundation," he said icily. "There is no record of any such thing happening a witness. If there was, the inhabitants of Ireland would have considerably less to say for themselves. You would be surprised the things respectable people will say in the witness box. Rot in their mouths indeed! Ah, dear me, no. With documents, of course, it would be different, but it is only our word against theirs. Can it be proved that you weren't knocking round with any other man at this time, Miss Carty?"

"Indeed, I was doing nothing of the sort," Delia said indignantly. "I swear to God I wasn't, Mr. Canty. I hardly spoke to a fellow the whole time, only when Tom and myself might have a row and I'd go out with Timmy Martin."

"Timmy Martin!" Canty cried dramatically, pointing an accusing finger at her. "There is their man!"

"But Tom did the same with Betty Daly," cried Delia on the point of tears, "and he only did it to spite me. I swear there was nothing else in it, Mr. Canty, nor he never accused me of it."

"Mark my words," chanted Jackie with a mournful smile, "he'll make up for lost time now."

In this he showed considerably more foresight than Delia gave him credit for. After the baby was born and the action begun, Tom and his father went to town to see their solicitor, Peter Humphreys. Peter, who knew all he wanted to know about the facts of life, liked the case much less than Jackie. A crosseyed, full-blooded man who had made his money when law was about land, not love, he thought it a terrible comedown. Besides, he didn't think it nice to be listening to such things.

"And so, according to you, Timmy Martin is the father?" he asked Tom.

"Oh, I'm not swearing he is," said Tom earnestly, giving himself a heave in his chair and crossing his legs. "How the hell could I? All I am saying is that I wasn't the only one, and what's more she boasted about it. Boasted about it, begod!" he added with a look of astonishment at such female depravity.

"Before witnesses?" asked Peter, his eyes doing a double cross with hopelessness.

"As to that," replied Tom with great solemnity, looking over his shoulder for an open window he could spit through, "I couldn't swear."

"But you understood her to mean Timmy Martin?"

"I'm not accusing Timmy Martin at all," said Tom in great alarm, seeing how the processes of law were tending to involve him in a row with the Martins, who were a turbulent family with ways of getting their own back unknown to any law. "Timmy Martin is one man she used to be round with. It might be Timmy Martin or it might be someone else, or what's more," he added with the look of a man who has had a sudden revelation, "it might be more than one." He looked from Peter to his father and back again to see what effect the revelation was having, but like other revelations it didn't seem to be going down too well. "Begod," he said, giving himself another heave, "it might be any God's number. . . . But, as to that," he added cautiously, "I wouldn't like to swear."

"Nor indeed, Tom," said his solicitor with a great effort at politeness, "no one would advise you. You'll want a good counsel."

"Begod, I suppose I will," said Tom with astonished resignation before the idea that there might be people in the world bad enough to doubt his word.

There was great excitement in the village when it became known that the Flynns were having the Roarer Cooper as counsel. Even as a first-class variety turn Cooper could always command attention, and everyone knew that the rights and wrongs of the case would be relegated to their proper position while the little matter of Eileen O'Grady's best frock received the attention it deserved.

On the day of the hearing the court was crowded. Tom and his father were sitting at the back with Peter Humphreys, waiting for Cooper, while Delia and her father were talking to Jackie Canty and their own counsel, Ivers. He was a well-built young man with a high brow, black hair, and half-closed, red-tinged sleepy eyes. He talked in a bland drawl.

"You're not worrying, are you?" he asked Delia kindly. "Don't be a bit afraid. . . . I suppose there's no chance of them settling, Jackie?"

"Musha, what chance would there be?" Canty asked scoldingly. "Don't you know yourself what sort they are?"

"I'll have a word with Cooper myself," said Ivers. "Dan isn't as bad as he looks." He went to talk to a coarse-looking man in wig and gown who had just come in. To say he wasn't as bad as he looked was no great compliment. He had a face that was almost a square, with a big jaw and blue eyes in wicked little slits that made deep dents across his cheekbones.

"What about settling this case of ours, Dan?" Ivers asked gently.

Cooper didn't even return his look; apparently he was not responsive to charm.

"Did you ever know me to settle when I could fight?" he growled.

"Not when you could fight your match," Ivers said, without taking offence. "You don't consider that poor girl your match?"

"We'll soon see what sort of girl she is," replied Cooper complacently as his eyes fell on the Flynns. "Tell me," he whispered, "what did she see in my client?"

"What you saw yourself when you were her age, I suppose," said Ivers. "You don't mean there wasn't a girl in a tobacconist's shop that you thought came down from heaven with the purpose of consoling you?"

"She had nothing in writing," Cooper replied gravely. "And, unlike your client, I never saw double."

"You don't believe that yarn, do you?"

"That's one of the things I'm going to inquire into."

"I can save you the trouble. She was too fond of him."

"Hah!" snorted Cooper as though this were a good joke. "And I suppose that's why she wants the cash."

"The girl doesn't care if she never got a penny. Don't you know

F

yourself what's behind it? A respectable father. Two respectable fathers! The trouble about marriage in this country, Dan Cooper, is that the fathers always insist on doing the coorting."

"Hah!" grunted Cooper, rather more uncertain of himself. "Show me this paragon of the female sex, Ivers."

"There in the brown hat beside Canty," said Ivers without looking round. "Come on, you old devil, and stop trying to pretend you're Buffalo Bill. It's enough going through what she had to go through. I don't want her to go through any more."

"And why in God's name do you come to me?" Cooper asked in sudden indignation. "What the hell do you take me for? A Society for Protecting Fallen Women? Why didn't the priest make him marry her?"

"When the Catholic Church can make a farmer marry a labourer's daughter the Kingdom of God will be at hand," said Ivers. "I'm surprised at you, Dan Cooper, not knowing better at your age."

"And what are the neighbours doing here if she has nothing to hide?"

"Who said she had nothing to hide?" Ivers asked lightly, throwing in his hand. "Haven't you daughters of your own? You know she played the fine lady in the O'Gradys' frocks. If 'tis any information to you she wore their jewellery as well."

"Ivers, you're a young man of great plausibility," said Cooper, "but you can spare your charm on me. I have my client's interests to consider. Did she sleep with the other fellow?"

"She did not."

"Do you believe that?"

"As I believe in my own mother."

"The faith that moves mountains," Cooper said despondently. "How much are ye asking?"

"Two hundred and fifty," replied Ivers, shaky for the first time.

"Merciful God Almighty!" moaned Cooper, turning his eyes to the ceiling. "As if any responsible Irish court would put that price on a girl's virtue. Still, it might be as well. I'll see what I can do."

He moved ponderously across the court and with two big arms outstretched like wings shepherded out the Flynns.

"Two hundred and fifty pounds?" gasped Ned, going white. "Where in God's name would I get that money?"

"My dear Mr. Flynn," Cooper said with coarse amiability, "that's only half the yearly allowance his Lordship makes the young lady that obliges him, and she's not a patch on that girl in court. After a lifetime of experience I can assure you that for two years' fornication with a fine girl like that you won't pay a penny less than five hundred."

Peter Humphreys's eyes almost grew straight with the shock of such reckless slander on a blameless judge. He didn't know what had come over the Roarer. But that wasn't the worst. When the settlement was announced and the Flynns were leaving he went up to them again.

"You can believe me when I say you did the right thing, Mr Flynn," he said. "I never like cases involving good-looking girls. Gentlemen of his Lordship's age are terribly susceptible. But tell me, why wouldn't your son marry her now as he's about it?"

"Marry her?" echoed Ned, who hadn't yet got over the shock of having to pay two hundred and fifty pounds and costs for a little matter he could have compounded for with Father Corcoran for fifty. "A thing like that!"

"With two hundred and fifty pounds, man?" snarled Cooper. " 'Tisn't every day you'll pick up a daughter-in-law with that. . . . What do you say to the girl yourself?" he asked Tom.

"Oh, begod, the girl is all right," said Tom.

Tom looked different. It was partly relief that he wouldn't have to perjure himself, partly astonishment at seeing his father so swiftly overthrown. His face said: "The world is wide."

"Ah, Mr. Flynn, Mr. Flynn," whispered Cooper scornfully, "sure you're not such a fool as to let all that good money out of the family?"

Leaving Ned gasping, he went on to where Dick Carty, aglow with pride and malice, was receiving congratulations. There were no congratulations for Delia who was standing near him. She felt a big paw on her arm and looked up to see the Roarer.

"Are you still fond of that boy?" he whispered.

"I have reason to be, haven't I?" she retorted bitterly.

"You have," he replied with no great sympathy. "The best. I got you that money so that you could marry him if you wanted to. Do you want to?"

Her eyes filled with tears as she thought of the poor broken china of an idol that was being offered her now.

"Once a fool, always a fool," she said sullenly.

"You're no fool at all, girl," he said, giving her arm an encouraging squeeze. "You might make a man of him yet. I don't know what the law in this country is coming to. Get him away to hell out of this till I find Michael Ivers and get him to talk to your father."

The two lawyers made the match themselves at Johnny Desmond's pub, and Johnny said it was like nothing in the world so much as a mission, with the Roarer roaring and threatening hellfire on all concerned, and Michael Ivers piping away about the joys of heaven. Johnny said it was the most instructive evening he ever had. Ivers was always recognized as a weak man so the marriage did him no great harm, but of course it was a terrible comedown for a true Roarer, and Cooper's reputation has never been the same since then.

PEASANTS

WHEN Michael John Cronin stole the funds of the Carricknabreena Hurling, Football and Temperance Association, commonly called the Club, everyone said: "Devil's cure to him!" " 'Tis the price of him!" "Kind father for him!" "What did I tell you?" and the rest of the things people say when an acquaintance has got what is coming to him.

And not only Michael John but the whole Cronin family, seed, breed, and generation, came in for it; there wasn't one of them for twenty miles round or a hundred years back but his deeds and sayings were remembered and examined by the light of this fresh scandal. Michael John's father (the heavens be his bed!) was a drunkard who beat his wife, and his father before him a land-grabber. Then there was an uncle or grand-uncle who had been a policeman and taken a hand in the bloody work at Mitchels-town long ago, and an unmarried sister of the same whose good name it would by all accounts have needed a regiment of hus-bands to restore. It was a grand shaking-up the Cronins got al-together, and anyone who had a grudge in for them, even if it was no more than a thirty-third cousin, had rare sport, dropping a friendly word about it and saying how sorry he was for the poor mother till he had the blood lighting in the Cronin eyes.

There was only one thing for them to do with Michael John; that was to send him to America and let the thing blow over, and that, no doubt, is what they would have done but for a certain unpleasant and extraordinary incident.

Father Crowley, the parish priest, was chairman of the com-mittee. He was a remarkable man, even in appearance; tall, powerfully built, but very stooped, with shrewd, loveless eyes that rarely softened to anyone except two or three old people. He was a strange man, well on in years, noted for his strong political views, which never happened to coincide with those of any party, and as obstinate as the devil himself. Now what should Father Crowley do but try to force the committee to prosecute Michael John?

The committee were all religious men who up to this had never as much as dared to question the judgments of a man of God: yes, faith, and if the priest had been a bully, which to give him his due he wasn't, he might have danced a jig on their backs and they wouldn't have complained. But a man has principles, and the like of this had never been heard of in the parish before. What? Put the police on a boy and he in trouble?

One by one the committee spoke up and said so. "But he did

wrong," said Father Crowley, thumping the table. "He did wrong and he should be punished."

"Maybe so, father," said Con Norton, the vice-chairman, who acted as spokesman. "Maybe you're right, but you wouldn't say his poor mother should be punished too and she a widow-woman?"

"True for you!" chorused the others.

"Serve his mother right!" said the priest shortly. "There's none of you but knows better than I do the way that young man was brought up. He's a rogue and his mother is a fool. Why didn't she beat Christian principles into him when she had him on her knee?"

"That might be, too," Norton agreed mildly. "I wouldn't say but you're right, but is that any reason his Uncle Peter should be punished?"

"Or his Uncle Dan?" asked another.

"Or his Uncle James?" asked a third.

"Or his cousins, the Dwyers, that keep the little shop in Lissna-carriga, as decent a living family as there is in County Cork?" asked a fourth.

"No, father," said Norton, "the argument is against you."

"Is it indeed?" exclaimed the priest, growing cross. "Is it so? What the devil has it to do with his Uncle Dan or his Uncle James? What are ye talking about? What punishment is it to them, will ye tell me that? Ye'll be telling me next 'tis a punish-ment to me and I a child of Adam like himself."

"Wisha now, father," asked Norton incredulously, "do you mean 'tis no punishment to them having one of their own blood made a public show? Is it mad you think we are? Maybe 'tis a thing you'd like done to yourself?"

"There was none of my family ever a thief," replied Father Crowley shortly.

"Begor, we don't know whether there was or not," snapped a little man called Daly, a hot-tempered character from the hills.

"Easy, now! Easy, Phil!" said Norton warningly.

"What do you mean by that?" asked Father Crowley, rising and grabbing his hat and stick.

"What I mean," said Daly, blazing up, "is that I won't sit here and listen to insinuations about my native place from any foreigner. There are as many rogues and thieves and vagabonds and liars in Cullough as ever there were in Carricknabreena—ay, begod, and more, and bigger! That's what I mean."

"No, no, no, no," Norton said soothingly. "That's not what he means at all, father. We don't want any bad blood between Cullough and Carricknabreena. What he means is that the Crowleys may be a fine substantial family in their own country, but that's fifteen long miles away, and this isn't their country, and the Cronins are neighbours of ours since the dawn of history and time, and 'twould be a very queer thing if at this hour we handed one of them over to the police. . . . And now, listen to me, father," he went on, forgetting his role of pacificator and hitting the table as hard as the rest, "if a cow of mine got sick in the morning, 'tisn't a Cremin or a Crowley I'd be asking for help, and damn the bit of use 'twould be to me if I did. And everyone knows I'm no enemy of the Church but a respectable farmer that pays his dues and goes to his duties regularly."

"True for you! True for you!" agreed the committee.

"I don't give a snap of my finger what you are," retorted the priest. "And now listen to me, Con Norton. I bear young Cronin no grudge, which is more than some of you can say, but I know my duty and I'll do it in spite of the lot of you."

He stood at the door and looked back. They were gazing blankly at one another, not knowing what to say to such an impossible man. He shook his fist at them.

"Ye all know me," he said. "Ye know that all my life I'm fighting the long-tailed families. Now, with the help of God, I'll shorten the tail of one of them."

Father Crowley's threat frightened them. They knew he was an obstinate man and had spent his time attacking what he called the "corruption" of councils and committees, which was all very well as long as it happened outside your own parish. They dared not oppose him openly because he knew too much about all of them and, in public at least, had a lacerating tongue. The solution they favoured was a tactful one. They formed themselves into a Michael John Cronin Fund Committee and canvassed the parishioners for subscriptions to pay off what Michael John had stolen. Regretfully they decided that Father Crowley would hardly countenance a football match for the purpose.

Then with the defaulting treasurer, who wore a suitably contrite air, they marched up to the presbytery. Father Crowley was at his dinner but he told the housekeeper to show them in. He looked up in astonishment as his dining-room filled with the seven committeemen, pushing before them the cowed Michael John.

"Who the blazes are ye?" he asked, glaring at them over the lamp.

"We're the Club Committee, father," replied Norton.

"Oh, are ye?"

"And this is the treasurer—the ex-treasurer, I should say."

"I won't pretend I'm glad to see him," said Father Crowley grimly.

"He came to say he's sorry, father," went on Norton. "He is sorry, and that's as true as God, and I'll tell you no lie. . . ." Norton made two steps forward and in a dramatic silence laid a heap of notes and silver on the table.

"What's that?" asked Father Crowley.

"The money, father. 'Tis all paid back now and there's nothing more between us. Any little crossness there was, we'll say no more about it, in the name of God."

The priest looked at the money and then at Norton.

"Con," he said, "you'd better keep the soft word for the judge. Maybe he'll think more of it than I do."

"The judge, father?"

"Ay, Con, the judge."

There was a long silence. The committee stood with open mouths, unable to believe it.

"And is that what you're doing to us, father?" asked Norton in a trembling voice. "After all the years, and all we done for you, is it you're going to show us up before the whole country as a lot of robbers?"

"Ah, ye idiots, I'm not showing ye up."

"You are then, father, and you're showing up every man,

woman, and child in the parish," said Norton. "And mark my words, 'twon't be forgotten for you."

The following Sunday Father Crowley spoke of the matter from the altar. He spoke for a full half hour without a trace of emotion on his grim old face, but his sermon was one long, venomous denunciation of the "long-tailed families" who, according to him, were the ruination of the country and made a mockery of truth, justice, and charity. He was, as his congregation agreed, a shockingly obstinate old man who never knew when he was in the wrong.

After Mass he was visited in his sacristy by the committee. He gave Norton a terrible look from under his shaggy eyebrows, which made that respectable farmer flinch.

"Father," Norton said appealingly, "we only want one word with you. One word and then we'll go. You're a hard character, and you said some bitter things to us this morning; things we never deserved from you. But we're quiet, peaceable poor men and we don't want to cross you."

Father Crowley made a sound like a snort.

"We came to make a bargain with you, father," said Norton, beginning to smile.

"A bargain?"

"We'll say no more about the whole business if you'll do one little thing—just one little thing—to oblige us."

"The bargain!" the priest said impatiently. "What's the bargain?"

"We'll leave the matter drop for good and all if you'll give the boy a character."

"Yes, father," cried the committee in chorus. "Give him a character! Give him a character!"

"Give him a what?" cried the priest.

"Give him a character, father, for the love of God," said Norton emotionally. "If you speak up for him, the judge will leave him off and there'll be no stain on the parish."

"Is it out of your minds you are, you halfwitted angashores?" asked Father Crowley, his face suffused with blood, his head trembling. "Here am I all these years preaching to ye about decency and justice and truth and ye no more understand me than that wall there. Is it the way ye want me to perjure myself? Is it the way ye want me to tell a damned lie with the name of Almighty God on my lips? Answer me, is it?"

"Ah, what perjure!" Norton replied wearily. "Sure, can't you say a few words for the boy? No one is asking you to say much. What harm will it do you to tell the judge he's an honest, good-living, upright lad, and that he took the money without meaning any harm?"

"My God!" muttered the priest, running his hands distractedly through his grey hair. "There's no talking to ye, no talking to ye, ye lot of sheep."

When he was gone the committeemen turned and looked at one another in bewilderment.

"That man is a terrible trial," said one.

"He's a tyrant," said Daly vindictively.

"He is, indeed," sighed Norton, scratching his head. "But in God's holy name, boys, before we do anything, we'll give him one more chance."

That evening when he was at his tea the committeemen called again. This time they looked very spruce, businesslike, and independent. Father Crowley glared at them.

"Are ye back?" he asked bitterly. "I was thinking ye would be. I declare to my goodness, I'm sick of ye and yeer old committee."

"Oh, we're not the committee, father," said Norton stiffly.

"Ye're not?"

"We're not."

"All I can say is, ye look mighty like it. And, if I'm not being impertinent, who the deuce are ye?"

"We're a deputation, father."

"Oh, a deputation! Fancy that, now. And a deputation from what?"

"A deputation from the parish, father. Now, maybe you'll listen to us."

"Oh, go on! I'm listening, I'm listening."

"Well, now, 'tis like this, father," said Norton, dropping his airs and graces and leaning against the table. " 'Tis about that little business this morning. Now, father, maybe you don't understand us and we don't understand you. There's a lot of misunderstanding in the world today, father. But we're quiet simple poor men that want to do the best we can for everybody, and a few words or a few pounds wouldn't stand in our way. Now, do you follow me?"

"I declare," said Father Crowley, resting his elbows on the table, "I don't know whether I do or not."

"Well, 'tis like this, father. We don't want any blame on the parish or on the Cronins, and you're the one man that can save us. Now all we ask of you is to give the boy a character—"

"Yes, father," interrupted the chorus, "give him a character! Give him a character!"

"Give him a character, father, and you won't be troubled by him again. Don't say no to me now till you hear what I have to say. We won't ask you to go next, nigh or near the court. You have pen and ink beside you and one couple of lines is all you need write. When 'tis over you can hand Michael John his ticket to America and tell him not to show his face in Carricknabreena again. There's the price of his ticket, father," he added, clapping a bundle of notes on the table. "The Cronins themselves made it up, and we have his mother's word and his own word that he'll clear out the minute 'tis all over."

"He can go to pot!" retorted the priest. "What is it to me where he goes?"

"Now, father, can't you be patient?" Norton asked reproachfully. "Can't you let me finish what I'm saying? We know 'tis no advantage to you, and that's the very thing we came to talk about. Now, supposing—just supposing for the sake of argument —that you do what we say, there's a few of us here, and between us, we'd raise whatever little contribution to the parish fund you'd think would be reasonable to cover the expense and trouble to yourself. Now do you follow me?"

"Con Norton," said Father Crowley, rising and holding the edge of the table, "I follow you. This morning it was perjury, and now 'tis bribery, and the Lord knows what 'twill be next. I see I've been wasting my breath. . . . And I see too," he added savagely, leaning across the table towards them, "a pedigree bull would be more use to ye than a priest."

"What do you mean by that, father?" asked Norton in a low voice.

"What I say."

"And that's a saying that will be remembered for you the longest day you live," hissed Norton, leaning towards him till they were glaring at one another over the table.

"A bull," gasped Father Crowley. "Not a priest."

" 'Twill be remembered."

"Will it? Then remember this too. I'm an old man now. I'm forty years a priest, and I'm not a priest for the money or power or glory of it, like others I know. I gave the best that was in me —maybe 'twasn't much but 'twas more than many a better man would give, and at the end of my days . . ." lowering his voice to a whisper he searched them with his terrible eyes, ". . . at the end of my days, if I did a wrong thing, or a bad thing, or an unjust thing, there isn't man or woman in this parish that would brave me to my face and call me a villain. And isn't that a poor story for an old man that tried to be a good priest?" His voice changed again and he raised his head defiantly. "Now get out before I kick you out!"

And true to his word and character not one word did he say in Michael John's favour the day of the trial, no more than if he was a black. Three months Michael John got and by all accounts he got off light.

He was a changed man when he came out of jail, downcast and dark in himself. Everyone was sorry for him, and people who had never spoken to him before spoke to him then. To all of them he said modestly: "I'm very grateful to you, friend, for overlooking my misfortune." As he wouldn't go to America, the committee made another whip-round and between what they had collected before and what the Cronins had made up to send him to America, he found himself with enough to open a small shop. Then he got a job in the County Council, and an agency for some shipping company, till at last he was able to buy a public-house.

As for Father Crowley, till he was shifted twelve months later, he never did a day's good in the parish. The dues went down and the presents went down, and people with money to spend on

Masses took it fifty miles away sooner than leave it to him. They said it broke his heart.

He has left unpleasant memories behind him. Only for him, people say, Michael John would be in America now. Only for him he would never have married a girl with money, or had it to lend to poor people in the hard times, or ever sucked the blood of Christians. For, as an old man said to me of him: "A robber he is and was, and a grabber like his grandfather before him, and an enemy of the people like his uncle, the policeman; and though some say he'll dip his hand where he dipped it before, for myself I have no hope unless the mercy of God would send us another Moses or Brian Boru to cast him down and hammer him in the dust."

IN THE TRAIN

"THERE!" said the sergeant's wife. "You would hurry me."

"I always like being in time for a train," replied the sergeant, with the equability of one who has many times before explained the guiding principle of his existence.

"I'd have had heaps of time to buy the hat," added his wife.

The sergeant sighed and opened his evening paper. His wife looked out on the dark platform, pitted with pale lights under which faces and faces passed, lit up and dimmed again. A uniformed lad strode up and down with a tray of periodicals and chocolates. Farther up the platform a drunken man was being seen off by his friends.

"I'm very fond of Michael O'Leary," he shouted. "He is the most sincere man I know."

"I have no life," sighed the sergeant's wife. "No life at all. There isn't a soul to speak to; nothing to look at all day but bogs and mountains and rain—always rain! And the people! Well, we've had a fine sample of them, haven't we?"

The sergeant continued to read.

"Just for the few days it's been like heaven. Such interesting people! Oh, I thought Mr. Boyle had a glorious face! And his voice—it went through me."

The sergeant lowered his paper, took off his peaked cap, laid it on the seat beside him, and lit his pipe. He lit it in the old-fashioned way, ceremoniously, his eyes blinking pleasurably like a sleepy cat's in the match-flare. His wife scrutinized each face that passed and it was plain that for her life meant faces and people and things and nothing more.

"Oh, dear!" she said again. "I simply have no existence. I was educated in a convent and play the piano; my father was a literary man, and yet I am compelled to associate with the lowest types of humanity. If it was even a decent town, but a village!"

"Ah," said the sergeant, gapping his reply with anxious puffs, "maybe with God's help we'll get a shift one of these days." But he said it without conviction, and it was also plain that he was well-pleased with himself, with the prospect of returning home, with his pipe and his paper.

"Here are Magner and the others," said his wife as four other policemen passed the barrier. "I hope they'll have sense enough to let us alone. . . . How do you do? How do you do? Had a nice time, boys?" she called with sudden animation, and her pale, sullen face became warm and vivacious. The policemen smiled and touched their caps but did not halt.

"They might have stopped to say good evening," she added sharply, and her face sank into its old expression of boredom and dissatisfaction. "I don't think I'll ask Delancey to tea again. The others make an attempt but, really, Delancey is hopeless. When I smile and say: 'Guard Delancey, wouldn't you like to use the butter-knife?' he just scowls at me from under his shaggy brows and says without a moment's hesitation: 'I would not.'"

"Ah, Delancey is a poor slob," the sergeant said affectionately.

"Oh, yes, but that's not enough, Jonathan. Slob or no slob, he should make an attempt. He's a young man; he should have a dinner jacket at least. What sort of wife will he get if he won't even wear a dinner jacket?"

"He's easy, I'd say. He's after a farm in Waterford."

"Oh, a farm! A farm! The wife is only an incidental, I suppose?"

"Well, now, from all I hear she's a damn nice little incidental."

"Yes, I suppose many a nice little incidental came from a farm," answered his wife, raising her pale brows. But the irony was lost on him.

"Indeed yes, indeed yes," he said fervently.

"And here," she added in biting tones, "come our charming neighbours."

Into the pale lamplight stepped a group of peasants. Not such as one sees near a capital but in the mountains and along the coasts. Gnarled, wild, with turbulent faces, their ill-cut clothes full of character, the women in pale brown shawls, the men wearing black sombreros and carrying big sticks, they swept in, ill at ease, laughing and shouting defiantly. And so much part of their natural environment were they that for a moment they seemed to create about themselves rocks and bushes, tarns, turf-ricks, and sea.

With a prim smile the sergeant's wife bowed to them through the open window.

"How do you do? How do you do?" she called. "Had a nice time?"

At the same moment the train gave a jolt and there was a rush in which the excited peasants were carried away. Some minutes passed; the influx of passengers almost ceased, and a porter began to slam the doors. The drunken man's voice rose in a cry of exultation.

"You can't possibly beat O'Leary," he declared. "I'd lay down my life for Michael O'Leary."

Then, just as the train was about to start, a young woman in a brown shawl rushed through the barrier. The shawl, which came low enough to hide her eyes, she held firmly across her mouth, leaving visible only a long thin nose with a hint of pale flesh at either side. Beneath the shawl she was carrying a large parcel.

She looked hastily around; a porter shouted to her and pushed her towards the nearest compartment, which happened to be that occupied by the sergeant and his wife. He had actually seized the handle of the door when the sergeant's wife sat up and screamed.

"Quick! Quick!" she cried. "Look who it is! She's coming in. Jonathan! Jonathan!"

The sergeant rose with a look of alarm on his broad red face. The porter threw open the door, with his free hand grasping the woman's elbow. But when she laid eyes on the sergeant's startled face she stepped back, tore herself free and ran crazily up the platform. The engine shrieked; the porter slammed the door with a curse; somewhere another door opened and shut, and the row of watchers, frozen into effigies of farewell, now dark now bright, began to glide gently past the window, and the stale, smoky air was charged with the breath of open fields.

II

The four policemen spread themselves out in a separate compartment and lit cigarettes.

"Poor old Delancey!" Magner said with his reckless laugh. "He's cracked on her all right."

"Cracked on her," agreed Fox. "Did ye see the eye he gave her?"

Delancey smiled sheepishly. He was a tall, handsome, black-haired young man with the thick eyebrows described by the sergeant's wife. He was new to the force and suffered from a mixture of natural gentleness and country awkwardness.

"I am," he said in his husky voice. "The devil admire me, I never hated anyone yet, but I think I hate the living sight of her."

"Oh now, oh now!" protested Magner.

"I do. I think the Almighty God must have put that one into the world with the one main object of persecuting me."

"Well indeed," said Foley, " 'tis a mystery to me how the sergeant puts up with her. If any woman up and called me by an outlandish name like Jonathan when everyone knew my name was plain John I'd do fourteen days for her—by God, I would, and a calendar month."

The four men were now launched on a favourite topic that held them for more than a hour. None of them liked the sergeant's wife and all had stories to tell against her. From these there emerged the fact that she was an incurable scandalmonger and mischiefmaker who couldn't keep quiet about her own business, much less about that of her neighbours. And while they talked the train dragged across a dark plain, the heart of Ireland, and in the moonless night tiny cottage-windows blew past like sparks from a fire, and a pale simulacrum of the lighted carriages leaped and frolicked over hedges and fields. Magner shut the window and the compartment began to fill with smoke.

"She'll never rest till she's out of Farranchreesht," he said.

"That she mightn't!" groaned Delancey.

"How would you like the city yourself, Dan?" asked Magner.

"Man dear," exclaimed Delancey with sudden brightness, "I'd like it fine. There's great life in a city."

"You're welcome to it," said Foley, folding his hands across his paunch.

"Why so? What's wrong with it?"

"I'm better off where I am."

"But the life!"

"Life be damned! What sort of life is it when you're always under someone's eye? Look at the poor devils in court."

"True enough, true enough," agreed Fox.

"Ah, yes, yes," said Delancey, "but the adventures they have!"

"What adventures?"

"There was a sergeant in court only yesterday telling me one thing that happened himself. 'Twas an old maid without a soul in the world that died in an old loft on the quays. The sergeant put a new man on duty outside the door while he went back to report, and all he had to do was kick the door and frighten off the rats."

"That's enough, that's enough!" cried Foley.

"Yes, yes, but listen now, listen can't you?" cried Delancey. "He was there ten minutes with a bit of candle when the door at the foot of the stairs began to open. "Who's there?" says he, getting a bit nervous. "Who's there I say?" No answer, and still the door kept opening. Then he gave a laugh. What was it only an old cat? "Puss, puss," says he, "come on up, puss." Thinking, you know, the old cat would be company. Then he gave another look and the hair stood up on his head. There was another bloody cat coming in. "Get out!" says he to scare them, and then another cat came in and then another, and in his fright he dropped the candle. The cats began to hiss and bawl and that robbed him of the last stitch of sense. He made down the stairs, and if he did he trod on a cat, and went down head over heels, and when he tried to grip something 'twas a cat he gripped, and he felt the claws tearing his face. He was out for three weeks after."

"That's a bloody fine adventure," said Foley with bitter restraint.

"Isn't it though?" Delancey said eagerly. "You'd be a long time in Farranchreesht before anything like that would happen you."

"That's the thing about Farranchreesht, lad," said Magner. " 'Tis a great ease to be able to put on your cap and go for a drink any hour of the day or night."

"Yes," added Foley, "and to know the worst case you're likely to have in ten years is a bit of a scrap about politics."

"I don't know," Delancey sighed dreamily. "Chrisht, there's great charm about the Criminal Courts."

"Damn the much they had for you when you were in the box," growled Foley.

"I know, sure, I know," admitted Delancey crestfallen. "I was sweating."

"Shutting your eyes you were," said Magner, "like a kid afraid he was going to get a box on the ear."

"Still," said Delancey, "this sergeant I'm talking about, he said after a while you wouldn't mind that no more than if 'twas a card party. He said you'd talk back to the judge as man to man."

"I dare say that's true," agreed Magner.

There was silence in the smoky compartment that jolted and

rocked on its way across Ireland, and the four occupants, each touched with that morning wit which afflicts no one so much as state witnesses, thought of how they'd speak to the judge now if only they had him before them as man to man. They looked up to see a fat red face behind the door, and a moment later it was dragged back.

"Is this my carriage, gentlemen?" asked a meek and boozy voice.

"No, 'tisn't. Go on with you!" snapped Magner.

"I had as nice a carriage as ever was put on a railway train," said the drunk, leaning in, "a handsome carriage, and 'tis lost."

"Try farther on," suggested Delancey.

"Ye'll excuse me interrupting yeer conversation, gentlemen."

"That's all right, that's all right."

"I'm very melancholic. My best friend, I parted him this very night, and 'tis unknown to anyone, only the Almighty and Merciful God (here the drunk reverently raised his bowler hat and let it slide down the back of his neck to the floor) if I'll ever lay eyes on him again in this world. Good night, gentlemen, and thanks, thanks for all yeer kindness."

As the drunk slithered away up the corridor Delancey laughed. Fox, who had remained thoughtful, resumed the conversation where it had left off.

"Delancey wasn't the only one that was sweating," he said.

"He was not," agreed Foley. "Even the sergeant was a bit shook."

"He was very shook. When he caught up the poison mug to identify it he was shaking, and before he could put it down it danced a jig on the table."

"Ah, dear God, dear God," sighed Delancey, "what killed me most entirely was the bloody old model of the house. I didn't mind anything else only the house. There it was, a living likeness, with the bit of grass in front and the shutter hanging loose, and every time I looked at it I was in the back lane in Farranchreesht, and then I'd look up and see the lean fellow in the wig pointing his finger at me."

"Well, thank God," said Foley with simple devotion, "this

time tomorrow I'll be in Ned Ivers's back with a pint in my fist."

Delancey shook his head, a dreamy smile playing upon his dark face.

"I don't know," he said. "'Tis a small place, Farranchreesht; a small, mangy old place with no interest or advancement in it." His face lit up as the sergeant appeared in the corridor.

"Here's the sergeant now," he said.

"He wasn't long getting tired of Julietta," whispered Magner maliciously.

The door was pushed back and the sergeant entered, loosening the collar of his tunic. He fell into a corner seat, crossed his legs, and accepted the cigarette which Delancey proffered.

"Well, lads," he exclaimed. "What about a jorum?"

"Isn't it remarkable?" said Foley. "I was only just talking about it."

"I have noted before now, Peter," said the sergeant, "that you and me have what might be called a simultaneous thirst."

III

The country folk were silent and exhausted. Kendillon drowsed now and then, but he suffered from blood-pressure, and after a while his breathing grew thicker and stronger till at last it exploded in a snort and he started up, broad awake and angry. In the silence rain spluttered and tapped along the roof and the dark windowpanes streamed with shining runnels of water that trickled to the floor. Moll Mhor scowled, her lower lip thrust out. She was a great flop of a woman with a big, coarse, powerful face. The other two women whose eyes were closed had their brown shawls drawn tight about their heads, but Moll's was round her shoulders and the gap above her breasts was filled with a blaze of scarlet.

"Aren't we home yet?" Kendillon asked crossly, starting awake after one of his drowsing fits.

Moll glowered at him.

"No, nor won't be. What scour is on you?"

"My little house," moaned Kendillon.

"My little house," mimicked Moll. "'Twasn't enough for you to board the windows and put barbed wire on the gate."

" 'Tis all very well for you that have someone to mind yours for you," he snarled.

One of the women laughed softly and turned a haggard virginal face within the cowl of her shawl.

" 'Tis that have me laughing," she explained apologetically. "Tim Dwyer this week past at the stirabout pot."

"And making the beds," chimed in the third woman.

"And washing the children's faces! Glory be to God, he'll be mad."

"Ay," said Moll, "and his chickens running off with Thade Kendillon's roof."

"My roof is it?" he asked.

"Yes."

" 'Tis a good roof," he said roughly. " 'Tis a better roof than ever was seen over your head since the day you married."

"Oh, Mary my mother!" sighed Moll, " 'tis a great pity of me this three hours and I looking at the likes of you instead of my own fine bouncing man."

" 'Tis a new thing to hear you praising Sean then," said a woman.

"I wronged him," Moll said contritely. "I did so. I wronged him before God and the world."

At this moment the drunken man pulled back the door of the compartment and looked from face to face with an expression of deepening melancholy.

"She's not here," he said in disappointment.

"Who's not here, mister?" asked Moll with a wink at the others.

"I'm looking for my own carriage, ma'am," said the drunk with melancholy dignity, "and whatever the bloody hell they done with it, 'tis lost. The railways in this country are gone to hell."

"Wisha, if that's all that's worrying you, wouldn't you sit here with me?" asked Moll. "I'm here so long I'm forgetting what a real man looks like."

"I would with great pleasure," replied the drunk politely, "but 'tisn't only the carriage. 'Tis my travelling-companion. I'm a lonely man; I parted my best friend this very night; I found one to console me, and then when I turned my back—God took her!"

And with a dramatic gesture he closed the door and continued on his way. The country folk sat up, blinking. The smoke of the men's pipes filled the compartment and the heavy air was laden with the smell of homespun and turf-smoke, the sweet pungent odour of which had penetrated every fibre of their clothes.

"Listen to the rain!" said one of the women. "We'll have a wet walk home."

" 'Twill be midnight before we're in," said another.

"Ah, what matter sure when the whole country will be up? There'll be a lot of talking done in Farranchreesht tonight."

"A lot of talking and no sleep."

"Oh, Farranchreesht! Farranchreesht!" cried the young woman with the haggard face, the ravaged lineaments of which were suddenly transfigured. "Farranchreesht and the sky over you, I wouldn't change places with the Queen of England tonight!"

And suddenly Farranchreesht, the bare bogland with the hump-backed mountain behind, the little white houses and the dark fortifications of turf that made it seem like the flame-blackened ruin of some mighty city, all was lit up in their minds. An old man sitting in a corner, smoking a broken clay pipe, thumped his stick on the floor.

"Well now," said Kendillon darkly, "wasn't it great impudence in her to come back?"

"Wasn't it indeed?" echoed one of the women.

"I'd say she won't be there long," he went on knowingly.

"You'll give her the hunt, I suppose?" asked Moll politely, too politely.

"If no one else do, I'll give her the hunt myself. What right have she in a decent place?"

"Oh, the hunt, the hunt," agreed a woman. "Sure, no one could ever darken her door again."

"And what the hell did we tell all the lies for?" asked Moll with her teeth on edge to be at Kendillon. "Thade Kendillon there swore black was white."

"What else would I do, woman? There was never an informer in my family."

"I'm surprised to hear it," said Moll vindictively, but the old man thumped his stick three or four times for silence.

"We all told our story," he said, "and we told it well. And no one told it better than Moll. You'd think to hear her she believed it herself."

"I declare to God I very nearly did," she said with a wild laugh.

"I seen great changes in my time, great changes," the old man said, shaking his head, "and now I see a greater change still."

A silence followed his words. There was profound respect in all their eyes. The old man coughed and spat.

"What change is that, Colm?" asked Moll.

"Did any of ye ever think the day would come when a woman in our parish would do the like of that?"

"Never, never."

"But she might do it for land?"

"She might."

"Or for money?"

"She might so."

"She might indeed. When the hunger is money people kill for the money; when the hunger is land people kill for the land. But what are they killing for now? I tell ye, there's a great change coming. In the ease of the world people are asking more. When I was a boy in the barony if you killed a beast you made six pieces of it, one for yourself and the rest for the neighbours. The same if you made a catch of fish. And that's how it was with us from the beginning of time. But now look at the change! The people aren't as poor or as good or as generous or as strong."

"Or as wild," added Moll with a vicious glance at Kendillon. " 'Tis in the men you'd mostly notice the change."

The door opened and Magner, Delancey and the sergeant entered. Magner was already drunk.

"I was lonely without you, Moll," he said. "You're the biggest and brazenest and cleverest liar of the lot and you lost me my sergeant's stripes, but I'll forgive you everything if you'll give us one bar of the 'Colleen Dhas Roo.' "

IV

"I'm a lonely man," said the drunk. "And I'm going back to a lonely habitation.

"My best friend," he continued, "I left behind me—Michael O'Leary, the most sincere man I know. 'Tis a great pity you don't know Michael and a great pity Michael don't know you. But look at the misfortunate way things happen! I was looking for someone to console me, and the moment I turned my back you were gone."

He placed his hand solemnly under the woman's chin and raised her face to the light. With the other hand he stroked her cheeks.

"You have a beautiful face," he said reverently, "a beautiful face. But what's more important, you have a beautiful soul. I look into your eyes and I see the beauty of your nature. Allow me one favour. Only one favour before we part."

He bent and kissed her. Then he picked up his bowler which had fallen once more, put it on back to front, took his dispatch case and got out.

The woman sat on alone. Her shawl was thrown open and beneath it she wore a bright blue blouse. The carriage was cold, the night outside black and cheerless, and within her something had begun to contract that threatened to crush the very spark of life in her. She could no longer fight it off even when for the hundredth time she went over the scenes of the previous day; the endless hours in the dock, the wearisome questions and speeches she could not understand, and the long wait in the cells till the jury returned. She felt again the shiver of mortal anguish that went through her when the chief warder beckoned angrily from the stairs and the wardress, glancing hastily in a hand-mirror, pushed her forward. She saw the jury with their expressionless faces. She was standing there alone, in nervous twitches jerking back the shawl from her face to give herself air. She was trying to say a prayer but the words were being drowned in her mind by the thunder of nerves, crashing and bursting. She could feel one which had escaped dancing madly at the side of her mouth, but was powerless to recapture it.

"The verdict of the jury is that Helena Maguire is not guilty."
Which was it? Death or life? She could not say. "Silence!
Silence!" shouted the usher though no one had tried to say anything. "Any other charge?" asked a weary voice. "Release the
prisoner." "Silence!" shouted the usher again. The chief warder
opened the door of the dock and she began to run. When she
reached the steps she stopped and looked back to see if she was
being followed. A policeman held open a door and she found
herself in an ill-lit, draughty stone corridor. She stood there, the
old shawl about her face. The crowd began to emerge. The first
was a tall girl with a rapt expression as though she were walking
on air. When she saw the woman she halted, her hands went
up in an instinctive gesture, as though to feel her, to caress her.
It was that look of hers, that gait as of a sleepwalker that brought
the woman to her senses. . . .

But now the memory had no warmth in her mind, and the
something within her continued to contract, smothering her with
loneliness, shame, and fear. She began to mutter crazily to herself. The train, now almost empty, was stopping at every little
wayside station. Now and again a blast from the Atlantic pushed
at it as though trying to capsize it.

She looked up as the door slammed open and Moll came in,
swinging her shawl behind her.

"They're all up the train. Wouldn't you come?"

"No, no, I couldn't."

"Why couldn't you? Who are you minding? Is it Thade
Kendillon?"

"No, no, I'll stop as I am."

"Here, take a sup of this." Moll fumbled in her shawl and
produced a bottle of liquor as pale as water. "Wait till I tell you
what Magner said! That fellow is a limb of the devil. 'Have you
e'er a drop, Moll?' says he. 'Maybe I have,' says I. 'What is
it?' says he. 'For God's sake, baptize it quick and call it whisky.' "

The woman took the bottle and put it to her lips. She shivered
as she drank.

" 'Tis a good drop," said Moll approvingly.

Next moment there were loud voices in the corridor. Moll
grabbed the bottle and hid it under her shawl. But it was only

Magner, the sergeant, and Delancey. After them came the two countrywomen, giggling. Magner held out his hand.

"Helena," he said, "accept my congratulations."

She took his hand, smiling awkwardly.

"We'll get you the next time though," he added.

"Musha, what are you saying, mister?"

"Not a word. You're a clever woman, a remarkable woman, and I give you full credit for it. You threw dust in all our eyes."

"Poison is supposed to be an easy thing to trace but it beat me to trace it," said the sergeant, barely concealing his curiosity.

"Well, well, there's things they're saying about me!" she said with a nervous laugh.

"Tell him," advised Magner. "There's nothing he can do to you now. You're as safe as the judge himself. Last night when the jury came in with the verdict you could have stood there in the dock and said: 'Ye're wrong. I did it. I got the stuff in such and such a place. I gave it to him because he was old and dirty and cantankerous and a miser. I did it and I'm proud of it.' You could have said every word of that and they couldn't have laid a finger on you."

"Indeed, what a thing I'd say!"

"Well, you could."

"The law is truly a remarkable phenomenon," said the sergeant, who was also rather squiffy. "Here you are, sitting at your ease at the expense of the state, and for one simple word of a couple of letters you could be up in Mountjoy, waiting for the rope and the morning jaunt."

The woman shuddered. The young woman with the ravaged face looked up.

" 'Twas the holy will of God," she said.

" 'Twas all the bloody lies Moll Mhor told," replied Magner.

" 'Twas the will of God."

"There was many hanged in the wrong," said the sergeant.

"Even so, even so, 'twas God's will."

"You have a new blouse, Helena," said the other woman in an envious tone.

"I seen it last night in a shop on the quays."

"How much was it?"

"Honour of God!" exclaimed Magner, looking at the woman in stupefaction. "Is that all you had to think of? You should have been on your bended knees before the altar."

"And sure I was," she answered indignantly.

"Women!" exclaimed Magner with a gesture of despair. He winked at Moll and they retired to the next compartment. But the interior was reflected clearly in the corridor window, and the others could see the pale quivering image of the policeman lift the bottle to his lips and blow a long silent blast on it. The young woman who had spoken of the blouse laughed.

"There'll be one good day's work done on the head of the trial," she said.

"How so?" asked the sergeant.

"Dan Canty will make a great brew of poteen while he have all yeer backs turned."

"I'll get Dan Canty yet," replied the sergeant stiffly.

"You will, the way you got Helena."

"I'll get him yet," he said as he consulted his watch. "We'll be in in another quarter of an hour. 'Tis time we were all getting back to our respective compartments."

Magner entered and the other policemen rose. The sergeant fastened his collar and buckled his belt. Magner swayed, holding the doorframe, a mawkish smile on his thin, handsome, dissipated face.

"Well, good night to you now, ma'am," said the sergeant primly. "I'm as glad for all our sakes things ended as they did."

"Good night, Helena," said Magner, bowing low and promptly tottering. "There'll be one happy man in Farranchreesht tonight."

"Come on, Joe," protested the sergeant.

"One happy man," Magner repeated obstinately. " 'Tis his turn now."

"You're drunk, man," said Delancey.

"You wanted him," Magner said heavily. "Your people wouldn't let you have him but you have him now in spite of them all."

"Do you mean Cady Driscoll?" hissed the woman with sudden anger, leaning towards Magner, the shawl tight about her head.

"Never mind who I mean. You have him."

"He's no more to me now than the salt sea."

The policemen went out first, the women followed, Moll Mhor laughing boisterously. The woman was left alone. Through the window she could see little cottages stepping down over wet and naked rocks to the water's edge. The flame of life had narrowed in her to a pinpoint, and she could only wonder at the force that had caught her up, mastered her and then thrown her aside.

"No more to me," she repeated dully to her own image in the glass, "no more to me than the salt sea."

THE MAJESTY OF THE LAW

OLD Dan Bride was breaking brosna for the fire when he heard a step on the path. He paused, a bundle of saplings on his knee.

Dan had looked after his mother while the life was in her, and after her death no other woman had crossed his threshold. Signs on it, his house had that look. Almost everything in it he had made with his own hands in his own way. The seats of the chairs were only slices of log, rough and round and thick as the saw had left them, and with the rings still plainly visible through the grime and polish that coarse trouser-bottoms had in the course of long years imparted. Into these Dan had rammed stout knotted ash-boughs that served alike for legs and back. The deal table, bought in a shop, was an inheritance from his mother and a great pride and joy to him though it rocked whenever he touched it. On the wall, unglazed and fly-spotted, hung in mysterious isolation a Marcus Stone print, and beside the door was a calendar with a picture of a racehorse. Over the door hung a gun, old but good, and in excellent condition; and before the fire was stretched an old setter who raised his head expectantly whenever Dan rose or even stirred.

He raised it now as the steps came nearer and when Dan, laying down the bundle of saplings, cleaned his hands thoughtfully in the seat of his trousers, he gave a loud bark, but this expressed no more than a desire to show off his own watchfulness. He was half human and knew people thought he was old and past his prime.

A man's shadow fell across the oblong of dusty light thrown over the half-door before Dan looked round.

"Are you alone, Dan?" asked an apologetic voice.

"Oh, come in, come in, sergeant, come in and welcome," exclaimed the old man, hurrying on rather uncertain feet to the door which the tall policeman opened and pushed in. He stood there, half in sunlight, half in shadow, and seeing him so, you would have realized how dark the interior of the house really was. One side of his red face was turned so as to catch the light, and behind it an ash tree raised its boughs of airy green against the sky. Green fields, broken here and there by clumps of red-brown rock, flowed downhill, and beyond them, stretched all across the horizon, was the sea, flooded and almost transparent with light. The sergeant's face was fat and fresh, the old man's face, emerging from the twilight of the kitchen, had the colour of wind and sun, while the features had been so shaped by the struggle with time and the elements that they might as easily have been found impressed upon the surface of a rock.

"Begor, Dan," said the sergeant, " 'tis younger you're getting."

"Middling I am, sergeant, middling," agreed the old man in a voice which seemed to accept the remark as a compliment of which politeness would not allow him to take too much advantage. "No complaints."

"Begor, 'tis as well because no one would believe them. And the old dog doesn't look a day older."

The dog gave a low growl as though to show the sergeant that he would remember this unmannerly reference to his age, but indeed he growled every time he was mentioned, under the impression that people had nothing but ill to say of him.

"And how's yourself, sergeant?"

"Well, now, like the most of us, Dan, neither too good nor too bad. We have our own little worries, but, thanks be to God, we have our compensations."

"And the wife and family?"

"Good, praise be to God, good. They were away from me for a month, the lot of them, at the mother-in-law's place in Clare."

"In Clare, do you tell me?"

"In Clare. I had a fine quiet time."

The old man looked about him and then retired to the bedroom, from which he returned a moment later with an old shirt. With this he solemnly wiped the seat and back of the log-chair nearest the fire.

"Sit down now, sergeant. You must be tired after the journey. 'Tis a long old road. How did you come?"

"Teigue Leary gave me the lift. Wisha now, Dan, don't be putting yourself out. I won't be stopping. I promised them I'd be back inside an hour."

"What hurry is on you?" asked Dan. "Look, your foot was only on the path when I made up the fire."

"Arrah, Dan, you're not making tea for me?"

"I am not making it for you, indeed; I'm making it for myself, and I'll take it very bad of you if you won't have a cup."

"Dan, Dan, that I mightn't stir, but 'tisn't an hour since I had it at the barracks!"

"Ah, whisht, now, whisht! Whisht, will you! I have something here to give you an appetite."

The old man swung the heavy kettle onto the chain over the open fire, and the dog sat up, shaking his ears with an expression of the deepest interest. The policeman unbuttoned his tunic, opened his belt, took a pipe and a plug of tobacco from his breast pocket, and crossing his legs in an easy posture, began to cut the tobacco slowly and carefully with his pocket knife. The old man went to the dresser and took down two handsomely decorated cups, the only cups he had, which, though chipped and handleless, were used at all only on very rare occasions; for himself he preferred his tea from a basin. Happening to glance into them, he noticed that they bore signs of disuse and had collected a lot of the fine white turf-dust that always circulated in the little smoky cottage. Again he thought of the shirt, and, rolling up his sleeves with a stately gesture, he wiped them inside and out till they shone. Then he bent and opened the cupboard. Inside was a quart bottle of pale liquid, obviously untouched. He removed the cork and smelt the contents, pausing for a moment in the act as though to recollect where exactly he had noticed that particular smoky smell before. Then, reassured, he stood up and poured out with a liberal hand.

"Try that now, sergeant," he said with quiet pride.

The sergeant, concealing whatever qualms he might have felt at the idea of drinking illegal whisky, looked carefully into the cup, sniffed, and glanced up at old Dan.

"It looks good," he commented.

"It should be good," replied Dan with no mock modesty.

"It tastes good too," said the sergeant.

"Ah, sha," said Dan, not wishing to praise his own hospitality in his own house, " 'tis of no great excellence."

"You'd be a good judge, I'd say," said the sergeant without irony.

"Ever since things became what they are," said Dan, carefully guarding himself against a too-direct reference to the peculiarities of the law administered by his guest, "liquor isn't what it used to be."

"I've heard that remark made before now, Dan," said the sergeant thoughtfully. "I've heard it said by men of wide experience that it used to be better in the old days."

"Liquor," said the old man, "is a thing that takes time. There was never a good job done in a hurry."

" 'Tis an art in itself."

"Just so."

"And an art takes time."

"And knowledge," added Dan with emphasis. "Every art has its secrets, and the secrets of distilling are being lost the way the old songs were lost. When I was a boy there wasn't a man in the barony but had a hundred songs in his head, but with people running here, there and everywhere, the songs were lost. . . . Ever since things became what they are," he repeated on the same guarded note, "there's so much running about the secrets are lost."

"There must have been a power of them."

"There was. Ask any man today that makes whisky do he know how to make it out of heather."

"And was it made of heather?" asked the policeman.

"It was."

"You never drank it yourself?"

"I didn't, but I knew old men that did, and they told me that no whisky that's made nowadays could compare with it."

"Musha, Dan, I think sometimes 'twas a great mistake of the law to set its hand against it."

Dan shook his head. His eyes answered for him, but it was not in nature for a man to criticize the occupation of a guest in his own home.

"Maybe so, maybe not," he said noncommittally.

"But sure, what else have the poor people?"

"Them that makes the laws have their own good reasons."

"All the same, Dan, all the same, 'tis a hard law."

The sergeant would not be outdone in generosity. Politeness required him not to yield to the old man's defence of his superiors and their mysterious ways.

"It is the secrets I'd be sorry for," said Dan, summing up. "Men die and men are born, and where one man drained another will plough, but a secret lost is lost forever."

"True," said the sergeant mournfully. "Lost forever."

Dan took his cup, rinsed it in a bucket of clear water by the door and cleaned it again with the shirt. Then he placed it carefully at the sergeant's elbow. From the dresser he took a jug of milk and a blue bag containing sugar; this he followed up with a slab of country butter and—a sure sign that he had been expecting a visitor—a round cake of homemade bread, fresh and uncut. The kettle sang and spat and the dog, shaking his ears, barked at it angrily.

"Go away, you brute!" growled Dan, kicking him out of his way.

He made the tea and filled the two cups. The sergeant cut himself a large slice of bread and buttered it thickly.

"It is just like medicines," said the old man, resuming his theme with the imperturbability of age. "Every secret there was is lost. And leave no one tell me that a doctor is as good a man as one that had the secrets of old times."

"How could he be?" asked the sergeant with his mouth full.

"The proof of that was seen when there were doctors and wise people there together."

"It wasn't to the doctors the people went, I'll engage?"

"It was not. And why?" With a sweeping gesture the old man took in the whole world outside his cabin. "Out there on the hillsides is the sure cure for every disease. Because it is written"—he tapped the table with his thumb—"it is written by the poets 'wherever you find the disease you will find the cure.' But people walk up the hills and down the hills and all they see is flowers. Flowers! As if God Almighty—honour and praise to Him!—had nothing better to do with His time than be making old flowers!"

"Things no doctor could cure the wise people cured," agreed the sergeant.

"Ah, musha, 'tis I know it," said Dan bitterly. "I know it, not in my mind but in my own four bones."

"Have you the rheumatics at you still?" the sergeant asked in a shocked tone.

"I have. Ah, if you were alive, Kitty O'Hara, or you, Nora Malley of the Glen, 'tisn't I'd be dreading the mountain wind or the sea wind; 'tisn't I'd be creeping down with my misfortunate red ticket for the blue and pink and yellow dribble-drabble of their ignorant dispensary."

"Why then indeed," said the sergeant, "I'll get you a bottle for that."

"Ah, there's no bottle ever made will cure it."

"That's where you're wrong, Dan. Don't talk now till you try it. It cured my own uncle when he was that bad he was shouting for the carpenter to cut the two legs off him with a handsaw."

"I'd give fifty pounds to get rid of it," said Dan magniloquently. "I would and five hundred."

The sergeant finished his tea in a gulp, blessed himself and struck a match which he then allowed to go out as he answered some question of the old man. He did the same with a second and third, as though titillating his appetite with delay. Finally he succeeded in getting his pipe alight and the two men pulled round their chairs, placed their toes side by side in the ashes, and in deep puffs, lively bursts of conversation, and long, long silences, enjoyed their smoke.

"I hope I'm not keeping you?" said the sergeant, as though struck by the length of his visit.

"Ah, what would you keep me from?"

"Tell me if I am. The last thing I'd like to do is waste another man's time."

"Begor, you wouldn't waste my time if you stopped all night."

"I like a little chat myself," confessed the policeman.

And again they became lost in conversation. The light grew thick and coloured and, wheeling about the kitchen before it disappeared, became tinged with gold; the kitchen itself sank into cool greyness with cold light on the cups and basins and plates of the dresser. From the ash tree a thrush began to sing. The open hearth gathered brightness till its light was a warm, even splash of crimson in the twilight.

Twilight was also descending outside when the sergeant rose to go. He fastened his belt and tunic and carefully brushed his clothes. Then he put on his cap, tilted a little to side and back.

"Well, that was a great talk," he said.

" 'Tis a pleasure," said Dan, "a real pleasure."

"And I won't forget the bottle for you."

"Heavy handling from God to you!"

"Good-bye now, Dan."

"Good-bye, sergeant, and good luck."

Dan didn't offer to accompany the sergeant beyond the door. He sat in his old place by the fire, took out his pipe once more, blew through it thoughtfully, and just as he leaned forward for a twig to kindle it, heard the steps returning. It was the sergeant. He put his head a little way over the half-door.

"Oh, Dan!" he called softly.

"Ay, sergeant?" replied Dan, looking round, but with one hand still reaching for the twig. He couldn't see the sergeant's face, only hear his voice.

"I suppose you're not thinking of paying that little fine, Dan?"

There was a brief silence. Dan pulled out the lighted twig, rose slowly and shambled towards the door, stuffing it down in the almost empty bowl of the pipe. He leaned over the half door while the sergeant with hands in the pockets of his trousers gazed rather in the direction of the laneway, yet taking in a considerable portion of the sea line.

"The way it is with me, sergeant," replied Dan unemotionally, "I am not."

"I was thinking that, Dan; I was thinking you wouldn't."

There was a long silence during which the voice of the thrush grew shriller and merrier. The sunken sun lit up rafts of purple cloud moored high above the wind.

"In a way," said the sergeant, "that was what brought me."

"I was just thinking so, sergeant, it only struck me and you going out the door."

"If 'twas only the money, Dan, I'm sure there's many would be glad to oblige you."

"I know that, sergeant. No, 'tisn't the money so much as giving that fellow the satisfaction of paying. Because he angered me, sergeant."

The sergeant made no comment on this and another long silence ensued.

"They gave me the warrant," the sergeant said at last, in a tone which dissociated him from all connection with such an unneighbourly document.

"Did they so?" exclaimed Dan, as if he was shocked by the thoughtlessness of the authorities.

"So whenever 'twould be convenient for you—"

"Well, now you mention it," said Dan, by way of throwing out a suggestion for debate, "I could go with you now."

"Ah, sha, what do you want going at this hour for?" protested the sergeant with a wave of his hand, dismissing the notion as the tone required.

"Or I could go tomorrow," added Dan, warming to the issue.

"Would it be suitable for you now?" asked the sergeant, scaling up his voice accordingly.

"But, as a matter of fact," said the old man emphatically, "the day that would be most convenient to me would be Friday after dinner, because I have some messages to do in town, and I wouldn't have the journey for nothing."

"Friday will do grand," said the sergeant with relief that this delicate matter was now practically disposed of. "If it doesn't they can damn well wait. You could walk in there yourself when it suits you and tell them I sent you."

"I'd rather have yourself there, sergeant, if it would be no inconvenience. As it is, I'd feel a bit shy."

"Why then, you needn't feel shy at all. There's a man from my own parish there, a warder; one Whelan. Ask for him; I'll tell him you're coming, and I'll guarantee when he knows you're a friend of mine he'll make you as comfortable as if you were at home."

"I'd like that fine," Dan said with profound satisfaction. "I'd like to be with friends, sergeant."

"You will be, never fear. Good-bye again now, Dan. I'll have to hurry."

"Wait now, wait till I see you to the road."

Together the two men strolled down the laneway while Dan explained how it was that he, a respectable old man, had had the grave misfortune to open the head of another old man in such a way as to require his removal to hospital, and why it was that he couldn't give the old man in question the satisfaction of paying in cash for an injury brought about through the victim's own unmannerly method of argument.

"You see, sergeant," Dan said, looking at another little cottage up the hill, "the way it is, he's there now, and he's looking at us as sure as there's a glimmer of sight in his weak, wandering, watery eyes, and nothing would give him more gratification than for me to pay. But I'll punish him. I'll lie on bare boards for him. I'll suffer for him, sergeant, so that neither he nor any of his children after him will be able to raise their heads for the shame of it."

On the following Friday he made ready his donkey and butt and set out. On his way he collected a number of neighbours who wished to bid him farewell. At the top of the hill he stopped to send them back. An old man, sitting in the sunlight, hastily made his way indoors, and a moment later the door of his cottage was quietly closed.

Having shaken all his friends by the hand, Dan lashed the old donkey, shouted: "Hup there!" and set out alone along the road to prison.

SONG WITHOUT WORDS

EVEN if there were only two men left in the world and both of them saints they wouldn't be happy. One of them would be bound to try and improve the other. That is the nature of things.

I am not, of course, suggesting that either Brother Arnold or Brother Michael was a saint. In private life Brother Arnold was a postman, but as he had a great name as a cattle doctor they had put him in charge of the monastery cows. He had the sort of face you would expect to see advertising somebody's tobacco; a big, innocent, contented face with a pair of blue eyes that were always twinkling. According to the rule he was supposed to look sedate and go about in a composed and measured way, but he could not keep his eyes downcast for any length of time and wherever his eyes glanced they twinkled, and his hands slipped out of his long white sleeves and dropped some remark in sign language. Most of the monks were good at the deaf and dumb language; it was their way of getting round the rule of silence, and it was remarkable how much information they managed to pick up and pass on.

Now, one day it happened that Brother Arnold was looking for a bottle of castor oil and he remembered that he had lent it to Brother Michael, who was in charge of the stables. Brother

Michael was a man he did not get on too well with; a dour, dull sort of man who kept to himself. He was a man of no great appearance, with a mournful wizened little face and a pair of weak red-rimmed eyes—for all the world the sort of man who, if you shaved off his beard, clapped a bowler hat on his head and a cigarette in his mouth, would need no other reference to get a job in a stable.

There was no sign of him about the stable yard, but this was only natural because he would not be wanted till the other monks returned from the fields, so Brother Arnold pushed in the stable door to look for the bottle himself. He did not see the bottle, but he saw something which made him wish he had not come. Brother Michael was hiding in one of the horse-boxes; standing against the partition with something hidden behind his back and wearing the look of a little boy who has been caught at the jam. Something told Brother Arnold that at that moment he was the most unwelcome man in the world. He grew red, waved his hand to indicate that he did not wish to be involved, and returned to his own quarters.

It came as a shock to him. It was plain enough that Brother Michael was up to some shady business, and Brother Arnold could not help wondering what it was. It was funny, he had noticed the same thing when he was in the world; it was always the quiet, sneaky fellows who were up to mischief. In chapel he looked at Brother Michael and got the impression that Brother Michael was looking at him, a furtive look to make sure he would not be noticed. Next day when they met in the yard he caught Brother Michael glancing at him and gave back a cold look and a nod.

The following day Brother Michael beckoned him to come over to the stables as though one of the horses was sick. Brother Arnold knew it wasn't that; he knew he was about to be given some sort of explanation and was curious to know what it would be. He was an inquisitive man; he knew it, and blamed himself a lot for it.

Brother Michael closed the door carefully after him and then leaned back against the jamb of the door with his legs crossed and his hands behind his back, a foxy pose. Then he nodded in the direction of the horse-box where Brother Arnold had almost caught him in the act, and raised his brows inquiringly. Brother Arnold nodded gravely. It was not an occasion he was likely to forget. Then Brother Michael put his hand up his sleeve and held out a folded newspaper. Brother Arnold shrugged his shoulders as though to say the matter had nothing to do with him, but the other man nodded and continued to press the newspaper on him.

He opened it without any great curiosity, thinking it might be some local paper Brother Michael smuggled in for the sake of the news from home and was now offering as the explanation of his own furtive behaviour. He glanced at the name and then a great light broke on him. His whole face lit up as though an electric torch had been switched on behind, and finally he burst out laughing. He couldn't help himself. Brother Michael did not laugh but gave a dry little cackle which was as near as he ever got to laughing. The name of the paper was *The Irish Racing News*.

Now that the worst was over Brother Michael grew more relaxed. He pointed to a heading about the Curragh and then at himself. Brother Arnold shook his head, glancing at him expectantly as though he were hoping for another laugh. Brother Michael scratched his head for some indication of what he meant. He was a slow-witted man and had never been good at the sign talk. Then he picked up the sweeping brush and straddled it. He pulled up his skirts, stretched out his left hand holding the handle of the brush, and with his right began flogging the air behind him, a grim look on his leathery little face. Inquiringly he looked again and Brother Arnold nodded excitedly and put his thumbs up to show he understood. He saw now that the real reason Brother Michael had behaved so queerly was that he read racing papers on the sly and he did so because in private life he had been a jockey on the Curragh.

He was still laughing like mad, his blue eyes dancing, wishing only for an audience to tell it to, and then he suddenly remembered all the things he had thought about Brother Michael and bowed his head and beat his breast by way of asking pardon. Then he glanced at the paper again. A mischievous twinkle came into his eyes and he pointed the paper at himself. Brother Michael pointed back, a bit puzzled. Brother Arnold chuckled and stowed the paper up his sleeve. Then Brother Michael winked and gave the thumbs-up sign. In that slow cautious way of his he went down the stable and reached to the top of the wall where the roof sloped down on it. This, it seemed, was his hiding-hole. He took down several more papers and gave them to Brother Arnold.

For the rest of the day Brother Arnold was in the highest spirits. He winked and smiled at everyone till they all wondered what the joke was. He still pined for an audience. All that evening and long after he had retired to his cubicle he rubbed his hands and giggled with delight whenever he thought of it; it was like a window let into his loneliness; it gave him a warm, mellow feeling, as though his heart had expanded to embrace all humanity.

It was not until the following day that he had a chance of looking at the papers himself. He spread them on a rough desk under a feeble electric-light bulb high in the roof. It was four years since he had seen a paper of any sort, and then it was only a scrap of local newspaper which one of the carters had brought wrapped about a bit of bread and butter. But Brother Arnold had palmed it, hidden it in his desk, and studied it as if it were a bit of a lost Greek play. He had never known until then the modern appetite for words—printed words, regardless of their meaning. This was merely a County Council wrangle about the appointment of seven warble-fly inspectors, but by the time he was done with it he knew it by heart.

So he did not just glance at the racing papers as a man would in the train to pass the time. He nearly ate them. Blessed words like fragments of tunes coming to him out of a past life; paddocks and point-to-points and two-year-olds, and again he was in the middle of a racecourse crowd on a spring day with silver streamers of light floating down the sky like heavenly bunting. He had only to close his eyes and he could see the refreshment tent again with the golden light leaking like spilt honey through the rents in the canvas, and the girl he had been in love with sitting on an upturned lemonade box. "Ah, Paddy," she had said, "sure there's bound to be racing in heaven!" She was fast, too fast for Brother Arnold, who was a steady-going fellow and had never got over the shock of discovering that all the time she had been running another man. But now all he could remember of her was her smile and the tone of her voice as she spoke the words which kept running through his head, and afterwards whenever his eyes met Brother Michael's he longed to give him a hearty slap on the back and say: "Michael, boy, there's bound to be racing in heaven." Then he grinned and Brother Michael, though he didn't hear the words or the tone of voice, without once losing his casual melancholy air, replied with a wall-faced flicker of the horny eyelid, a tick-tack man's signal, a real, expressionless, horsy look of complete understanding.

One day Brother Michael brought in a few papers. On one he pointed to the horses he had marked, on the other to the horses who had won. He showed no signs of his jubilation. He just winked, a leathery sort of wink, and Brother Arnold gaped as he saw the list of winners. It filled him with wonder and pride to think that when so many rich and clever people had lost, a simple little monk living hundreds of miles away could work it all out. The more he thought of it the more excited he grew. For one wild moment he felt it might be his duty to tell the Abbot, so that the monastery could have the full advantage of Brother Michael's intellect, but he realized that it wouldn't do. Even if Brother Michael could restore the whole abbey from top to bottom with his winnings, the ecclesiastical authorities would disapprove of it. But more than ever he felt the need of an audience.

He went to the door, reached up his long arm, and took down a loose stone from the wall above it. Brother Michael shook his head several times to indicate how impressed he was by Brother Arnold's ingenuity. Brother Arnold grinned. Then he took down a bottle and handed it to Brother Michael. The ex-jockey gave him a questioning look as though he were wondering if this wasn't cattle-medicine; his face did not change but he took out the cork and sniffed. Still his face did not change. All at once he went to the door, gave a quick glance up and a quick glance down and then raised the bottle to his lips. He reddened and coughed; it was good beer and he wasn't used to it. A shudder as of delight went through him and his little eyes grew moist as he watched Brother Arnold's throttle working on well-oiled hinges.

The big man put the bottle back in its hiding-place and indicated by signs that Brother Michael could go there himself whenever he wanted a drink. Brother Michael shook his head doubtfully, but Brother Arnold nodded earnestly. His fingers moved like lightning while he explained how a farmer whose cow he had cured had it left in for him every week.

The two men were now fast friends. They no longer had any secrets from one another. Each knew the full extent of the other's little weakness and liked him the more for it. Though they couldn't speak to one another they sought out one another's company and whenever other things failed they merely smiled. Brother Arnold felt happier than he had felt for years. Brother Michael's successes made him want to try his hand, and whenever Brother Michael gave him a racing paper with his own selections marked, Brother Arnold gave it back with his, and they waited impatiently till the results turned up three or four days late. It was also a new lease of life to Brother Michael, for what comfort is it to a man if he has all the winners when not a soul in the world can ever know whether he has or not. He felt now that if only he could have a bob each way on a horse he would ask no more of life.

It was Brother Arnold, the more resourceful of the pair, who solved that difficulty. He made out dockets, each valued for so many Hail Marys, and the loser had to pay up in prayers for the other man's intention. It was an ingenious scheme and it worked admirably. At first Brother Arnold had a run of luck. But it wasn't for nothing that Brother Michael had had the experience; he was too tough to make a fool of himself even over a few Hail Marys, and everything he did was carefully planned. Brother Arnold began by imitating him, but the moment he struck it lucky he began to gamble wildly. Brother Michael had often seen it happen on the Curragh and remembered the fate of those it had happened to. Men he had known with big houses and cars were now cadging drinks in the streets of Dublin. It struck him that God had been very good to Brother Arnold in calling him to a monastic life where he could do no harm to himself or to his family.

And this, by the way, was quite uncalled for, because in the world Brother Arnold's only weakness had been for a bottle of stout and the only trouble he had ever caused his family was the discomfort of having to live with a man so good and gentle, but Brother Michael was rather given to a distrust of human nature, the sort of man who goes looking for a moral in everything even when there is no moral in it. He tried to make Brother Arnold take an interest in the scientific side of betting but the man seemed to treat it all as a great joke. A flighty sort of fellow! He bet more and more wildly with that foolish good-natured grin on his face, and after a while Brother Michael found himself being owed a deuce of a lot of prayers, which his literal mind insisted on translating into big houses and cars. He didn't like that either. It gave him scruples of conscience and finally turned him against betting altogether. He tried to get Brother Arnold to drop it, but as became an inventor, Brother Arnold only looked hurt and indignant, like a child who has been told to stop his play. Brother Michael had that weakness on his conscience too. It suggested that he was getting far too attached to Brother Arnold, as in fact he was. It would have been very difficult not to. There was something warm and friendly about the man which you couldn't help liking.

Then one day he went in to Brother Arnold and found him with a pack of cards in his hand. They were a very old pack which had more than served their time in some farmhouse, but Brother Arnold was looking at them in rapture. The very sight of them gave Brother Michael a turn. Brother Arnold made the gesture of dealing, half playfully, and the other shook his head sternly. Brother Arnold blushed and bit his lip but he persisted, seriously enough now. All the doubts Brother Michael had been having for weeks turned to conviction. This was the primrose path with a vengeance, one thing leading to another. Brother Arnold grinned and shuffled the deck; Brother Michael, biding his time, cut for deal and Brother Arnold won. He dealt two hands of five and showed the five of hearts as trump. He wanted to play twenty-five. Still waiting for a sign, Brother Michael looked at his own hand. His face grew grimmer. It was not the sort of sign he had expected but it was a sign all the same; four hearts in a bunch; the ace, jack, two other trumps, and the three of spades. An unbeatable hand. Was that luck? Was that coincidence or was it the Adversary himself, taking a hand and trying to draw him deeper in the mire.

He liked to find a moral in things, and the moral in this was plain, though it went to his heart to admit it. He was a lonesome, melancholy man and the horses had meant a lot to him in his bad spells. At times it had seemed as if they were the only thing that kept him sane. How could he face twenty, perhaps thirty, years more of life, never knowing what horses were running or what jockeys were up—Derby Day, Punchestown, Leopardstown, and the Curragh all going by while he knew no more of them than if he were already dead?

"O Lord," he thought bitterly, "a man gives up the whole world for You, his chance of a wife and kids, his home and his family, his friends and his job, and goes off to a bare mountain where he can't even tell his troubles to the man alongside him; and still he keeps something back, some little thing to remind him of what he gave up. With me 'twas the horses and with this man 'twas the sup of beer, and I dare say there are fellows inside who have a bit of a girl's hair hidden somewhere they can go and look at it now and again. I suppose we all have our little hiding-hole if the truth was known, but as small as it is, the whole world is in it, and bit by bit it grows on us again till the day You find us out."

Brother Arnold was waiting for him to play. He sighed and put his hand on the desk. Brother Arnold looked at it and at him. Brother Michael idly took away the spade and added the heart and still Brother Arnold couldn't see. Then Brother Michael shook his head and pointed to the floor. Brother Arnold bit his lip again as though he were on the point of crying, then threw down his own hand and walked to the other end of the cowhouse. Brother Michael left him so for a few moments. He could see the struggle going on in the man, could almost hear the Devil whisper in his ear that he (Brother Michael) was only an old woman—Brother Michael had heard that before; that life was long and a man might as well be dead and buried as not have some little innocent amusement—the sort of plausible whisper that put many a man on the gridiron. He knew, however hard it was now, that Brother Arnold would be grateful to him in the other world. "Brother Michael," he would say, "I don't know what I'd ever have done without your example."

Then Brother Michael went up and touched him gently on the shoulder. He pointed to the bottle, the racing paper, and the cards. Brother Arnold fluttered his hands despairingly but he nodded. They gathered them up between them, the cards, the bottle, and the papers, hid them under their habits to avoid all occasion of scandal, and went off to confess their guilt to the Prior.

UPROOTED

SPRING had only come and already he was tired to death; tired of the city, tired of his job. He had come up from the country intending to do wonders, but he was as far as ever from that. He would be lucky if he could carry on, be at school each morning at half past nine and satisfy his half-witted principal.

He lodged in a small red-brick house in Rathmines that was kept by a middle-aged brother and sister who had been left a bit of money and thought they would end their days enjoyably in a city. They did not enjoy themselves, regretted their little farm in Kerry, and were glad of Ned Keating because he could talk to them about all the things they remembered and loved.

Keating was a slow, cumbrous young man with dark eyes and a dark cow's-lick that kept tumbling into them. He had a slight stammer and ran his hand through his long limp hair from pure nervousness. He had always been dreamy and serious. Sometimes on market days you saw him standing for an hour in Nolan's shop, turning the pages of a schoolbook. When he could not afford it he put it back with a sigh and went off to find his father in a pub, just raising his eyes to smile at Jack Nolan. After his elder brother Tom had gone for the church he had his father had constant rows. Nothing would do Ned now but to be a teacher. Hadn't he all he wanted now? his father asked. Hadn't he the place to himself? What did he want going teaching? But Ned was stubborn. With an obstinate, almost despairing determination he had fought his way through the training college into a city job. The city was what he had always wanted. And now the city had failed him. In the evenings you could still see him poking round the second-hand bookshops on the quays, but his eyes were already beginning to lose their eagerness.

It had all seemed so clear. But then he had not counted on his own temper. He was popular because of his gentleness, but how many concessions that involved! He was hesitating, good-natured, slow to see guile, slow to contradict. He felt he was constantly underestimating his own powers. He even felt he lacked spontaneity. He did not drink, smoked little, and saw dangers and losses everywhere. He blamed himself for avarice and cowardice. The story he liked best was about the country boy and the letter box. "Indeed, what a fool you think I am! Put me letther in a pump!"

He was in no danger of putting his letter in a pump or anywhere else for the matter of that. He had only one friend, a nurse in Vincent's Hospital, a wild, light-hearted, light-headed girl. He was very fond of her and supposed that some day when he had money enough he would ask her to marry him; but not yet: and at the same time something that was both shyness and caution kept him from committing himself too far. Sometimes he planned excursions beside the usual weekly walk or visit to the pictures but somehow they seldom came to anything.

He no longer knew why he had come to the city, but it was not for the sake of the bed-sitting-room in Rathmines, the oblong of dusty garden outside the window, the trams clanging up and down, the shelf full of second-hand books, or the occasional visit to the pictures. Half humorously, half despairingly, he would sometimes clutch his head in his hands and admit to himself that he had no notion of what he wanted. He would have liked to leave it all and go to Glasgow or New York as a labourer, not because he was romantic, but because he felt that only when he had to work with his hands for a living and was no longer sure of his bed would he find out what all his ideals and emotions meant and where he could fit them into the scheme of his life.

But no sooner did he set out for school next morning, striding slowly along the edge of the canal, watching the trees become green again and the tall claret-coloured houses painted on the quiet surface of the water, than all his fancies took flight. Put his letter in a pump indeed! He would continue to be submissive and draw his salary and wonder how much he could save and when he would be able to buy a little house to bring his girl into; a nice thing to think of on a spring morning: a house of his own and a wife in the bed beside him. And his nature would continue to contract about him, every ideal, every generous impulse another mesh to draw his head down tighter to his knees till in ten years time it would tie him hand and foot.

II

Tom who was a curate in Wicklow wrote and suggested that they might go home together for the long weekend, and on Saturday morning they set out in Tom's old Ford. It was Easter weather, pearly and cold. They stopped at several pubs on the way and Tom ordered whiskies. Ned was feeling expansive and joined him. He had never quite grown used to his brother, partly because of old days when he felt that Tom was getting the education he should have got, partly because his ordination seemed to have shut him off from the rest of the family, and now it was as though he were trying to surmount it by his boisterous manner and affected bonhomie. He was like a man shouting to his comrades across a great distance. He was different from Ned; lighter in colour of hair and skin; fat-headed, fresh-complexioned, deep-voiced, and autocratic; an irascible, humorous, friendly man who was well-liked by those he worked for. Ned, who was shy and all tied up within himself, envied him his way with men in garages and barmaids in hotels.

It was nightfall when they reached home. Their father was in his shirtsleeves at the gate waiting to greet them, and imme-

diately their mother rushed out as well. The lamp was standing
in the window and threw its light as far as the whitewashed gate-
posts. Little Brigid, the girl from up the hill who helped their
mother now she was growing old, stood in the doorway in half-
silhouette. When her eyes caught theirs she bent her head in confusion.

Nothing was changed in the tall, bare, whitewashed kitchen.
The harness hung in the same place on the wall, the rosary on the
same nail in the fireplace, by the stool where their mother usually
sat; table under the window, churn against the back door, stair
without banisters mounting straight to the attic door that yawned
in the wall—all seemed as unchanging as the sea outside. Their
mother sat on the stool, her hands on her knees, a coloured shawl
tied tightly about her head, like a gipsy woman with her battered
yellow face and loud voice. Their father, fresh-complexioned like
Tom, stocky and broken-bottomed, gazed out the front door,
leaning with one hand on the dresser in the pose of an orator
while Brigid wet the tea.

"I said ye'd be late," their father proclaimed triumphantly,
twisting his moustache. "Didn't I, woman? Didn't I say they'd be
late?"

"He did, he did," their mother assured them. " 'Tis true for
him."

"Ah, I knew ye'd be making halts. But damn it, if I wasn't put
astray by Thade Lahy's car going east!"

"And was that Thade Lahy's car?" their mother asked in a
shocked tone.

"I told ye 'twas Thade Lahy's," piped Brigid, plopping about
in her long frieze gown and bare feet.

"Sure I should know it, woman," old Tomas said with chagrin.
"He must have gone into town without us noticing him."

"Oye, and how did he do that?" asked their mother.

"Leave me alone now," Tomas said despairingly. "I couldn't
tell you, I could not tell you."

"My goodness, I was sure that was the Master's car," their
mother said wonderingly, pulling distractedly at the tassels of
her shawl.

"I'd know the rattle of Thade Lahy's car anywhere," little Brigid said very proudly and quite unregarded.

It seemed to Ned that he was interrupting a conversation that had been going on since his last visit, and that the road outside and the sea beyond it, and every living thing that passed before them, formed a pantomime that was watched endlessly and passionately from the darkness of the little cottage.

"Wisha, I never asked if ye'd like a drop of something," their father said with sudden vexation.

"Is it whisky?" boomed Tom.

"Why? Would you sooner whisky?"

"Can't you pour it out first and ask us after?" growled Tom.

"The whisky, is it?"

"'Tis not. I didn't come all the ways to this place for what I can get better at home. You'd better have a bottle ready for me to take back."

"Coleen will have it. Damn it, wasn't it only last night I said to Coleen that you'd likely want a bottle? Some way it struck me you would. Oh, he'll have it, he'll have it."

"Didn't they catch that string of misery yet?" asked Tom with the cup to his lips.

"Ah, man alive, you'd want to be a greyhound to catch him. God Almighty, hadn't they fifty police after him last November, scouring the mountains from one end to the other and all they caught was a glimpse of the white of his ass. Ah, but the priest preached a terrible sermon against him—by name, Tom, by name!"

"Is old Murphy blowing about it still?" growled Tom.

"Oh, let me alone now!" Tomas threw his hands to heaven and strode to and fro in his excitement, his bucket-bottom wagging. Ned knew to his sorrow that his father could be prudent, silent, and calculating; he knew only too well the cock of the head, the narrowing of the eyes, but, like a child, the old man loved innocent excitement and revelled in scenes of the wildest passion, all about nothing. Like an old actor he turned everything to drama. "The like of it for abuse was never heard, never heard, never heard! How Coleen could ever raise his head again after it!

And where the man got the words from! Tom, my treasure, my son, you'll never have the like."

"I'd spare my breath to cool my porridge," Tom replied scornfully. "I dare say you gave up your own still so?"

"I didn't, Tom, I didn't. The drop I make, 'twould harm no one. Only a drop for Christmas and Easter."

The lamp was in its own place on the rear wall, and made a circle of brightness on the fresh lime wash. Their mother was leaning over the fire with joined hands, lost in thought. The front door was open and night thickening outside, the coloured night of the west; and as they ate their father walked to and fro in long ungainly strides, pausing each time at the door to give a glance up and down the road and at the fire to hoist his broken bottom to warm. Ned heard steps come up the road from the west. His father heard them too. He returned to the door and glued his hand to the jamb. Ned covered his eyes with his hands and felt that everything was as it had always been. He could hear the noise of the strand as a background to the voices.

"God be with you, Tomas," the voice said.

"God and Mary be with you, Teig." (In Irish they were speaking.) "What way are you?"

"Well, honour and praise be to God. 'Tis a fine night."

" 'Tis, 'tis, 'tis so indeed. A grand night, praise be to God."

"Musha, who is it?" their mother asked, looking round.

" 'Tis young Teig," their father replied, looking after him.

"Shemus's young Teig?"

" 'Tis, 'tis, 'tis."

"But where would Shemus's young Teig be going at this hour of night? 'Tisn't to the shop?"

"No, woman, no, no, no. Up to the uncle's I suppose."

"Is it Ned Willie's?"

"He's sleeping at Ned Willie's," Brigid chimed in in her high-pitched voice, timid but triumphant. " 'Tis since the young teacher came to them."

There was no more to be said. Everything was explained and Ned smiled. The only unfamiliar voice, little Brigid's, seemed the most familiar of all.

III

Tom said first Mass next morning and the household, all but Brigid, went. They drove, and Tomas in high glee sat in front with Tom, waving his hand and shouting greetings at all they met. He was like a boy, so intense was his pleasure. The chapel was perched high above the road. Outside the morning was grey and beyond the windy edge of the cliff was the sea. The wind blew straight in, setting cloaks and petticoats flying.

After dinner as the two boys were returning from a series of visits to the neighbours' houses their father rushed down the road to meet them, shaking them passionately by the hand and asking were they well. When they were seated in the kitchen he opened up the subject of his excitement.

"Well," he said, "I arranged a grand little outing for ye to-morrow, thanks be to God," and to identify further the source of his inspiration he searched at the back of his neck for the peak of his cap and raised it solemnly.

"Musha, what outing are you talking about?" their mother asked angrily.

"I arranged for us to go over the bay to your brother's."

"And can't you leave the poor boys alone?" she bawled. "Haven't they only the one day? Isn't it for the rest they came?"

"Even so, even so, even so," Tomas said with mounting passion. "Aren't their own cousins to lay eyes on them?"

"I was in Carriganassa for a week last summer," said Tom.

"Yes, but I wasn't, and Ned wasn't. 'Tis only decent."

"'Tisn't decency is worrying you at all but drink," growled Tom.

"Oh!" gasped his father, fishing for the peak of his cap to swear with, "that I might be struck dead!"

"Be quiet, you old heathen!" crowed his wife. "That's the truth, Tom my pulse. Plenty of drink is what he wants where he won't be under my eye. Leave ye stop at home."

"I can't stop at home, woman," shouted Tomas. "Why do you be always picking at me? I must go whether they come or not. I must go, I must go, and that's all there is about it."

"Why must you?" asked his wife.

"Because I warned Red Pat and Dempsey," he stormed. "And the woman from the island is coming as well to see a daughter of hers that's married there. And what's more, I borrowed Cassidy's boat and he lent it at great inconvenience, and 'twould be very bad manners for me to throw his kindness back in his face. I must go."

"Oh, we may as well all go," said Tom.

It blew hard all night and Tomas, all anxiety, was out at break of day to watch the whitecaps on the water. While the boys were at breakfast he came in and, leaning his arms on the table with hands joined as though in prayer, he announced in a caressing voice that it was a beautiful day, thank God, a pet day with a moist gentle little bit of a breezheen that would only blow them over. His voice would have put a child to sleep, but his wife continued to nag and scold, and he stumped out again in a fury and sat on the wall with his back to the house and his legs crossed, chewing his pipe. He was dressed in his best clothes, a respectable blue tailcoat and pale frieze trousers with only one patch on the seat. He had turned his cap almost right way round so that the peak covered his right ear.

He was all over the boat like a boy. Dempsey, a haggard, pockmarked, melancholy man with a soprano voice of astounding penetration, took the tiller and Red Patrick the sail. Tomas clambered into the bows and stood there with one knee up, leaning forward like a figurehead. He knew the bay like a book. The island woman was perched on the ballast with her rosary in her hands and her shawl over her eyes to shut out the sight of the waves. The cumbrous old boat took the sail lightly enough and Ned leaned back on his elbows against the side, rejoicing in it all.

"She's laughing," his father said delightedly when her bows ran white.

"Whose boat is that, Dempsey?" he asked, screwing up his eyes as another brown sail tilted ahead of them.

" 'Tis the island boat," shrieked Dempsey.

" 'Tis not, Dempsey. 'Tis not indeed, my love. That's not the island boat."

"Whose boat is it then?"

"It must be some boat from Carriganassa, Dempsey."

" 'Tis the island boat I tell you."

"Ah, why will you be contradicting me, Dempsey, my treasure?
'Tis not the island boat. The island boat has a dark brown sail;
'tis only a month since 'twas tarred, and that's an old tarred sail,
and what proves it out and out, Dempsey, the island-boat sail has
a patch in the corner."

He was leaning well over the bows, watching the rocks that
fled beneath them, a dark purple. He rested his elbow on his
raised knee and looked back at them, his brown face sprinkled
with spray and lit from below by the accumulated flickerings of
the water. His flesh seemed to dissolve, to become transparent,
while his blue eyes shone with extraordinary brilliance. Ned
half-closed his eyes and watched sea and sky slowly mount and
sink behind the red-brown, sun-filled sail and the poised and
eager figure.

"Tom!" shouted his father, and the battered old face peered at
them from under the arch of the sail, with which it was almost
one in tone, the silvery light filling it with warmth.

"Well?" Tom's voice was an inexpressive boom.

"You were right last night, Tom, my boy. My treasure, my
son, you were right. 'Twas for the drink I came."

"Ah, do you tell me so?" Tom asked ironically.

" 'Twas, 'twas, 'twas," the old man said regretfully. " 'Twas for
the drink. 'Twas so, my darling. They were always decent people, your mother's people, and 'tis her knowing how decent they
are makes her so suspicious. She's a good woman, a fine woman,
your poor mother, may the Almighty God bless her and keep her
and watch over her."

"Aaaa-men," Tom chanted irreverently as his father shook his
old cap piously towards the sky.

"But Tom! Are you listening, Tom?"

"Well, what is it now?"

"I had another reason."

"Had you indeed?" Tom's tone was not encouraging.

"I had, I had, God's truth, I had. God blast the lie I'm telling
you, Tom, I had."

" 'Twas boasting out of the pair of ye," shrieked Dempsey from the stern, the wind whipping the shrill notes from his lips and scattering them wildly like scraps of paper.

" 'Twas so, Dempsey, 'twas so. You're right, Dempsey. You're always right. The blessing of God on you, Dempsey, for you always had the true word." Tomas's laughing leprechaun countenance gleamed under the bellying, tilting, chocolate-coloured sail and his powerful voice beat Dempsey's down. "And would you blame me?"

"The O'Donnells hadn't the beating of them in their own hand," screamed Dempsey.

"Thanks be to God for all His goodness and mercy," shouted Tomas, again waving his cap in a gesture of recognition towards the spot where he felt the Almighty might be listening, "they have not. They have not so, Dempsey. And they have a good hand. The O'Donnells are a good family and an old family and a kind family, but they never had the like of my two sons."

"And they were stiff enough with you when you came for the daughter," shrieked Dempsey.

"They were, Dempsey, they were. They were stiff. They were so. You wouldn't blame them, Dempsey. They were an old family and I was nothing only a landless man." With a fierce gesture the old man pulled his cap still further over his ear, spat, gave his moustache a tug and leaned at a still more precarious angle over the bow, his blue eyes dancing with triumph. "But I had the gumption, Dempsey. I had the gumption, my love."

The islands slipped past; the gulf of water narrowed and grew calmer, and white cottages could be seen scattered under the tall ungainly church. It was a wild and rugged coast, the tide was full, and they had to pull in as best they could among the rocks. Red Patrick leaped lightly ashore to draw in the boat. The others stepped after him into several inches of water and Red Patrick, himself precariously poised, held them from slipping. Rather shamefastly, Ned and Tom took off their shoes.

"Don't do that!" shrieked their father. "We'll carry ye up. Mother of God, yeer poor feet!"

"Will you shut your old gob?" Tom said angrily.

They halted for a moment at the stile outside Caheraghs. Old Caheragh had a red beard and a broad, smiling face. Then they went on to O'Donnell's who had two houses, modern and old, separated by a yard. In one lived Uncle Maurice and his family and in the other Maurice's married son, Sean. Ned and Tom remained with Sean and his wife. Tom and he were old friends. When he spoke he rarely looked at Tom, merely giving him a sidelong glance that just reached to his chin and then dropped his eyes with a peculiar timid smile. " 'Twas," Ned heard him say, and then: "He did," and after that: "Hardly." Shuvaun was tall, nervous and matronly. She clung to their hands with an excess of eagerness as though she couldn't bear to let them go, uttering ejaculations of tenderness, delight, astonishment, pity, and admiration. Her speech was full of diminutives: "childeen," "handeen," "boateen." Three young children scrambled about the floor with a preoccupation scarcely broken by the strangers. Shuvaun picked her way through them, filling the kettle and cutting the bread, and then, as though afraid of neglecting Tom, she clutched his hand again. Her feverish concentration gave an impression that its very intensity bewildered her and made it impossible for her to understand one word they said. In three days time it would all begin to drop into place in her mind and then she would begin quoting them.

Young Niall O'Donnell came in with his girl; one of the Deignans from up the hill. She was plump and pert; she had been in service in town. Niall was a well-built boy with a soft, wild-eyed, sensuous face and a deep mellow voice of great power. While they were having a cup of tea in the parlour where the three or four family photos were skyed, Ned saw the two of them again through the back window. They were standing on the high ground behind the house with the spring sky behind them and the light in their faces. Niall was asking her something but she, more interested in the sitting-room window, only shook her head.

"Ye only just missed yeer father," said their Uncle Maurice when they went across to the other house for dinner. Maurice was a tightlipped little man with a high bald forehead and a snappy voice. "He went off to Owney Pat's only this minute."

"The devil!" said Tom. "I knew he was out to dodge me. Did you give him whisky?"

"What the hell else could I give him?" snapped Maurice. "Do you think 'twas tea the old coot was looking for?"

Tom took the place of honour at the table. He was the favourite. Through the doorway into the bedroom could be seen a big canopy bed and on the whiteness of a raised pillow a skeleton face in a halo of smoke-blue hair surmounted with what looked suspiciously like a mauve tea-cosy. Sometimes the white head would begin to stir and everyone fell silent while Niall, the old man's pet, translated the scarcely audible whisper. Sometimes Niall would go in with his stiff ungainly swagger and repeat one of Tom's jokes in his drawling, powerful bass. The hens stepped daintily about their feet, poking officious heads between them, and rushing out the door with a wild flutter and shriek when one of the girls hooshed them. Something timeless, patriarchal and restful about it made Ned notice everything. It was as though he had never seen his mother's house before.

"Tell me," Tom boomed with mock concern, leaning over confidentially to his uncle and looking under his brows at young Niall, "speaking as a clergyman and for the good of the family and so on, is that son of yours coorting Delia Deignan?"

"Why? Was the young blackguard along with her again?" snapped Maurice in amusement.

"Of course I might be mistaken," Tom said doubtfully.

"You wouldn't know a Deignan, to be sure," Sean said dryly.

"Isn't any of them married yet?" asked Tom.

"No, by damn, no," said Maurice. "Isn't it a wonder?"

"Because," Tom went on in the same solemn voice, "I want someone to look after this young brother of mine. Dublin is a wild sort of place and full of temptations. Ye wouldn't know a decent little girl I could ask?"

"Cait! Cait!" they all shouted, Niall's deep voice loudest of all.

"Now all the same, Delia looks a smart little piece," said Tom.

"No, Cait! Cait! Delia isn't the same since she went to town. She has notions of herself. Leave him marry Cait!"

Niall rose gleefully and shambled in to the old man. With a gamesome eye on the company Tom whispered:

"Is she a quiet sort of girl? I wouldn't like Ned to get anyone rough."

"She is, she is," they said, "a grand girl!"

Sean rose quietly and went to the door with his head bowed.

"God knows, if anyone knows he should know and all the times he manhandled her."

Tom sat bolt upright with mock indignation while the table rocked. Niall shouted the joke into his grandfather's ear. The mauve tea-cosy shook; it was the only indication of the old man's amusement.

IV

The Deignans' house was on top of a hill high over the road and commanded a view of the countryside for miles. The two brothers with Sean and the O'Donnell girls reached it by a long winding boreen that threaded its way uncertainly through little grey rocky fields and walls of unmortared stone which rose against the sky along the edges of the hill like lacework. On their way they met another procession coming down the hill. It was headed by their father and the island woman, arm in arm, and behind came two locals with Dempsey and Red Patrick. All the party except the island woman were well advanced in liquor. That was plain when their father rushed forward to shake them all by the hand and ask them how they were. He said that divil such honourable and kindly people as the people of Carriganassa were to be found in the whole world, and of these there was no one a patch on the O'Donnells; kings and sons of kings as you could see from one look at them. He had only one more call to pay and promised to be at Caheraghs within a quarter of an hour.

They looked over the Deignans' half-door. The kitchen was empty. The girls began to titter. They knew the Deignans must have watched them coming from Maurice's door. The kitchen was a beautiful room; woodwork and furniture, homemade and shapely, were painted a bright red-brown and the painted dresser shone with pretty ware. They entered and looked about them. Nothing was to be heard but the tick of the cheap alarm-clock on the dresser. One of the girls began to giggle hysterically. Sean raised his voice.

"Are ye in or are ye out, bad cess to ye!"

For a moment there was no reply. Then a quick step sounded in the attic and a girl descended the stairs at a run, drawing a black knitted shawl tighter about her shoulders. She was perhaps twenty-eight or thirty, with a narrow face, sharp like a ferret's, and blue nervous eyes. She entered the kitchen awkwardly sideways, giving the customary greetings but without looking at anyone.

"A hundred welcomes. . . . How are ye? . . . 'Tis a fine day."

The O'Donnell girls giggled again. Nora Deignan looked at them in astonishment, biting nervously at the tassel of her shawl. She had tiny sharp white teeth.

"What is it, aru?" she asked.

"Musha, will you stop your old cimeens," boomed Tom, "and tell us where's Cait from you? You don't think 'twas to see your ugly puss that we came up here?"

"Cait!" Nora called in a low voice.

"What is it?" another voice replied from upstairs.

"Damn well you know what it is," bellowed Tom, "and you crosseyed expecting us since morning. Will you come down out of that or will I go up and fetch you?"

There was the same hasty step and a second girl descended the stairs. It was only later that Ned was able to realize how beautiful she was. She had the same narrow pointed face as her sister, the same slight features sharpened by a sort of animal instinct, the same blue eyes with their startled brightness; but all seemed to have been differently composed, and her complexion had a transparency as though her whole nature were shining through it. "Child of Light, thy limbs are burning through the veil which seems to hide them," Ned found himself murmuring. She came on them in the same hostile way, blushing furiously. Tom's eyes rested on her; soft, bleary, emotional eyes incredibly unlike her own.

"Have you nothing to say to me, Cait?" he boomed, and Ned thought his very voice was soft and clouded.

"Oh, a hundred welcomes." Her blue eyes rested for a moment on him with what seemed a fierce candour and penetration and went past him to the open door. Outside a soft rain was beginning to fall; heavy clouds crushed down the grey landscape, which grew clearer as it merged into one common plane; the little grey bumpy fields with the walls of grey unmortared stone that drifted hither and over across them like blown sand, the whitewashed farmhouses lost to the sun sinking back into the brown-grey hillsides.

"Nothing else, my child?" he growled, pursing his lips.

"How are you?"

"The politeness is suffocating you. Where's Delia?"

"Here I am," said Delia from the doorway immediately behind him. In her furtive way she had slunk round the house. Her bland impertinence raised a laugh.

"The reason we called," said Tom, clearing his throat, "is this young brother of mine that's looking for a wife."

Everyone laughed again. Ned knew the oftener a joke was repeated the better they liked it, but for him this particular joke was beginning to wear thin.

"Leave him take me," said Delia with an arch look at Ned who smiled and gazed at the floor.

"Be quiet, you slut!" said Tom. "There are your two sisters before you."

"Even so, I want to go to Dublin. . . . Would you treat me to lemonade, mister?" she asked Ned with her impudent smile. "This is a rotten hole. I'd go to America if they left me."

"America won't be complete without you," said Tom. "Now, don't let me hurry ye, ladies, but my old fellow will be waiting for us in Johnny Kit's."

"We'll go along with you," said Nora, and the three girls took down three black shawls from inside the door. Some tension seemed to have gone out of the air. They laughed and joked between themselves.

"Ye'll get wet," said Sean to the two brothers.

"Cait will make room for me under her shawl," said Tom.

"Indeed I will not," she cried, starting back with a laugh.

"Very shy you're getting," said Sean with a good-natured grin.

" 'Tisn't that at all but she'd sooner the young man," said Delia.

"What's strange is wonderful," said Nora.

Biting her lip with her tiny front teeth, Cait looked angrily at her sisters and Sean, and then began to laugh. She glanced at Ned and smilingly held out her shawl in invitation, though at the same moment angry blushes chased one another across her forehead like squalls across the surface of a lake. The rain was a mild, persistent drizzle and a strong wind was blowing. Everything had darkened and grown lonely and, with his head in the blinding folds of the shawl, which reeked of turf-smoke, Ned felt as if he had dropped out of Time's pocket.

They waited in Caheragh's kitchen. The bearded old man sat in one chimney corner and a little barelegged boy in the other. The dim blue light poured down the wide chimney on their heads in a shower with the delicacy of light on old china, picking out surfaces one rarely saw; and between them the fire burned a bright orange in the great whitewashed hearth with the black, swinging bars and pothook. Outside the rain fell softly, almost soundlessly, beyond the half door. Delia, her black shawl trailing from her shoulders, leaned over it, acting the part of watcher as in a Greek play. Their father's fifteen minutes had strung themselves out to an hour and two little barefooted boys had already been sent to hunt him down.

"Where are they now, Delia?" one of the O'Donnells would ask.

"Crossing the fields from Patsy Kit's."

"He wasn't there so."

"He wouldn't be," the old man said. "They'll likely go on to Ned Kit's now."

"That's where they're making for," said Delia. "Up the hill at the far side of the fort."

"They'll find him there," the old man said confidently.

Ned felt as though he were still blanketed by the folds of the turf-reeking shawl. Something seemed to have descended on him that filled him with passion and loneliness. He could scarcely take his eyes off Cait. She and Nora sat on the form against the back wall, a composition in black and white, the black shawl drawn tight under the chin, the cowl of it breaking the curve of her dark hair, her shadow on the gleaming wall behind. She did not speak except to answer some question of Tom's about her brother, but sometimes Ned caught her looking at him with naked eyes. Then she smiled swiftly and secretly and turned her eyes again to the door, sinking back into pensiveness. Pensiveness or vacancy? he wondered. While he gazed at her face with the animal instinctiveness of its overdelicate features it seemed like a mirror in which he saw again the falling rain, the rocks and hills and angry sea.

The first announced by Delia was Red Patrick. After him came the island woman. Each had last seen his father in a different place. Ned chuckled at a sudden vision of his father, eager and impassioned and aflame with drink, stumping with his broken bottom across endless fields through pouring rain with a growing procession behind him. Dempsey was the last to come. He doubted if Tomas would be in a condition to take the boat at all.

"What matter, aru?" said Delia across her shoulder. "We can find room for the young man."

"And where would we put him?" gaped Nora.

"He can have Cait's bed," Delia said innocently.

"Oye, and where would Cait sleep?" Nora asked and then skitted and covered her face with her shawl. Delia scoffed. The men laughed and Cait, biting her lip furiously, looked at the floor. Again Ned caught her eyes on him and again she laughed and turned away.

Tomas burst in unexpected on them all like a sea-wind that scattered them before him. He wrung Tom's hand and asked him how he was. He did the same to Ned. Ned replied gravely that he was very well.

"In God's holy name," cried his father, waving his arms like a windmill, "what are ye all waiting for?"

The tide had fallen. Tomas grabbed an oar and pushed the boat on to a rock. Then he raised the sail and collapsed under it and had to be extricated from its drenching folds, glauming and swearing at Cassidy's old boat. A little group stood on a naked rock against a grey background of drifting rain. For a long time

Ned continued to wave back to the black shawl that was lifted to him. An extraordinary feeling of exultation and loss enveloped him. Huddled up in his overcoat he sat with Dempsey in the stern, not speaking.

"It was a grand day," his father declared, swinging himself to and fro, tugging at his Viking moustache, dragging the peak of his cap farther over his ear. His gestures betrayed a certain lack of rhythmical cohesion; they began and ended abruptly. "Dempsey, my darling, wasn't it a grand day?"

" 'Twas a grand day for you," shrieked Dempsey as if his throat would burst.

" 'Twas, my treasure, 'twas a beautiful day. I got an honourable reception and my sons got an honourable reception."

By this time he was flat on his belly, one leg completely over the edge of the boat. He reached back a clammy hand to his sons.

" 'Twas the best day I ever had," he said. "I got porter and I got whisky and I got poteen. I did so, Tom, my calf. Ned, my brightness, I went to seven houses and in every house I got seven drinks and with every drink I got seven welcomes. And your mother's people are a hand of trumps. It was no slight they put on me at all even if I was nothing but a landless man. No slight, Tom. No slight at all."

Darkness had fallen, the rain had cleared, the stars came out of a pitch-black sky under which the little tossing, nosing boat seemed lost beyond measure. In all the waste of water nothing could be heard but the splash of the boat's sides and their father's voice raised in tipsy song.

> *The evening was fair and the sunlight was yellow,*
> *I halted, beholding a maiden bright*
> *Coming to me by the edge of the mountain,*
> *Her cheeks had a berry-bright rosy light.*

V

Ned was the first to wake. He struck a match and lit the candle. It was time for them to be stirring. It was just after dawn, and at half past nine he must be in his old place in the schoolroom before the rows of pinched little city-faces. He lit a cigarette and

closed his eyes. The lurch of the boat was still in his blood, the
face of Cait Deignan in his mind, and as if from far away he
heard a line of the wild love-song his father had been singing:
"And we'll drive the geese at the fall of night."

He heard his brother mumble something and nudged him.
Tom looked big and fat and vulnerable with his fair head rolled
sideways and his heavy mouth dribbling on to the sleeve of his
pyjamas. Ned slipped quietly out of bed, put on his trousers, and
went to the window. He drew the curtains and let in the thin
cold daylight. The bay was just visible and perfectly still. Tom began to mumble again in a frightened voice and Ned shook him.
He started out of his sleep with a cry of fear, grabbing at the bedclothes. He looked first at Ned, then at the candle and drowsily
rubbed his eyes.

"Did you hear it too?" he asked.

"Did I hear what?" asked Ned with a smile.

"In the room," said Tom.

"There was nothing in the room," replied Ned. "You were
ramaishing so I woke you up."

"Was I? What was I saying?"

"You were telling no secrets," said Ned with a quiet laugh.

"Hell!" Tom said in disgust and stretched out his arm for a
cigarette. He lit it at the candle flame, his drowsy red face puck-
ered and distraught. "I slept rotten."

"Oye!" Ned said quietly, raising his eyebrows. It wasn't often
Tom spoke in that tone. He sat on the edge of the bed, joined
his hands and leaned forward, looking at Tom with wide gentle
eyes.

"Is there anything wrong?" he asked.

"Plenty."

"You're not in trouble?" Ned asked without raising his voice.

"Not that sort of trouble. The trouble is in myself."

Ned gave him a look of intense sympathy and understanding.
The soft emotional brown eyes were searching him for a judg-
ment. Ned had never felt less like judging him.

"Ay," he said gently and vaguely, his eyes wandering to the
other side of the room while his voice took on its accustomed
stammer, "the trouble is always in ourselves. If we were contented

in ourselves the other things wouldn't matter. I suppose we must
only leave it to time. Time settles everything."

"Time will settle nothing for me," Tom said despairingly.
"You have something to look forward to. I have nothing. It's the
loneliness of my job that kills you. Even to talk about it would be
a relief but there's no one you can talk to. People come to you
with their troubles but there's no one you can go to with your
own."

Again the challenging glare in the brown eyes and Ned realized with infinite compassion that for years Tom had been living
in the same state of suspicion and fear, a man being hunted down
by his own nature; and that for years to come he would continue
to live in this way, and perhaps never be caught again as he was
now.

"A pity you came down here," stammered Ned flatly. "A pity
we went to Carriganassa. 'Twould ϳe better for both of us if we
went somewhere else."

"Why don't you marry her, Ned?" Tom asked earnestly.

"Who?" asked Ned.

"Cait."

"Yesterday," said Ned with the shy smile he wore when he confessed something, "I nearly wished I could."

"But you can, man," Tom said eagerly, sitting upon his elbow.
Like all men with frustration in their hearts he was full of
schemes for others. "You could marry her and get a school down
here. That's what I'd do if I was in your place."

"No," Ned said gravely. "We made our choice a long time ago.
We can't go back on it now."

Then with his hands in his trouser pockets and his head bowed
he went out to the kitchen. His mother, the coloured shawl about
her head, was blowing the fire. The bedroom door was open and
he could see his father in shirtsleeves kneeling beside the bed, his
face raised reverently towards a holy picture, his braces hanging
down behind. He unbolted the half-door, went through the garden and out on to the road. There was a magical light on everything. A boy on a horse rose suddenly against the sky, a startling
picture. Through the apple-green light over Carriganassa ran
long streaks of crimson, so still they might have been enamelled.

Magic, magic, magic! He saw it as in a children's picture-book with all its colours intolerably bright; something he had out-grown and could never return to, while the world he aspired to was as remote and intangible as it had seemed even in the despair of youth.

It seemed as if only now for the first time was he leaving home; for the first time and forever saying good-bye to it all.

THE BABES IN THE WOOD

Whenever Mrs. Early made Terry put on his best trousers and gansey he knew his aunt must be coming. She didn't come half often enough to suit Terry, but when she did it was great gas. Terry's mother was dead and he lived with Mrs. Early and her son, Billy. Mrs. Early was a rough, deaf, scolding old woman, doubled up with rheumatics, who'd give you a clout as quick as she'd look at you, but Billy was good gas too.

This particular Sunday morning Billy was scraping his chin frantically and cursing the bloody old razor while the bell was ringing up the valley for Mass, when Terry's aunt arrived. She come into the dark little cottage eagerly, her big rosy face toasted with sunshine and her hand out in greeting.

"Hello, Billy," she cried in a loud, laughing voice, "late for Mass again?"

"Let me alone, Miss Conners," stuttered Billy, turning his lath-ered face to her from the mirror. "I think my mother shaves on the sly."

"And how's Mrs. Early?" cried Terry's aunt, kissing the old woman and then fumbling at the strap of her knapsack in her ex-citable way. Everything about his aunt was excitable and high-

H

powered; the words tumbled out of her so fast that sometimes she became incoherent.

"Look, I brought you a couple of things—no, they're fags for Billy ("God bless you, Miss Conners," from Billy)—this is for you, and here are a few things for the dinner."

"And what did you bring me, Auntie?" Terry asked.

"Oh, Terry," she cried in consternation, "I forgot about you."

"You didn't."

"I did, Terry," she said tragically. "I swear I did. Or did I? The bird told me something. What was it he said?"

"What sort of bird was it?" asked Terry. "A thrush?"

"A big grey fellow?"

"That's the old thrush all right. He sings in our back yard."

"And what was that he told me to bring you?"

"A boat!" shouted Terry.

It was a boat.

After dinner the pair of them went up the wood for a walk. His aunt had a long, swinging stride that made her hard to keep up with, but she was great gas and Terry wished she'd come to see him oftener. When she did he tried his hardest to be grown-up All the morning he had been reminding himself: "Terry, remember you're not a baby any longer. You're nine now, you know." He wasn't nine, of course; he was still only five and fat, but nine, the age of his girl friend Florrie, was the one he liked pretending to be. When you were nine you understood everything. There were still things Terry did not understand.

When they reached the top of the hill his aunt threw herself on her back with her knees in the air and her hands under her head. She liked to toast herself like that. She liked walking; her legs were always bare; she usually wore a tweed skirt and a pullover. Today she wore black glasses, and when Terry looked through them he saw everything dark; the wooded hills at the other side of the valley and the buses and cars crawling between the rocks at their feet, and, still farther down, the railway track and the river. She promised him a pair for himself next time she came, a small pair to fit him, and he could scarcely bear the thought of having to wait so long for them.

"When will you come again, Auntie?" he asked. "Next Sunday?"

"I might," she said and rolled on her belly, propped her head on her hands, and sucked a straw as she laughed at him. "Why? Do you like it when I come?"

"I love it."

"Would you like to come and live with me altogether, Terry?"

"Oh, Jay, I would."

"Are you sure now?" she said, half-ragging him. "You're sure you wouldn't be lonely after Mrs. Early or Billy or Florrie?"

"I wouldn't, Auntie, honest," he said tensely. "When will you bring me?"

"I don't know yet," she said. "It might be sooner than you think."

"Where would you bring me? Up to town?"

"If I tell you where," she whispered, bending closer, "will you swear a terrible oath not to tell anybody?"

"I will."

"Not even Florrie?"

"Not even Florrie."

"That you might be killed stone dead?" she added in a blood-curdling tone.

"That I might be killed stone dead!"

"Well, there's a nice man over from England who wants to marry me and bring me back with him. Of course, I said I couldn't come without you and he said he'd bring you as well. . . . Wouldn't that be gorgeous?" she ended, clapping her hands.

" 'Twould," said Terry, clapping his hands in imitation. "Where's England?"

"Oh, a long way off," she said, pointing up the valley. "Beyond where the railway ends. We'd have to get a big boat to take us there."

"Chrisht!" said Terry, repeating what Billy said whenever something occurred too great for his imagination to grasp, a fairly common event. He was afraid his aunt, like Mrs. Early, would give him a wallop for it, but she only laughed. "What sort of a place is England, Auntie?" he went on.

"Oh, a grand place," said his aunt in her loud, enthusiastic way. "The three of us would live in a big house of our own with lights that went off and on, and hot water in the taps, and every morning I'd take you to school on your bike."

"Would I have a bike of my own?" Terry asked incredulously.

"You would, Terry, a two-wheeled one. And on a fine day like this we'd sit in the park—you know, a place like the garden of the big house where Billy works, with trees and flowers and a pond in the middle to sail boats in."

"And would we have a park of our own, too?"

"Not our own; there'd be other people as well; boys and girls you could play with. And you could be sailing your boat and I'd be reading a book, and then we'd go back home to tea and I'd bath you and tell you a story in bed. Wouldn't it be massive, Terry?"

"What sort of story would you tell me?" he asked cautiously. "Tell us one now."

So she took off her black spectacles and, hugging her knees, told him the story of the Three Bears and was so carried away that she acted it, growling and wailing and creeping on all fours with her hair over her eyes till Terry screamed with fright and pleasure. She was really great gas.

II

Next day Florrie came to the cottage for him. Florrie lived in the village so she had to come a mile through the woods to see him, but she delighted in seeing him and Mrs. Early encouraged her. "Your young lady" she called her and Florrie blushed with pleasure. Florrie lived with Miss Clancy in the Post Office and was very nicely behaved; everyone admitted that. She was tall and thin, with jet-black hair, a long ivory face, and a hook nose.

"Terry!" bawled Mrs. Early. "Your young lady is here for you," and Terry came rushing from the back of the cottage with his new boat.

"Where did you get that, Terry?" Florrie asked, opening her eyes wide at the sight of it.

"My auntie," said Terry. "Isn't it grand?"

"I suppose 'tis all right," said Florrie, showing her teeth in a smile which indicated that she thought him a bit of a baby for making so much of a toy boat.

Now, that was one great weakness in Florrie, and Terry regretted it because he really was very fond of her. She was gentle, she was generous, she always took his part; she told creepy stories so well that she even frightened herself and was scared of going back through the woods alone, but she was jealous. Whenever she had anything, even if it was only a raggy doll, she made it out to be one of the seven wonders of the world, but let anyone else have a thing, no matter how valuable, and she pretended it didn't even interest her. It was the same now.

"Will you come up to the big house for a pennorth of goose-gogs?" she asked.

"We'll go down the river with this one first," insisted Terry, who knew he could always override her wishes when he chose.

"But these are grand goosegogs," she said eagerly, and again you'd think no one in the world but herself could even have a gooseberry. "They're that size. Miss Clancy gave me the penny."

"We'll go down the river first," Terry said cantankerously. "Ah, boy, wait till you see this one sail—sssss!"

She gave in as she always did when Terry showed himself headstrong, and grumbled as she always did when she had given in. She said it would be too late; that Jerry, the under-gardener, who was their friend, would be gone and that Mr. Scott, the head gardener, would only give them a handful, and not even ripe ones. She was terrible like that, an awful old worrier.

When they reached the riverbank they tied up their clothes and went in. The river was deep enough, and under the trees it ran beautifully clear over a complete pavement of small, brown, smoothly rounded stones. The current was swift, and the little sailing-boat was tossed on its side and spun dizzily round and round before it stuck in the bank. Florrie tired of this sport sooner than Terry did. She sat on the bank with her hands under her bottom, trailing her toes in the river, and looked at the boat with growing disillusionment.

"God knows, 'tisn't much of a thing to lose a pennorth of goosegogs over," she said bitterly.

"What's wrong with it?" Terry asked indignantly. " 'Tis a fine boat."

"A wonder it wouldn't sail properly so," she said with an accusing, school-marmish air.

"How could it when the water is too fast for it?" shouted Terry.

"That's a good one," she retorted in pretended grown-up amusement. " 'Tis the first time we ever heard of water being too fast for a boat." That was another very aggravating thing about her —her calm assumption that only what she knew was knowledge. " 'Tis only a cheap old boat."

" 'Tisn't a cheap old boat," Terry cried indignantly. "My aunt gave it to me."

"She never gives anyone anything only cheap old things," Florrie replied with the coolness that always maddened other children. "She gets them cost price in the shop where she works. Everyone knows that."

"Because you're jealous," he cried, throwing at her the taunt the village children threw whenever she enraged them with her supercilious airs.

"That's a good one too," she said in a quiet voice, while her long thin face maintained its air of amusement. "I suppose you'll tell us now what we're jealous of?"

"Because Auntie brings me things and no one ever brings you anything."

"She's mad about you," Florrie said ironically.

"She is mad about me."

"A wonder she wouldn't bring you to live with her so."

"She's going to," said Terry, forgetting his promise in his rage and triumph.

"She is, I hear!" Florrie said mockingly. "Who told you that?"

"She did; Auntie."

"Don't mind her at all, little boy," Florrie said severely. "She lives with her mother, and her mother wouldn't let you live with her."

"Well, she's not going to live with her any more," Terry said, knowing he had the better of her at last. "She's going to get married."

"Who is she going to get married to?" Florrie asked casually, but Terry could see she was impressed.

"A man in England, and I'm going to live with them. So there!"

"In England?" Florrie repeated, and Terry saw he had really knocked the stuffing out of her this time. Florrie had no one to bring her to England, and the jealousy was driving her mad. "And I suppose you're going?" she asked bitterly.

"I am going," Terry said, wild with excitement to see her overthrown; the grand lady who for all her airs had no one to bring her to England with them. "And I'm getting a bike of my own. So now!"

"Is that what she told you?" Florrie asked with a hatred and contempt that made him more furious still.

"She's going to, she's going to," he shouted furiously.

"Ah, she's only codding you, little boy," Florrie said contemptuously, splashing her long legs in the water while she continued to fix him with the same dark, evil, round-eyed look, exactly like a witch in a storybook. "Why did she send you down here at all so?"

"She didn't send me," Terry said, stooping to fling a handful of water in her face.

"But sure, I thought everyone knew that," she said idly, merely averting her face slightly to avoid the splashes. "She lets on to be your aunt but we all know she's your mother."

"She isn't," shrieked Terry. "My mother is dead."

"Ah, that's only what they always tell you," Florrie replied quietly. "That's what they told me too, but I knew it was lies. Your mother isn't dead at all, little boy. She got into trouble with a man and her mother made her send you down here to get rid of you. The whole village knows that."

"God will kill you stone dead for a dirty liar, Florrie Clancy," he said and then threw himself on her and began to pummel her with his little fat fists. But he hadn't the strength, and she merely pushed him off lightly and got up on the grassy bank, flushed and triumphant, pretending to smooth down the front of her dress.

"Don't be codding yourself that you're going to England at all, little boy," she said reprovingly. "Sure, who'd want you? Jesus knows I'm sorry for you," she added with mock pity, "and I'd like to do what I could for you, but you have no sense."

Then she went off in the direction of the wood, turning once or twice to give him her strange stare. He glared after her and danced and shrieked with hysterical rage. He had no idea what she meant, but he felt that she had got the better of him after all. "A big, bloody brute of nine," he said, and then began to run through the woods to the cottage, sobbing. He knew that God would kill her for the lies she had told, but if God didn't, Mrs. Early would. Mrs. Early was pegging up clothes on the line and peered down at him sourly.

"What ails you now didn't ail you before?" she asked.

"Florrie Clancy was telling lies," he shrieked, his fat face black with fury. "Big bloody brute!"

"Botheration to you and Florrie Clancy!" said Mrs. Early. "Look at the cut of you! Come here till I wipe your nose."

"She said my aunt wasn't my aunt at all," he cried.

"She what?" Mrs. Early asked incredulously.

"She said she was my mother—Auntie that gave me the boat," he said through his tears.

"Aha," Mrs. Early said grimly, "let me catch her round here again and I'll toast her backside for her, and that's what she wants, the little vagabond! Whatever your mother might do, she was a decent woman, but the dear knows who that one is or where she came from."

III

All the same it was a bad business for Terry. A very bad business! It is all very well having fights, but not when you're only five and live a mile away from the village, and there is nowhere for you to go but across the footbridge to the little railway station and the main road where you wouldn't see another kid once in a week. He'd have been very glad to make it up with Florrie, but she knew she had done wrong and that Mrs. Early was only lying in wait for her to ask her what she meant.

And to make it worse, his aunt didn't come for months. When she did, she came unexpectedly and Terry had to change his clothes in a hurry because there was a car waiting for them at the station. The car made up to Terry for the disappointment (he had never been in a car before), and to crown it, they were going to the seaside, and his aunt had brought him a brand-new bucket and spade.

They crossed the river by the little wooden bridge and there in the yard of the station was a posh grey car and a tall man beside it whom Terry hadn't seen before. He was a posh-looking fellow too, with a grey hat and a nice manner, but Terry didn't pay him much attention at first. He was too interested in the car.

"This is Mr. Walker, Terry," his aunt said in her loud way. "Shake hands with him nicely."

"How're ye, mister?" said Terry.

"But this fellow is a blooming boxer," Mr. Walker cried, letting on to be frightened of him. "Do you box, young Samson?" he asked.

"I do not," said Terry, scrambling into the back of the car and climbing up on the seat. "Hey, mister, will we go through the village?" he added.

"What do you want to go through the village for?" asked Mr. Walker.

"He wants to show off," said his aunt with a chuckle. "Don't you, Terry?"

"I do," said Terry.

"Sound judge!" said Mr. Walker, and they drove along the main road and up through the village street just as Mass was ending, and Terry, hurling himself from side to side, shouted to all the people he knew. First they gaped, then they laughed, finally they waved back. Terry kept shouting messages but they were lost in the noise and rush of the car. "Billy! Billy!" he screamed when he saw Billy Early outside the church. "This is my aunt's car. We're going for a spin. I have a bucket and spade." Florrie was standing outside the Post Office with her hands behind her back. Full of magnanimity and self-importance, Terry gave her a special shout and his aunt leaned out and waved, but though Florrie looked up she let on not to recognize them. That was Florrie all out, jealous even of the car!

Terry had not seen the sea before, and it looked so queer that he decided it was probably England. It was a nice place enough but a bit on the draughty side. There were whitewashed houses all along the beach. His aunt undressed him and made him put on bright blue bathing-drawers, but when he felt the wind he shivered and sobbed and clasped himself despairingly under the armpits.

"Ah, wisha, don't be such a baby!" his aunt said crossly.

She and Mr. Walker undressed too and led him by the hand to the edge of the water. His terror and misery subsided and he sat in a shallow place, letting the bright waves crumple on his shiny little belly. They were so like lemonade that he kept on tasting them, but they tasted salt. He decided that if this was England it was all right, though he would have preferred it with a park and a bicycle. There were other children making sand-castles and he decided to do the same, but after a while, to his great annoyance, Mr. Walker came to help him. Terry couldn't see why, with all that sand, he wouldn't go and make castles of his own.

"Now we want a gate, don't we?" Mr. Walker asked officiously.

"All right, all right, all right," said Terry in disgust. "Now, you go and play over there."

"Wouldn't you like to have a daddy like me, Terry?" Mr. Walker asked suddenly.

"I don't know," replied Terry. "I'll ask Auntie. That's the gate now."

"I think you'd like it where I live," said Mr. Walker. "We've much nicer places there."

"Have you?" asked Terry with interest. "What sort of places?"

"Oh, you know—roundabouts and swings and things like that."

"And parks?" asked Terry.

"Yes, parks."

"Will we go there now?" asked Terry eagerly.

"Well, we couldn't go there today; not without a boat. It's in England, you see; right at the other side of all that water."

"Are you the man that's going to marry Auntie?" Terry asked, so flabbergasted that he lost his balance and fell.

"Now, who told you I was going to marry Auntie?" asked Mr. Walker, who seemed astonished too.

"She did," said Terry.

"Did she, by jove?" Mr. Walker exclaimed with a laugh. "Well, I think it might be a very good thing for all of us, yourself included. What else did she tell you?"

"That you'd buy me a bike," said Terry promptly. "Will you?"

"Sure thing," Mr. Walker said gravely. "First thing we'll get you when you come to live with me. Is that a bargain?"

"That's a bargain," said Terry.

"Shake," said Mr. Walker, holding out his hand.

"Shake," replied Terry, spitting on his own.

He was content with the idea of Mr. Walker as a father. He could see he'd make a good one. He had the right principles.

They had their tea on the strand and then got back late to the station. The little lamps were lit on the platform. At the other side of the valley the high hills were masked in dark trees and no light showed the position of the Earlys' cottage. Terry was tired; he didn't want to leave the car, and began to whine.

"Hurry up now, Terry," his aunt said briskly as she lifted him out. "Say night-night to Mr. Walker."

Terry stood in front of Mr. Walker, who had got out before him, and then bowed his head.

"Aren't you going to say good night, old man?" Mr. Walker asked in surprise.

Terry looked up at the reproach in his voice and then threw himself blindly about his knees and buried his face in his trousers. Mr. Walker laughed and patted Terry's shoulder. His voice was quite different when he spoke again.

"Cheer up, Terry," he said. "We'll have good times yet."

"Come along now, Terry," his aunt said in a brisk official voice that terrified him.

"What's wrong, old man?" Mr. Walker asked.

"I want to stay with you," Terry whispered, beginning to sob. "I don't want to stay here. I want to go back to England with you."

"Want to come back to England with me, do you?" Mr. Walker repeated. "Well, I'm not going back tonight, Terry, but, if you ask Auntie nicely we might manage it another day."

"It's no use stuffing up the child with ideas like that," she said sharply.

"You seem to have done that pretty well already," Mr. Walker said quietly. "So you see, Terry, we can't manage it tonight. We must leave it for another day. Run along with Auntie now."

"No, no, no," Terry shrieked, trying to evade his aunt's arms. "She only wants to get rid of me."

"Now, who told you that wicked nonsense, Terry?" Mr. Walker said severely.

"It's true, it's true," said Terry. "She's not my auntie. She's my mother."

Even as he said it he knew it was dreadful. It was what Florrie Clancy said, and she hated his auntie. He knew it even more from the silence that fell on the other two. His aunt looked down at him and her look frightened him.

"Terry," she said with a change of tone, "you're to come with me at once and no more of this nonsense."

"Let him to me," Mr. Walker said shortly. "I'll find the place."

She did so and at once Terry stopped kicking and whining and nosed his way into Mr. Walker's shoulder. He knew the Englishman was for him. Besides he was very tired. He was half asleep already. When he heard Mr. Walker's step on the planks of the wooden bridge he looked up and saw the dark hillside, hooded with pines, and the river like lead in the last light. He woke again in the little dark bedroom which he shared with Billy. He was sitting on Mr. Walker's knee and Mr. Walker was taking off his shoes.

"My bucket," he sighed.

"Oh, by gum, lad," Mr. Walker said, "I'd nearly forgotten your bucket."

IV

Every Sunday after, wet or fine, Terry found his way across the footbridge and the railway station to the main road. There was a pub there, and men came from up from the valley and sat on the wall outside, waiting for the coast to be clear to slip in for a drink. In case there might be any danger of having to leave them behind, Terry brought his bucket and spade as well. You never knew when you'd need things like those. He sat at the foot of the wall near the men, where he could see the buses and cars coming from both directions. Sometimes a grey car like Mr. Walker's appeared from round the corner and he waddled up the road towards it, but the driver's face was always a disappointment. In the evenings when the first buses were coming back he returned to the cottage and Mrs. Early scolded him for moping and whining. He blamed himself a lot because all the trouble began when he broke his word to his aunt.

One Sunday, Florrie came up the main road from the village. She went past him slowly, waiting for him to speak to her, but he wouldn't. It was all her fault, really. Then she stopped and turned to speak to him. It was clear that she knew he'd be there and had come to see him and make it up.

"Is it anyone you're waiting for, Terry?" she asked.

"Never mind," Terry replied rudely.

"Because if you're waiting for your aunt, she's not coming," Florrie went on gently.

Another time Terry wouldn't have entered into conversation, but now he felt so mystified that he would have spoken to anyone who could tell him what was keeping his aunt and Mr. Walker. It was terrible to be only five, because nobody ever told you anything.

"How do you know?" he asked.

"Miss Clancy said it," replied Florrie confidently. "Miss Clancy knows everything. She hears it all in the post office. And the man with the grey car isn't coming either. He went back to England."

Terry began to snivel softly. He had been afraid that Mr. Walker wasn't really in earnest. Florrie drew closer to him and then sat on the grass bank beside him. She plucked a stalk and began to shred it in her lap.

"Why wouldn't you be said by me?" she asked reproachfully. "You know I was always your girl and I wouldn't tell you a lie."

"But why did Mr. Walker go back to England?" he asked.

"Because your aunt wouldn't go with him."

"She said she would."

"Her mother wouldn't let her. He was married already. If she went with him he'd have brought you as well. You're lucky he didn't."

"Why?"

"Because he was a Protestant," Florrie said primly. "Protestants have no proper religion like us."

Terry did his best to grasp how having a proper religion made up to a fellow for the loss of a house with lights that went off and on, a park and a bicycle, but he realized he was too young. At five it was still too deep for him.

"But why doesn't Auntie come down like she always did?"

"Because she married another fellow and he wouldn't like it."

"Why wouldn't he like it?"

"Because it wouldn't be right," Florrie replied almost pityingly. "Don't you see the English fellow have no proper religion, so he wouldn't mind, but the fellow she married owns the shop she works in, and Miss Clancy says 'tis surprising he married her at all, and he wouldn't like her to be coming here to see you. She'll be having proper children now, you see."

"Aren't we proper children?"

"Ah, no, we're not," Florrie said despondently.

"What's wrong with us?"

That was a question that Florrie had often asked herself, but she was too proud to show a small boy like Terry that she hadn't discovered the answer.

"Everything," she sighed.

"Florrie Clancy," shouted one of the men outside the pub, "what are you doing to that kid?"

"I'm doing nothing to him," she replied in a scandalized tone, starting as though from a dream. "He shouldn't be here by himself at all. He'll get run over. . . . Come on home with me now, Terry," she added, taking his hand.

"She said she'd bring me to England and give me a bike of my own," Terry wailed as they crossed the tracks.

"She was only codding," Florrie said confidently. Her tone changed gradually; it was becoming fuller, more scornful. "She'll forget all about you when she has other kids. Miss Clancy says they're all the same. She says there isn't one of them worth bothering your head about, that they never think of anyone only themselves. She says my father has pots of money. If you were in with me I might marry you when you're a bit more grown-up."

She led him up the short cut through the woods. The trees were turning all colours. Then she sat on the grass and sedately smoothed her frock about her knees.

"What are you crying for?" she asked reproachfully. "It was all your fault. I was always your girl. Even Mrs. Early said it. I always took your part when the others were against you. I wanted you not to be said by that old one and her promises, but you cared more for her and her old toys than you did for me. I told you what she was, but you wouldn't believe me, and now, look at you! If you'll swear to be always in with me I'll be your girl again. Will you?"

"I will," said Terry.

She put her arms about him and he fell asleep, but she remained solemnly holding him, looking at him with detached and curious eyes. He was hers at last. There were no more rivals. She fell asleep too and did not notice the evening train go up the valley. It was all lit up. The evenings were drawing in.

THE MISER

He used to sit all day, looking out from behind the dirty little window of his dirty little shop in Main Street; a man with a smooth oval pate and bleared, melancholy-looking, unblinking eyes; a hanging lip with a fag dangling from it, and hanging unshaven chins. It was a face you'd remember; swollen, ponderous, crimson, with a frame of jet-black hair plastered down on either side with bear's grease; and though the hair grew grey and the face turned yellow it seemed to make no difference: because he never changed his position you did not notice the change which came over him from within, and saw him at the end as you had seen him at first, planted there like an oak or a rock. He scarcely stirred even when someone pushed in the old glazed door and stumbled down the steps from the street. The effort seemed to be too much for him; the bleary, bloodshot eyes travelled slowly to some shelf, the arm reached lifelessly out; the coins dropped in the till. Then he shrugged himself and gazed out into the street again. Sometimes he spoke, and it always gave you a shock, for it was as if the statue of O'Connell had descended from its pedestal and inquired in a melancholy bass voice and with old-fashioned politeness for some member of your family. It was a thing held greatly in his favour that he never forgot an old neighbour.

Sometimes the children tormented him, looking in and making faces at him through the glass, so that they distracted him from his vigil, and then he roared at them without stirring. Sometimes they went too far and his face swelled and grew purple; he staggered to the door and bellowed after them in a powerful resonant voice that echoed to the other end of the town. But mostly he stayed there silent and undisturbed, and the dirt and disorder round him grew and greased his hair and clothes, while his face and chin with their Buddha-like gravity were shiny with spilt gravy. His only luxury was the Woodbine that went out between his lips. The cigarettes were on the shelf behind him, and all he had to do was to reach out for them; he didn't need to turn his head.

He was the last of a very good family, the Devereuxs, who had once been big merchants in the town. People remembered his old father driving into town in his own carriage; indeed, they remembered Tom Devereux himself as a bit of a masher, smoking a cigar and wearing a new flower in his buttonhole every day. But then he married beneath him and the match turned out badly. There was a daughter called Joan but she turned out badly too, started a child and went away, God knows where, and now he had no one to look after him but an old soldier called Faxy, a tall, stringy, ravaged-looking man, toothless and half mad. Faxy had attached himself to Tom years before as a batman. He boiled the kettle and brought the old man a cup of tea in the mornings.

"Orders for the day, general!" he would say then, springing to attention; and Devereux, after a lot of groaning, would fish out sixpence from under his pillow.

"And what the hell do you think I'm going to get for that?" Faxy would snarl, the smile withering from his puss.

"Oh, indeed," Devereux would bellow complacently, "you can get a very nice bit of black pudding for that."

"And is it black pudding you're going to drink instead of tea?"

"But when I haven't it, man?" the old man would shout, turning purple.

"You haven't, I hear!" Faxy would hiss with a wolfish grin, stepping from one foot to the other like a child short-taken. "Come on now, can't you? I can't be waiting the whole day for it. Baksheesh! Baksheesh for the sahib's tiffin!"

"I tell you to go away and not be annoying me," Devereux would shout, and that was all the satisfaction Faxy got. It was a nightmare to Faxy, trying to get money or credit.

"But he have it, man, he have it," he would hiss, leaning over the counters, trying to coax more credit out of the shopkeepers. "Boxes of it he have, man; nailed down and flowing over. He have two big trunks of it under the bed alone."

That was the report in town as well; everyone knew that the Devereuxs always had the tin and that old Tom hadn't lessened it much, and at one time or other, every shopkeeper had given him credit, and all ended by refusing it, seeing the old man in the window, day after day, looking as though he were immortal.

II

At long last he did have a stroke and had to take to his bed, upstairs in a stinking room with the sagging windowpanes padded and nailed against draughts from the Main Street, and the flowery wallpaper, layer on layer of it, hanging in bangles from the walls, while Faxy looked after the shop and made hay of the Woodbines and whatever else came handy. Not that there was much, only paraffin oil and candles and maybe a few old things like cards of castor-oil bottles that the commercials left on spec. Whenever a customer went out, bang, bang, bang! old Devereux thumped on the floor for Faxy.

"Who was that went out, Faxy?" he would groan. "I didn't recognize the voice."

"That was the Sheehan girl from the lane."

"Did you ask her how her father was?"

"I did not, indeed, ask how her father was. I have something else to think about."

"You ought to have asked her all the same," the old man grumbled. "What did she want?"

"A couple of candles," hissed Faxy. "Is there anything else you'd like to know?"

"It wasn't a couple of candles, Donnell. Don't you try and deceive me. I heard every word of it. I distinctly heard her asking for something else as well."

"A pity the stroke affected your hearing," snarled Faxy.

"Don't you try and deceive me, I say," boomed Devereux. "I have it all checked, Donnell, every ha'p'orth. Mind now what I'm saying!"

Then one morning while Faxy was smoking a cigarette and studying the racing on the previous day's paper, the shop door opened gently and Father Ring came in. Father Ring was a plausible little Kerryman with a sand-coloured face and a shock of red hair. He was always very deprecating, with an excuse-me air, and came in sideways, on tiptoe, wearing a shocked expression—it is only Kerryman who can do things like that.

"My poor man," he whispered, leaning over the counter to Faxy. "I'm sorry for your trouble. Himself isn't well on you."

"If he isn't," snarled Faxy, looking as much like the Stag at Bay as made no difference, "he's well looked after."

"I know that, Faxy," the priest said, nodding. "I know that well. Still, 'twould be no harm if I had a few words with him. A man like that might go in a flash. . . . Tell me, Faxy," he whispered with his hand across his lips and his head to one side, "are his affairs in order?"

"How the hell would I know when the old devil won't even talk about them?" asked Faxy.

"That's bad, Faxy," said Father Ring gravely. "That's very bad. That's a great risk you're running, a man like you that must be owed a lot of money. If anything happened him you might be thrown on the road without a ha'penny. Whisper here to me," he went on, drawing Faxy closer and whispering into his ear the way no one but a Kerryman can do it, without once taking his eyes off Faxy's face. "If you want to make sure of your rights, you'd better see he has his affairs in order. Leave it to me and I'll do what I can." Then he nodded and winked, and away with him upstairs, leaving Faxy gaping after him.

He opened the bedroom door a couple of inches, bowed, and smiled in with his best excuse-me-God-help-me expression. The smile was one of the hardest things he had ever had to do, because the smell was something shocking. Then he tiptoed in respectfully, his hand outstretched.

"My poor man!" he whispered. "My poor fellow! How are you at all? I needn't ask."

"Poorly, father, poorly," rumbled Devereux, rolling his lazy bloodshot eyes at him.

"I can see that. I can see you are. Isn't there anything I can do for you?" Father Ring tiptoed back to the door and gave a glance out at the landing. "I'm surprised that man of yours didn't send for me," he said reproachfully. "You don't look very comfortable. Wouldn't you be better off in hospital?"

"I won't tell you a word of a lie, father," Devereux said candidly. "I couldn't afford it."

"No, to be sure, to be sure, 'tis expensive, 'tis, 'tis," Father Ring agreed feelingly. "And you have no one to look after you?"

"I have not, father, I'm sorry to say."

"Oh, my, my, my! At the end of your days! You couldn't get in touch with the daughter, I suppose?"

"No, father, I could not," Devereux said shortly.

"I'm sorry about that. Wisha, isn't life queer. A great disappointment, that girl, Julia."

"Joan, father."

"Joan I mean. To be sure, to be sure, Joan. A great disappointment."

"She was, father."

And then, when Devereux had told his little story, Father Ring, bending forward with his hairy hands joined, whispered:

"Tell me, wouldn't it be a good thing if you had a couple of nuns?"

"A couple of what, father?" asked Devereux in astonishment.

"A couple of nuns. From the hospital. They'd look after you properly."

"Ah, father," Devereux said indignantly as though the priest had accused him of some nasty mean action, "sure I have no money for nuns."

"Well now," Father Ring said thoughtfully, "that's a matter you might leave to me. Myself and the nuns are old friends. Sure, that man, that What's-his-name, that fellow you have downstairs— sure, that poor unfortunate could do nothing for you."

"Only break my heart, father," Devereux sighed gustily. "I won't tell you a word of a lie. He have me robbed."

"Well, leave it to me," Father Ring said with a wink. "He might meet his match."

Downstairs he whispered into Faxy's ear with his hand shading his mouth and his eyes following someone down the street:

"I'd say nothing just at present, Faxy. I'll get a couple of nuns to look after him. You might find him easier to deal with after that."

III

It wasn't until the following morning that Faxy understood the full implications of that. Then it was too late. The nuns were installed and couldn't be shifted; one old, tough, and hairy, whom Faxy instantly christened "the sergeant-major," the other young and good-looking.

"Come now," the sergeant-major said to Faxy. "Put on this apron and give that floor a good scrubbing."

"Scrubbing?" bawled Faxy. "Name of Ja—" and stopped himself just in time. "What's wrong with that floor?" he snarled. "You could eat your dinner off that floor."

"You'd have the makings of it anyway," the sergeant-major said dryly, "only 'twouldn't be very appetizing. I have a bath of water on for you. And mind and put plenty of Jeyes' Fluid."

"I was discharged from the army with rheumatics," Faxy said, grabbing his knee illustratively. "Light duty is all I'm fit for. I have it on my discharge papers. And who's going to look after the shop?"

It was all no use. Down he had to go on his knees like any old washerwoman with a coarse apron round his waist and scrub every inch of the floor with carbolic soap and what he called Jeyes's Fluid. The sergeant-major was at his heels the whole time, telling him to change the water and wash the brush and cracking jokes about his rheumatics till she had him leaping. Then, under the eyes of the whole street, he had to get out on the window-ledge, wash the window, and strip away the comforting felt that had kept out generations of draughts; and afterwards scrape the walls while the young nun went after him with a spray, killing the bugs, she said—as if a couple of bugs ever did anyone any harm!

Faxy muttered rebelliously to himself about people who never saw anything of life only to plank their ass in a featherbed while poor soldiers had to sleep out with nothing but gravestones for mattresses and corpses all round them and never complained. From his Way of the Cross he glared at Devereux, only asking for one word of an order to mutiny, but the old man only looked away at the farther wall with bleared and frightened eyes. He seemed to imagine that all he had to do was lie doggo to make the sergeant-major think he was dead.

But then his own turn came and Faxy, on face and hands on the landing, looked up through the chink in the door and saw them strip Devereux naked to God and the world and wash him all down the belly. "Sweet Christ preserve us!" he muttered. It looked to him like the end of the world. Then they turned the old man over and washed him all down the back. He never uttered a groan or a moan, and relaxed like a Christian martyr in the flames, looking away with glassy eyes at floor and ceiling so that he would not embarrass them seeing what they had no right to see.

He contained himself till he couldn't contain himself any longer and then burst into a loud wail for Faxy and the bucket, but Faxy realized to his horror that even this little bit of decency was being denied him and that he was being made to sit up in bed with the young one holding him under the armpits while the sergeant-major planted him on top of some new-fangled yoke she was after ordering up from the chemist's.

It was too much for Faxy. At heart he was a religious man and to see women dressed as nuns behaving with no more modesty than hospital orderlies broke his spirit entirely. He moaned and tore his hair and cursed his God. He didn't wait to see the old man's hair cut, and his mattress and bedclothes that he had lain in so comfortably all the long years taken out to be burned, but prowled from shop to street and street back to shop, looking up at the window or listening at the foot of the stairs, telling his sad tale to all who passed. "We didn't know how happy we were," he snarled. "God pity the poor that fall into their hands! We had a king's life and look at us now, like paupers in the workhouse without a thing we can call our own!"

He was even afraid to go into his own kitchen for fear the sergeant-major would fall on him and strip him as well. The woman had no notion of modesty. She might even say he was dirty. A woman who'd say what she had said about the bedroom floor would stop at nothing. It was only when her back was turned that he crept up the stairs on tiptoe and silently pushed in the bedroom door. The change from the morning was terrible. It went to Faxy's heart. He knew now he no longer had a home to call his own: windows open above and below, a draught that would skin a brass monkey and flowers in a vase on a table near the bed. The old man was lying there like a corpse, clean, comfortable, and collapsed. It was only after a few moments that he opened his weary bloodshot eyes and gazed at Faxy with a faraway, heartbroken air. Faxy glared down at him like a great gaunt bird of prey, clutching his ragged old shirt back from his chest and shaking his skeleton head.

"Jasus!" he whispered in agony. " 'Tis like a second crucifixion."

"Would you gimme a fag, Faxy, if you please?" pleaded Devereux in a dying voice.

"Ask your old jenny-asses for one!" hissed Faxy malevolently.

IV

Devereux was just beginning to get over the shock when Father Ring called again. Whatever it might have cost himself and Faxy, the clean-up was a great ease to Father Ring.

"My poor man!" he said, shaking Devereux's hand and casting a sly glance round the room, "how are you today? You're looking better. Well, now, aren't they great little women? Tell me, are they feeding you properly?"

"Very nice, father," Devereux said feebly in a tone of astonishment, as if he thought after the shocking way they had already behaved to him, starvation was the only thing he could have expected. "Very nice indeed. I had a nice little bit of chicken and a couple of poppies and a bit of cabbage."

"Sure, you couldn't have nicer," said Father Ring, smacking his own lips over it.

"I had, indeed," Devereux boomed, raising his arm and looking at the clean hairy skin inside the shirtband as though he wondered whom it belonged to. "And I had rice pudding," he added reflectively, "and a cup of tea."

"Ah, man, they'll have you trotting like a circus pony before they're done with you," said Father Ring.

"I'm afraid it come too late, father," sighed the old man as if the same notion had crossed him mind. "I had a lot of hardship."

"You had, you poor soul, you had," sighed Father Ring. "And, of course, when it comes to our turn we must be resigned. I say we must be resigned," he added firmly. "It comes to us all, sooner or later, and if our conscience is clear and our—oh, by the way, I nearly forgot it; my head is going—I suppose your own little affairs are in order?"

"What's that you say, father?" Devereux whispered with a timid, trapped air, raising his head from the pillow.

"Your affairs," murmured Father Ring. "Are they in order? I mean, have you your will made?"

"I won't tell you a word of a lie, father," the old man said bashfully. "I have not."

"Well, now, listen to me," Father Ring said persuasively, pulling his chair closer to the bed, "wouldn't it be a good thing for you to do? 'Tisn't, God knows, for the little that either of us will leave, but for the sake of peace and quietness after we've gone. You saw them as I did myself, fighting over a few sticks."

"I did, father, I did."

" 'Tis the scandal of it," said Father Ring. "And God between us and all harm, the hour might come for any of us. It might come for myself and I a younger man than you."

"Wouldn't I want an attorney, father?" Devereux asked timidly.

"Ah, what attorney?" exclaimed Father Ring. "Aren't I better than any attorney? 'Pon my soul, I don't know why I didn't go in for the law. As it happens," he added, scowling and fumbling in his pockets, "I have some writing paper with me. I hope I didn't leave my specs behind. I did! As sure as you're there, I did. What sort of old head have I? . . . No, I declare to my goodness, I brought them for once. Ah, man alive," he exclaimed, looking at Devereux over the specs, "I have to do this every month of my life. 'Tis astonishing, the number of people that put it on the long finger. . . . I may as well get it down as I'm here. I can write the rigmarole in after. . . . What'll we say to begin with? You'd like to leave a couple of pounds for Masses, I suppose?"

"God knows I would, father," Devereux said devoutly.

"Well, what'll we say? Give me a figure! Ten? Twenty?"

"I suppose so, father," Devereux replied hesitatingly.

"Well, now, make it whatever you like," said Father Ring, pointing the fountain pen like a dart at him and giving him a long look through the spectacles, a sort of professional look, quite different from the ones he gave over and round them. "But, remember, Masses are the only investment you can draw on in the next world. The only friends you can be sure won't forget you. Think again before you say the last word on Masses."

"How much would you say yourself, father?" asked Devereux, hypnotised by the gleam of the spectacles like a rabbit by the headlights of a car.

"Well, that's a matter for you. You know what you can afford. You might like to make it a hundred. Or even more."

"We'll say a hundred so," said Devereux.

"Good man! Good man! I like a man that knows his own mind. You'd be astonished, the people that don't seem to be able to say 'yes' or 'no.' And what'll we do about the—" he nodded towards the door—"the holy ladies? 'Twould be expected."

"Would the same thing be enough, father?"

"To tell you the truth, Mr. Devereux, I think it would," said Father Ring, bobbing his head and giving Devereux an unprofessional dart over the top of his spectacles. "I'll go farther. I'd say 'twould be generous. Women are lick alike. I don't know how it is, Mr. Devereux, but a woman crossed in love finds some fatal attraction in building. Building is the ruin of those poor women. A fool and his money—but you know the old proverb."

"I do, father."

"And the monks? As we're on the subject of charities, what are we going to do about the monks?"

Devereux gave him an appealing glance. Father Ring rose, pursing his lips and putting his hands behind his back. He stood at the window and gazed down the street, his head on his chest and his eyes strained over his glasses.

"Look at that scut, Foley, sneaking into Johnny Desmond's," he said as though to himself. "That fellow will be the death of his poor unfortunate wife. . . . I think so, Mr. Devereux," he added in a loud voice, turning on his heel and raising his head like a man who has received a sudden illumination. "I think so. Religious orders! 'Tisn't for me to be criticizing them, God knows, but they'd surprise you. 'Pon my soul, they'd surprise you! The jealousy between them over a miserable couple of hundred pounds! Those poor fellows would be fretting over a slight like that for years to come."

" 'Twouldn't be wishing to me," said Devereux, shaking his head regretfully.

" 'Twouldn't, man, 'twouldn't, 'twouldn't," cried Father Ring as if astonished at Devereux's perspicacity, and implying by his tone that if the bad wishes of the monks didn't actually follow the old man to the next world they'd make very heavy weather for any prayers which did. "You're right, Mr. Devereux, it would not be wishing to you. . . . Now, coming nearer home," he whispered with a nervous glance over his shoulder, "what about that man of yours? They'll be expecting you to provide for him."

"He robbed me, father," Devereux said sullenly, his heavy face settling into the expression of an obstinate child.

"Ah, let me alone, let me alone!" said Father Ring, waving the paper in his face with exasperation. "I know all about it. That British Army! 'Tis the ruination of thousands."

"The couple of cigarettes I'd have," the old man went on, turning his red eyes on the priest while his deep voice throbbed like a 'cello with the dint of self-pity, "he'd steal them on me. Often and often—I won't tell you a word of a lie, father—I'd go down to the shop of a morning and I wouldn't have a smoke. Not a smoke!"

"Oh, my, my!" said Father Ring, clucking and nodding over the villainy of man.

"The packets of Lux," intoned Devereux solemnly, raising his right hand in affirmation, "that's as true as the Almighty God is looking down on me this moment, father, he'd take them and sell them from door to door, a half dozen for the price of a medium. And I sitting here, gasping for a cigarette!"

"Well, well!" sighed the priest. "But still, Mr. Devereux, you know you're after forgiving him all that."

"Forgiving him is one thing," the old man said stubbornly, "but leaving him a legacy is another thing entirely, father. Oh, no."

"But as a sign you forgive him!" the priest said coaxingly. "A— what'll I call it?—a token! Some little thing."

"Not a ha'penny, father," said Devereux in the voice of a judge with the black cap on. "Not one solitary ha'penny."

"Well, now, Mr. Devereux," Father Ring pleaded, "fifty pounds. What is it? 'Tis neither here nor there and 'twould mean a lot to that poor wretch."

Suddenly the door burst open and Faxy, who had been listening at the keyhole, charged in on them, a great, gaunt skeleton of a man with mad eyes and clenched fists.

"Fifty pounds?" he shouted. "Fifty pounds? Is it mad ye are, the pair of ye?"

Old Devereux began to struggle frantically up in the bed,

throwing off the clothes with his swollen old hands and gasping for breath so that he could tell Faxy what he thought of him.

"You robber!" he croaked away back in his throat. "If I done you justice I'd have you up in the body of the jail."

"Come now, Mr. Devereux, come, come!" cried Father Ring, alarmed that the old man might drop dead on him before the will was even sketched. "Compose yourself," he said, putting down his papers and trying to get Devereux to lie back.

"I won't give him a ha'penny," roared Devereux in a voice that could be heard at the opposite side of the street. "Not one ha'penny! Leave him support himself out of all he stole from the till!"

"And a hell of a lot there ever was to steal!" hissed Faxy with his gaunt head bowed, grinning back at him.

"Not a ha'penny!" repeated the old man frantically, pummeling his knees with his fists and blowing himself up like a balloon till he turned all colours.

"Two hundred and fifty pounds," snarled Faxy with his toothless gums, pointing at the palm of his left hand as if he had it all noted there. "That's what I'm owed. I have it all down in black and white. Back wages. The War Office won't see me wronged."

"You robber!" panted Devereux.

"Sister!" cried Father Ring, throwing the door open. "Sister Whatever-your-name is, send for the police! Tell them I want this fellow locked up."

"Leave that one out of it!" hissed Faxy, dragging Father Ring back from the door. Faxy wasn't afraid of the police, but he was scared out of his wits by the sergeant-major of the nuns. "We want no women in it. Play fair and fight like a man. Fair play is all I ask. I done for him what no one else would do."

"Mr. Devereux," Father Ring said earnestly, "he's right. The man is right. He's entitled to something. He could upset the will."

"God knows, father, that's not what I want," said Faxy. He sat on the edge of the bed, began to sob, and brushed away the tears with his hand. "I deserved better after my years of hardship. No one knows what I went through with him."

"You sweet God, listen to him!" croaked Devereux despairingly. "Black puddings and old sausages. Not one decent bite of food crossed my lips, father, all the long years he's with me. Not till the blessed nuns came."

"Because they can get the credit," snarled Faxy, shaking his fist at his boss while his tears dried as though by magic. "If you handed me out the money instead of locking it up, you could have bacon and cabbage every day of the week. I was batman to better men than you. You were too near, you old bugger, you, and now 'tis going on you whether you like it or not on medicines and Jeyses Fluid and chamberpots. That's all you have out of it at the end of your days."

"Be quiet now, be quiet!" said Father Ring. "You'll get something, even though you don't deserve it. I'll take it on myself to put him down for another hundred, Mr. Devereux. You won't deny me that?"

"A hundred strokes of the cat-and-nine-tails," grumbled the old man. "But I won't deny you, father. I'll offer it up. . . . That it might choke you!" he added charitably to Faxy.

"And now, Mr. D., I won't keep you much longer. There's just Julia."

"Joan, father."

"Joan I mean. To be sure, Joan. Or the little—you know who I'm talking of. Was it a little boy? 'Pon my soul, my memory is gone."

"Nothing, father," Devereux said firmly, settling himself back in his pillows and gazing out the window.

"What's that?" Faxy shouted, scandalized. "Your daughter!"

"This have nothing to do with you, Donnell," said Devereux. "It have nothing to do with anyone."

"Now, you're wrong there, Mr. Devereux," Father Ring said with a quelling professional glance. "I say you're wrong there. Whatever little disagreement ye might have or whatever upset she might cause you, this is no time to remember it."

"I won't leave her a ha'penny, father," Devereux said firmly. " 'Tis no use to be at me. Anything that's over can go to the Church."

"Christ look down on the poor!" cried Faxy, raising his arms to heaven. "Stick and stone instead of flesh and bone."

"Will you be quiet?" snapped Father Ring. "Now, Mr

Devereux, I understand your feelings; I understand them perfectly, but 'tisn't right. Do you know what they'd say? Have you any notion of the wickedness of people in this town? They'd say there was undue influence, Mr. Devereux. You might have the whole will upset on you for the sake of—what'll I say? A hundred? Two hundred? A trifle anyway."

"This is my will, father, not yours," Devereux said with sudden, surprising dignity. "I'm after telling you my wishes, and Donnell here is a witness. Everything else is to go to the Church, barring a few pounds to keep the family vault in order. The Devereuxs are an old family, father," he added with calm pride. "They were a great family in their day, and I'd like the grave to be respected when I'm gone."

That night the will was signed and the substance of it was the talk of the town. Many blamed old Devereux for being hard and unnatural; more blamed Father Ring for being so grasping. Faxy got credit on the strength of it and came home fighting drunk, under the impression that the old man was already dead and that the priest had cheated him out of his inheritance; but the nuns locked him out and he slept in the straw in Kearney's yard, waking in the middle of the night and howling like a dog for his lost master.

But Devereux had no intention of dying. He began to improve visibly under the nuns' care. He had a little handbell on the table by his bed, and whenever he felt bored he rang for the sergeant-major to keep him company. He had taken a great fancy to her, and he just rang whenever he remembered anything more about the history of the Devereuxs. When he tired of this he held her hand while she read him a chapter from the Imitation of Christ or the Lives of the Saints.

"That's beautiful reading, sister," he said, stroking her hand.

"Sure, there's nothing like it," said the sergeant-major.

"Beautiful reading," sighed Devereux with a far-away air. "Don't we miss a lot in life, sister?"

"Ah, musha, we all miss a lot, but God will make it up to us, we hope. Sunshine in this life, shadow in the next."

"I'd like a bit of sunshine too, sister," he said. "Ye're very good to me and I didn't forget ye in my will."

He talked a lot about his will and even said he was thinking of changing it in favour of the nuns. The only trouble was that Father Ring wouldn't approve, being a strong-minded man himself, and Devereux could never warm to solicitors from the time they started sending him letters. The rudeness of some of those solicitors' letters was still on his mind. He got really lively at times and even suggested that the sergeant-major might read him some novels by Mrs. Braddon. He was very fond of the works of Mrs. Braddon, he said.

"I suppose you'll be renewing that bottle for me, sister?" he said on one occasion. "I wonder would you get me something else at the same time?"

"I will to be sure, Mr. Devereux. What is it?"

"Well," he said bashfully, "I'd like a little drop of hair-oil, if you please. My hair doesn't lie down well without it. The scented kind is the kind I like."

She got him the hair-oil and did his hair for him while he looked at her fondly and commented on her hands. Beautiful, gentle hands she had, he said. Then she gave him the mirror to see himself, and he was so shocked that tears came to his eyes.

"Now," she said briskly, "there's a fine handsome man for you!"

"I was very handsome once, sister," he said mournfully. "The handsomest man in the town, I was supposed to be. People used to stop and look after me in the street. Dandy Devereux they used to call me."

Then he asked for the scissors to clip his moustache.

He made a most beautiful and edifying death, with the nuns at either side of him saying the prayers for the dying, and when they had laid him out the sergeant-major went down to the kitchen and had a good cry to herself.

" 'Tis a hard old life," she said to the young nun. "You're left with them long enough to get fond of them, and then either they get better or they die on you, and you never see them again. If 'twas only an old dog you'd be sorry for him, and he was a fine gentlemanly old man, God rest him."

Then, having tidied away her pots and pans and had a last look at old Tom Devereux, the man who had stroked her hands and praised them as no one else had done since she was a girl, she washed her eyes and went back to her convent.

After Requiem High Mass next day Devereux went to join the rest of his family within the ruined walls of the abbey they had founded in the fifteenth century, and by the time Father Ring got back from the funeral Faxy had already started prying. The great iron-bound chests were in the centre of the floor and Faxy had borrowed a set of tools. They opened the chests between them but there was nothing inside only old screws, bolts, washers, bits of broken vases and an enormous selection of pipe-bowls and stems. Father Ring was so incredulous that he put on his glasses to examine them better. By that time he was ready to believe they were pieces of eight in disguise.

"I made a great mistake," he said, sitting back on the floor beside the chest. "I should have asked him where he had it."

He still had not even faced the possibility that Devereux hadn't it. They stayed on till midnight, searching. Next day they had two men from the builders in. Every floor was ripped up, every chimney searched, every hollow bit of wall burst in. Faxy was first everywhere with a lighted candle, and Father Ring followed, stroking his chin. A crowd had gathered in the street, and at intervals the priest stood at the window and surveyed them moodily over his glasses. He had a nasty feeling that the crowd would be well pleased if he failed.

Eddie Murphy, the undertaker, came up the stairs looking anxious. Eddie was owed thirty quid so he had good cause for anxiety.

"Did ye find it, father?" he asked.

"I'm afraid, Eddie," Father Ring said, looking round his glasses, "we were had. We were had, boy, all of us. 'Tis a great disappointment, a great disappointment, Eddie, but 'pon my soul, he was a remarkable man."

Then he took his shabby old soft hat and went home.

THE HOUSE THAT
JOHNNY BUILT

EVERY morning about the same time Johnny Desmond came to the door of his shop for a good screw up and down the street. He was like an old cat stretching himself after a nap. He had his cap down over his left eye and his hands in his trouser pockets, and first he inspected the sky, then the Square end of Main Street, then the Abbey end, and finally there were a lot of small personal stares at other shops and at people who passed. Johnny owned the best general store in town, a man who came in from the country without, as you might say, a boot to his foot. He had a red face, an apoplectic face which looked like a plum pudding you'd squeezed up and down till it bulged sideways, so that the features were all flattened and spread out and the two eyes narrowed into slits. As if that was not enough he looked at you from under the peak of his cap as though you were the headlights of a car, his right eye cocked, his left screwed up, till his whole face was as wrinkled as a roasted apple.

Now, one morning as Johnny looked down towards the Abbey, what should he see but a handsome woman in a white coat coming up towards him with her head bowed and her hands in her coat pockets. She was a woman he had never before, to his knowledge, laid eyes on, and he stared at her and saluted, and then stood looking after her with his left eye closed as though he were still a bit blinded by her headlights.

"Tom!" he called without looking round.

"Yes, Mr. D.?" said his assistant from behind the counter.

"Who's that, Tom?" asked Johnny, knowing he needn't specify.

"That's the new doctor," said Tom.

"Doctor?" echoed Johnny, swinging his head right round.

"Doctor O'Brien in the dispensary."

"Which O'Briens are they, Tom?" asked Johnny in a baffled tone.

"Micky the Miser," said Tom.

"Micky of Asragh?" exclaimed Johnny, as if it were too much for human reason.

Every morning after that he waited for her, and even strode up the street alongside her, rolling along like a barrel on props and jingling the coin in his trouser pocket.

"Tom!" he called when he returned.

"Yes, Mr. D.?"

"There's style for you!" grunted Johnny.

"She can damn well afford it," grunted Tom.

"There's breeding for you!" said Johnny.

"She's a bitch for her beer," said Tom.

But beer or no beer—and Johnny had a light hand on the liquor himself—he was impressed. He was more than impressed; he was inspired. He ordered a new brown suit and a new soft hat, put on a new gold watch-chain, and set off one night for the doctor's digs. They showed him into the parlour. Parlours always fascinated Johnny. Leave alone the furniture, which is a book in itself, a roomful of photos will set up a man of inquiring mind for life.

The doctor came in, a bit bosomy in a yellow blouse, and Johnny saw with interest and amusement that at the very first glance she took in the gold chain. She was a shy sort of girl, and the most you got from her as a rule was a hasty glance, but that same would blister you. He liked that in her. He liked a girl not to be a fool.

"I suppose you're surprised to see me?" said Johnny.

"I'm delighted, of course," she said in a high singsong, the way they speak in Asragh. "I hope there's nothing the matter?"

"Well, now," said Johnny, who was by way of being a bit of a joker, "you put your finger on it. 'Tis the old heart."

I

"Is it codding me you are?" she asked with a shocked look, her head bowed.

"Oh, the devil a cod," said Johnny, delighted with his reception. "I came to you because there's no one else I'd trust."

"'Tis probably indigestion," she said. "Are you sleeping all right?"

"Poorly," said Johnny.

"Is it palpitations?"

"Thumps," said Johnny, indicating how his heart went pit-a-pat.

"Go to God!" she exclaimed, drawing down the blind a little and giving an inquisitive look down the street at the same time. "Open that old shirt and give us a look at you."

"I'd be too shy," said Johnny drawing back in mock alarm.

"Shy, my nanny!" she exclaimed. "What old nonsense you have! Will you open it before I drag it off you?"

"And besides," Johnny said confidentially, "what's wrong with my heart wouldn't show through the speaking-tube. Sit down there till I be talking to you."

"Ah, botheration to you and your old jokes!" she cried in exasperation. "Will you have a drop of whisky?—though God knows you don't deserve it."

"Whisky?" chuckled Johnny, well-pleased with the success of his act. "What's that? Give us a drop till I try it?"

As she poured out the whisky Johnny took out his cigarettes, and at once her eye was caught by the silver case—a girl in a thousand!

"That's a new cigarette-case you have," she said. "Is it silver?"

"'Tis," said Johnny.

"Ah, God, Johnny," she said, screwing up her eyes as she struck a light, "you must be rolling in money."

"I am," said Johnny.

"Aren't you the selfish old devil wouldn't share it with some poor woman?"

"I'm coming to that," said Johnny.

He took the tumbler from her, put one thumb in the armhole of his vest and waited till she sat down on the sofa, her goldy-brown hair coming loose and the finest pair of legs in the county tucked under her. Then he leaned back in his chair and gave his mouth a wiggle to limber it up.

"I'm fifty," he said to the fire-screen. "Fifty or near it," he added to herself. "I'm a well-to-do man. I never had a day's sickness, barring one rupture I got about twelve year ago. 'Twas the way I was lugging an old packing-case from the shop to the van."

"Was it an operation you had?" she asked with professional curiosity.

" 'Twas."

"Was it Caulfield did it?"

"That fellow!" Johnny said contemptuously. "I wouldn't leave him sew on a button for me. I had Surgeon Hawthorne. Forty guineas he charged me."

"Forty?" she exclaimed. "He saw you coming."

"And sixteen for the nursing home," Johnny added bitterly. "I wish I could make my money as easy. But anyway, between the jigs and the reels, I never thought much about marriage, and besides, the women in this town wouldn't suit me at all." He let his chair fall back into position and leaned across the table towards her, his glass to one side, his pudgy hands clasped before him. "The sort of man I am, I like a woman with a bit of style, and the women in this town that have style have no nature, and the ones that have nature have no style. I declare to my God," he burst out indignantly, waving one hand in the air, "whatever the hell they do to them in convent schools you couldn't get a laugh out of them. They're killed with grandeur. But you're different. You have the nature and you have the style."

"Ah, hold on, Johnny!" cried the doctor in alarm. "What ails you? 'Tisn't asking me to marry you you are?"

"If 'tisn't that same, 'tis no less," said Johnny stoutly.

"Why then, I'll do nothing of the sort," she retorted with the Asragh lilt in her voice like a dive-bomber swooping and soaring; as pretty a tune as ever you'd hear in the mouth of a good-looking girl unless she actually happened to be pitching you to blazes. "Sure, God Almighty, Johnny, you're old enough to be my father."

"If I'm older I'm steadier," said Johnny, not liking the turn the conversation was taking.

"Like the Rock of Cashel," she said cuttingly. "But I never had much of a smack for history."

"Now, what you ought to do," said Johnny cunningly, "is to talk to your father. See what advice will he give you. He's the smartest businessman in this part of the world, and the man that says it is no fool."

"Ah, Johnny, will you have a bit of sense?" she begged. "Sure, that sort of family haggling is over and done with these fifty years. You wouldn't get a girl in the whole county to let her father put a halter round her neck like that."

"Are you sure now?" asked Johnny, feeling he might be just a little behind the times.

"Ah, of course I'm sure. God Almighty, Johnny," she added, with the same dive-bomber swoop in her voice, "isn't it the one little bit of pleasure we have?"

"I see, I see," muttered Johnny, meaning that he didn't, and he stood up, dug his hands in his trouser pockets, and spun on one leg, studying the pattern in the carpet.

"Of course," he went on in torment, "you might be misled about what I'm worth. I'm worth a lot of money. Even your friend the bank manager doesn't know all I'm worth. No, nor half it."

"Ah, Con Doody never even mentioned your name to me," she said furiously, jumping up and giving him a glare. "Sure, I wouldn't give a snap of my fingers for all your old money."

"And you won't ask your father?"

"What a thing I'd do!"

"There's no harm done so," Johnny said stiffly. "You'll excuse my asking."

And off he went in a huff. Next morning when she passed on her way to the dispensary, there was no sign of him. That vexed her, because she was just beginning to be sorry for not having taken him easier, and she worked herself up into such a temper that she told all about it at the bridge party that evening.

"And I declare to God," she concluded innocently, "he went out the door on me as if I was a bad neighbour that wouldn't give him the loan of my flatiron."

II

But at the same time you couldn't help admiring Johnny's obstinacy. He was the sort who can do without something all the days of their lives, but from the moment the idea occurs to them, it gives them no peace. A month passed; two months passed; Johnny, everything awake in him, never stopped brooding and planning. And finally he went to John O'Connor, the County Council architect.

"Tell me," he said, leaning his two arms on the table, his left eye screwed up and his lower lip thrust out, "the couple of old houses I have there at the corner of the Skehenagh Road—what sort of place could you make of them?"

"Begor, I don't know, Johnny," O'Connor said blandly, "unless you were thinking of giving them to the National Museum."

"I'm thinking of knocking them down," said Johnny grimly.

"I see," said O'Connor, sitting back and folding his hands. "You could do a nice little job there all right if you had the tenants."

"Never mind about the tenants," said Johnny. "What I'm thinking of is a shop."

"What sort of shop?" O'Connor asked with new interest.

"That's for me to know and you to find out," retorted Johnny with a chuckle. "I want a new shop and a new house."

"And I suppose I have to find out what sort of house you want as well?" O'Connor asked innocently.

"How many rooms would there be in that house of the bank manager's?" asked Johnny.

"Doody's!" O'Connor exclaimed. "But that's a big place, man."

"You couldn't swing a cat in that old place I have now," said Johnny.

"I see," said O'Connor dryly. " 'Tis cats you're going in for."

But it wasn't cats Johnny was going in for at all, but chemistry. A chemist's shop, if you please! And Johnny a man that never in his life sold more in that line than a cake of soap or a bottle of castor oil. The funny thing was that no one seemed to see that it might have anything to do with the doctor. The true grandeur of Johnny's fantasy was something beyond the conception of the town.

The house was a handsome affair. O'Connor got a free hand with everything, furniture and all, and he might have chosen the pictures as well, only that by way of a joke he suggested a lot of Old Masters as being suitable for an old bachelor. That settled it. Johnny didn't like being reminded of his failure with the doctor, so he said explosively that he was in no hurry; the pictures could wait.

He had the car to the station the night the new chemist arrived. She was a very pretty girl, just out of training, and with a nice, pleasing, unaffected air. Johnny had selected her himself from among a half-dozen candidates, principally for her manners, and he was glad to see that he had been right about these. Affectation in girls was the one thing Johnny couldn't stand; he said it frightened customers away.

All that day he had been driving himself and the maid crazy seeing that everything in the house was right for the new chemist; flowers on her dressing-table, the towels fresh, the water boiling. When Johnny was that way he was like a hen with an egg, poking round the kitchen and picking things up to ask what they were for. While the girl was upstairs he walked from one room to another and stopped in the hall with his head cocked to hear what she was up to now. He was waiting for her in the hall when she came down. She was looking grand. No wonder she would, after all the stories she had heard of the awful lives of chemists in Irish small towns.

"Was everything all right?" growled Johnny.

"Oh, grand, Mr. Desmond, thanks," she said cheerfully.

"Be sure and ask if there's anything you want," he added. "The girl is new. She might forget. You'll have a drop of sherry?"

"I'd love it," she said and went into the sitting-room with him. O'Connor had furnished it beautifully. She warmed her hands while Johnny filled out the drinks.

"Here's health!" he said.

"Good health!" she replied and chuckled. "A good job Daddy can't see me now."

"Why's that?" asked Johnny.

"The poor man has no notion that I ever take a drink," she said. "If he had his way, we'd never be let do anything. He won't even have a book in the house unless 'tis by a priest, and he makes us be in every night by ten. He's in for a surprise one of these days."

"I see I'll have to keep you in order," said Johnny, but he didn't really hear more than half she was saying. He was thinking too much about the supper. At table he gave her more wine, red wine this time, and the result was that she continued to improve. The more she drank the more ladylike she became.

"Isn't Mrs. Desmond well?" she asked at last in a confidential tone and with great concern.

"Mrs. Desmond?" chuckled Johnny. "Who's that?" He was beginning to feel easier, and thanked God sincerely that the meat part of it was over—a mistake wouldn't matter so much with the sweet.

"Your wife, I mean," said the chemist.

"Ah, 'tis only the job in the shop that's filled," laughed Johnny, feeling the wine warm him up. "The other one is still vacant."

"You mean you're not married?" asked the chemist.

"Aren't I great?" said Johnny.

"You're wonderful," said the chemist, but a less enthusiastic man would have noticed there was something wrong in her tone. Johnny didn't even notice how her chatter dried up. He was talking too much himself. Supper had gone off splendidly, and when they went to the sitting-room for coffee he was beginning to get into his stride. Johnny's knowledge was personal and peculiar, when he chose to share it, which wasn't often, and a student of the social sciences would have got rare value out of his talk. Holding a cigarette in the hollow of his hand like a candle in a turnip, he strode up and down the room, holding forth about the shop he had made his money in and how he'd done it, and about the rival chemist's shop, which would prove no rival at all, for it was run by a poor benighted banshee of a man with no business sense. Johnny had it all taped. He told her about the doctors in the town. "Woolley and Hyde and a woman doctor called O'Brien. Her father is a rich man. I dare say 'twas he got it for her."

It gave him a certain satisfaction to get his own back like this on Doctor O'Brien, but the chemist didn't seem to be listening as carefully as you'd expect.

"You wouldn't mind if I run down to the chapel to say a little prayer, Mr. Desmond?" she asked suddenly.

"The chapel?" Johnny echoed in astonishment, for his brain didn't adjust itself too rapidly and it was now going full speed ahead in another direction.

"I won't be a minute."

" 'Tis raining cats and dogs, girl," he said crossly. "You'd be drenched. Wait a minute and I'll run you down in the car."

"Oh, no, no, you mustn't do that," she said hastily, clasping her hands. "It's the air I want as much as anything else. Really, I won't be a minute."

"Oh, just as you like," growled Johnny, flustered and hot and upset. He could have sworn that there was nothing in the world wrong with that supper. He stood in the hall as she went out in the rain, peered after her down the street and shouted: "Don't be long!" His plum-pudding face was screwed up in mystification. Nine o'clock! What sense was there in that? He took up a paper and laid it down every time he heard a woman's step. The chapel was only a couple of hundred yards away. At ten he got up and began to prowl about the room with his hands in his pockets. The devil was in it if she didn't come home now, for the chapel shut at ten. The sweat broke out on him and he cursed himself and cursed his luck. The Town Hall clock struck eleven; he heard the maid go up to bed and surrendered himself to despair. Man or no man, eleven meant scandal. Nothing but misfortune ever came of women. What bad luck was on him the first day he saw a strange one in town? It was the doctor who was behind all his misfortunes.

Then he heard the sound of a car and his heart gave a jump. All the bad language he had been saving up for hours rose in him and, after one savage glance at the clock, he ran to the front door determined to give her a good lick of his tongue. The car was drawn up at the curb, the engine stopped and the side-lights on. More blackguarding!

"Is that you?" he snarled, leaning out into the spitting rain.

"Why?" asked a familiar woman's voice. "Were you waiting up for me?"

The door of the car opened and the doctor scuttled for shelter.

"Is there something up with the chemist?" he asked in holy terror, backing in before her.

"With who?" asked the doctor, screwing up her face in the bright light and pulling off her motoring gloves. "I don't know what you're talking about. Aren't you going to ask whether we have a mouth on us?"

"There's whisky on the sideboard," snapped Johnny distractedly. "Take it and leave me alone! I'm demented with the whole damn lot of ye. I thought you were the new chemist."

"Wisha, Johnny," asked the doctor in great concern as she filled her glass, "is this the sort of hours she's keeping?"

"She went down to the chapel to say a prayer," Johnny ground out through the side of his mouth. "Three hours ago!" he ended in a thunderclap.

"Three hours ago?" she said incredulously, leaning her elbow on the sideboard and looking a million times prettier than Johnny had ever seen her look, in her tight-fitting coat and skirt with the little wisps of goldy-brown hair straying from under the cocky hat. "Wisha, Johnny, I don't know would I like an old one like that around the house at all. Sure, she'd have you persecuted with piety."

"Hell to your soul, woman!" roared Johnny, stopping dead in his bearlike shamble about the room. "Sure, the chapel is shut since ten!"

"And this her first night here and all!" exclaimed the doctor. "She must have drink taken. Did you try the guards' barracks?"

"Drink?" said Johnny unsuspectingly. "Where the hell would she get drink? She had nothing here only a couple of glasses of wine to her supper."

"And do you tell me she had wine to her supper?" asked the doctor. "Begor, 'tisn't everyone can have that, Johnny. So what happened then?"

"What happened then was she said she wanted to go to the chapel," shouted Johnny, well aware of how unconvincing it sounded.

"And after having wine and everything?" said the doctor incredulously. "Ah, Johnny, you must take me for a great gom entirely. You're not telling me the whole story at all, Johnny.

Go on now, and tell us what did you do to the unfortunate girl to drive her out of a night like this."

"Me?" Johnny cried indignantly. "I done nothing to her."

"Not as much as a squeeze?"

"Not as much as a what?" he boomed in bellowing fury. "What do you take me for? Go out of my sight, you malicious, wicked, mocking jade! I have no time to waste on the likes of you."

"What do I take you for?" retorted the doctor. "And what were the pair of ye doing with sofas and cushions and whisky and wine? How do I know what you'd do if you had a few drinks in you? Maybe you'd be just as lively as the rest of them. Is she living here with you, Johnny?" she asked with interest.

"Where else would she live?" growled Johnny.

"And ye not married or anything!" the doctor said reproachfully. " 'Twouldn't be down to the priest she went to ease her conscience about it?"

"What in God's name do you mean, woman?" Johnny asked, brought to a dead halt like a wild horse the trainer has exhausted.

"Wisha, Johnny, are you ever going to get a bit of sense?" she continued pityingly. "At your age oughtn't you know damn well that in a town like this you couldn't bring a girl just out of school to live with you?"

"But, God above!" Johnny said in an anguished whisper, his hands clasped, his face gone white. "I meant no harm to the girl."

"And how do you expect her to know?" asked the doctor. "How would a little gom like that know that 'twasn't the White Slave traders had hold of her? She's up in my digs now, if you want to know, doing hysterics on the landlady. At least she was when I left. She's probably doped or dead by now, because I gave her enough to quieten a dancehall."

"But why—why did she go to your house?"

"Because the priest was out at a party, and you mentioned my name to her—thanks for the reference! And now give us her things and let us go home to our bed. God knows, Johnny Desmond, you should have more sense!"

As she was driving away she suddenly put her head out of the window.

"Johnny!" she called.

"What is it now?" Johnny asked irritably, pulling up the collar of his coat and running across the pavement to her.

"Tell us, Johnny," she asked innocently, "why haven't you a few pictures on the walls?"

"Ask my arse!" hissed Johnny malevolently and rushed back to shelter.

"Johnny!" she called again. "Aren't you going to kiss and be friends?"

"Kiss my arse!" shouted Johnny as he banged the door.

III

Next day about lunchtime he dropped into the new shop. He had deliberately left it alone till then. Everything inside seemed to be going grand. The new chemist was serving a customer and she turned to give him a smile like a sunbeam. It filled his heart with bitterness. The devil a hair astray on her, and the night she had given him! He waited till the customer left and then called her into the parlour. She stopped to give a few instructions to the assistant and followed him.

"You're comfortable where you are?" he asked gruffly.

"Oh, grand, Mr. Desmond, thanks," she replied and had the grace to blush.

" 'Twas a mistake about last night," he said awkwardly, lifting his cap and scratching his head. " 'Twas my fault. I blame myself a lot for it. It should have occurred to me. But I'll make it up on the wages."

"Oh, it's all right," she said. " 'Tis only on Daddy's account. He'd kill me."

"I wouldn't wish for a thousand pounds you'd think anything wrong was intended," Johnny said in a choking voice. "If you saw Father Ring last night instead of the—person you did see (the doctor's name stuck in his gullet), he'd tell you. If I made a mistake 'twas because the likes of it would never cross my mind. I was never in all my days mixed up in work like that."

"Ah, there's no reason for you to apologize," she said earnestly. "It was my own fault. I see now I was foolish. The doctor told me."

"It might be for the best," said Johnny. He pulled a chair closer to him, rested his foot on it, his elbow on his knee, and then joined his hands as he studied her. "There's a certain thing I was going to say," he said thickly. "I wasn't going to say it in a hurry. I wanted to give you time to look round you and see what sort of man I am and what sort of home I have. I'm afraid of no inquiry. I have nothing to hide. That's the sort I am. But," he went on, growing purple at the very thought of the doctor and her gibing tongue, "after the people you might see and the things you might hear, I'd sooner say it now. Here's the house and here's the man!"

"It's a lovely house, isn't it?" she said admiringly.

"It ought to be," he said complacently. "It cost two thousand eight hundred pounds. You might notice I left the pictures on one side. It seems what suits one doesn't suit all. You could choose the pictures yourself."

"You want me to choose the pictures, Mr. Desmond?" she asked in bewilderment.

"I want you to choose myself, girl," Johnny said passionately, kicking the chair to the other side of the room. "That was why I picked you out in Dublin. I was sure you were the right girl for me."

"Oh, I couldn't do that, Mr. Desmond," she said in alarm, backing away from him.

"Why couldn't you?"

"Daddy would never allow it."

"I'll talk to your father."

"Oh, I'd rather you didn't," she said in panic. "You have no idea, the sort of man he is. He'd blame it all on me. Besides, I have no inclination for marriage."

"Don't say no till you have time to look round you," Johnny advised her shrewdly. "You'll see what people will say about me. I'd make you a good husband. My money is safe, and when I die I'll leave you the richest woman in these parts. And, mind," he added, pointing a finger at her, "I'd make no conditions. I saw too much of the dead man's meanness. If you wanted to marry again there would be nothing to stop you."

She was really frightened now. She had never seen anyone

like this before, and was half afraid that by sheer will-power Johnny would make her marry him in spite of herself.

"Oh, I couldn't, I couldn't really," she said desperately. "I'd sooner not get married at all, but if I have to, I'll have to marry the fellow I'm going with. I'm not sure that he's suitable at all; I don't think he has the right attitude—I have terrible doubts about him sometimes—but I could never think of anyone else."

"Think over it," Johnny said hopelessly. "You might change."

But he knew she wouldn't. Women were like that. It was a lingo he couldn't speak, and it was too late for him to learn. His fortune and his beautiful house and his furniture were in a different language altogether, a language this chit of a girl wouldn't understand for another thirty years, if she ever learned it at all.

He died less than a year later and the story goes in town that the chagrin killed him. The Foxy Desmonds of the Glen blew the labours of a lifetime on fur coats and motor cars. Only the doctor believes that it was all on her account and that what Johnny really died of was a broken heart. Women are great on broken hearts.

THE CHEAPJACK

EVERYONE was sorry after Sam Higgins, the headmaster. Sam was a right good skin, one of the decentest men in Ireland, but too honest.

He was a small fat man with a round, rosy, good-natured face, a high bald brow, and specs. He wore a bowler hat and a stiff collar the hottest day God sent, because no matter how sociable he might be, he never entirely forgot his dignity. He lived with his sister, Delia, in a house by the station and suffered a good deal from nerves and dyspepsia. The doctors tried to make out that they were one and the same thing but they weren't; they worked on entirely different circuits. When it was the nerves were bad Sam went on a skite. The skite, of course, was good for the nerves but bad for the dyspepsia, and for months afterwards he'd be on a diet and doing walks in the country. The walks, on the other hand, were good for the dyspepsia but played hell with the nerves, so Sam had to try and take the harm out of them by dropping into Johnny Desmond's on the way home for a pint. Johnny had a sort of respect for him as an educated man, which Johnny wasn't, and a sort of contempt for him as a man who, for all his education, couldn't keep his mind to himself—an art Johnny was past master of.

One day they happened to be discussing the Delea case, which Johnny, a cautious, religious man, affected to find peculiar. There was nothing peculiar about it. Father Ring had landed another big fish; that was all. Old Jeremiah Delea had died and left everything to the Church, nothing to his wife and family. There was to be law about that, according to what Johnny had heard—ah, a sad business, a peculiar business! But Sam, who hated Father Ring with a hate you might describe as truly religious, rejoiced.

"Fifteen thousand, I hear," he said with an ingenuous smile.

"So I believe," said Johnny with a scowl. "A man that couldn't write his own name for you! Now what do you say to the education?"

"Oh, what I always said," replied Sam with his usual straightforwardness. " 'Tis nothing only a hindrance."

"Ah, I wouldn't go so far as that," said Johnny, who, though he tended to share this view, was too decent to criticize any man's job to his face, and anyway had a secret admiration for the polish which a good education can give. "If he might have held onto the wireless shares he'd be good for another five thousand. I suppose that's where the education comes in."

Having put in a good word for culture, Johnny now felt it was up to him to say something in the interests of religion. There was talk about Father Ring and Johnny didn't like it. He didn't think it was lucky. Years of observation of anticlericals in his pub had convinced Johnny that none of them ever got anywhere.

"Of course, old Jerry was always a very good-living man," he added doubtfully.

"He was," Sam said dryly. "Very fond of the Children of Mary."

"That so?" said Johnny, as if he didn't know what a Child of Mary would be.

"Young and old," Sam said enthusiastically. "They were the poor man's great hobbies."

That was Sam all out; too outspoken, too independent! No one like that ever got anywhere. Johnny went to the shop door and looked after him as he slouched up Main Street with his sailor's roll and his bowler hat and wondered to himself that an educated man wouldn't have more sense.

II

Delia and Mrs. MacCann, the new teacher in the girls' school, were sitting on deck-chairs in the garden when Sam got back. It did more than the pint to rouse his spirits after that lonesome rural promenade. Mrs. MacCann was small, gay and go-as-you-please. Sam thought her the pleasantest woman he had ever met and would have told her as much only that she was barely out of mourning for her first husband. He felt it was no time to approach any woman with proposals of marriage, which showed how little Sam knew of women.

"How're ye, Nancy?" he cried heartily, holding out a fat paw.

"Grand, Sam," she replied, sparkling with pleasure. "How's the body?"

"So-so," said Sam. He took off his coat and squatted to give the lawnmower a drop of oil. "As pleasant a bit of news as I heard this long time I'm after hearing today."

"What's that, Sam?" Delia asked in her high-pitched, fluting voice.

"Chrissie Delea that's going to law with Ring over the legacy."

"Ah, you're not serious, Sam?" cried Nancy.

"Oh, begod I am," growled Sam. "She has Canty the solicitor in Asragh on to it. Now Ring will be having Sister Mary Milkmaid and the rest of them making novenas to soften Chrissie's hard heart. By God I tell you 'twill take more than novenas to do that."

"But will she get it, Sam?" asked Nancy.

"Why wouldn't she get it?"

"Anyone that got money out of a priest ought to have a statue put up to her."

"She'll get it all right," Sam said confidently. "After all the other scandals the bishop will never let it go to court. Sure, old Jerry was off his rocker years before he made that will. I'd give evidence myself that I saw him stopping little girls on their way from school to try and look up their clothes."

"Oh, God, Sam, the waste of it!" said Nancy with a chuckle. "Anyway, we'll have rare gas with a lawcase and a new teacher."

"A new what?" asked Sam, stopping dead in his mowing.

"Why? Didn't Ormond tell you he got the shift?" she asked in surprise.

"No, Nancy, he did not," Sam said gravely.

"But surely, Ormond would never keep a thing like that from you?"

"He wouldn't," said Sam, "and I'll swear he knows nothing about it. Where did you hear it?"

"Plain Jane told me." (She meant Miss Daly, the head.)

"And she got it from Ring, I suppose," Sam said broodingly. "And Ring was in Dublin for the last couple of days. Now we know what he was up for. You didn't hear who was coming in Ormond's place?"

"I didn't pay attention, Sam," Nancy said with a frown. "But she said he was from Kerry. Isn't that where Father Ring comes from?"

"Oh, a cousin of Ring's for a fortune!" Sam said dolefully, wiping his sweaty brow. He felt suddenly very depressed and very tired. Even the thought of Chrissie Delea's lawcase couldn't cheer him. He felt the threat of Ring now shadowing himself. A bad manager is difficult enough. A bad manager with a spy in the school can destroy a teacher.

He was right about the relationship with Ring. The new teacher arrived in a broken-down two-seater which he seemed to think rather highly of. His name was Carmody. He was tall and thin with a high, bumpy forehead, prominent cheekbones, and a dirty complexion. He held himself stiffly, obviously proud of his figure. He wore a tight-fitting cheap city suit with stripes, and Sam counted two fountain pens and a battery of coloured pencils in his breast pocket. He had a little red diary sticking from the top pocket of his waistcoat, and while Sam was talking he made notes—a businesslike young fellow. Then he pushed the pencil behind his ear, stuck his thumbs in the armholes of his vest, and giggled at Sam. Giggled was the only way Sam could describe it. It was almost as though he found Sam funny. Within five minutes he was giving him advice on the way they did things in Kerry. Sam, his hands in his trouser pockets and wearing his most innocent air, looked him up and down and his tone grew dryer.

"You seem to get on very well with your class," he said later in the day.

"I make a point of it," Carmody explained pompously.

"Treat them as man to man, like?" Sam said, luring him on.

"That's the modern method, of course," said Carmody.

"That so?" Sam said dryly, and at the same moment he made a face. It was the first twinge of the dyspepsia.

He and Nancy usually had their lunch together in the open air, sitting on the low wall between the two schools. They were there a few minutes when Carmody came out. He stood on the steps and sunned himself, thrusting out his chest and drawing in deep gulps of what a Kerryman would call the ozone.

"Fine figure of a man, Sam," Nancy said, interpreting and puncturing his pose.

As though he had heard her and taken it in earnest Carmody came up to them with an air which he probably thought quizzical.

"That's a fine view you have," he said jocularly.

"You won't be long getting tired of it," Sam said coldly.

"I believe 'tis a quiet sort of place," said Carmody, unaware of any lack of warmth.

"It must be simply shocking after Kerry," Sam said, giving Nancy a nudge. "Were you ever in Kerry, Mrs. Mac?"

"Never, Mr. Higgins," said Nancy, joining in the sport. "But I believe 'tis wonderful."

"Wonderful," Sam agreed mournfully. "You'd wonder where the people got the brains till you saw the scenery."

Carmody, as became a modest man, overlooked the implication that the intellect of a Kerryman might be due to environment rather than heredity; he probably didn't expect better from a native.

"Tell me," he asked with great concern, "what *do* you do with yourselves?"

The impudence of this was too much even for Sam. He gaped at Carmody to see was he in earnest. Then he pointed to the town.

"See the bridge?"

"I do."

"See the abbey tower near it?"

"Yes."

"When we get tired of life we chuck ourselves off that."

"I was being serious," Carmody said icily.

"Oh, begor, so was I," said Sam. "That tower is pretty high."

"I believe you have some sort of dramatic society," Carmody went on to Nancy as though he couldn't be bothered carrying on conversation at Sam's level.

"We have," said Nancy brightly. "Do you act?"

"A certain amount," said Carmody. "Of course, in Kerry we go in more for the intellectual drama."

"Go on!" said Sam. "That'll be a shock to the dramatic society."

"It probably needs one," said Carmody.

"It does," said Sam blithely, getting down and looking at Carmody with his lower lip hanging and the sunlight dazzling on his spectacles. "The town needs a bit of attention too. You might notice 'tis on the downgrade. And then you can have the whole country to practice on. It often struck me it needed a bombshell to wake it up. Maybe you're the bombshell."

It wasn't often that Sam, who was a bit tongue-tied, made a speech as long as that. It should have shut anyone up, but Carmody only stuck his thumbs in his armholes, thrust out his chest, and giggled.

"But of course I'm a bombshell," he said with a sidelong glance at Nancy. You couldn't pierce Carmody's complacency so easily.

III

A week or two later Sam dropped into Johnny Desmond's for his pint.

"Mrs. Mac and the new teacher seem to be getting very great," Johnny said by way of no harm.

"That so, Johnny?" Sam replied in the same tone.

"I just saw them going off for a spin together," added Johnny.

"Probably giving her a lift home," said Sam. "He does it every day. I hope she's insured."

" 'Twasn't that at all," Johnny said, opening a bottle of boiled sweets and cramming a fistful into his mouth. "Out Bauravullen way they went. Have a couple of these, Mr. Higgins!"

"Thanks, Johnny, I won't," Sam said sourly, glancing out the door the way Johnny wouldn't notice how he was hit. There was damn little Johnny didn't notice, though. He went to the door and stood there, crunching sweets.

"Widows are the devil," he said reflectively. "Anything at all so long as 'tis in trousers. I suppose they can't help it."

"You seem to know a lot about them," said Sam.

"My own father died when I was only a boy," Johnny explained discreetly. "Clever chap, young Carmody," he added with his eyes on the ground.

"A human bombshell," said Sam with heavy irony.

"So I believe, so I believe," said Johnny, who didn't know what irony was but who was going as far as a man like himself could go towards indicating that there were things about Carmody he didn't approve of. "A pity he's so quarrelsome in drink," he said, looking back at Sam.

"Is he so?" said Sam.

"Himself and Donovan of the Exchange were at it here last night. I believe Father Ring is hoping he'll settle down. I dunno will he?"

"God forbid!" said Sam.

He went home but he couldn't read or rest. It was too cold for the garden, too hot for the room. He put on his hat again and went for a walk. At least, he explained it to himself as going for a walk, but it took him past Nancy's bungalow. There was no sign of life in that and Sam didn't know whether this was a good sign or a bad one. He dropped into Johnny's, expecting to find the Bombshell there, but there were only a couple of fellows from the County Council inside, and Sam had four drinks which was three more than was good for him. When he came out the moon was up. He returned the same way, and there, sure enough, was a light in Nancy's sitting-room window and the Bombshell's car standing outside.

For two days Sam didn't show his nose in the playground at lunchtime. When he looked out he saw Carmody leaning over the wall, talking to Nancy, and giggling.

On the afternoon of the third day, while Sam was in the garden, Nancy called and Delia opened the door.

"Oh, my!" Delia cried in her laughing, piping voice. "Such a stranger as you're becoming!"

"You'd never guess what I was up to?" Nancy asked.

"I believe you were motoring," replied Delia with a laugh.

"Ah, you can't do anything in this old town," Nancy said with a shrug of disgust. "Where the blazes is Sam? I didn't see him these ages."

"He's in the workshop," said Delia. "Will I call him in?"

"Time enough," Nancy said gaily, grabbing her by the arm. "Come on in till I talk to you."

"And how's your friend, Mr. Carmody?" asked Delia, trying to keep the hurt out of her voice.

"He's all right as long as you don't go out in a motor car with him," laughed Nancy, not noticing Delia's edginess. "Whoever gave him that car was no friend."

"I'm not in much danger of being asked, dear, am I?" Delia asked, half joking, half wincing. "And is he still homesick for Kerry? I dare say not."

"He'll settle down," said Nancy, blithely unconscious of the volcano of emotion under her feet. "A poor gom like that, brought up in the wilds, what more could you expect?"

"I dare say," said Delia. "He has every inducement."

Just then Sam came up the garden and in the back door without noticing Nancy's presence. He stood at the door, wiping his boots, his hat shading his eyes, and laughed in an embarrassed way. Even then, if only he could have welcomed her as he longed to do, things might have been all right, but no more than Delia was he able to conceal his feelings.

"Oh, hullo," he drawled idly. "How're you?"

"Grand, Sam," Nancy said, sitting up and flashing him an extra-special look. "Where were you the last couple of days?"

"Working," said Sam. "Or trying to. It's hard to do anything with people pinching your things. Did you take the quarter-inch chisel, Delia?"

"Is that a big chisel, Sam?" she asked innocently.

"No," he drawled. "Not much bigger than a quarter of an inch, if you know what that is."

"I think it might be on top of the press, Sam," she said guiltily.

"Why the hell women can't put things back where they find them!" he grunted as he got a chair. He pawed about on top of the press till he found the chisel. Then he held it up to the light and closed one eye. "Holy God!" he moaned. "Were you using it as a screwdriver or what?"

"I thought it was a screwdriver, Sam," she replied with a nervous laugh.

"You ought to use it on yourself," he said with feeling, and went out again.

Nancy frowned. Delia laughed again, even more nervously. She knew what the scene meant, but Nancy was still incredulous.

"He seems very busy," she said in a hurt tone.

"He's always pulling the house to pieces," Delia explained apologetically.

"There's nothing wrong with him?" Nancy asked suspiciously.

"No, dear," Delia said. "Only his digestion. That's always a trouble to him."

"I suppose it must be," said Nancy, growing pale. Only now was she beginning to realize that the Higginses wanted to have no more to do with her. Deeply offended, she began to collect her things.

"You're not going so soon, Nancy?"

"I'd better. I promised Nellie the afternoon off."

"Oh, dear, Sam will be so disappointed," sighed Delia.

"He'll get over it," said Nancy. "So long, Delia."

"Good-bye, dear," said Delia and, after shutting the door, began to cry. In a small town the end of a friendship has something of death about it. Delia had had hopes of something closer than friendship. Nancy had broken down her jealousy of other women; when she came to the house Sam was more cheerful and Delia found herself more cheerful too. She brought youth and gaiety into their lives.

Delia had a good long cry before Sam came in from the back. He said nothing about Nancy but went into the front room and took down a book. After a while Delia washed her eyes and went in. It was dark inside, and when she opened the door he started, always a bad sign.

"You wouldn't like to come for a little walk with me, dear?" Delia asked in a voice that went off into a squeak.

"No, Dee," he said without looking round. "I wouldn't be able."

"I'm sure a little drink in Johnny's would cheer you up," she persisted.

"No, Dee," he went on dully. "I couldn't stand his old guff."

"Then wouldn't you run up to town and see a doctor, Sam?"

"Ah, what good are doctors?"

"But it must be something, Sam," she said. She wished he'd say it and be done with it and let her try to comfort him as best she could: the two of them there, growing old, in a lonesome, unfriendly place.

"I know what it is myself," he said. "It's that cheapjack, Carmody. Twenty years I'm in that school and I was never laughed at to my face before. Now he's turning the boys against me."

"I think you only fancy that, dear," she said timidly. "I don't believe Mr. Carmody could ever turn anybody against you."

"There's where you're wrong, Dee," he replied, shaking his head, infallible even in despair. "That fellow was put there with a purpose. Ring chose his man well. They'll be having a new head one of these days."

IV

School had become a real torture to Sam. Carmody half-suspected his jealousy and played on it. He sent boys to the girls' school with notes and read the replies with a complacent smirk. Sam went about as though he was doped. He couldn't find things he had just left out of his hand, he forgot the names of the boys, and sometimes sat for a quarter of an hour at a time in a desk behind his class, rubbing his eyes and brow in a stupor.

He came to life only when he wrangled with Carmody. There was a window that Sam liked open and Carmody liked shut. That was enough to set the pair of them off. When Carmody sent a boy to shut the window Sam asked the boy who gave him permission. Then Carmody came up, stiff and blustering, and said no one was going to make him work with a draught down the back of his neck and Sam replied that a better man had worked there for ten years without noticing any draught at all. It was all as silly as that, and Sam knew it was silly, but that was how it took him, and no amount of good resolutions made it any better.

All through November he ate his lunch by the school fire, and when he looked out it was to see Carmody and Nancy eating theirs outside and Nancy putting up her hand to tidy her hair and breaking into a sudden laugh. Sam always felt the laugh was at him.

One day he came out, ringing the school bell, and Carmody, who had been sitting on the wall, jumped off with such an affectation of agility that the diary fell from his vest pocket. He was so occupied with Nancy that he didn't notice it, and Sam was so full of his own troubles that he went on down the playground and he didn't notice it either. He saw a bit of paper that someone's lunch had been wrapped in, picked it up and crumpled it into a ball. At the same time he noticed the diary, and, assuming that one of the boys had dropped it, picked it up and glanced through it. It puzzled him, for it did not seem like the notebook of a schoolboy. It was all about some girl that the writer was interested in. He couldn't help reading on till he came to a name that caused him to blush. Then he recognized the writing; it was Carmody's. When he turned the pages and saw how much of it there was, he put it in his pocket. Afterwards, he knew what he had done and saw it was wrong, but at the time he never even thought of an alternative. During the first lesson he sat at a desk and read on, his head in his hands.

Now, Carmody was a conceited young man who thought that everything about himself was of such importance that it had to be recorded for the benefit of posterity. Things Sam would have been ashamed even to think about himself he had all written down. Besides, Sam had led a sheltered life. He didn't know much of any woman but Delia. He had thought of Nancy as an angelic little creature whose life had been wrecked by her husband's death and who spent most of her time thinking of him. It was clear from the diary that this was not how she spent her time at all, but that, like any other bad, flighty, sensual girl, she let herself be made love to in motor cars by cheapjacks like Carmody, who even on his own admission had no respect for her and only wanted to see how far a widow like that would go: "Anything at all so long as 'tis in trousers," as Johnny said. Johnny was right. Johnny knew the sort of woman she was. That was all Sam needed to make him hate Nancy as much as he already hated Carmody. She was another cheapjack.

Then he looked at the clock. Dictation came next. Without a moment's thought he went to the blackboard, wiped out the sums on it, and wrote in a neat, workmanlike hand: "The Diary of a Cheapjack." Even then he had no notion of what he was actually going to do, but as the boys settled themselves he took a deep breath and began to read.

"October 21st," he dictated in a dull voice. "I think I have bowled the widow over."

There was a shocked silence and some boy giggled.

"It's all right," Sam explained blandly, pointing to the blackboard. "I told you this fellow was only a cheapjack, one of those lads you see at the fair, selling imitation jewellery. You'll see it all in a minute."

And on he went again in a monotonous voice, one hand holding the diary, the other in his trouser pocket. He knew he was behaving oddly, even scandalously, but it gave him an enormous feeling of release, as though all the weeks of misery and humiliation were being paid for at last. It was everything he had ever thought of Carmody, only worse. Worse, for how could Sam have suspected that Carmody would admit the way he had first made love to Nancy, just to keep his hand in (his own very words!), or describe the way love came to him at last one evening up Bauravullen when the sun was setting behind the pine trees and he found he no longer despised Nancy.

The fellows began to titter. Sam raised his brows and looked at them with a wondering smile as if he did not quite know what they were laughing at. In a curious way he was beginning to enjoy it himself. He began to parody it in the style of a bad actor, waving one arm, throwing back his head and cooing out the syrupy pseudo-Byronic sentences. "And all for a widow!" he read, raising his voice and staring at Carmody. "A woman who went through it all before."

Carmody heard him and suddenly recognized the diary. He came up the classroom in a few strides and tore the book out of Sam's hand. Sam let it go with him and only gaped.

"Hi, young man," he asked amiably, "where are you going with that?"

"What are you doing with it?" Carmody asked in a terrible voice, equally a caricature of a bad actor's. He was still incredulous; he could not believe that Sam had actually been reading it aloud to his class.

"Oh, that's our piece for dictation," Sam said and glanced at the blackboard. "I'm calling it 'The Diary of a Cheapjack.' I think that about hits it off."

"You stole my diary!" hissed Carmody.

"Your diary?" Sam replied with assumed concern. "You're not serious?"

"You knew perfectly well it was mine," shouted Carmody beside himself with rage. "You saw my name and you know my writing."

"Oh, begod I didn't," Sam protested stolidly. "If anyone told me that thing was written by an educated man I'd call him a liar."

Then Carmody did the only thing he could do, the thing that

Sam in his heart probably hoped for—he gave Sam a punch in the jaw. Sam staggered, righted himself and made for Carmody. They closed. The boys left their desks, shouting. One or two ran out of the school. In a few moments the rest had formed a cheering ring about the two struggling teachers. Sam was small and gripped his man low. Carmody punched him viciously and effectively about the head but Sam hung on, pulling Carmody right and left till he found it hard to keep his feet. At last Sam gave one great heave and sent Carmody flying. His head cracked off the iron leg of a desk. He lay still for some moments and then rose, clutching his head.

At the same moment Miss Daly and Nancy came in.

"Sam!" Nancy cried. "What's the matter?"

"Get out of my way," Carmody shouted, skipping round her. "Get out of my way till I kill him."

"Come on, you cheapjack!" drawled Sam. His head was down, his hands were hanging, and he was looking dully at Carmody over his spectacles. "Come on and I'll give you more of it."

"Mr. Higgins, Mr. Higgins!" screamed Miss Daly. "Is it mad ye are, the pair of ye?"

They came to their senses at that. Miss Daly took charge. She rang the bell and cleared the school. Sam turned away and began fumbling blindly with the lid of a chalk-box. Carmody began to dust himself. Then, with long backward glances, he and the two women went into the playground, where Sam heard them talking in loud, excited voices. He smiled vaguely, took off his glasses and wiped them carefully before he picked up his books, his hat, and his coat, and locked the school door behind him. He knew he was doing it for the last time and wasn't sorry. The three other teachers drew away and he went past them without a glance. He left the keys at the presbytery and told the housekeeper he'd write. Next morning he went away by an early train and never came back.

We were all sorry for him. Poor Sam! As decent a man as ever drew breath but too honest, too honest!

THE MASCULINE PRINCIPLE

MYLES REILLY was a building contractor in a small way of business that would never be any larger owing to the difficulty he
found in doing sums. For a man of expansive nature sums are
hell; they narrow and degrade the mind. And Myles was expansive, a heavy, shambling man, always verging on tears or
laughter, with a face like a sunset, and something almost physi-
cally boneless about his make-up. A harassed man too, for all
his fat, because he was full of contradictory impulses. He was a
first-rate worker, but there was no job, however fascinating,
which he wouldn't leave for the sake of a chat, and no conversation, however delightful, which did not conceal a secret sense of
guilt. "God, I promised Gaffney I'd be out of that place by
Saturday, Joe. I know I ought to be going; I declare to my God
I ought, but I love an intelligent talk. That's the thing I miss
most, Joe—someone intelligent to talk to."

But even if he was no good at sums he was great at daughters.
He had three of these, all stunners, but he never recognized his
real talent and continued to lament the son he wanted. This was
very shortsighted of him because there wasn't a schoolboy in
town who didn't raise his cap to Myles in hopes of impressing
his spotty visage on him, so that one day he might say to his
daughters "Who's that charming fellow from St. Joseph's Terrace
—best-mannered boy in the town. Why don't we ever have him
round here?" There was no recorded instance of his saying anything of the sort, which might have been as well, because if the
boys' mothers didn't actually imply that the girls were fast, they
made no bones about saying they were flighty. Mothers, unfortunately, are like that.

They were three grand girls. Brigid, the eldest, was tall and bossy like a reverend mother; Joan, the youngest, was small and ingratiating, but Evelyn was a bit of a problem. She seemed to have given up early any hope of competing with her sisters and resigned herself to being the next best thing to the missing son. She slouched, she swore, she drank, she talked with the local accent which her sisters had discarded; and her matey air inspired fierce passions in cripples, out-of-works, and middle-aged widowers, who wrote her formal proposals beginning: "Dearest Miss Reilly, since the death of my dear wife R. I. P. five years ago I gave up all hopes of meeting another lady that would mean the same to me till I had the good fortune to meet your charming self. I have seven children; the eldest is eighteen and will soon be leaving home and the other six are no trouble."

Then Jim Piper came on the scene. Nobody actually remembered inviting him, nobody pressed him to come again, but he came and hung on. It was said that he wasn't very happy at home. He was a motor mechanic by trade. His mother kept a huxter shop, and in her spare time was something of a collector, mostly of shillings and sixpenny bits. This was supposed to be why Jim was so glad to get out of the house. But, as Father Ring was the first to discover, Jim had a tough streak too.

Father Ring was also a collector. Whatever pretty girls he had banished from his conscious mind came back to him in dreams, disguised as pound notes, except the plainer, coarser types who took the form of ten-shilling notes. Mrs. Piper was shocked by this, and when Father Ring came for his dues, she fought him with all the guile and passion of a fellow collector. When Jim was out of his time Father Ring decided that it would be much more satisfactory to deal with him; a nice, easy-going boy with nothing of the envy and spite of his mother.

Jim agreed at once to pay the dues himself. He took out his wallet and produced a ten-shilling note. Now, ten shillings was a lot of money to a working man, and at least four times what his mother had ever paid, but the sight of it sent a fastidious shudder through Father Ring. As I say, he associated it with the coarser type of female.

"Jim," he said roguishly, "I think you could make that a pound."

"I'm afraid I couldn't, father," Jim replied respectfully, trying to look Father Ring in the eye, a thing that was never easy.

"Of course, Jim," Father Ring said in a tone of grief, " 'tis all one to me what you pay; I won't touch a penny of it; but at the same time, I'd only be getting into trouble taking it from you. 'Twouldn't be wishing to me."

"I dare say not, father," said Jim. Though he grew red he behaved with perfect respect. "I won't press you."

So Father Ring went off in the lofty mood of a man who has defended a principle at a great sacrifice to himself, but that very night he began to brood and he continued to brood till that sickly looking voluptuary of a ten-shilling note took on all the radiance and charm of a virgin of seventeen. Back he went to Jim for it.

"Don't say a word to anybody," he whispered confidentially. "I'll put that through."

"At Christmas you will, father," Jim said with a faint smile, apparently quite unaware of the favour Father Ring thought he was doing him. "The Easter dues were offered and refused."

Father Ring flushed and almost struck him. He was a passionate man; the lovers' quarrel over, the reconciliation complete, the consummation at hand, he saw her go off to spend the night with another man—his beautiful, beautiful ten-shilling note!

"I beg your pardon," he snapped. "I thought I was talking to a Christian."

It was more than a man should be asked to bear. He had been too hasty, too hasty! A delicate, high-spirited creature like her! Father Ring went off to brood again, and the more he brooded, the dafter his schemes became. He thought of having a special collection for the presbytery roof but he felt the bishop would probably only send down the diocesan architect. Bishops, like everything else, were not what they used to be; there was no gravity in them, and excommunication was practically unknown. A fortnight later he was back to Jim.

"Jim, boy," he whispered, "I'll be wanting you for a concert at the end of the month."

Now, Jim wasn't really much of a singer; only a man in the throes of passion would have considered him a singer at all, but such was his contrariness that he became convinced that Father Ring was only out to get his money, by hook or crook.

"All right, father," he said smoothly. "What's the fee?"

"Fee?" gasped Father Ring. "What fee?"

"The fee for singing, father."

And not one note would Jim sing without being paid for it! It was the nearest thing to actual free-thinking Father Ring had ever encountered, the reflection among the laity of the bishops' cowardice, and he felt that at last he understood the sort of man Voltaire must have been. A fee!

Myles Reilly loved telling that story, not because he was against the church but because he was expansive by temperament and felt himself jailed by the mean-spiritedness of life about him. "God, I love a man!" he muttered and turned to his pint. "A man, not a pincushion," he added, drinking and looking fiercely away. He liked Jim because he was what he would have wished a son of his own to be. When Evelyn and Jim became engaged he was deeply moved. "You picked the best of the bunch," he muttered to Jim with tears in his eyes. "God, I'm not criticizing any of them because I love them all, but Evvie is out on her own. She may have a bit of a temper, but what good is anyone without it?"

He said the same things about Jim to the girls, but they, being romantic, didn't pay much heed to him, even Evelyn herself. He had no patience with the sort of fellows they knocked round with; counter-jumpers and bank-clerks with flannel bags and sports coats; tennis-players, tea-party gents carrying round plates of sandwiches—"Will you have some of this or some of that, please?" God Almighty, how could anyone put up with it? When Jim started bringing Evelyn ten shillings a week out of his wages to put in her Post Office account towards the wedding, Myles drew the lesson for them. There was the good, steady tradesman—the man, the *man*—not like the sports coats and the flannel bags who'd have been more likely to touch them for the ten bob. When Evelyn had two hundred saved he'd build a house for them himself. It would be like no house they ever saw; modern, if you wished, and with every labour-saving device, but it would be a house, a *house,* not a bloody concrete box. The girls listened to him with amusement; they always enjoyed their father's temperamental grumblings and moanings without ever taking them seriously.

"You don't know what you're letting yourself in for," Evelyn said dryly to Jim. "You may be engaged to me but you're going to marry my da. Greatest mistake anyone could make, getting too thick with their in-laws."

In fact, Jim was more popular with father than with daughters. They, of course, were not haunted by the image of a son they could not have. Evelyn liked Jim well enough, and, given a chance, she might even have loved him, but the sense of inferiority towards her sisters left her peculiarly vulnerable to their criticisms. They didn't understand what she could see in Jim, a poor fish of a fellow who only came to their house because he wasn't happy at home. The ten shillings a week put the finishing touches to him. How any girl of feeling could go with a man who saved ten shillings a week towards his wedding was beyond them. Evelyn defended him as best she could, but secretly she felt they were right, and that as usual she had got the second best out of life, a decent poor slob of a mechanic whom her sisters would turn up their noses at.

Then, at Christmas, she went out to do the shopping with the week's housekeeping in her purse, ran into a crowd of fellows home from Dublin for the holidays, and started to drink with them. She kept saying she had all the money in the house and must really go off and do the shopping, but all the Reillys had a remarkable capacity for reminding themselves of what they should be doing without doing it, and what began as a protest ended up as a turn. The fellows said she was a great card. When she came home half tight with only half the shopping done Brigid smacked her face.

Evelyn knew she ought to kill Brigid, but she didn't do that either. Instead she went to her room and wept. Jim came up later to go to Midnight Mass with her. He was a bit lit up too but drink only gave Jim words without warmth. It roused his sense of abstract justice, and instead of soothing Evelyn as he should have done he set out to prove to her how unreasonable she was.

"My goodness," he said with a feeble oratorical gesture, "what do you expect? Here's poor Brigid trying to get things ready for Christmas and you drinking yourself stupid down in Johnny Desmond's with Casserley and Doyle and Maurice the Slug. Sure, of course, she was mad."

"That's right," Evelyn said, beginning to flame. "It's all my fault as usual."

"There's nothing usual about it," Jim went on with futile reasonableness, "only you don't know what a good sister you have. The girl was a mother to you. A mother! I only wish I had a mother like her."

"You have time still," said Evelyn, beside herself.

"I wouldn't be good enough for her," said Jim with sickly servility.

"If you're not good enough for her you're not good enough for me."

"I never said I was. Are you going to make it up and come to Mass?"

"Go to Hell!" snapped Evelyn.

All through the holidays she brooded over him and over her own weak character and rotten luck, and the day after the holidays, in the mood of disillusionment that follows Christmas, while still feeling that no one in the world gave a damn for her, she took out Jim's savings and caught the boat for London. The Reillys had friends there; a disorderly family called Ronan who had once lived on the terrace and had to get out of it in a hurry.

This was a scandal, if you like! The only one who really had a tolerant word to say for Evelyn was Joan, who said that, though, of course, it was wrong of Evelyn to have stolen the money, running away was the only decent way out of an impossible marriage. But then, Joan, as well as disliking Jim, loved romance and excitement. In Brigid the romantic was subdued a little by the mother; she knew it would be her responsibility to get Joan off her father's hands and that it had all been made ten times more difficult by the reports that were now going round that the Reilly girls were really what the schoolboys' mothers had always proclaimed them to be.

As for Myles, he was brokenhearted, or as near brokenhearted as his temperament permitted him to be. "The one decent boy that ever came to the house," he said with his face in his hands, "and he had to be robbed, and robbed by a daughter of mine. God, Bridgie, isn't it cruel?" After that he began to cry quietly to himself. "I loved that boy: I loved him as if he was my own son. I could have spent my last days happily with him. And the little house I was going to build for him and all—everything gone!" Then he beat the wall with his fists and cried: "God, if only I could lay my hands on her I'd strangle her! Evelyn, Evelyn, you were the last I thought would shame me."

Jim took it as you'd expect a fellow like that to take it. The person he seemed most concerned about was Myles. When he took Myles out for a drink, the old boy sat with the tears in his eyes and then spread out his big paws like claws and silently closed them round the spot where he imagined his daughter's neck to be.

"That's what I'd like to do to her, Jim," he said.

"Ah, you're not still chewing over that!" Jim said reproachfully.

Myles closed his eyes and shook his head.

"What the hell else can I do?" he asked, almost sobbing. "It's not the money, Jim; it's not the money, boy. I'll pay that back."

"You'll do nothing of the sort," Jim said quietly. "That's a matter between Evelyn and me. It has nothing to do with you."

"No, no, it's my responsibility, my responsibility entirely, Jim," cried Myles in agony, swaying to and fro. He was indignant at the very suggestion that he wasn't responsible; if he'd had it he would have paid it ten times over sooner than carry the burden of it on his mind. But Jim knew his capacity for discussing what was the right thing to do without doing it, and indeed, without any prospect of doing it. Within a few weeks it had boiled down to the skilled assistance Jim would receive in any house he built for the girl who replaced Evelyn. But Jim

K

showed no signs of even wanting to replace her. For months he was drinking more than he should have been.

II

Then, when all the commotion had died away, when Jim ceased to go to the Reillys' and there was no longer even a question of the ninety pounds being paid back, Evelyn came home. There was no nonsense about her slinking in the back door in the early hours of the morning. She wore a grand new tailormade with a hat like a hoop and arrived at the house in a car. Brigid watched her pay off the driver, and her face looked old and grim.

"I suppose that was the last of the money?" she asked bitterly.

"What money?" Evelyn asked, on the defensive at once.

"Why? Did you rob some other man as well?" Brigid asked. "What money, indeed?"

"That's gone long ago," Evelyn said haughtily. "I'm paying it back. I suppose I can get a job, can't I?"

"I suppose so," said Brigid. "If Jim Piper will give you a character."

Myles got up and stumped upstairs to his room. He was very agitated. He told Brigid that he'd kill Evelyn with his own two hands, and became still more agitated when Brigid told him sharply that it would be better if he used a stick. He told Brigid that he didn't like being spoken to in that way. He didn't either. The truth was that Myles was in a very difficult position. Ever since Evelyn's fall Brigid had developed a high moral tone which was far too like her mother's to be wholesome. Unlike her mother's it could not be short-circuited by blandishments or embraces or even softened by tears. The girl wanted him to keep regular hours; she wanted him, suffering as he was from cruel responsibilities, to deny himself the consolation of a friendly chat after his day's work. There was a hard streak in Brigid; she never realized the strain he was living under.

For all her faults, no one could say that of Evelyn. She might be weak and a thief and deserve strangling, but she always knew the proper tone to adopt to a father a bit the worse for drink who knew he had done wrong and didn't want to be reminded of it. He knew he had sworn that she should never set foot in the house again, but damn it, she was his daughter, and—though it was something he wouldn't like to say—he was glad to see her home.

Joan too was glad, and she showed it. She was doing a tearing line with a bank clerk, a gorgeous fellow of violent passions, and Brigid, regardless of the way she had behaved herself with Ben Hennessy, chaperoned her like mad. Brigid herself had contracted a regular, a draper called Considine, and drapers being exceedingly respectable, she was taking no more chances. The Reillys were to be respectable if it killed them. Again and again with her cutting tongue she made it plain that Evelyn wasn't wanted. Joan thought it disgusting.

Besides, Evelyn's descriptions of life in London were a revelation to her. It seemed that in disgust with herself and life she had begun a sordid and idiotic love affair, and used it merely to lacerate herself further. It was only when she realized that the man she was associating with despised her almost as much as she despised herself that she broke it off and came home. Joan put this down to her sister's unfortunate character and her inability to get the best out of life. In Evelyn's position she would have acted quite differently. She wouldn't have permitted any man to despise her; she would certainly not have despised herself, and under no circumstances would she have come home. It worked so much on Joan's imagination that she even thought of going away, just to show Evelyn how it should be done.

But there was still one thing Evelyn had to reckon with. She had to face Jim. This is one of the tests which the small town imposes, which cannot be avoided and cannot really be worked out in advance. One evening late when she was coming home from a friend's she ran into Jim. There was no getting out of it. He was taken aback though he tried not to show it. He raised his cap and stopped. Evelyn stopped too. When it came to the test she found she couldn't walk past him; she was a girl of weak character.

"Hullo, Evelyn," he said in a tone of surprise.

"Hullo," she replied chokingly.

"Back for a holiday?" he asked—as if he didn't know!

"No, for good."

"Homesick?" he added, still trying to make talk.

"Ah, for God's sake," she cried with sudden violence, "if you want to talk, come away where we won't have the whole town looking at us."

She led the way, walking fast and silently, full of suppressed anger and humiliation. Jim loped along beside her, his hands in the pockets of his trench coat. She turned up Lovers' Lane, a place they had used in their courting days. It was a long, dark, winding boreen with high walls, between two estates. Then she turned on him, at bay.

It is extraordinary what women can do in self-defence. She shouted at him. She said it was all his fault for being such a doormat; that no one with a spark of manliness in him could have let her be treated as she was at home, and that he knew she was heart-scalded and hadn't the spirit to stand up for her. She all but implied that it was he who had pinched her savings. He didn't try to interrupt her.

"Well," he said lamely when she had talked herself out, "it's no use crying over spilt milk."

"Oh, if it was only milk!" she said and began to cry. "Ronans is no better than a kip. I never meant to take your money. I meant to get a job and send it back to you, but they kept cadging and cadging until every penny was gone."

"I suppose we can be thankful it was no worse," he said, and then held out his hand. "Anyway, are we quits now?"

She threw her arms about him and squeezed him fiercely. She was weeping hysterically and he patted her back gently, talking to her in a low, soothing voice. She did not tell him about the fellow in London. She wanted to forget it, for it made her ashamed every time she thought of it. Besides, she couldn't see that it was any business of Jim's.

After that night they continued to meet, but in a peculiar way, unknown to their families. Both were self-conscious about it. Evelyn would not invite Jim to the house and he was too proud to invite himself. The truth was that she felt Jim was behaving with his usual lack of manliness. He should have cut her dead when they met or, failing that, should have got drunk and beaten her up, all the more because she had behaved so badly in London. The fact that she hadn't told him of what took place in London only made his conduct more indefensible, and she suffered almost as much on his account as if the fault had been her own. They met after dark in out-of-the-way places, and it was weeks before word got round that they were walking out again. Joan was bitterly disappointed; she had thought better of Evelyn. Brigid, seeing a grand chance of washing out the scandal of the stolen money, changed her tune and demanded that Jim should see her sister at the house, but Evelyn refused sulkily. By this time her main anxiety was to keep Jim and Joan apart so that the London scandal mightn't leak out: not that she thought Joan would wish to betray her but because for some reason she was enormously proud of Evelyn's conduct and would be bound to boast of it. That was the worst of a romantic sister.

"If you're going to marry Jim Piper it's only right," said Brigid.

"Jim Piper didn't say he wanted to marry me," said Evelyn.

"Then what are ye walking out for?" cried Brigid.

"What do people usually walk out for?" Evelyn asked scornfully.

It was months before Brigid realized why Evelyn was so stubborn about not inviting Jim to the house, and by that time it was too late. Joan knew but Joan wouldn't tell. Evelyn told Jim one summer evening at the edge of a wood. She did it with an air of boyish toughness and braggadocio, smoking a cigarette. Jim was aghast.

"Are you sure, Evvie?" he asked mildly.

"Certain," said Evelyn. "Joan looked it up in the library."

Jim gave a bitter, embarrassed laugh and lay back with his hands under his head.

"That's a bit of a shock all right," he said. "What are we going to do about it?"

"I suppose I'll only have to go back to Ronan's," Evelyn said lightly. "They won't mind. What would shock them would sweat a black."

"I suppose so," Jim said ruefully. "We can't afford to rush into anything now."

"No one is trying to rush you into anything," she said hotly. "Get that out of your head."

She was silent for a moment; then she got up quickly, brushed her skirt and crossed the fence into the lane. Jim came after her with a hangdog air. As he jumped down she turned and faced him, all ablaze.

"Don't attempt to follow me!" she cried.

"Why not?" he asked in surprise.

"Why not?" she repeated mockingly. "As if you didn't know! Oh, you codded me nicely! You wanted to get your own back for the money and you did, if that's any satisfaction to you."

"It's no satisfaction at all to me," Jim said, raising his voice. There was a queer, unhappy doggedness about his air. He put his hands in his trouser pockets and stood with his legs wide. His voice lacked resonance. "And I wasn't trying to get my own back for anything, though I had plenty of cause."

"You had; you and your old money; I wish I never saw it."

"It's not the money."

"Then what is it?"

He didn't reply. He had no need to. Under his accusing eyes she reddened again. It had never crossed her mind that he might know.

"I suppose Joan was chattering," she said bitterly.

"Nobody was chattering at all," he said scornfully. "I knew all about it from the first night I saw you. You couldn't conceal it."

"I wasn't trying to conceal it," she blazed. "I have nothing to hide from you."

"I'm not throwing it up at you," he protested. "I'll marry you just the same when I can."

"Marry me?" she spat. "I wouldn't marry you if you were the last living thing left in the world—you worm!"

Then she strode off down the lane, humiliated to the very depth of her being. If she had gone away without saying anything to him she could have kept her pride, but she knew that in her desperation she had as good as asked him to marry her and, what was worse, asked him under false pretences. This was not what she had intended when she shut up about the London affair; then her only idea had been to protect her own wounded sensibilities, but now she realized that if ever the story got round, she would appear no better than any other little tart, pretending to be innocent so as to kid a man into marrying her. Nothing she could now do would alter that interpretation. She went home in such a fury of rage and misery that she blurted it out in a few sentences to Brigid.

"You'd better get some money for me somewhere. I'm going to have a kid, and I'll have to go to London to have it."

"You're going to—?" began Brigid, growing pale.

"Have a kid, I said," shouted Evelyn savagely.

"Is it Jim Piper?"

"Never mind!"

"He'll have to marry you."

"He won't. I asked him and he told me to go to hell."

"We'll soon see about that."

"You won't. I did the same thing with another fellow in London and he found out."

"You—so that's what you were up to in London."

"That's what I was up to," sneered Evelyn. "Anyway, I wouldn't marry that fellow now if he came to me on his knees."

Then she went to bed and Joan, for once a little awed, brought up her tea. Myles first wept and then went out and got drunk. He said if it was anyone else he'd go out at once and kill him with his own two hands, but a fellow who had had his savings stolen on him! That was the real tragedy of being poor, that it destroyed a man's self-respect and made it impossible for him to wipe out his humiliations in blood. *Blood,* that was what he wanted. But Brigid didn't want anyone's blood. She wanted to marry Considine, the draper, and though Considine was broadminded enough as drapers go, she didn't want to give him anything more to be broadminded about. She stormed out to interview Jim's mother.

With all her responsibilities, Brigid was still something of a child. Standing with one hand on the table and the other on her hip, Mrs. Piper dominated the scene from the first moment. She asked in the most ingenuous way in the world how such a thing could happen in a well-conducted house, and when Brigid assured her that it hadn't happened there Mrs. Piper said wasn't it lucky that Evelyn didn't get pneumonia as well. Brigid had as much chance against her as an innocent naked savage against a machine-gun post.

While they were arguing Jim came in and hung up his cap.

"You know what I came about, Jim," Brigid said challengingly.

"If I don't I can guess, Brigid," he replied with a tight smile.

"The girl has no mother."

"She has something as good, Brigid," Jim replied simply, and Brigid suddenly realized that his respect for her was something he did not put off and on as it suited him. It gave her new dignity and confidence.

"You'll marry her for my sake, Jim?" she asked.

"I'll marry her the minute I'm able, Brigid," he said stubbornly, putting his hands in his trouser pockets, a trick he had to give him the feeling of stability. "I may be able to marry her in a year's time, but I can't do it now."

"A year's time will be too late, Jim," Brigid cried. "A girl in her position can afford to do without a house but she can't do without a husband."

"And start off in furnished rooms with a kid?" Jim replied scornfully. "I saw too many do that, and I never saw one that came to any good."

Brigid looked at him doubtfully. She didn't believe him; she felt he was holding out on her only because of his bitterness about Evelyn's betrayal. It caused her to make a false move.

"I know she behaved like a bitch about that fellow in London," she said. "I only heard it today for the first time. But surely, seeing the state she's in, you're big enough to forgive her."

The look on Jim's face convinced her that she was right. His expression showed pain, humiliation, and bewilderment, but his voice remained firm.

"If I didn't forgive her I wouldn't be in the fix I'm in now," he said.

"What's that?" his mother cried. "What's that about a fellow in London? So that's what she was up to, the vagabond! And now she's trying to put the blame on my innocent boy!"

"She's not trying to put the blame on anybody," Jim said with the first sign of real anger he had shown. "I'm responsible, and

I'm not denying it, but I can't marry her now. She'll have to go to London."

"But we haven't the money to send her to London," Brigid cried in exasperation. "Don't you know well the way we're situated?"

"I'll pay my share," Jim said. "And I'll pay for the kid, but I won't do any more."

"Leave her pay for it out of what she stole!" hissed his mother. "Oh, my, that many a fine family was reared on less!"

"I'm going straight up to Father Ring," Brigid said desperately.

"You can spare yourself the trouble," said Jim flatly. "Ring isn't going to make me marry Evelyn, nor anyone else either."

This was strong language from a young fellow of Jim's age, but it was no more than Father Ring himself expected.

"Brigid," he said, squeezing the girl's arm sympathetically, "I'll do what I can but I wouldn't have much hope. To tell you the truth I never expected better. The best thing I can do is to see Lane."

So off he went to interview Jim's employer, Mick Lane, at his own home.

"You could warn him he'd get the sack if he didn't marry her," he suggested.

"Oh, begod, father, I could not," replied Lane in alarm. "I wouldn't mind anyone else, but Jim is the sort of fellow would walk out the door on me if he thought I was threatening him, and I'd be a hell of a long time getting as good a man. I might talk to him myself in a friendly way."

"Mick," said Father Ring in a disappointment, "you'd only be wasting your time. Is it a fellow that wouldn't sing at a parish concert without a fee? It might be the best thing for the poor girl in the long run."

III

Next time Evelyn came back from London without any finery; the baby was put out to nurse up the country and not referred to again. It caused a lot of talk. There were plenty to say that Jim was in the wrong, that, even allowing that the girl was damaged goods, a fellow might swallow his pride. Better men had had to do it. But Jim in his quiet, stubborn way went on as though he didn't even know there was talk.

Ultimately, it did the Reillys no great harm, because Joan became engaged to the gorgeous passionate fellow at the bank and Brigid married Considine. Evelyn set her teeth and stuck it out. She went twice to see Owen, her baby, but gave it up when she realized that you can't retain a child's affection by visiting him two or three times a year.

For months she didn't see Jim. Then one evening when she went for a walk in the country, she came on him about a mile out of town, studying the wreck of a car which he was trying to make something of. It was one of those occasions when anyone is at a disadvantage; when it depends on the weather or your digestion—or, going further back, what sort your parents were—what you do. Evelyn was her father's daughter and, having no true feminine pride to direct her, she naturally did the wrong thing.

"Hello," she said.

"Oh, hello, Evelyn," Jim said, raising his cap. "How are you getting on?"

"All right," she replied curtly, with the sinking of the heart she would have felt anyhow, knowing that the decision of a lifetime had been taken, and that, as usual, it was the wrong one.

"Can I give you a lift?"

"I wasn't going anywhere in particular," she said, realizing the enormous effort of will it would take to restore the situation to what it had been a moment before.

That night, crazy with rage, she wrote him a blistering letter, asking how he had dared to speak to her and warning him that if he did it again she would slap his face. Then, remembering the lonesome evening she would spend if she posted it, she put it in her bag and went off to meet him. While they were sitting on a gate up a country lane she realized that now she would never send the letter, and the thought of it in her bag irritated her. It was as though she saw the two women in her fighting for mastery. She took it out and tore it up.

"What's that?" asked Jim.

"A letter to you."

"Can't I see it?"

"You'd hate it."

That extraordinary man threw back his head and laughed like a kid. There was no doubt about it, he was a worm, but at any rate he was her worm; he didn't divide his attentions, and even if she didn't think much of him, there was no one else she thought more of. She couldn't merely sit at home, waiting for someone who'd overlook her past. Fellows in Ireland were death on girls' pasts.

But now the sense of guilt was ingrained: when she met Jim in town she merely saluted him, and if she had anyone with her she tried to avoid doing even that. It was funny, but she felt if she stopped to speak to him she would suddenly be overcome by the popular feeling and tear his eyes out. It was again that feeling that she was really two women and didn't know which of them she wanted to be.

As a result it was months before people knew they were walking out again. This time there was a thundering row and the Reillys were the most scandalized of all. Even Joan deserted her. It was all very well for Brigid, who had her draper where he couldn't escape, but Joan's bank-clerk was still a toss-up and everyone knew the unmannerly way the banks had of prying into their officials' business.

"Honest to God," Joan said contemptuously, "you haven't a spark of pride or decency."

"Well, neither has he, so we're well matched," Evelyn said despondently.

"God knows, 'tis a pity to spoil two houses with ye."

"It's all very well for you, Joan," said Evelyn, "but I have the kid's future to think of."

This wasn't true; it was a long time since Evelyn had thought of Owen's future because it was only too plain that he had none, but it was the best excuse she could think of.

"You'd hate him to be an only child," snapped Joan.

"I'm not such a fool," said Evelyn, deeply hurt.

"Fool is the word," retorted Joan.

Her father ignored her presence in the house. The latest scandal was the final touch. He was disappointed in Evelyn but he was far more disappointed in Jim, who had once shown signs of character. Up to this he had felt it was only daughters who threatened a man's peace of mind; now he began to think a son might be as bad.

When Joan married it made things easier for him, though not for Evelyn. It is always a lonesome thing for a girl when the last of her sisters has gone and the prams have begun to come back. It was worse on her because she had never pushed her own pram, and the babies she fussed over were getting something her own would never get. It fixed and confirmed her feeling of inferiority to Brigid and Joan, almost as though she had done it deliberately. She sometimes wondered whether she hadn't.

But it gradually dawned on her father that if God had tried to reward him for a well-spent life with a secure old age, He couldn't well have planned anything more satisfactory than a more or less unmarriageable daughter who could never take a high moral line. If he came in drunk every night of the week and cut her down on the housekeeping, her sins would still outnumber his. A man like Myles in such an unassailable position of moral superiority could not help being kind. "God's truth," he muttered to his cronies, "I can't blame the girl. I'm as bad myself. It's a thing you can't talk about, but since the missis died I had my own temptations." Sometimes when he saw her getting ready to go out and see Jim Piper he patted her on the shoulder, mumbled a few words of encouragement, and went out with his eyes wet. Myles was like that, a man of no character!

IV

One evening while he and Evelyn were having their tea the latch was lifted and Jim Piper himself walked in. It was his first visit since the far-away night when he had called to console Myles for his daughter's crime.

"God save all here," he said and beamed at them with unusual magnanimity.

Myles looked up, drew a deep breath through his nose and looked away. It was all damn well condoning his daughter's misbehaviour, but he refused to condone Jim's. Even Evelyn was embarrassed and cross. It wasn't like Jim.

"Hello," she replied with no great warmth. "What do you want?"

"Oh, just a few words with you," Jim replied cheerfully, placing a chair for himself in the middle of the kitchen. "Nothing important. Don't interrupt yourself. Finish your supper. If you have a paper I could look at it."

"There you are," she said, mystified, but no newspaper was capable of halting Jim's unusual flow of garrulity.

"Good evening, Mr. Reilly," he said to her father, and then as Myles ignored him he threw back his head and laughed. "I don't know what's coming over Irish hospitality," he added with a touch of indignation. "You pass the time of day to a man and he won't even answer. Begod," he added with growing scorn, "they won't even ask you to sit down. Go on with their tea overright you, and not ask have you a mouth on you! 'What do you want?'" he echoed Evelyn.

She realized in a flash what was the matter with him. He was drunk. She had never seen him so bad before, and he was not the type which gets drunk gracefully. He was too angular for that. He threw his limbs about in a dislocated way like a rag doll. All the same it put her at her ease. She was always more comfortable with men like that.

"Far from tea you were today, wherever you were," she said, fetching a cup and saucer. "Do you want tea?"

"Oh, no," said Jim bitterly with another dislocated motion of his arm. "I'm only making conversation. I didn't have a bit to eat since morning and then I'm asked if I want tea!"

"You'd better have something to eat so," she said. "Will you have sausages?"

"Isn't it about time you asked me?" Jim asked with grave reproach, looking at her owlishly.

It was only with the greatest difficulty that she kept from laughing outright. But her father, who had recognized Jim's condition from the start, had the toper's sensitiveness. He drew a deep breath through his nose, banged his fist on the table, and exploded in a "Christ! In my own house!" Then he got up, went upstairs and slammed the bedroom door behind him. No doubt he was resisting the temptation to kill Jim with his own hands. Jim laughed. Apparently he had no notion of his peril.

"Call him back," he said, tossing his head.

"Why?"

"I want to ask him to my wedding."

"Go on!" she said with amusement. "Are you getting married?"

"I can't stand this bloody bachelor life," Jim said pathetically.

"So I noticed," she said. "Who's the doll?"

"One moment, please!" he said severely. "We're coming to that. First, I have a crow to pluck with you."

"Go on!" she said, her smile fading. People always seemed to have crows to pluck with Evelyn, and she was getting tired of it.

"You said you wouldn't marry me if I was the last living thing in the world," he said, wagging his finger sternly at her. "I'm not a man to bear malice but I'm entitled to remind you of what you said. As well as that, you said I was a worm. I'm not complaining about that either. All I'm doing is asking are you prepared—prepared to withdraw those statements?" he finished up successfully.

"You never know," she said, her lip beginning to quiver. "You might ask me again some time you're sober."

"You think I don't know what I'm saying?" he asked triumphantly as he rose to his feet—but he rose unsteadily.

"Do you?" she asked.

"I banked the last of two hundred quid today," said Jim in the same tone. "Two hundred quid and five for Ring, and if that's not enough for the old bastard I'll soon find someone that will be glad of it. I drank the rest. You can go down the country now, to-morrow if you like, and bring Ownie back, and tell the whole bloody town to kiss your ass. Now, do I know what I'm saying?" he shouted with the laughter bubbling up through his words.

It was a great pity he couldn't remain steady. But Evelyn no longer noticed that. She only noticed the laughter and triumph and realized how much of Jim's life she had wasted along with her own. She gave a low cry and ran upstairs after her father. Jim looked after her dazedly and collapsed with another dislocated gesture. It was useless trying to carry on a discussion with an unstable family like the Reillys who kept running up and down stairs the whole time.

It was her father's turn now. He stumped heavily down the stairs, gripping the banisters with both hands as though he were about to spring, and then stood at the foot. This time it was clear that Jim's hour had come. He didn't mind. He knew he was going to be sick anyway.

"What's wrong with that girl?" Myles asked in a shaking voice.

"I don't know," Jim said despondently, tossing the limp wet hair back from his forehead. "Waiting, I suppose."

"Waiting?" Myles asked. "Waiting for what?"

"This," shouted Jim, waving his arm wildly and letting it collapse by his side. "The money is there now. Two hundred quid, and five for the priest. You start work on that house at eight tomorrow morning. See?"

Myles took a few moments to digest this. Even for a man of expansive nature, from murder to marriage is a bit of a leap. He stroked his chin and looked at Jim, lying there with his head hanging and one arm dead by his side. He chuckled. Such a story! Christ, such a story!

"And not a drop of drink in the house!" he exclaimed. "Evelyn!" he called up the stairs.

There was no reply.

"Evelyn!" he repeated peremptorily, as though he were a man accustomed to instant obedience. "We'll let her alone for a while," he mumbled, scratching his head. "I suppose it came as a bit of shock to her. She's a good girl, Jim, a fine girl. You're making no mistake. Take it from me." But even in that state, Jim, he realized, was not the sort to need encouragement, and he beamed and rubbed his hands. For more than anything else in the world Myles loved a man, a *man*. He stood looking fondly down on his semiconscious son-in-law.

"You thundering ruffian!" he chuckled, shaking his head. "Oh, God, if only I might have done it thirty years ago I'd be a made man today."

THE LUCEYS

It's extraordinary, the bitterness there can be in a town like ours
between two people of the same family. More particularly between two people of the same family. I suppose living more or
less in public as we do we are either killed or cured by it, and the
same communal sense that will make a man be battered into a
reconciliation he doesn't feel gives added importance to whatever
quarrel he thinks must not be composed. God knows, most of
the time you'd be more sorry for a man like that than anything
else.

The Luceys were like that. There were two brothers, Tom and
Ben, and there must have been a time when the likeness between
them was greater than the difference, but that was long before
most of us knew them. Tom was the elder; he came in for the
drapery shop. Ben had to have a job made for him on the County
Council. This was the first difference and it grew and grew. Both
were men of intelligence and education but Tom took it more
seriously. As Ben said with a grin, he could damn well afford to
with the business behind him.

It was an old-fashioned shop which prided itself on only stocking the best, and though the prices were high and Tom in his
irascible opinionated way refused to abate them—he said haggling
was degrading!—a lot of farmer's wives would still go nowhere
else. Ben listened to his brother's high notions with his eyes
twinkling, rather as he read the books which came his way, with
profound respect and the feeling that this would all be grand for
some other place, but was entirely inapplicable to the affairs of
the County Council. God alone would ever be able to disentangle

these, and meanwhile the only course open to a prudent man was to keep his mind to himself. If Tom didn't like the way the County Council was run, neither did Ben, but that was the way things were, and it rather amused him to rub it in to his virtuous brother.

Tom and Ben were both married. Tom's boy, Peter, was the great friend of his cousin, Charlie—called "Charliss" by his Uncle Tom. They were nice boys; Peter a fat, heavy, handsome lad who blushed whenever a stranger spoke to him, and Charles with a broad face that never blushed at anything. The two families were always friendly; the mothers liked to get together over a glass of port wine and discuss the fundamental things that made the Lucey brothers not two inexplicable characters but two aspects of one inexplicable family character; the brothers enjoyed their regular chats about the way the world was going, for intelligent men are rare and each appreciated the other's shrewdness.

Only young Charlie was occasionally mystified by his Uncle Tom; he hated calling for Peter unless he was sure his uncle was out, for otherwise he might be sent into the front room to talk to him. The front room alone was enough to upset any high-spirited lad, with its thick carpet, mahogany sideboard, ornamental clock, and gilt mirror with cupids. The red curtains alone would depress you, and as well as these there was a glass-fronted mahogany bookcase the length of one wall, with books in sets, too big for anyone only a priest to read: *The History of Ireland, The History of the Popes, The Roman Empire, The Life of Johnson,* and *The Cabinet of Literature.* It gave Charlie the same sort of shivers as the priest's front room. His uncle suited it, a small, frail man, dressed in clerical black with a long pinched yellow face, tight lips, a narrow skull going bald up the brow, and a pair of tin specs.

All conversations with his uncle tended to stick in Charlie's mind for the simple but alarming reason that he never understood what the hell they were about, but one conversation in particular haunted him for years as showing the dangerous state of lunacy to which a man could be reduced by reading old books. Charlie was no fool, far from it; but low cunning and the most genuine benevolence were mixed in him in almost equal parts, producing a blend that was not without charm but gave no room for subtlety or irony.

"Good afternoon, Charliss," said his uncle after Charlie had tied what he called "the ould pup" to the leg of the hallstand. "How are you?"

"All right," Charlie said guardedly. (He hated being called Charliss; it made him sound such a sissy.)

"Take a seat, Charliss," said his uncle benevolently. "Peter will be down in a minute."

"I won't," said Charlie. "I'd be afraid of the ould pup."

"The expression, Charliss," said his uncle in that rasping little voice of his, "sounds like a contradiction in terms, but, not being familiar with dogs, I presume 'tis correct."

"Ah, 'tis," said Charlie, just to put the old man's mind at rest.

"And how is your father, Charliss?"

"His ould belly is bad again," said Charlie. "He'd be all right only the ould belly plays hell with him."

"I'm sorry to hear it," his uncle said gravely. "And tell me, Charliss," he added, cocking his head on one side like a bird, "what is he saying about me now?"

This was one of the dirtiest of his Uncle Tom's tricks, assuming that Charlie's father was saying things about him, which to give Ben his due, he usually was. But on the other hand, he was admitted to be one of the smartest men in town, so he was entitled to do so, while everyone without exception appeared to agree that his uncle had a slate loose. Charlie looked at him cautiously, low cunning struggling with benevolence in him, for his uncle though queer was open-handed, and you wouldn't want to offend him. Benevolence won.

"He's saying if you don't mind yourself you'll end up in the poorhouse," he said with some notion that if only his uncle knew the things people said about him he might mend his ways.

"Your father is right as always, Charliss," said his uncle, rising and standing on the hearth with his hands behind his back and his little legs well apart. "Your father is perfectly right. There are two main classes of people, Charliss—those who gravitate

towards the poorhouse and those who gravitate towards the
jail. . . . Do you know what 'gravitate' means, Charliss?"

"I do not," said Charlie without undue depression. It struck
him as being an unlikely sort of word.

" 'Gravitate,' Charliss, means 'tend' or 'incline.' Don't tell me
you don't know what they mean!"

"I don't," said Charlie.

"Well, do you know what this is?" his uncle asked smilingly
as he held up a coin.

"I do," said Charlie, humouring him as he saw that the conversation was at last getting somewhere. "A tanner."

"I am not familiar with the expression, Charliss," his uncle
said tartly and Charlie knew, whatever he'd said out of the way,
his uncle was so irritated that he was liable to put the tanner
back. "We'll call it sixpence. Your eyes, I notice, gravitate towards
the sixpence," (Charlie was so shocked that his eyes instantly
gravitated towards his uncle) "and in the same way, people
gravitate, or turn naturally, towards the jail or poorhouse. Only
a small number of either group reach their destination, though—
which might be just as well for myself and your father," he added
in a low impressive voice, swaying forward and tightening his
lips. "Do you understand a word I'm saying, Charliss?" he added
with a charming smile.

"I do not," said Charlie.

"Good man! Good man!" his uncle said approvingly. "I admire an honest and manly spirit in anybody. Don't forget your
sixpence, Charliss."

And as he went off with Peter, Charlie scowled and muttered
savagely under his breath: "Mod! Mod! Mod! The bleddy mon
is mod!"

II

When the boys grew up Peter trained for a solicitor while
Charlie, one of a large family, followed his father into the County
Council. He grew up a very handsome fellow with a square,
solemn, dark-skinned face, a thick red lower lip, and a mass of
curly black hair. He was reputed to be a great man with grey-

hounds and girls and about as dependable with one as with the other. His enemies called him "a crooked bloody bastard" and his father, a shrewd man, noted with alarm that Charlie thought him simpleminded.

The two boys continued the best of friends, though Peter, with an office in Asragh, moved in circles where Charlie felt himself lost; professional men whose status was calculated on their furniture and food and wine. Charlie thought that sort of entertainment a great pity. A man could have all the fun he wanted out of life without wasting his time on expensive and unsatisfactory meals and carrying on polite conversation while you dodged between bloody little tables that were always falling over, but Charlie, who was a modest lad, admired the way Peter never knocked anything over and never said: "Chrisht!" Wine, coffee-cups, and talk about old books came as easy to him as talk about a dog or a horse.

Charlie was thunderstruck when the news came to him that Peter was in trouble. He heard it first from Mackesy the detective, whom he hailed outside the courthouse. (Charlie was like his father in that; he couldn't let a man go by without a greeting.)

"Hullo, Matt," he shouted gaily from the courthouse steps. "Is it myself or my father you're after?"

"I'll let ye off for today," said Mackesy, making a garden-seat of the crossbar of his bicycle. Then he lowered his voice so that it didn't travel further than Charlie. "I wouldn't mind having a word with a relative of yours, though."

"A what, Matt?" Charlie asked, skipping down the steps on the scent of news. (He was like his father in that, too.) You don't mean one of the Luceys is after forgetting himself?"

"Then you didn't hear about Peter?"

"Peter! Peter in trouble! You're not serious, Matt?"

"There's a lot of his clients would be glad if I wasn't, Cha," Mackesy said grimly. "I thought you'd know about it as ye were such pals."

"But we are, man, we are," Charlie insisted. "Sure, wasn't I at the dogs with him—when was it?—last Thursday? I never noticed a bloody thing, though, now you mention it, he was lashing pound notes on that Cloonbullogue dog. I told him the Dalys could never train a dog."

Charlie left Mackesy, his mind in a whirl. He tore through the cashier's office. His father was sitting at his desk, signing paying-orders. He was wearing a grey tweed cap, a grey tweed suit, and a brown cardigan. He was a stocky, powerfully built man with a great expanse of chest, a plump, dark, hairy face, long quizzical eyes that tended to close in slits; hair in his nose, hair in his ears; hair on his high cheekbones that made them like small cabbage-patches.

He made no comment on Charlie's news, but stroked his chin and looked worried. Then Charlie shot out to see his uncle. Quill, the assistant, was serving in the shop and Charlie stumped in behind the counter to the fitting-room. His uncle had been looking out the back, all crumpled up. When Charlie came in he pulled himself erect with fictitious jauntiness. With his old black coat and wrinkled yellow face he had begun to look like an old rabbi.

"What's this I hear about Peter?" began Charlie, who was never one to be ceremonious.

"Bad news travels fast, Charlie," said his uncle in his dry little voice, clamping his lips so tightly that the wrinkles ran up his cheeks from the corners of his mouth. He was so upset that he forgot even to say "Charliss."

"Have you any notion how much it is?" asked Charlie.

"I have not, Charlie," Tom said bitterly. "I need hardly say my son did not take me into his confidence about the extent of his robberies."

"And what are you going to do?"

"What can I do?" The lines of pain belied the harsh little staccato that broke up every sentence into disjointed phrases as if it were a political speech. "You saw yourself, Charliss, the way I reared that boy. You saw the education I gave him. I gave him the thing I was denied myself, Charliss. I gave him an honourable profession. And now for the first time in my life I am ashamed to show my face in my own shop. What can I do?"

"Ah, now, ah, now, Uncle Tom, we know all that," Charlie

said truculently, "but that's not going to get us anywhere. What can we do now?"

"Is it true that Peter took money that was entrusted to him?" Tom asked oratorically.

"To be sure he did," replied Charlie without the thrill of horror which his uncle seemed to expect. "I do it myself every month, only I put it back."

"And is it true he ran away from his punishment instead of standing his ground like a man?" asked Tom, paying no attention to him.

"What the hell else would he do?" asked Charlie, who entirely failed to appreciate the spiritual beauty of atonement. "Begod, if I had two years' hard labour facing me you wouldn't see my heels for dust."

"I dare say you think I'm old-fashioned, Charliss," said his uncle, "but that's not the way I was reared, nor the way my son was reared."

"And that's where the ferryboat left ye," snorted Charlie. "Now that sort of thing may be all very well, Uncle Tom, but 'tis no use taking it to the fair. Peter made some mistake, the way we all make mistakes, but instead of coming to me or some other friend, he lost his nerve and started gambling. Chrisht, didn't I see it happen to better men? You don't know how much it is?"

"No, Charliss, I don't."

"Do you know where he is, even?"

"His mother knows."

"I'll talk to my old fellow. We might be able to do something. If the bloody fool might have told me on Thursday instead of backing that Cloonbullogue dog!"

Charlie returned to the office to find his father sitting at his desk with his hands joined and his pipe in his mouth, staring nervously at the door.

"Well?"

"We'll go over to Asragh and talk to Toolan of the Guards ourselves," said Charlie. "I want to find out how much he let himself in for. We might even get a look at the books."

"Can't his father do it?" Ben asked gloomily.

"Do you think he'd understand them?"

"Well, he was always fond of literature," Ben said shortly.

"God help him," said Charlie. "He has enough of it now."

"'Tis all his own conceit," Ben said angrily, striding up and down the office with his hands in his trouser pockets. "He was always good at criticizing other people. Even when you got in here it was all influence. Of course, he'd never use influence. Now he wants us to use it."

"That's all very well," Charlie said reasonably, "but this is no time for raking up old scores."

"Who's raking up old scores?" his father shouted angrily.

"That's right," Charlie said approvingly. "Would you like me to open the door so that you can be heard all over the office?"

"No one is going to hear me at all," his father said in a more reasonable tone—Charlie had a way of puncturing him. "And I'm not raking up any old scores. I'm only saying now what I always said. The boy was ruined."

"He'll be ruined with a vengeance unless we do something quick," said Charlie. "Are you coming to Asragh with me?"

"I am not."

"Why?"

"Because I don't want to be mixed up in it at all. That's why. I never liked anything to do with money. I saw too much of it. I'm only speaking for your good. A man done out of his money is a mad dog. You won't get any thanks for it, and anything that goes wrong, you'll get the blame."

Nothing Charlie could say would move his father, and Charlie was shrewd enough to know that everything his father said was right. Tom wasn't to be trusted in the delicate negotiations that would be needed to get Peter out of the hole; the word here, the threat there; all the complicated machinery of family pressure. And alone he knew he was powerless. Despondently he went and told his uncle and Tom received the news with resignation, almost without understanding.

But a week later Ben came back to the office deeply disturbed. He closed the door carefully behind him and leaned across the desk to Charlie, his face drawn. For a moment he couldn't speak.

"What ails you?" Charlie asked with no great warmth.

"Your uncle passed me just now in the Main Street," whispered his father.

Charlie wasn't greatly put out. All of his life he had been made a party to the little jabs and asides of father and uncle, and he did not realize what it meant to a man like his father, friendly and popular, this public rebuke.

"That so?" he asked without surprise. "What did you do to him?"

"I thought you might know that," his father said, looking at him with a troubled air from under the peak of his cap.

"Unless 'twas something you said about Peter?" suggested Charlie.

"It might, it might," his father agreed doubtfully. "You didn't —ah—repeat anything I said to you?"

"What a bloody fool you think I am!" Charlie said indignantly. "And indeed I thought you had more sense. What did you say?"

"Oh, nothing. Nothing only what I said to you," replied his father and went to the window to look out. He leaned on the sill and then tapped nervously on the frame. He was haunted by all the casual remarks he had made or might have made over a drink with an acquaintance—remarks that were no different from those he and Tom had been passing about one another all their lives. "I shouldn't have said anything at all, of course, but I had no notion 'twould go back."

"I'm surprised at my uncle," said Charlie. "Usually he cares little enough what anyone says of him."

But even Charlie, who had moments when he almost understood his peppery little uncle, had no notion of the hopes he had raised and which his more calculating father had dashed. Tom Lucey's mind was in a rut, a rut of complacency, for the idealist too has his complacency and can be aware of it. There are moments when he would be glad to walk through any mud, but he no longer knows the way; he needs to be led; he cannot degrade himself even when he is most ready to do so. Tom was ready to beg favours from a thief. Peter had joined the Air Force under an assumed name, and this was the bitterest blow of all to him, the extinction of the name. He was something of an amateur genealogist, and had managed to convince himself, God knows how, that his family was somehow related to the Gloucestershire Lucys. This was already a sort of death.

The other death didn't take long in coming. Charlie, in the way he had, got wind of it first, and, having sent his father to break the news to Min, he went off himself to tell his uncle. It was a fine spring morning. The shop was empty but for his uncle, standing with his back to the counter studying the shelves.

"Good morning, Charliss," he crackled over his shoulder. "What's the best news?"

"Bad, I'm afraid, Uncle Tom," Charlie replied, leaning across the counter to him.

"Something about Peter, I dare say?" his uncle asked casually, but Charlie noticed how, caught unawares, he had failed to say "my son," as he had taken to doing.

"Just so."

"Dead, I suppose?"

"Dead, Uncle Tom."

"I was expecting something of the sort," said his uncle. "May the Almighty God have mercy on his soul! . . . Con!" he called at the back of the shop while he changed his coat. "You'd better close up the shop. You'll find the crepe on the top shelf and the mourning-cards in my desk."

"Who is it, Mr. Lucey?" asked Con Quill. " 'Tisn't Peter?"

" 'Tis, Con, 'tis, I'm sorry to say," and Tom came out briskly with his umbrella over his arm. As they went down the street two people stopped them: the news was already round.

Charlie, who had to see about the arrangements for the funeral, left his uncle outside the house and so had no chance of averting the scene that took place inside. Not that he would have had much chance of doing so. His father had found Min in a state of collapse. Ben was the last man in the world to look after a woman, but he did manage to get her a pillow, put her legs on a chair and cover her with a rug, which was more than Charlie would have given him credit for. Min smelt of brandy. Then Ben strode up and down the darkened room with his hands in his pockets and his cap over his eyes, talking about the horrors of airplane travel. He knew he was no fit company for a woman of sensibility like Min, and he almost welcomed Tom's arrival.

"That's terrible news, Tom," he said.

"Oh, God help us!" cried Min. "They said he disgraced us but he didn't disgrace us long."

"I'd sooner 'twas one of my own, Tom," Ben said excitedly. "As God is listening to me I would. I'd still have a couple left, but he was all ye had."

He held out his hand to Tom. Tom looked at it, then at him, and then deliberately put his own hands behind his back.

"Aren't you going to shake hands with me, Tom?" Ben asked appealingly.

"No, Ben," Tom said grimly. "I am not."

"Oh, Tom Lucey!" moaned Min with her crucified smile. "Over your son's dead body!"

Ben looked at his brother in chagrin and dropped his hand. For a moment it looked as though he might strike him. He was a volatile, hot-tempered man.

"That wasn't what I expected from you, Tom," he said, making a mighty effort to control himself.

"Ben," said his brother, squaring his frail little shoulders, "you disrespected my son while he was alive. Now that he's dead I'd thank you to leave him alone."

"I disrespected him?" Ben exclaimed indignantly. "I did nothing of the sort. I said things I shouldn't have said. I was upset. You know the sort I am. You were upset yourself and I dare say you said things you regret."

" 'Tisn't alike, Ben," Tom said in a rasping, opinionated tone. "I said them because I loved the boy. You said them because you hated him."

"I hated him?" Ben repeated incredulously. "Peter? Are you out of your mind?"

"You said he changed his name because it wasn't grand enough for him," Tom said, clutching the lapels of his coat and stepping from one foot to another. "Why did you say such a mean, mocking, cowardly thing about the boy when he was in trouble?"

"All right, all right," snapped Ben. "I admit I was wrong to say it. There were a lot of things you said about my family, but I'm not throwing them back at you."

"You said you wouldn't cross the road to help him," said Tom. Again he primmed up the corners of his mouth and lowered his head. "And why, Ben? I'll tell you why. Because you were jealous of him."

"I was jealous of him?" Ben repeated. It seemed to him that he was talking to a different man, discussing a different life, as though the whole of his nature was being turned inside out.

"You were jealous of him, Ben. You were jealous because he had the upbringing and education your own sons lacked. And I'm not saying that to disparage your sons. Far from it. But you begrudged my son his advantages."

"Never!" shouted Ben in a fury.

"And I was harsh with him," Tom said, taking another nervous step forward while his neat waspish little voice grew harder, "I was harsh with him and you were jealous of him, and when his hour of trouble came he had no one to turn to. Now, Ben, the least you can do is to spare us your commiserations."

"Oh, wisha, don't mind him, Ben," moaned Min. "Sure, everyone knows you never begrudged my poor child anything. The man isn't in his right mind."

"I know that, Min," Ben said, trying hard to keep his temper. "I know he's upset. Only for that he'd never say what he did say—or believe it."

"We'll see, Ben, we'll see," said Tom grimly.

III

That was how the row between the Luceys began, and it continued like that for years. Charlie married and had children of his own. He always remained friendly with his uncle and visited him regularly; sat in the stuffy front room with him and listened with frowning gravity to Tom's views, and no more than in his childhood understood what the old man was talking about. All he gathered was that none of the political parties had any principle and the country was in a bad way due to the inroads of the uneducated and ill-bred. Tom looked more and more like a rabbi. As is the way of men of character in provincial towns, he tended more and more to become a collection of mannerisms, a caricature of himself. His academic jokes on his simple customers became more elaborate; so elaborate, in fact, that in time he gave up trying to explain them and was content to be set down as merely queer. In a way it made things easier for Ben; he was able to treat the breach with Tom as another example of his brother's cantankerousness, and spoke of it with amusement and good nature.

Then he fell ill. Charlie's cares were redoubled. Ben was the world's worst patient. He was dying and didn't know it, wouldn't go to hospital, and broke the heart of his wife and daughter. He was awake at six, knocking peremptorily for his cup of tea; then waited impatiently for the paper and the post. "What the hell is keeping Mick Duggan? That fellow spends half his time gossiping along the road. Half past nine and no post!" After that the day was a blank to him until evening when a couple of County Council chaps dropped in to keep him company and tell him what was afoot in the courthouse. There was nothing in the long low room, plastered with blue and green flowered wallpaper, but a bedside table, a press, and three or four holy pictures, and Ben's mind was not on these but on the world outside—feet passing and repassing on errands which he would never be told about. It broke his heart. He couldn't believe he was as bad as people tried to make out; sometimes it was the doctor he blamed, sometimes the chemist who wasn't careful enough of the bottles and pills he made up—Ben could remember some shocking cases. He lay in bed doing involved calculations about his pension.

Charlie came every evening to sit with him. Though his father didn't say much about Tom, Charlie knew the row was always there in the back of his mind. It left Ben bewildered, a man without bitterness. And Charlie knew he came in for some of the blame. It was the illness all over again: someone must be slipping up somewhere; the right word hadn't been dropped in the right quarter or a wrong one had been dropped instead. Charlie, being so thick with Tom, must somehow be to blame. Ben did not understand the inevitable. One night it came out.

"You weren't at your uncle's?" Ben asked.

"I was," Charlie said with a nod. "I dropped in on the way up."

"He wasn't asking about me?" Ben asked, looking at him out of the corner of his eye.

"Oh, he was," Charlie said with a shocked air. "Give the man his due, he always does that. That's one reason I try to drop in every day. He likes to know."

But he knew this was not the question his father wanted answered. That question was: "Did you say the right words? Did you make me out the feeble figure you should have made me out, or did you say the wrong thing, letting him know I was better?" These things had to be managed. In Charlie's place Ben would have managed it splendidly.

"He didn't say anything about dropping up?" Ben asked with affected lightness.

"No," Charlie said with assumed thoughtfulness. "I don't remember."

"There's blackness for you!" his father said with sudden bitterness. It came as a shock to Charlie; it was the first time he had heard his father speak like that, from the heart, and he knew the end must be near.

"God knows," Charlie said, tapping one heel nervously, "he's a queer man. A queer bloody man!"

"Tell me, Charlie," his father insisted, "wouldn't you say it to him? 'Tisn't right and you know 'tisn't right."

" 'Tisn't," said Charlie, tearing at his hair, "but to tell you the God's truth I'd sooner not talk to him."

"Yes," his father added in disappointment. "I see it mightn't do for you."

Charlie realized that his father was thinking of the shop, which would now come to him. He got up and stood against the fireplace, a fat, handsome, moody man.

"That has nothing to do with it," he said. "If he gave me cause I'd throw his bloody old shop in his face in the morning. I don't want anything from him. 'Tis just that I don't seem to be able to talk to him. I'll send Paddy down tonight and let him ask him."

"Do, do," his father said with a knowing nod. "That's the very thing you'll do. And tell Julie to bring me up a drop of whisky and a couple of glasses. You'll have a drop yourself?"

"I won't."

"You will, you will. Julie will bring it up."

Charlie went to his brother's house and asked him to call on Tom and tell him how near the end was. Paddy was a gentle good-natured boy with something of Charlie's benevolence and none of his guile.

"I will to be sure," he said. "But why don't you tell him? Sure he thinks the world of you."

"I'll tell you why, Paddy," Charlie whispered with his hand on his brother's sleeve. "Because if he refused me I might do him some injury."

"But you don't think he will?" Paddy asked in bewilderment.

"I don't think at all, Paddy," Charlie said broodingly. "I know."

He knew all right. When he called on his way home the next afternoon his mother and sister were waiting for him, hysterical with excitement. Paddy had met with a cold refusal. Their hysteria was infectious. He understood now why he had caught people glancing at him curiously in the street. It was being argued out in every pub, what Charlie Lucey ought to do. People couldn't mind their own bloody business. He rapped out an oath at the two women and took the stairs three at a time. His father was lying with his back to the window. The whisky was still there as Charlie had seen it the previous evening. It tore at his heart more than the sight of his father's despair.

"You're not feeling too good?" he said gruffly.

"I'm not, I'm not," Ben said, lifting the sheet from his face. "Paddy didn't bring a reply to that message?" he added questioningly.

"Do you tell me so?" Charlie replied, trying to sound shocked.

"Paddy was always a bad man to send on a message," his father said despondently, turning himself painfully in the bed, but still not looking at Charlie. "Of course, he hasn't the sense. Tell me, Charlie," he added in a feeble voice, "weren't you there when I was talking about Peter?"

"About Peter?" Charlie exclaimed in surprise.

"You were, you were," his father insisted, looking at the window. "Sure, 'twas from you I heard it. You wanted to go to Asragh to look at the books, and I told you if anything went wrong you'd get the blame. Isn't that all I said?"

Charlie had to readjust his mind before he realized that his father had been going over it all again in the long hours of loneliness and pain, trying to see where he had gone wrong. It seemed to make him even more remote. Charlie didn't remember what his father had said; he doubted if his uncle remembered.

"I might have passed some joke about it," his father said, "but sure I was always joking him and he was always joking me. What the hell more was there in it?"

"Oh, a chance remark!" agreed Charlie.

"Now, the way I look at that," his father said, seeking his eyes for the first time, "someone was out to make mischief. This town is full of people like that. If you went and told him he'd believe you."

"I will, I will," Charlie said, sick with disgust. "I'll see him myself today."

He left the house, cursing his uncle for a brutal egotist. He felt the growing hysteria of the town concentrating on himself and knew that at last it had got inside him. His sisters and brothers, the people in the little shops along the street, expected him to bring his uncle to book, and failing that, to have done with him. This was the moment when people had to take their side once and for all. And he knew he was only too capable of taking sides.

Min opened the door to him, her red-rimmed eyes dirty with tears and the smell of brandy on her breath. She was near hysterics, too.

"What way is he, Charlie?" she wailed.

"Bad enough, Aunt Min," he said as he wiped his boots and went past her. "He won't last the night."

At the sound of his voice his uncle had opened the sitting-room door and now he came out and drew Charlie in by the hand. Min followed. His uncle didn't release his hand, and betrayed his nervousness only by the way his frail fingers played over Charlie's hand, like a woman's.

"I'm sorry to hear it, Charliss," he said.

"Sure, of course you are, Uncle Tom," said Charlie, and at the first words the feeling of hysteria within him dissolved and left only a feeling of immense understanding and pity. "You know what brought me?"

His uncle dropped his hand.

"I do, Charliss," he said and drew himself erect. They were neither of them men to beat about the bush.

"You'll come and see the last of him," Charlie said, not even marking the question.

"Charliss," Tom said with that queer tightening at the corners of his mouth, "I was never one to hedge or procrastinate. I will not come."

He almost hissed the final words. Min broke into a loud wail.

"Talk to him, Charlie, do! I'm sick and tired of it. We can never show our faces in the town again."

"And I need hardly say, Charliss," his uncle continued with an air of triumph that was almost evil, "that that doesn't trouble me."

"I know," Charlie said earnestly, still keeping his eyes on the withered old face with the narrow-winged, almost transparent nose. "And you know that I never interfered between ye. Whatever disagreements ye had, I never took my father's side against you. And 'twasn't for what I might get out of you."

In his excitement his uncle grinned, a grin that wasn't natural, and that combined in a strange way affection and arrogance, the arrogance of the idealist who doesn't realize how easily he can be fooled.

"I never thought it, boy," he said, raising his voice. "Not for an instant. Nor 'twasn't in you."

"And you know too you did this once before and you regretted it."

"Bitterly! Bitterly!"

"And you're going to make the same mistake with your brother that you made with your son?"

"I'm not forgetting that either, Charliss," said Tom. "It wasn't today nor yesterday I thought of it."

"And it isn't as if you didn't care for him," Charlie went on remorselessly. "It isn't as if you had no heart for him. You know he's lying up there waiting for you. He sent for you last night and you never came. He had the bottle of whisky and the two glasses by the bed. All he wants is for you to say you forgive him. . . . Jesus Christ, man," he shouted with all the violence in him roused, "never mind what you're doing to him. Do you know what you're doing to yourself?"

"I know, Charliss," his uncle said in a cold, excited voice. "I know that too. And 'tisn't as you say that I have no heart for him. God knows it isn't that I don't forgive him. I forgave him long years ago for what he said about—one that was very dear to me. But I swore that day, Charliss, that never the longest day I lived would I take your father's hand in friendship, and if God was to strike me dead at this very moment for my presumption I'd say the same. You know me, Charliss," he added, gripping the lapels of his coat. "I never broke my word yet to God or man. I won't do it now."

"Oh, how can you say it?" cried Min. "Even the wild beasts have more nature."

"Some other time I'll ask you to forgive me," added Tom, ignoring her.

"You need never do that, Uncle Tom," Charlie said with great simplicity and humbleness. "'Tis yourself you'll have to forgive."

At the door he stopped. He had a feeling that if he turned he would see Peter standing behind him. He knew his uncle's barren pride was all he could now offer to the shadow of his son, and that it was his dead cousin who stood between them. For a moment he felt like turning and appealing to Peter. But he was never much given to the supernatural. The real world was trouble enough for him, and he went slowly homeward, praying that he might see the blinds drawn before him.

THE HOLY DOOR

Polly Donegan and Nora Lawlor met every morning after eight o'clock Mass. They were both good-living girls; indeed, they were among the best girls in town. Nora had a round soft face and great round wondering eyes. She was inquisitive, shy, and a dreamer—an awkward combination. Her father, a builder called Jerry Lawlor, had been vice-commandant of the Volunteers during the Troubles.

Polly was tall, with coal-black hair, a long, proud, striking face, and an air of great calm and resolution. As they went down the hill from the church she saluted everyone with an open pleasant smile and accepted whatever invitations she got. Nora went through the torments of the damned whenever anyone invited her anywhere; curiosity and timidity combined made her visualize every consequence of accepting or not accepting, down to the last detail.

Now Nora, with that peculiar trait in her make-up, had a knack which Polly found very disconcerting of bringing the conversation round to the facts of life. To Nora the facts of life were the ultimate invitation; acceptance meant never-ending embarrassment, refusal a curiosity unsatisfied till death. While she struggled to put her complex in words Polly adopted a blank and polite air and without the least effort retreated into her own thoughts of what they should have for dinner.

"You're not listening to a word I say," Nora said on a note of complaint.

"Oh, I am, Nora, I am," Polly said impatiently. "But I'll have to be rushing or I'll be late for breakfast."

Nora could see that Polly wasn't even interested in the facts of life. She wondered a lot about that. Was Polly natural? Was it possible not to be curious? Was she only acting sly like all the Donegans? Nora had thought so long about God's inscrutable purpose in creating mankind in two sexes that she could hardly see the statue of a saint without wondering what he'd be like without his clothes. That was no joke in our church, where there are statues inside the door and in each of the sidechapels and along the columns of the arcade. It makes the church quite gay, but it was a terrible temptation to Nora, who found it hard not to see them all like Greek statues, and whatever it was about their faces and gestures they seemed worse like that than any Greek divinities. To the truly pious mind there is something appalling in the idea of St. Aloysius Gonzaga without his clothes.

That particular notion struck Polly as the height of nonsense. "Wisha, Nora," she said with suppressed fury, "what things you think about!"

"But after all," retorted Nora with a touch of fire, "they must have had bodies like the rest of us."

"Why then indeed, Nora, they'd be very queer without them," said Polly serenely, and it was clear to Nora that she hadn't a glimmer. "Anyway, what has it to do with us?"

"You might find it has a lot to do with you when you get married," said Nora darkly.

"Ah, well, it'll never worry me so," said Polly confidently.

"Why, Polly? Won't you ever get married?"

"What a thing I'd do!" said Polly.

"But why, Polly?" asked Nora eagerly, hoping that at last she might discover some point where Polly's fastidiousness met her own.

"Ah," Polly sighed, "I could never imagine myself married. No matters how fond of them you'd be. Like Susie. I always hated sharing a room with Susie. She was never done talking."

"Oh, if talking was all that was in it!" exclaimed Nora with a dark brightness like a smile.

"I think talking is the worst of all, Nora," Polly said firmly. "I can't imagine anything worse."

"There's a shock in store for you if you do marry," said Nora darkly.

"What sort of shock, Nora?" asked Polly.

"Oh, of course, you can't even describe it," said Nora fretfully. "No one will even tell you. People you knew all your life go on as if you were only a child and couldn't be told."

"Do they really, Nora?" Polly said with a giggle, inspired less by thought of what the mystery could be than by that of Nora's inquisitiveness brought to a full stop for once.

"If you get married before me will you tell me?" Nora asked.

"Oh, I will to be sure, girl," said Polly in the tone of one promising to let her know when the coal man came.

"But I mean everything, Polly," Nora said earnestly.

"Oh, why wouldn't I, Nora?" Polly cried impatiently, showing that Nora's preoccupation with the facts of life struck her as being uncalled-for. "Anyway, you're more likely to be married than I am. Somehow I never had any inclination for it."

It was clear that her sister's garrulity had blighted some man's chance of Polly.

II

Charlie Cashman was a great friend of Nora's father and a regular visitor to her home. He had been her father's Commandant during the Troubles. He owned the big hardware store in town and this he owed entirely to his good national record. He and his mother had never got on, for she hated the Volunteers as she hated the books he read; she looked on him as a flighty fellow and had determined early in his life that the shop would go to her second son, John Joe. As Mrs. Cashman was a woman who had never known what it was not to have her own way, Charlie had resigned himself to this, and after the Troubles, cleared out and worked as a shop assistant in Asragh. But then old John Cashman died, having never in his liftime contradicted his wife, and his will was found to be nothing but a contradiction. It seemed that he had always been a violent nationalist and admired culture and hated John Joe, and Charlie, as in the novels, got every damn thing, even his mother being left in the house only on sufferance.

Charlie was a good catch and there was no doubt of his liking for Nora, but somehow Nora couldn't bear him. He was an airy, excitable man with a plump, sallow, wrinkled face that always looked as if it needed shaving, a pair of keen grey eyes in slits under bushy brows; hair on his cheekbones, hair in his ears, hair even in his nose. He wore a dirty old tweed suit and a cap. Nora couldn't stand him—even with his clothes on. She told herself that it was the cleft in his chin, which someone had once told her betokened a sensual nature, but it was really the thought of all the hair. It made him look so animal!

Besides, there was something sly and double-meaning about him. He was, by town standards, a very well-read man. Once he found Nora reading St. Francis de Sales and asked her if she'd ever read *Romeo and Juliet* with such a knowing air that he roused her dislike even further. She gave him a cold and penetrating look which should have crushed him but didn't—he was so thick.

"As a matter of fact I have," she said steadily, just to show him that true piety did not exclude a study of the grosser aspects of life.

"What did you think of it?" he asked.

"I thought it contained a striking moral lesson," said Nora.

"Go on!" Charlie exclaimed with a grin. "What was that, Nora?"

"It showed where unrestrained passion can carry people," she said.

"Ah, I wouldn't notice that," said Charlie. "Your father and myself were a bit wild too, in our time."

Her father, a big, pop-eyed, open-gobbed man, looked at them both and said nothing, but he knew from their tone that they were sparring across him and he wanted to know more about it. That night after Charlie had gone he looked at Nora with a terrible air.

"What's that book Charlie Cashman was talking about?" he asked. "Did I read that?"

"*Romeo and Juliet*?" she said with a start. "It's there on the shelf behind you. In the big Shakespeare."

Jerry took down the book and looked even more astonished.

"That's a funny way to write a book," he said. "What is it about?"

She told him the story as well as she could, with a slight tendency to make Friar Laurence the hero, and her father looked more pop-eyed than ever. He had a proper respect for culture.

"But they were married all right?" he asked at last.

"They were," said Nora. "Why?"

"Ah, that was a funny way to take him up so," her father said cantankerously. " 'Tisn't as if there was anything wrong in it." He went to the foot of the stairs with his hands in his trouser pockets while Nora watched him with a hypnotised air. She knew what he was thinking of. "Mind," he said, "I'm not trying to force him on you, but there's plenty of girls in this town would be glad of your chance."

That was all he said but Nora wanted no chances. She would have preferred to die in the arena like a Christian martyr sooner than marry a man with so much hair. She never even gave Charlie the opportunity of proposing, though she knew her father and he had discussed it between themselves.

And then, to her utter disgust, Charlie transferred his attentions to Polly, whom he had met at her house. Of course, her disgust had nothing to do with jealousy of Polly. Mainly it was inspired by the revelation it afforded of masculine character, particularly of Charlie's. Sensual, flighty, he had not had the decency to remain a celibate for the rest of his life; he hadn't threatened suicide, hadn't even to be taken away for a long holiday by his friends. He merely cut his losses as though she were a type of car he couldn't afford and took the next cheapest.

It left her depressed about human nature in general. Only too well had her father gauged the situation. Not only did the Donegans go all-out to capture Charlie but Polly herself seemed quite pleased. After all she had said against marriage, this struck Nora as sly. In more judicious moments she knew she was not being quite fair to Polly. The truth was probably that Polly, being a good-natured, dutiful girl, felt if she were to marry at all, she should do so in such a way as to oblige her family. She did not mind the hair and had a genuine liking for Charlie. She was a modest girl who made no claim to brains; she never even knew which of the two parties was the government of the moment, and Charlie could explain it all to her in the most interesting way. To her he seemed a man of really gigantic intellect, and listening to him was like listening to a great preacher.

Yet, even admitting all this, Nora thought her conduct pretty strange. The Donegans were all sly. It caused a certain coldness between the two girls, but Polly was self-centred and hard-hearted and Nora got the worst of that.

III

Like all young brides-to-be, Polly was full of plans. When Charlie asked where they should go on their honeymoon she looked troubled.

"Ah, 'twould cost too much," she said in her tangential way.

"What would cost too much, girl?" Charlie replied recklessly. "Never mind what it costs. Where do you want to go?"

"Lourdes?" Polly asked, half as a question. "Is that far, Charlie?"

"Lourdes," repeated Charlie in bewilderment. "What do you want to go to Lourdes for?"

"Oh, only for the sake of the pilgrimage," said Polly. "You never read *The Life of Bernadette,* Charlie?"

"Never," said Charlie promptly, in dread he was going to be compelled to read it. "We'll go to Lourdes."

It was all arranged when one day Polly and Nora met in the street. Nora was self-conscious; she was thinking of all the things she had said of Charlie to Polly and certain they had got back (they hadn't, but Nora judged by herself).

"Where are ye going for the honeymoon?" she asked.

"You'd never guess," replied Polly joyously.

"Where?" Nora asked, her eyes beginning to pop.

"Lourdes, imagine!"

"Lourdes?" cried Nora aghast. "But didn't you know?"

"Know what, Nora?" Polly asked, alarmed in her turn. "Don't tell me 'tis forbidden."

" 'Tisn't that at all but 'tis unlucky," said Nora breathlessly. "I only knew one girl that did it and she died inside a year."

"Oh, Law, Nora," Polly cried with bitter disappointment, "how is it nobody told me that, or what sort of people do they have in those travel agencies?"

"I suppose they took it for granted you'd know," said Nora.

"How *could* I know, Nora?" Polly cried despairingly. "Even Charlie doesn't know, and he's supposed to be an educated man."

Away she rushed to challenge Charlie and they had their first big row. Charlie was now reconciled to Lourdes by the prospect of a few days in Paris, and he stamped and fumed about Nora Lawlor and her blasted pishrogues, but you did not catch a prudent girl like Polly risking fortune and happiness by defying the will of God, and a few days before the wedding everything was cancelled. They went to Connemara instead.

They arrived there on a wet evening and Polly said dismally that it wasn't in the least like what she expected. This was not the only thing that failed to come up to expectations, nor was hers the only disappointment. She had brought a little statue of the Blessed Virgin and put it on the table by her bed. Then she said her night prayers and undressed. She was rather surprised at the way Charlie looked at her but not really upset. She was exhausted after the journey and remarked to Charlie on the comfort of the bed. "Oh," she said with a yawn, "I don't think there's anything in the world like bed." At this Charlie gave her a wolfish grin, not like any grin she'd ever seen before, and it filled her with alarm. "Oh, Charlie, what did I say?" she asked. Charlie didn't reply, which was still more alarming; he got into bed beside her and she gave a loud gasp that could be heard right through the hotel.

For the rest of the night her brain, not usually retentive of ideas, had room only for one. "Can it be? Is it possible? Why did nobody tell me?" She kept herself from flying out of the room in hysterics only by repeating aspirations like "Jesus, mercy! Mary, help!" She thought of all the married women she had known from her mother on—fat pious, good-natured women you saw every morning at Mass—and wondered if they had lived all those years with such a secret in their hearts. Now she knew exactly what Nora had been trying to find out and why no one had ever told her. It was something that couldn't be told, only endured. One faint hope remained; that after years she might get used to it as the others seemed to have done. But then it all began again and she muttered aspirations to herself loud enough for Charlie to hear, and knew she could never, never get used to it; and when it was over a bitter anger smouldered in her against all the nonsense that had been written about it by old gasbags like Shakespeare. "Oh, what liars they are!" she thought, wishing she could just lay hands on one of them for five minutes. "What liars!"

The day after they returned from the honeymoon Nora called. She had managed to bottle her curiosity just so far. Charlie was in the shop and she smiled shyly at him. Polly and herself sat in the best room overlooking the Main Street and had their tea. Nora noticed with satisfaction that she looked a bit haggard. Then Nora lit a cigarette and sat back.

"And what does it feel like to be married?" she asked with a smile.

"Oh, all right, Nora," Polly replied, though for a moment her face looked more haggard than before.

"And how do you find Charlie?"

"Oh, much like anyone else, I suppose," Polly said doubtfully, and her eyes strayed in the direction of the window.

"And is that all you're going to tell us?" Nora went on with a nervous laugh.

"Oh, whatever do you mean, Nora?" Polly asked indignantly.

"I thought you were going to advise me," Nora said lightly, though with a growing feeling that there was nothing to be got out of Polly.

"Oh, Law, Nora," Polly said with a distraught air, "I don't think it can ever be right to talk about things like that."

Nora knew she would never get anything out of Polly. She would never get anything out of anybody. They were all the same. They went inside and the door closed behind them forever. She felt like crying.

"Was it as bad as that?" she asked with chagrin.

"I think I'd sooner not talk about it at all, Nora," Polly said firmly. She bowed her head; her smooth forehead became fenced with wrinkles and a second chin began to peep from beneath the first.

IV

Charlie's shop was on Main Street; a store like a cave, with buckets and spades hanging and stacked at either side of the opening. When you went in there was hardware on your right and the general store on the left. Charlie looked after the hardware and Polly and a girl assistant after the rest. Charlie's end of it was really well run; there wasn't a bit of agricultural machinery for miles around that he didn't know the workings of and for which, at a pinch, he couldn't produce at least the substitute for a spare part.

Polly wasn't brilliant in that way, but she was conscientious and polite. In every way she was all a wife should be; obliging, sweet-tempered, good-humoured, and so modest that she wouldn't even allow Charlie to put on the light while she dressed for Mass on a winter morning. Mrs. Cashman had always had a great selection of holy pictures but Polly had brought a whole gallery with her. There was also a Lourdes clock which played the Lourdes hymn at the Angelus hours—very soothing and devotional—but at the same time Charlie was just the least bit disappointed.

He was disappointed and he couldn't say why. "Romeo, Romeo, wherefore art thou, Romeo?" he would suddenly find himself declaiming about nothing at all. Italian women were probably different. No doubt it was the sun! He was a restless man and he had hoped marriage would settle him. It hadn't settled him. When he had closed the shop for the night and should have been sitting upstairs with his book and his pipe, the longing would suddenly seize him to go out to Johnny Desmond's pub instead. He would walk in and out the hall and peer up and down the street till the restlessness became too much for him. It was all very disconcerting. Sometimes for consolation he went back to the shop, switched on the lamp over his desk, and took out the copy of his father's will. This was the will from which he had expected nothing and which gave him everything. He read it through again with a reverent expression. He had always liked the will; admired its massive style, the way it carefully excluded all possibility of misunderstanding; it had given him a new respect for lawyers; indeed, in its own way it was as powerful as Shakespeare.

One murky, gloomy afternoon when business had stopped his mother came in and found him at it. He gave her a sly grin. She was a cranky, crafty, monotonous old woman, twisted with rheumatics and malice.

"I was just saying my office," he said.

"Oh, I see what you're at," she said with resignation. "I saw it long ago."

"Fine, devotional reading!" said Charlie, slapping a hairy paw on the will.

"Go on, you blasphemous bosthoon!" she said without rancour. "You were always too smart for your poor slob of a brother. But take care you wouldn't be keeping the bed warm for him yet!"

"What's that you say?" asked Charlie, startled.

"God spoke first," intoned his mother. "Many a better cake didn't rise."

She went out, banging the door behind her, and left Charlie gasping, naked to the cruel day. The will had lost its magical power. There was one clause in it to which he had never paid attention—there never had been any reason why he should do so —entailing the shop on his children, and, failing those, on John Joe's. And John Joe had four with another coming while Charlie still had none.

Another man only a year married wouldn't have given it a thought but Charlie wasn't that kind. The man was a born worrier. With his hands in his pockets he paced moodily to the shop door and stood there, leaning against the jamb, his legs crossed and his cap pulled down over his eyes.

His mother read him like a book. The least thing was enough to set him off. At the first stroke of the Angelus he put up the shutters and ate his supper. Then he lit his pipe and strolled to the hall door for a look up and down the Main Street on the off chance of seeing somebody or something. He never did, but it was as well to make sure. Then he returned to the kitchen, his feet beginning to drag as they usually did before he set out for Johnny Desmond's. It was their way of indicating that they weren't moving in the right direction. His mother had gone to the chapel and Polly was sitting by the table under the window. Charlie took a deep breath, removed his hands from his pockets, raised his head, and squared his shoulders.

"Well," he said briskly, "I might as well take a little turn."

"Wisha, you might as well, Charlie," Polly replied without resentment.

It was only what she always said, but in Charlie's state of depression it sounded like a dead key on the piano. He felt it was a hard thing that a married man of a year's standing had no inclination to stop at home and that his wife had no inclination to make him. Not that she could have made him even if she had tried but he felt that a little persuasion wouldn't have been out of place.

"The mother wasn't talking to you?" he asked keenly.

"No, Charlie," Polly said in surprise. "What would she talk to me about?"

"Oh, nothing in particular. . . . Only she was remarking that you were a long time about having a family," he added with a touch of reproach.

"Oh, Law, Charlie," Polly cried, "wasn't that a very queer thing for her to say?"

"Was it, I wonder?" Charlie said as though to himself but giving her a sideway glance.

"But Charlie, you don't think I won't have children, do you?" she exclaimed.

"Oh, no, no, no," Charlie replied hastily, in dread he might have said too much. "But 'twould suit her fine if you hadn't. Then she'd have the place for John Joe's children."

"But how would John Joe's children get it?" asked Polly. "Didn't your father leave it to you?"

"To me and my children," said Charlie. "If I hadn't children 'twould go to John Joe's."

"Oh, Law, Charlie, isn't that a great worry to you?"

"Well, it is, a bit," Charlie conceded, scratching his poll. "I put a lot of work into the place. No one likes working for another man's family. You wouldn't see a doctor?"

"I'd have to ask Father Ring first."

That upset Charlie again. He nearly told her it was Father Ring she should have married, but remembered in time that she'd be bound to confess it. There's nothing a good-living woman likes so much as confessing her husband's sins.

V

Charlie's remarks brought Polly for the first time up against the facts of life. This made her very thoughtful, but it was a week before she could even bring herself to discuss it with Nora. It was a subject you could only discuss with a woman, and an intellectual woman at that, and Nora was the only intellectual woman Polly knew.

Nora was not inclined to treat it as seriously as Charlie had done. According to her there was a lot of chance in it. Some people went on for years before they had a child; others didn't even wait for their time to be up. It was quite shocking when you came to think of it, but somehow Polly never did get round to thinking of it. If you were really in trouble, there was always the Holy Door. Johnny Fleming the barrister and his wife had been married ten years without having children, and they had made the pilgrimage to the Holy Door, and now people were beginning to say it was about time they made another to shut off the power.

"I suppose I could go next year if I had to," said Polly doubtfully.

"You'll have to go this year if you're going at all," said Nora. "It's only opened once in seven years."

"Seven years!" cried Polly. "Oh, I could never wait as long as that."

"It would be too dangerous anyway," said Nora. "There was a woman up our road waited till she was thirty-eight to have a child, and she died."

"Oh, Law!" cried Polly, a little peeved. "I suppose 'tis wrong to be criticizing, but really, the Lord's ways are very peculiar."

So back she went to Charlie with her story. Charlie screwed up his face as though he were hard of hearing, a favourite trick of his whenever he wanted to gain time. He wanted to gain it now.

"Where did you say?" he asked searchingly.

"Rome," repeated Polly.

"Rome?" echoed Charlie with a mystified air. "And what did you say you wanted to go to Rome for?"

"It's the pilgrimage to the Holy Door," said Polly. "You wouldn't know about that?" she asked in the trustful tone she used to indicate the respect she had for his learning.

"No," replied Charlie doubtfully, playing up to the part of the well-informed husband. "What sort of door?"

"A holy door."

"A holy door?"

" 'Tis only opened once in seven years, and 'tis good for people that want families," prompted Polly hopefully.

"Is that so?" asked Charlie gravely. "Who told you about that?"

"Nora Lawlor."

"Tut, tut, tut," clucked Charlie impatiently, "ah, I wouldn't say there would be any truth in that, Polly."

"Oh, Law, Charlie," she cried in ringing tones, outraged at his lack of faith, "you surely don't think the Flemings would go all that way unless there was something in it?"

"Oh, no, no, no, I dare say not," Charlie said hastily, seeing that any further objections he made were likely to be reported back to Father Ring. "I'm afraid I couldn't get away, though."

"Well, I'll have to get away, Charlie," Polly said with quiet decision. "It might be too late if I left it for another seven years. Nora says 'tis very dangerous."

"And a hell of a lot of danger that one will ever be in!" snapped Charlie fierily.

His bad temper did not last long. This was an excuse for an outing, and Charlie loved an outing. He had never been farther than London before; Paris staggered him; he experimented with green drinks, pink drinks, and yellow drinks with the satisfied expression of a child in a pantry; and while the train passed through the Alps in the late evening he wedged himself in the corridor with his elbows on the rail, humming "Home to Our Mountains," while tears of excitement poured down his hairy cheeks. He couldn't forget that he was going to the homeland of Romeo and Juliet.

He quickly made friends with the other two occupants of the carriage, a fat Dutchman in shirtsleeves who ate sausages and embraced the woman beside him who he said was his wife. The sight was too gross for Polly and she went and stood in the corridor but not to look at the scenery.

"Isn't she beautiful?" said the Dutchman, stroking his companion affectionately under the chin.

"Grand! grand!" agreed Charlie enthusiastically, nodding and smiling encouragement to the woman, who couldn't speak English and to all appearances didn't know much of any other language either.

"That's a nice-looking girl with you," said the Dutchman. "Who is she?"

"Polly?" said Charlie, looking at the gloomy figure in the corridor. "Oh, that's the wife."

"Whose wife?" asked the Dutchman.

"Mine," said Charlie.

"And don't you love her?"

"Love her?" echoed Charlie, giving another peep out. "I'm cracked on her, of course."

"Then why don't you make love to her?" asked the Dutchman in surprise. "Women can't have enough of it. Look at this!"

"Ah, mine wouldn't like it," said Charlie in alarm. "In Ireland we don't go in much for that sort of thing."

"And what do you go in for?"

"Well," said Charlie doubtfully, seeing that he didn't quite know, himself—apart from politics, which didn't sound right— "we're more in the sporting line; horses and dogs, you know."

"Ah," said the Dutchman earnestly, "you can't beat women."

Charlie went out to Polly, who was leaning with her back to the compartment and with a brooding look on her face.

"Charlie, how do they do it?" she asked in a troubled voice. "Wouldn't you think the woman would drop dead with shame? I suppose they're Protestants, are they, Charlie?"

"I dare say, I dare say," said Charlie, thinking it was better not to try and explain.

VI

It was a great outing and it lasted Charlie in small talk for a month. The grapes like gooseberries, and from nightfall on every little café with soprano or tenor or baritone bawling away about love—*amore, mio cuore, traditore*—you could see where Juliet got it. But they weren't there long enough for Polly to be infected, and all the wonders she brought back was her astonishment at the way the men in St. Peter's pinched her bottom. "Your what, Polly?" the neighbours asked in surprise. "My bottom," repeated Polly incredulously. "Would you believe it?"

After that, Morgan, the wit of Johnny Desmond's pub, began dropping nasty remarks about doors of one sort and another, while old Mrs. Cashman, getting over her alarm at the possibility of divine intervention, declared loudly that it would be a poor lookout for a woman like her to be relying on a son who had to take his wife to Rome. It didn't take a miracle to start John Joe's wife off, for the poor wretch had only to look at her.

But Polly, to give her her due, was every bit as upset as Charlie. Sixty pounds odd the pilgrimage had cost, and they had absolutely nothing to show for it. If the Holy Door couldn't do a thing like that it couldn't be so holy after all. She scolded Nora Lawlor a lot over her bad advice.

"But after all, Polly," Nora said reasonably, "you mustn't expect too much. It might be something mental."

"Oh, how could it, Nora?" Polly cried in a fury. "What a thing to say!"

"But why not?" asked Nora with a touch of asperity. "If you didn't feel attracted to Charlie—"

"Oh," said Polly vaguely and guardedly but with a dim comprehension dawning in her eyes, "would that make a difference?"

"It might make all the difference in the world, Polly," Nora said severely. "After all, there was Kitty Daly. She was married eight years without having a family, and one night she pretended to herself that her husband was Rudolph Valentino, and everything was all right."

"Rudolph Valentino?" said Polly. "Who's he?"

"He was a film actor," said Nora.

"But why would she do that?"

"Well, I suppose he was a nice-looking man, and you know what sort Jerome Daly is."

"Would there be a picture of that fellow that I could see?" asked Polly.

"I wouldn't say so," replied Nora. "Anyway, he's dead now, so I suppose it wouldn't be right. But, of course, there are plenty of others just as nice-looking."

"Oh, I don't think it could ever be right," cried Polly with a petulant toss of her head. She was feeling very sorry for herself. She knew quite well that that sly thing, Nora, was trying to worm out of her what Charlie really did to her and she was torn asunder between the need for revealing something and the desire not to reveal anything at all. "I'm sure Father Ring would say it was wrong."

"I don't see why he would," Nora said coolly. "After all, it was done with a good purpose."

Polly had no reply to that, for she knew the importance of doing things with a good purpose, but at the same time the temptation lingered. The following Saturday evening she went to confession to Father Ring. Her sins didn't take long to tell. They were never what you'd call major ones.

"Father," she said when she had done, "I want to ask your advice."

"What about, my child?" asked Father Ring.

"It's my husband, father," said Polly. "You see, we have no children, and I know it's a terrible worry to him, so I went on the pilgrimage to the Holy Door but it didn't do me any good."

"Go on," said Father Ring.

"So a friend of mine was telling me about another woman that was in the same position. It seems she imagined her husband was Rudolph Valentino."

"Who was he?"

"Some sort of fellow on the pictures."

"But what made her think he was her husband?" asked Father Ring with a puzzled frown.

"Oh, she didn't think it," said Polly in distress. "She only pretended. It seems he was a very nice-looking fellow and her husband is an insignificant little man. . . . Of course, I could understand that," she added candidly. "My husband is a very good fellow, but somehow he doesn't look right."

"Is it Charlie?" exclaimed Father Ring, so astonished that he broke the tone of decent anonymity in which the discussion was being conducted. "Sure, Charlie is a grand-looking man."

"Oh, would you think so?" asked Polly with real interest. "Of course I might be wrong. But anyway, this woman had a child after."

"What did she call him?" asked Father Ring.

"I don't know, father. Why? Does it make any difference?"

"No. I was just wondering."

"But tell me, father, would that ever be right?" asked Polly.

"Ah, I don't say there would be anything wrong about it," said Father Ring, pulling aside the curtain before the confessional and peeping out into the darkened church. "Of course she did it with a good object."

"That's what my friend said," said Polly, amazed at the intellect of that little gligeen of a girl.

"Provided, of course, she didn't get any pleasure from it," Father Ring added hastily. "If she got carnal pleasure out of it that would be a different thing."

"Oh!" exclaimed Polly, aghast. "You don't think she'd do that?"

"What I mean," the priest explained patiently, "is more than the natural pleasure."

"The natural pleasure?" repeated Polly with a stunned air.

"However," said Father Ring hastily, "I don't think you're in much danger of that."

It was shortly after this that Charlie began to notice a change in the atmosphere in Johnny Desmond's. Charlie was very sensitive to atmosphere. First Morgan passed a remark about Polly and the new teacher, Carmody. Now, Carmody was a relative of Father Ring's, as has been said, a good-looking plausible Kerryman who put on great airs with the women. Charlie greeted the remark with a sniff and a laugh and was almost on the point of telling how Polly wouldn't let him switch on the light while she dressed for Mass. Then he began to wonder. The remark

had stuck. The next time Polly's name was mentioned in connection with Carmody he scowled. It was clear that something
was going on and that he was the victim. He couldn't bear the
thought of that. It might be that in her innocence Polly was being indiscreet. On the other hand it might well be that like
many another woman before her, she was only letting on to be
innocent to get the chance of being indiscreet. A man could never
tell. He went home feeling very upset.

He strode in the hall and snapped a command to Polly, who
was sitting in the darkness over the range. She rose in surprise
and followed him meekly up the stairs. In the sitting-room he lit
the gas and stooped to look up under the mantel as though to
see if the burner was broken. Like all worriers Charlie considered
nothing beneath him.

"Sit down," he said curtly over his shoulder.

"Oh, Law, what is it at all, Charlie?" Polly asked nervously.

Charlie turned and stood on the hearthrug, his legs apart like
buttresses, his cap drawn down over his eyes, and seemed as if
he were studying her through his hairy cheekbones. It was a
matter that required study. He had no precedent for inquiring
whether or not Polly had been unfaithful to him.

"Tell me, Polly," he said at last in a reasonable tone which
seemed to suit the part, "did I do anything to you?"

"Oh, whatever do you mean, Charlie?" she asked in bewilderment. "What could you do to me?"

"That's just what I'd like to know," said Charlie, nodding
sagaciously. "What I did out of the way."

"Oh, Charlie," she exclaimed in alarm, "what a thing to say
to me! I never said you did anything out of the way."

"I'm glad to hear it," said Charlie, nodding again and looking
away across the room at the picture of a sailing-ship in distress.
"I suppose you don't know the new teacher in the school?" he
added with the innocent air of a cross-examining lawyer.

"Is it Mr. Carmody?" she asked, giving herself away at once
by the suspicion of a blush.

"Aha, I see you do," said Charlie.

"I met him a couple of times with Mrs. MacCann," Polly explained patiently. "What about him?"

"Now is that all?" Charlie asked accusingly. "You might as well tell me the truth now and not have me drag it out of you."

"Oh, what do you mean?" cried Polly, sitting erect with indignation. "What would you drag out of me? I don't know what's coming over you at all, Charlie."

"Hold on now, hold on!" Charlie said commandingly, raising one hand for silence. "Just sit where you are for a minute." He put his hands behind his back, tilted forward on his toes and studied his feet for a moment. "Do you know," he added gravely, barely raising his head to fix her with his eyes, "that 'tis all over the town that you and Carmody are carrying on behind my back? Isn't that a nice thing to have said about your wife?" he added, raising his voice.

Up to that moment he had only partly believed in her guilt, but he no longer had any doubt when he saw how she changed colour. It was partly anger, partly shame.

"Oh," she cried in a fury, tossing her handsome black head, "the badness of people! This is all Nora Lawlor's fault. Father Ring would never repeat a thing like that."

"Father Ring?" exclaimed Charlie with a start, seeing that, whatever her crime was, it was already public property. "What has he to do with it?"

"I see it all now," Polly cried dramatically with a large wave of her arm. "I should never have trusted her. I might have known she'd bell it all over the town."

"What would she bell?" snapped Charlie impatiently. At the very best of times Polly was not what you'd call lucid, but whenever anything happened to upset her, every joint in her mind flew asunder.

"She said," explained Polly earnestly, wagging a long arm at him, "that Kitty Daly had a child after imagining her husband was Rudolph Valentino."

"Rudolph who?" asked Charlie with a strained air.

"You wouldn't know him," replied Polly impatiently. "He's an old fellow on the pictures. He's dead now."

"And what has he to do with Carmody?" Charlie asked anxiously.

"He has nothing to do with Carmody," shouted Polly, enraged at his stupidity.

"Well, go on, woman, go on!" said Charlie, his face screwed up in a black knot as he tried to disentangle the confusion she had plunged him in.

"Oh, I know it couldn't be wrong, Charlie," Polly said positively, flying off at another tangent. "I asked Father Ring myself was it wrong for her."

"Wrong for who?" snarled Charlie, beside himself.

"Kitty Daly, of course," shouted Polly.

"Christ Almighty!" groaned Charlie. "Do you want to drive me mad?"

"But when you won't listen to me!" Polly cried passionately. "And Father Ring said there was no harm in it so long as she was doing it for a good purpose and didn't get any pleasure out of it. . . . Though indeed," she added candidly, "I'm sure I have no idea what pleasure she could get out of it."

"Ah, botheration!" shouted Charlie, shaking his fists at her. "What goings-on you have about Rudolph Valentino! Don't you see I'm demented with all this hugger-mugger? What did you do then, woman?"

"I went to the pictures," replied Polly with an aggrieved air.

"You went to the pictures with Carmody?" asked Charlie encouragingly, only too willing to compound for an infidelity with an indiscretion.

"Oh, what a thing I'd do!" cried Polly in a perfect tempest of indignation. "Who said I went to the pictures with Mr. Carmody? This town is full of liars. I went with Nora, of course."

"Well?" asked Charlie.

"Well," Polly continued in a more reasonable tone, "I thought all the old men in the pictures were terrible, Charlie. How people can bear the sight of them night after night I do not know. And as we were coming out Nora asked me wasn't there any man at all I thought was good-looking, and I said: 'Nora,' I said, 'I always liked Mr. Carmody's appearance.' 'Oh, did you?' said Nora. 'I did, Nora,' said I. Now that," said Polly flatly, bringing her palm down on her knee, "was all that either of us said; and, of course, I might be wrong about his appearance, though I al-

ways thought he kept himself very nicely; but anyone that says
I went to the pictures with him, Charlie, all I can say is that they
have no conscience. Absolutely no conscience."

Charlie stared at her for a moment in stupefaction. For that one
moment he wondered at his own folly in ever thinking that Polly
would have it in her to carry on with a man and in thinking that
any man would try to carry on with her. *Amore, mio cuore,
traditore,* he thought despairingly. Quite clearly Italian women
must be different. And then the whole thing began to dawn on
him and he felt himself suffocating with rage.

"And do you mean to tell me," he asked incredulously, "that
you went to Father Ring and asked him could you pretend that
I was Charlie Carmody?"

"Rudolph Valentino, Charlie," corrected Polly. "It was Nora
Lawlor who suggested Mr. Carmody. . . . You don't think it
makes any difference?" she added hastily, terrified that she might
unwittingly have drifted into mortal sin.

"You asked Father Ring could you pretend that I was Rudolph
Valentino?" repeated Charlie frantically.

"Oh, surely Charlie," Polly said, brushing this aside as mere
trifling, "you don't think I'd do it without finding out whether
'twas a sin or not?"

"God Almighty!" cried Charlie, turning to the door. "I'm the
laughing-stock of the town!"

"Oh, you think too much about what people say of you," Polly
said impatiently. "What need you care what they say so long as
'tis for a good object?"

"Good object!" cried Charlie bitterly. "I know the object I'd
like to lay my hands on this minute. It's that Nora Lawlor with
her cesspool of a mind. By God, I'd wring her bloody neck!"

VII

That was nothing to what Nora did later. Somebody, Charlie
discovered, had put round the story that it was really his fault
and not Polly's that they had no children. Of course, that might
well have been a misconception of Polly's own, because he learned
from a few words she dropped that she thought his mother was

a witch and was putting spells on her. A girl who would believe that was quite capable of blaming it on the butcher's boy. But the obvious malice identified the story as Nora's. The Carmody business was only a flea-bite to it, because it lowered him in the estimation of everybody. Morgan made great play with it. And it was clever because Charlie was in no position to prove it a lie. Worst of all, he doubted himself. He was a nervous man; the least thing set him off; and for weeks and weeks he worried till he almost convinced himself that Nora was right, that he wasn't like other men. God had heaped so many burdens on him that this was all he could expect.

Now, the Cashmans had a maid called Molly O'Regan, a country girl with a rosy, laughing, good-natured face and a shrill penetrating voice. She was one of the few people Charlie knew who were not afraid of his mother, and in his bachelor days when she brought him his shaving-water of a morning, she had always leaned in the door and shown him just enough of herself to interest a half-wakened man. "Come in, girl," he would whisper, "come in and shut the door." "What would I come in for?" Molly would ask with a great air of surprise. "'Pon my soul," Charlie would say admiringly, "you're most captivating." "Captivating?" Molly would shriek. "Listen to him, you sweet God! There's capers for you!" "You're like a rose," Charlie would say and then give one wild bound out of the bed that landed him within a few feet of her, while Molly, shrieking with laughter, banged the door behind her.

It was undoubtedly the slander on his manhood which interested Charlie in Molly, though it would be going too far to say that he had no other object than to disprove it. He liked Molly, and more than ever with Polly and his mother round the house she seemed like a rose. Sometimes when they were out he followed her upstairs and skirmished with her. She let on to be very shocked. "Sweet Jesus!" she cried, "What would I do if one of them walked in on me? And all the holy pictures!" She flashed a wondering look at all the coloured pictures, the statues, and the Lourdes clock. "Isn't it true for me?" she cried. "A wonder you wouldn't have a bit of shame in you!"

"As a matter of fact," said Charlie gravely, "that's the idea. You knew I was starting a religious order of my own here, didn't you?"

"A religious order?" echoed Molly. "I did not."

"Oh, yes, yes," said Charlie importantly. "I'm only waiting on the authority from Rome."

"What sort of religious order?" asked Molly suspiciously—she was not too bright in the head and, as she said herself, with that thundering blackguard, Charlie Cashman, you'd never know where you were.

"An order of Christian married couples," replied Charlie. "The old sort of marriage is a washout. Purity is what we're going in for."

"Purity?" shrieked Molly in a gale of laughter. "And you in it!"

Secretly she was delighted to see Charlie among all "them old holy ones," as she called them, showing such spunk, and couldn't bear to deprive him of his little pleasure. She didn't deprive him of it long.

And then one autumn evening she whispered to him that she was going to have a baby. She wept and said her old fellow would have her sacred life, which was likely enough, seeing that her father preferred to correct his large family with a razor. Charlie shed a few tears as well and told her not to mind her old fellow; while he had a pound in the bank he'd never see her short of anything. He meant it too, because he was a warm-hearted man and had always kept a soft spot for Molly. But what really moved and thrilled him was that in spite of everybody he was at last going to be a father. His doubts about his manhood were set at rest. In the dusk he went up to Johnny Desmond's overflowing with delight and good humour. He cracked half a dozen jokes at Morgan in quick succession and made them all wonder what he had up his sleeve. From this out they could pass what dirty remarks they liked, but these would be nothing compared with his secret laugh at them. It didn't matter if it took twenty years before they knew. He was in the wildest spirits, drinking and joking and making up rhymes.

Next morning, coming on to dawn, he woke with a very bad

taste in his mouth. He glanced round and there, in the light of the colza-oil lamp that burned before the statue of the Sacred Heart, saw Polly beside him in the bed. She looked determined even in sleep. The Lourdes clock, which was suffering from hallucinations and imagining it was an alarm clock, was kicking up merry hell on the mantelpiece. He knew it was really playing "The bell of the Angelus calleth to pray," which is a nice, soothing, poetic thought, but what it said in his mind was: "You're caught, Charlie Cashman, you can't get away." He realized that, instead of escaping, he had only wedged himself more firmly in the trap, that if ever the truth about Molly became known, Polly would leave him, the Donegans would hound him down, Father Ring would denounce him from the altar, and his little business would go to pot. And in spite of it all he would not be able to leave the business to his son. "You're caught, Charlie Cashman, you can't get away," sang the clock with a sort of childish malice.

The skill with which he manœuvred Molly out of the house would have done credit to an international statesman. He found her lodgings in Asragh and put some money to her name in the bank without anyone being the wiser. But in crises it is never the difficulties you can calculate on that really upset you. How could anyone have guessed that Molly, without a job to do, would find her time a burden and spend hours in the Redemptorist church? After a couple of months Charlie started to receive the most alarming letters. Molly talked of telling Polly, of telling her father, of spending the rest of her days in a home doing penance. Charlie was getting thoroughly fed up with religion. When he saw her one night in a back street in Asragh—the only place where they could meet in comparative safety—he was shocked at the change in her. She was plumper and better-looking but her eyes were shadowy and her voice had dropped to a sort of whine.

"Oh, Charlie," she sighed with a lingering, come-to-Christ air, "what luck or grace could we have and the life of sin and deception we're leading?"

"A lot of deception and damn little sin," Charlie said bitterly. "What the hell do you want?"

"Oh, Charlie, I want you to put an end to the deception as well as the sin. Be said by me and confess it to your wife."

"What a thing I'd do!" Charlie said, scowling and stamping. "Do you know what she'd do?"

"What would any woman do and she finding you truly repentant?" asked Molly ecstatically.

"She'd take bloody good care I had cause," said Charlie.

He persuaded her out of that particular mood but all the same he wasn't sure of her. It was a nerve-racking business. In the evenings after his supper he lit his pipe and took his usual prowl to the door but he couldn't bring himself to leave the house. Nora Lawlor might drop in while he was away and tell the whole thing to Polly. He had a trick of making up little rhymes to amuse himself, and one that he made at this time ran:

> Brass, boys, brass, and not only buttons,
> The older we gets, the more we toughens.

Charlie didn't toughen at all, unfortunately.

"Wisha, wouldn't you go for a little stroll?" Polly would ask considerately.

"Ah, I don't feel like it," Charlie would say with a sigh.

"Oh, Law!" she would cry in gentle surprise. "Isn't that a great change for you, Charlie?"

Once or twice he nearly snapped at her and asked whose fault it was. Sometimes he went to the house door and stood there for a full half-hour with his shoulder against the jamb, drinking in the misery of the view in the winter dusk: the one mean main street where everyone knew him and no one wished him well. It was all very fine for Romeo, but Romeo hadn't to live in an Irish country town. Each morning he prowled about in wait for Christy Flynn, the postman, to intercept any anonymous letter there might be for Polly. As he didn't know which of them were anonymous, he intercepted them all.

Then one morning the blow fell. It was a solicitor's letter. He left the shop in charge of Polly and went down to Curwen Street to see his own solicitor, Timsy Harrington. Curwen Street is a nice quiet Georgian street, rosy and warm even on a winter's day, and signs on it; the cheapest call you could pay there would cost you a pound. Charlie knew his call would cost him more than that, but he smoked his pipe and tried to put a brave face on it, as though he thought actions for seduction the best sport in the world. That didn't go down with Timsy Harrington, though.

"Mr. Cashman," he said in his shrill, scolding, old woman's voice, "I'm surprised at you. I'm astonished at you. An educated man like you! You had the whole country to choose from and no one would do you but a daughter of Jim Regan, that stopped in bed with his son for eight months, hoping to get a couple of pounds out of the insurance company."

Charlie went back along the main street feeling as though he were bleeding from twenty gashes. He swore that if ever he got out of this scrape he'd live a celibate for the rest of his days. People said the woman always paid, but the particular occasion when she did was apparently forgotten. Outside the shop he was accosted by an old countryman with a long innocent face.

"Good morrow, Charlie," he said confidentially, giving Charlie a glimpse of a plug in the palm of his hand. "I wonder would you have the comrade of this?"

"I'll try, Tom," said Charlie with a sigh, taking it from him and turning it over in his hand. "Leave me this and I'll see what I can do. I'm very busy at the moment."

He opened the shop door, and knew at once that there was trouble in the wind. There was no one in the shop. He stood at the door with his ear cocked. He heard Polly moving with stallion strides about the bedroom and his heart misgave him. He knew well the Lawlor one had profited by his absence. Already the solicitor's letter was public property. He went up the stairs and opened the bedroom door a few inches. Polly was throwing clothes, shoes, and statues all together in a couple of suitcases with positive frenzy. Charlie pushed in the door a little further, looked at the suitcases, then at her, and finally managed to work up what he thought of as an insinuating smile.

"What's up, little girl?" he asked with a decent show of innocent gaiety.

He saw from her look that this particular line was a complete washout, so he entered cautiously, closing the door behind him for fear of being overheard from the shop.

"Aren't I in trouble enough?" he asked bitterly. "Do you know what the O'Regans want out of me?"

"Oh," cried Polly with the air of a tragedy queen, "if there was a man among them he'd shoot you!"

"Two hundred pounds!" hissed Charlie, his high hairy cheek-bones twitching. "Isn't that a nice how-d'ye-do?"

"Oh," she cried distractedly, "you're worse than the wild beasts. The wild beasts have some modesty but you have none. It was my own fault. Nora Lawlor warned me."

"Nora Lawlor will be the ruination of you," Charlie said severely. "She was in here again this morning—you needn't tell me. I can see the signs of her."

"Don't attempt to criticize her to me!" stormed Polly. "Get out of my sight or I won't be responsible. The servant!"

"Whisht, woman, whisht, whisht, whisht!" hissed Charlie, dancing in a fury of apprehension. "You'll be heard from the shop."

"Oh, I'll take care to be heard," said Polly, giving her rich voice full play. "I'll let them know the sort of man they're dealing with. I'll soho you well."

"So this is married life!" muttered Charlie in a wounded voice, turning away. Then he paused and looked at her over his shoulder as if he couldn't believe it. "Merciful God," he said, "what sort of woman are you at all? How well I didn't go on like this about the schoolmaster!"

"What schoolmaster?" Polly asked in bewilderment, her whole face taking on a ravaged air.

"Carmody," said Charlie reproachfully. "You thought it was my fault and I thought it was yours—what more was in it? We both acted with a good purpose. Surely to God," he added anxiously, "you don't think I did it for pleasure?"

"Oh," she cried, beside herself, "wait till I tell Father Ring! Wait till he knows the sort of comparisons you're making! With a good purpose! Oh, you blasphemer! How the earth doesn't open and swallow you!"

She pushed him out and slammed the door behind him. Charlie stood on the landing and gave a brokenhearted sigh. "So this is married life!" he repeated despairingly. He returned to the shop and stood far back at the rear, leaning against the stovepipe. It was a sunny morning and the sunlight streamed through the windows and glinted on the bright buckets hanging outside the door. He saw Nora Lawlor, wearing a scarlet coat, come out of the butcher's and give a furtive glance across the street. If he had had a gun with him he would have shot her dead.

He heard Polly come downstairs and open the hall door. Slowly and on tiptoe he went to the door of the shop, leaned his shoulder against the jamb and looked up the street after Nora. He saw her red coat disappear round the corner by the chapel. The old farmer who was waiting outside the Post Office thought that Charlie was hailing him, but Charlie frowned and shook his head. From the hall he heard Polly address a small boy in that clear voice of hers which he knew could be heard all along the street.

"Dinny," she said, "I want you to run down to Hennessey's and ask them to send up a car."

Charlie was so overcome that he retreated to the back of the shop again. Polly was leaving him. It would be all round the town in five minutes. Yet he knew he wasn't a bad man; there were plenty worse and their wives didn't leave them. For one wild moment he thought of making a last appeal to her love, but one glance into the hall at Polly sitting bolt-upright in her blue serge costume, her cases beside her and her gloves and prayer-book on the hall stand, and he knew that love wasn't even in the running. He went to the shop door and beckoned to another small boy.

"I want you to find Father Ring and bring him here quick," he whispered fiercely, pressing a coin into the child's palm. "Mr. Cashman sent you, say. And tell him hurry!"

"Is it someone sick, Mr. Cashman?" asked the little boy eagerly.

"Yes," hissed Charlie. "Dying. Hurry now!"

After that he paced up and down the shop like a caged tiger till he saw Father Ring rounding the corner by the chapel. He went up to meet him.

"What is it at all, Charlie?" the priest asked anxiously. "Is it the mother?"

"No, father," Charlie said desperately, seeing the twitching of curtains in top rooms. "I only wish to God it was," he ground out in a frenzy.

"Is it as bad as that, Charlie?" Father Ring asked in concern as they entered the shop.

"Ah, I'm in great trouble, father," Charlie said, tossing his head like a wounded animal. Then he fixed his gaze on a spot of light at the back of the shop and addressed himself to it. "I don't know did you hear any stories about me," he inquired guardedly.

"Stories, Charlie?" exclaimed Father Ring, who, being a Kerryman, could fight a better delaying-action than Charlie himself. "What sort of stories?"

"Well, now, father, not the sort you'd like to hear," replied Charlie with what for him was almost candour.

"Well, now you mention it, Charlie," said Father Ring with equal frankness, "I fancy I did hear something. . . . Not, of course, that I believed it," he added hastily, for fear he might be committing himself too far.

"I'm sorry to say you can, father," said Charlie, bowing his head and joining his hands before him as he did at Mass on Sunday.

"Oh, my, my, Charlie," said Father Ring, giving him a look out of the corner of his eye, "that's bad."

Charlie looked at the floor and nodded glumly a couple of times to show he shared the priest's view of it.

"And tell me, Charlie," whispered Father Ring, pivoting on his umbrella as he leaned closer, "what way did herself take it?"

"Badly, father," replied Charlie severely. "Very badly. I must say I'm disappointed in Polly."

This time it was he who looked out of the corner of his eye and somehow it struck him that Father Ring was not as shocked-looking as he might have been.

"I'd expect that, mind you," Father Ring said thoughtfully.

"By God, he isn't shocked!" thought Charlie. There was something that almost resembled fellow-feeling in his air.

"But heavens above, father," Charlie said explosively, "the woman is out of her mind. And as for that Lawlor girl, I don't know what to say to her." Father Ring nodded again, as though to say that he didn't know either. "Of course, she's a good-living girl and all the rest of it," Charlie went on cantankerously, "but girls with no experience of life have no business interfering between married couples. It was bad enough without her—I needn't tell you that. And there she is now," he added, cocking his thumb in the direction of the hall, "with her bags packed and after ordering a car up from Hennessey's. Sure that's never right."

"Well, now, Charlie," Father Ring whispered consolingly, "women are contrairy; they are contrairy, there's no denying that. I'll have a word with her myself."

He opened the house door gently, peeped in, and then went into the hall on tiptoe, as if he were entering a room where someone was asleep. Charlie held the door slightly open behind him to hear what went on. Unfortunately, the sight of the priest going in had given the old farmer the notion of business as usual. Charlie looked round and saw his long mournful face in the doorway.

"Charlie," he began, "if I'm not disturbing you—"

Charlie, raising his clenched fists in the air, did a silent war dance. The old farmer staggered back, cut to the heart, and then sat on the sill of the window with his stick between his legs. When another farmer came by the old man began to tell him his troubles with long, accusing glances back at Charlie, who was glued to the door with an agonized look on his face.

"My poor child!" he heard Father Ring say in a shocked whisper. "You were in the wars. I can see you were."

"Well, I'm going home now, father," Polly replied listlessly.

"Sure, where better could you go?" exclaimed Father Ring as if trying to disabuse her of any idea she might have of staying on. " 'Tis that husband of yours, I suppose? 'Tis to be sure. I need hardly ask."

"I'd rather not talk about it, father," Polly said politely but firmly. "I dare say you'll hear all about it soon enough."

"I dare say I will," he agreed. "People in this town don't seem to have much better to do. 'Pon my word, I believe I saw a few curtains stirring on my way down. You'll have an audience."

"I never minded much what they saw," said Polly wearily.

"Sure, you never had anything to conceal," said Father Ring, overwhelming her with agreement, as his way was. "I suppose you remember the case of that little girl from Parnell Street a few weeks ago?"

"No, father, I'm afraid I don't," replied Polly without interest.

"Sure, you couldn't be bothered. Ah, 'twas a sad business, though. Married at ten and the baby born at one."

"Oh, my, father," said Polly politely, "wasn't that very quick?"

"Well, now you mention it, Polly, it was. But that wasn't what I was going to say. The poor child came home at four in the morning to avoid attracting attention, and would you believe me, Polly, not a soul in Parnell Street went to bed that night! Sure, that's never natural! I say that's not natural. Where's that blackguard of a husband of yours till I give him a bit of my mind? Charlie Cashman! Charlie Cashman! Where are you, you scoundrel?"

"I'm here, father," said Charlie meekly, taking two steps forward till he stood between the crimson curtains with a blaze of silver from the fanlight falling on his bowed head.

"Aren't you ashamed of yourself?" shouted the priest, raising the umbrella to him.

"I am, father, I am, I am," replied Charlie in a broken voice without looking up.

"Oh, that's only all old connoisseuring, father," Polly cried distractedly, jumping to her feet and grabbing gloves and prayerbook. "No one knows what I went through with that man." She opened the hall door; the hall was flooded with silver light, and she turned to them, drawing a deep breath through her nose, as beautiful and menacing as a sibyl. "I'm going home to my father now," she continued in a firm voice. "I left my keys on the dressing-table and you can give Hennessey's boy the bags."

"Polly," Father Ring said sternly, leaning on his umbrella, "what way is this for a Child of Mary to behave?"

"As, 'tis all very fine for you to talk, father," Polly cried scoldingly. "You don't have to live with him. I'd sooner live with a wild beast than with that man," she added dramatically.

"Polly," Father Ring said mildly, "what you do in your own house is your business. What you do in the public view is mine. Polly, you're in the public view."

For the first time in Charlie's life he found himself admiring Father Ring. There was a clash and a grating of wills like the bending of steel girders, and suddenly Polly's girders buckled. She came in and closed the door. "Now, Polly," Father Ring said affectionately, "inside that door I don't want to interfere between ye, good or bad. Make what arrangements you like. Live with him or don't live with him; sleep in the loft or sleep in the stable, but don't let me have any more scandal like we had this morning."

"I wouldn't be safe from him in the stable," Polly said rebelliously. She felt that for the first time in her life she had been met and mastered by a man, and it rankled. There was more than a joke in Charlie's suggestion that it was Father Ring she should have married. If only she could have gone to bed with him then and there she would probably have risen a normal woman. But deprived of this consolation she was ready to turn nasty, and Father Ring saw it. Charlie only noticed the falsehood about himself.

"You wouldn't be what?" he cried indignantly. "When did I ever raise a finger or say a cross word to you?"

"Now, Charlie, now!" Father Ring said shortly, raising his hand for silence. "And woman alive," he asked good-humouredly, "can't you bolt your door?"

"How can I," stormed Polly, as sulky as a spoiled child, "when there's no bolt on it?"

"That's easily remedied."

"Then tell him send out for a carpenter and have it done now," she said vindictively.

"Send out for a what?" shouted Charlie, cocking his head as if he couldn't believe what he heard. "Is it mad you are? What a thing I'd do!"

"Very well," she said, opening the hall door again. "I'll go home to my father."

"Hold on now, hold on!" Charlie cried frantically, dragging her back and closing the door behind her. "I'll do it myself."

"Then do it now!" she cried.

"Do what she says, Charlie," the priest said quietly. He saw that the danger wasn't over yet. Charlie gave her a murderous glare and went out to the shop. A crowd had gathered outside on the pavement, discussing the wrongs of the poor farmer, who was an object of the most intense sympathy. Charlie returned with a brass bolt, a screwdriver, and a couple of screws.

"Show me that bolt!" said Polly menacingly. The devil was up in her now. The priest might have bested her but she still saw a way of getting her own back. Charlie knew that next day she and Nora Lawlor would be splitting their sides over it; women were like that, and he vowed a holy war against the whole boiling of them to the day of his death. "I'm going home to my father's," she said, clamping her long lips. "That bolt is too light."

"Get a heavier one, Charlie," Father Ring said quietly. "Don't argue, there's a good man!"

Argument was about the last thing in Charlie's mind at that moment. Murder would have been nearer the mark. He flung the bolt at Polly's feet but she didn't even glance at him. When he returned to the shop the crowd was surging round the door.

"Bad luck and end to ye!" he snarled, taking out his spleen on them. "Have ye no business of yeer own to mind without nosing round here?"

"Mr. Cashman," said a young man whom Charlie recognized as the old farmer's son, "you have a plug belonging to my father."

"Then take it and to hell with ye!" snarled Charlie, taking the plug from his pocket and throwing it into the midst of them.

"Oh, begor, we won't trouble you much from this day forth," the young man said fierily. "Nor more along with us."

That was the trouble in a quarrel with a country man. There always were more along with him. Charlie, aware that he might have seriously injured his business, returned to the hall with an iron bolt. "That's a stable bolt," he said, addressing no one in particular.

"Put it on," said Polly.

Charlie went upstairs. Father Ring followed him. The priest stood in awe, looking at all the holy pictures. Then he held the bolt while Charlie used the screwdriver. Charlie was so mad that he used it anyhow.

You're putting that screw in crooked, Charlie," said the priest. "Wait now till I put on my specs and I'll do it for you."

"Let her go! Let her go!" said Charlie on the point of a break-down. "It doesn't matter to me whether she goes or stays. I'm nothing only a laughing-stock."

"Now, Charlie, Charlie," said the priest good-naturedly, "you have your little business to mind."

"For my nephews to walk into," said Charlie bitterly.

"God spoke first, Charlie," the priest said gravely. "You're a young man yet. Begor," he added, giving Charlie a quizzical look over the specs, "I did a few queer jobs in my time but this is the queerest yet." He saw that Charlie was in no state to appreciate the humour of it, and gave him a professional look through the spectacles. "Ah, well, Charlie," he said, "we all have our burdens. You have only one, but I have a dozen, not to mention the nuns, and they reckon two on a count."

As they came down the stairs Charlie's mother appeared out of the kitchen as if from nowhere, drying her hands in her apron; a little bundle of rags, bones and malice, with a few wisps of white hair blowing about her.

"Aha," she cackled as if she were speaking to herself, "I hear the Holy Door is shut for the next seven years."

VIII

But, as she was so fond of saying herself, "God spoke first." It seemed as if Polly never had another day's luck. She fell into a slow decline and made herself worse instead of better by drinking the stuff Mrs. Cashman brought her from the Wise Woman, and by changing from the Nine Fridays to the Nine Tuesdays and from the Nine Tuesdays to the Nine Mondays on the advice of Nora Lawlor, who had tried them all.

A scandal of that sort is never good for a man's business. The Donegans and their friends paid their accounts and went elsewhere. The shop began to go down and Charlie went with it. He paid less attention to his appearance, served the counter unshaven and without collar and tie; grew steadily shabbier and more irritable and neglected-looking. He spent most of his evenings in Johnny Desmond's, but even there people fought shy of him. The professional men and civil servants treated him as a sort of town character, a humorous, unreliable fellow without much balance. To Charlie, who felt they were only cashing in on the sacrifices of men like himself, this was the bitterest blow, and in his anxiety to keep his end up before them he boasted, quarrelled, and generally played the fool.

But the funny thing was that from the time she fell ill Polly herself softened towards him. Her family were the first to notice it. Like everything else in Polly it went to extremes, and indeed it occurred to her mother that if the Almighty God in His infinite mercy didn't release her soon, she'd have no religion left.

"I don't know is he much worse than anyone else," she said broodingly. "I had some very queer temptations myself that no one knew about. Father Ring said once that I was very unforgiving. I think now he was right. Our family were always vindictive."

After that she began to complain about being nervous alone and Mrs. Cashman offered to sleep with her.

"Oh, I could never bear another woman in the room with me," Polly said impatiently. "What I want is a man. I think I'll ask Charlie to make it up."

"Is it that fellow?" cried Charlie's mother, aghast. "That scut—that—I have no words for him. Oh, my! A man that would shame his poor wife the way that ruffian did!"

"Ah, the way ye talk one'd think he never stopped," Polly said fractiously. "Ye have as much old goings-on about one five minutes!"

At this Mrs. Cashman decided she was going soft in the head. When a married woman begins to reckon her husband's infidelities in terms of hours and minutes she is in a bad state. Polly asked Charlie meekly enough to come back and keep her company. Charlie would have been as well pleased to stay as he was, where he could come and go as he liked, but he saw it was some sort of change before death.

It was cold comfort for Polly. Too much mischief had been made between them for Charlie to feel about her as a man should feel for his wife. They would lie awake in the grey, flickering light of the colza-oil lamp, with all the holy pictures round them and the Lourdes clock on the mantelpiece ticking away whenever it remembered it and making wild dashes to catch up on lost time, and Charlie's thoughts would wander and he would think that if Polly were once out of the way he would have another chance of a woman who would fling herself into his arms without asking Father Ring's permission, like the Yeoman Captain's daughter in the old song:

> *A thousand pounds I'll give thee*
> *And fly from home with thee;*
> *I'll dress myself in man's attire*
> *And fight for Liberty.*

Charlie was a romantic, and he couldn't get over his boyish notion that there must be women like the Captain's Daughter, if only you could meet them. And while he was making violent love to her, Polly, lying beside him, thought of how her poor bare bones would soon be scattered in the stony little patch above Kilmurray while another woman would be lying in her bed. It made her very bitter.

"I suppose you're only waiting till the sod is over me?" she said one night in a low voice when Charlie was just fancying that she must have dropped off.

"What's that?" he asked in astonishment and exasperation, looking at her with one arm under her head, staring into the shadows.

"You're only waiting till I'm well rotten to get another woman in my place," she went on accusingly.

"What a thing I'd think of!" Charlie snapped, as cross as a man jolted out of his sleep, for her words had caught the skirts of the Captain's Daughter as she slipped out of the room, and Charlie felt it was shameful for him in his health and strength to be contriving like that against a sick woman.

"Nothing matters to you now only to best John Joe and have a son that'll come in for the shop," said Polly with the terrible insight of the last loneliness. "Only for the shop you might have some nature for me."

"And when the hell had I anything but nature for you?" he shouted indignantly, sitting up. "What do you think I married you for? Money?"

"If you had any nature for me you wouldn't disrespect me," Polly went on stubbornly, clinging to her grievance.

"And what about you?" said Charlie. "You had to think I was some old devil on the pictures before you could put up with me. There's nature for you!"

"I did it with a good object," said Polly.

"Good object!" snorted Charlie. He almost told her that Juliet and the Captain's Daughter didn't do it with a good object or any object at all only getting the man they wanted, but he knew she wouldn't understand. Polly lay for a long time drawing deep breaths through her nose.

"Don't think or imagine I'll rest quiet and see you married to another woman," she added in a very determined voice. "You may think you'll be rid of me but I'll make full sure you won't. All our family would go to hell's gates to be revenged."

"Christ Almighty," snarled Charlie, giving one wild leap out of the bed, "leave me out of this! This is my thanks for coming back here! Leave me out!"

"Mind what I say now," said Polly in an awe-inspiring voice, pointing a bony arm at him from the shadows. She knew she had him on a sore spot. Herself or Mrs. Cashman would have made no more fuss about meeting a ghost than about meeting the postman, but Charlie had enough of the rationalist in him to be terrified. His mother had brought him up on them. "Our family was ever full of ghosts," she added solemnly. "You won't have much comfort with her."

"My trousers!" cried Charlie, beside himself with rage and terror. "Where the hell is my trousers?"

"I'm giving you fair warning," Polly cried in blood-curdling tones as he poked his way out of the room in his nightshirt. "I'll soho ye well, the pair of ye!"

IX

She died very peacefully one evening when no one was in the room but old Mrs. Cashman. Even in death she made trouble for Charlie. Her last wish was to be buried in Closty, the Donegan graveyard. It wasn't that she bore any malice to Charlie, but the thought of the two wives in one grave upset her. She said it wouldn't be nice, and Nora agreed with her. Of course, when it got out it made things worse for Charlie, for it suggested that, at the very least, he had some hand in her death.

Nora felt rather like that too, but then a strange thing happened. She was coming down from the bedroom when she heard a noise from the shop. The door was closed, all but an inch or two, but Nora was of a very inquisitive disposition. She pushed it in. The shop was dark, several of the outside shutters being up, but in the dim light she saw the figure of a man and realized that the noise she had heard was weeping. It gave her a shock, for it had never once occurred to her that Charlie was that sort of man. She was a warm-hearted girl. She went up and touched his arm.

"I'm sorry, Charlie," she said timidly.

"I know that, Nora," he muttered without looking round. "I know you are."

"She'll be a terrible loss," she added, more from want of something to say than the feeling that she was speaking the truth.

"Ah, she was unfortunate, Nora," Charlie said with a sob. "She was a fine woman, a lovely woman. I don't know what bad luck was on us."

"What better luck could ye have and the poor orphan cheated?" cried a harsh, inexpressive voice from the hall. Nora started. Mrs. Cashman was standing in the doorway with her hands on her hips. Her voice and appearance were like those of an apparition, and for the first time Nora wondered if there wasn't something in Polly's fancy that she was really a witch. "She's better off, Nora girl."

"I suppose so," Nora agreed doubtfully, resenting her intrusion just at the moment when Charlie was ready for confidences. People with tears in their eyes will tell you things they'd never tell you at other times.

"She was a good girl and a just girl and she loved her God," hissed Mrs. Cashman, aiming every word at Charlie under Nora's guard. "It would be a bad man that would go against her dying wishes."

"Who talked of going against them?" snarled Charlie with the savagery of a goaded beast, and lunging past them went out and banged the hall door behind him.

"Poor Charlie is very upset," said Nora.

"Upset?" cackled Mrs. Cashman. "How upset he is! She's not in her grave yet, and already he's planning who he'll get instead of her. That's how upset he is! But he's not done with me yet, the blackguard!"

For the first time it occurred to Nora that perhaps Charlie had been misjudged—if men could ever be misjudged. From all accounts of what they did to poor women when they had them stripped, they could not, but something about Mrs. Cashman made her suspicious.

She went to the funeral in Mrs. Cashman's carriage. The moment she got out of it at the graveyard she knew there was trouble in store. The Donegans were there, a half dozen different families, and on their own ground they had taken complete command. Charlie was only an outsider. He stood by the hearse with his hands crossed before him, holding his hat, and a look of desperation on his dark face. Others besides herself had noticed the signs, and a group of men was standing in a semicircle a hundred yards down the road, where they wouldn't get involved. Her father was between them and the hearse, but sufficiently far away to keep out of it as well. He was scowling, his lips pouted, his eyes were half shut while he noticed everything that went on.

The procession into the graveyard would be the signal. Charlie would be shouldered away from the cemetery gate, and he knew it, and knew he was no match for half a dozen men younger than himself. He'd fight, of course; everyone who knew Charlie knew that, but he could be very quickly dragged down the lane and no one much the wiser. Just at the moment when the coffin was eased out of the hearse and four Donegans got under it Nora left Mrs. Cashman's side and stood by Charlie.

It was exactly as though she had blown a policeman's whistle. Her father raised his head and beckoned to the semicircle of men behind and then, pulling the lapels of his coat together, placed himself at the other side of her. One by one half a dozen middle-aged men came up and joined Charlie's party. They were all old Volunteers and could not stand aside and let their commandant and vice-commandant be hustled about by the seed of land-grabbers and policemen. Not a word was spoken, not a cross look exchanged, but everyone knew that sides had been taken and that Charlie could now enter the graveyard unmolested. As he and Nora emerged at the grave Father Ring looked up at them from under his bushy brows. He had missed none of the drama. There was very little that foxy little man missed.

"Thanks, Nora, thanks," said Charlie in a low voice as the service ended. "You were always a good friend."

Even Nora at her most complacent wouldn't have described herself as a friend of Charlie's, but the fact that he had understood what she had done proved him to have better feelings than she had given him credit for. She was embarrassed by the feelings she had roused. The old volunteers all came up and shook her formally by the hand. Her father was the most surprising of all. He stood aside sniffing, with tears in his eyes, too overcome even to tell her what he felt.

After that, everyone noticed the change in Charlie. His clothes were brushed, his boots were polished, his face was shaved, and no matter what hour of the morning you went in he had collar and tie on. He spent more time in the shop and less in Johnny Desmond's. He even gave up going to Johnny's altogether. That could only mean that he was looking for someone to take Polly's place. But who would have him? A respectable woman would be lowering herself. The general impression was that he'd marry Molly O'Regan, and Nora supposed that this would only be right, but somehow she couldn't help feeling it would be a pity. Mrs. Cashman, who saw all her beautiful plans for her grandchildren go up in smoke, felt the same. For the first time Nora included Charlie in her prayers, and asked the Holy Ghost to help him in making the right choice.

One night a few weeks later on her way back from the church she looked in on him. She was astonished at Mrs. Cashman's sourness.

"You'll have a cup of tea?" said Charlie.

"I won't Charlie, honest," she said hastily, alarmed at the puss the old woman had on her. "I'm rushing home."

"I'll see you home," he said at once, giving himself a glance in the mirror.

"If you're back before me, the key will be in the window," Mrs. Cashman said sourly.

"You're not going out again?" he asked.

"I'm not going to stop in this house alone," she bawled.

"Really, Charlie, there's no reason for you to come," said Nora in distress.

"Nonsense!" he snapped crossly. "Herself and her ghosts!"

It was a moonlit night and the street was split with silver light. The abbey tower was silhouetted against it, and the light broke through the deeply splayed chancel lancets, making deep shadows among the foundered tombstones.

"I only came to know how you were getting on," she said.

"Ah, I'm all right," said Charlie. "Only a bit lonesome, of course."

"Ah," she said with a half-smile, "I suppose you won't be long that way."

She could have dropped dead with shame as soon as she had said it. Nora was never one to make any bones about her inquisitiveness, but this sounded positively vulgar. It wasn't in line at all with her behaviour at the funeral. Charlie didn't seem to notice. He gave her a long look through screwed-up eyes, and then crossed the road to lean his back against the bridge.

"Tell me, Nora," he asked, folding his arms and looking keenly at her from under the peak of his cap, "what would you do in my position?"

"Oh, I don't know, Charlie," she replied in alarm, wondering how she could extricate herself from the consequences of her own curiosity. "What's to prevent you?"

"You know the sort of things Polly said?" he said with a sigh.

"I don't think I'd mind that at all," she replied. "After all, Polly was a very sick woman."

"She was," agreed Charlie. "Do you think 'twould be right to go against her wishes like that?"

"Well, of course, that would depend, Charlie," said Nora with sudden gravity, for like many of her race she combined a strong grasp of the truths of religion with a hazy notion of the facts of life.

"You mean on whether 'twas done with a good object or not?" Charlie asked keenly. All he had learned from years with Polly was the importance of doing things with a good object.

"And whether the wishes were reasonable or not," she added, surprised to find him so well-versed in religious matters.

"And you don't think they were?"

"I wouldn't say so. Father Ring could tell you that better than I could."

"I dare say, I dare say. Tell me, Nora, do you believe in things like that?"

"Like what, Charlie?" she asked in surprise.

"Ghosts, and things of that sort," he said with a nervous glance in the direction of the abbey, whose slender tapering tower soared from the rubbish-tip of ruined gables, with its tall irregular battlements that looked like cockades in the moonlight.

"We're taught to believe in them," she replied with a little shudder.

"I know we are," sighed Charlie. "But you never saw one yourself?"

"I didn't."

"Nor I."

They resumed their walk home. Nora saw now what was fretting him. Polly had said she'd haunt him and Polly was a woman of her word. Anything she had ever said she'd do she had done, and there was no saying that as a pure spirit she'd have changed much. Charlie himself had lost a lot of the cocksure rationalism of his fighting days. He had lived so long with women that he was becoming almost as credulous as they. He was reckoning up his chances in case Polly's ghost got out of hand. Nora couldn't give him much comfort, for her own belief in ghosts was determined by the time of day, and at ten o'clock of a moonlight night is was always particularly strong.

When they parted she blamed herself a lot. It was most unmaidenly of her first to call at all and, secondly, to ask point blank what his intentions were, for that was what it amounted to, and for a terrible few minutes she had dreaded that he might think it mattered to her. Of course it didn't, except for his own sake, because though she had begun to like him better, she knew there was no possibility of a Child of Mary like herself marrying him—even if Polly had been an unobtrusive ghost.

She would have been surprised and upset to know that her views were not shared by others. When Charlie got home he stood in the hall in surprise. There was something queer about the house. The hall was in darkness; there was light in the kitchen but it was very feeble. With all the talk of ghosts it upset him. "Are you there, mother?" he called nervously, but there was no reply, only the echo of his own voice. He went to the kitchen door and his heart almost stopped beating. The fire was out, the greater part of the room in shadow, but two candles in two brass candlesticks were burning on the mantelpiece, and between them, smiling down at him, a large, silver-framed photo of Polly.

Next moment, seeing how he was being baited, he went mad with rage. His mother, the picture of aged innocence, was kneeling by her bed when he went in, and she looked round at him in surprise.

"Was it you left that in the kitchen?" he shouted.

"What is it?" she asked in mock ignorance, rising and screwing up her eyes as she reached for the picture. "Oh, isn't it pretty?" she asked. "I found it today in one of her drawers."

"Put it back where you found it," he stormed.

"Oye, why?" she asked with a pretence of concern. "Wouldn't anyone like it—his poor, dead wife? Unless he'd have something on his conscience."

"Never mind my conscience," shouted Charlie. "Fitter for you to look after your own."

"Aha," she bawled triumphantly, throwing off the mask, "my conscience have nothing to trouble it."

"You have it too well seasoned."

"And don't think but she sees it all, wherever she is," the old woman cried, raising her skinny paw in the direction in which Polly might be supposed to exist. "Take care she wouldn't rise from the grave and haunt you, you and that litle whipster you were out gallivanting with!"

"What gallivanting?" snarled Charlie. "You don't know what you're talking about."

"Maybe I'm blind!" bawled his mother. "Walking into the graveyard alongside you, as if she had you caught already! Aha, the sly-boots, the pussycat, with her novenas and her Nine Fridays! She thinks we don't know what she's up to, but God sees ye, and the dead woman sees ye, and what's more, I see ye. And mark my words, Charlie Cashman, that's the hand that'll never rock a cradle for you!"

X

Two days later Charlie happened to be serving behind the counter when he saw Father Ring busily admiring the goods in the shop window. The priest smiled and nodded, but when Charlie made to come out to him he shook his head warningly. Then he raised one finger and pointed in the direction of the house door. Charlie nodded gloomily. Father Ring made another sign with his thumb to indicate the direction he was going in and Charlie nodded again. He knew Father Ring wanted to talk to him somewhere his mother wouldn't know.

He found Father Ring letting on to be studying the plant life in the river. When Charlie appeared he indicated surprise and pleasure at such an unexpected meeting.

"Whisper, Charlie," he said at last, putting his left hand on Charlie's shoulder and bending his head discreetly across the other one, "I had a visit from your mother."

"My mother?"

"Your mother," the priest said gravely, studying his face again before making another little excursion over his shoulder. "She's afraid you're going to get married again," he whispered in amusement.

"She's easy frightened."

"That's what I told her. I know you'll keep this to yourself. She seems to think there's some special commandment to stop you. Of course," added the priest with a shocked air, "I told her I wouldn't dream of interfering."

"You did to be sure," said Charlie watchfully, knowing that

this was the one thing in the world that no one could prevent
Father Ring from doing.

"You know the girl I mean?"

"I do."

"A nice girl."

"A fine girl."

"And a courageous girl," said Father Ring. "Mind you, 'tisn't
every girl would do what she did the day of the funeral. Of
course," he admitted, "she should have been married ten years
ago. They get very contrairy." Then he pounced. "Tell me,
Charlie, you wouldn't be thinking about her, would you? I'm
not being inquisitive?"

"You're not, to be sure."

"Because it struck me that if you were, I might be able to do
you a good turn. Of course, she hasn't much experience. You
know what I mean?"

"I do, father," said Charlie who realized as well as the priest
did that it would be no easy job to coax a pious girl like Nora
into marriage with a public sinner like himself. But at the same
time he was not going to be bounced into anything. He had
made a fool of himself once before. "Well now," he added with
a great air of candour, turning towards the river as though for
recollection, "I'll tell you exactly the way I'm situated, father.
You know the old saying: 'Once bitten, twice shy.' "

"I do, I do," said Father Ring, turning in the same direction
as if his thought and Charlie's might meet and mingle over the
river. Then he started and gave Charlie a look of astonishment.
"Ah, I wouldn't say that, Charlie."

"Well, maybe I'm putting it a bit strongly, father."

"I think so, Charlie, I think you are," Father Ring said eagerly.
"I'd say she was a different class altogether. More feminine, more
clinging—that's under the skin, of course.

"You might be right, father," Charlie said but he stuck to his
point all the same. "But there's one thing you might notice about
me," he went on, looking at the priest out of the corner of his
eye. "You mightn't think it but I'm a highly strung man."

"You are, you are," said Father Ring with great anxiety. "I

noticed that myself. I wonder would it be blood pressure, Charlie?"

"I was never the same since the Troubles," said Charlie. "But whatever it is, I want something to steady me."

"You do, you do," said the priest, trying to follow his drift.

"If I had a family I'd be different."

"You would," said Father Ring with a crucified air. "I can see you're a domesticated sort of man."

"And," added Charlie with a wealth of meaning in his tone, "if the same thing happened me again I might as well throw myself in there." He pointed at the river, scowling, and then took a deep breath and stepped back from the priest.

"But you don't think it would, Charlie?"

"But you see, father, I don't know."

"You don't, you don't, to be sure you don't," said Father Ring in a glow of understanding. "I see it now. And, of course, having doubts like that, they might come against you."

"You put your finger on it."

"And, of course, if you were to marry the other girl—what's that her name is?—Peggy or Kitty or Joan, you'd have no doubts, and, as well as that, you'd have the little fellow. You could look after him."

"That's the very thing, father," Charlie said savagely. "That's what has me demented."

"It has, it has, of course," said Father Ring, smiling at the sheer simplicity of it. "Of course, Nora is a nicer girl in every way but a bird in the hand is worth two in the bush. I know exactly how you feel. I'd be the same myself."

So Charlie returned to the shop, feeling worse than ever. Nora, as Father Ring said, was a nice girl, but a bird in the hand was worth two in the bush and Charlie felt he never really had a bird of any breed; nothing but a few tailfeathers out of Molly before she flew into the bush after the others. And even Father Ring didn't know how badly he felt about Molly's son. He was a warm-hearted man; how else could he feel? Once he had got out the car and driven to the village where the boy had been nursed, watched him come home from school, and then followed him to slip a half crown into his hand. If only he could bring the little fellow home and see him go to a good school like a Christian, Charlie felt he could put up with a lot from Molly. And he knew that he wouldn't really have to put up with much from her. Under normal circumstances, there was no moral or intellectual strain that Molly could be subjected to which could not be cured by a hearty smack on the backside.

But then his mind would slip a cog and he would think of the scene outside the graveyard, and Nora, grave and pale, stepping over to his side. "In comes the Captain's Daughter, the Captain of the Yeos"; "Romeo, Romeo, wherefore art thou Romeo?"—a couple of lines like those and Charlie would feel himself seventeen again, ready to risk his life for Ireland or anything else that came handy. Whatever misfortune was on him, he knew his mother was right all the time; that he could never be like any other sensible man but would keep on to the day he died, pining for something a bit larger than life.

That night the temptation to go to the pub was almost irresistible. He went as far as the door and then walked on. That was where people went only when their problems had grown too much for them. Instead he went for a lonesome stroll in the country, and as he returned his feet, as if by magic, led him past Nora's door. He passed that too, and then turned back.

"God bless all here," he said pushing in the door. She was sitting in the dusk and rose to meet him, flushed and eager.

"Come in, Charlie," she said with real pleasure in her tone. "You'll have a cup?"

"I'll have a bucket," said Charlie. "Since I gave up the booze I have a throat like a lime-kiln."

"And did you give it up entirely?" she asked with awe.

"Entirely," said Charlie. "There's no other way of giving it up."

"Aren't you great?" she said, but Charlie didn't know whether he was or not. Like all worriers he had at last created a situation for himself that he could really worry about. As she rose to light the gas he stopped her, resting his big paws on her shoulder.

"Sit down," he said shortly. "I want to have a word with you."

Her face grew pale and her big brown eyes took on a wide, unwinking stare as she did what he told her. If Charlie could only have forgotten his own problem for a moment he would have realized that Nora had also hers. Her problem was what she would say if he asked her to marry him.

"I'm in great trouble," he said.

"Oh, Law!" she exclaimed. "What is it?"

"I had a talk with Father Ring today."

"I heard about that." (There was very little she didn't hear about.)

"He wanted me to get married."

" 'Tisn't much when you say it quick," said Nora with rising colour. From Charlie's announcement that he was in trouble she had naturally concluded that Father Ring wanted him to marry Molly and, now that it had come to the point, she didn't really want him to marry Molly. "I wonder how people can have the audacity to interfere in other people's business like that."

"Ah, well," said Charlie, surprised at her warmth, "he intended it as a kindness."

"It mightn't turn out to be such a kindness," said Nora.

"That's the very thing," said Charlie. "It might not turn out to be a kindness. That's what I wanted to ask your advice about. You know the way I'm situated. I'm lonely down there with no one only the mother. I know it would probably be the makings of me, but 'tis the risk that has me damned. 'Twould be different if I knew I was going to have a family, someone to come in for the business when I'm gone."

"You mean the same thing as happened with Polly might happen with her?" Nora exclaimed in surprise.

"I mean I broke my heart once before," snapped Charlie, "and I don't want to do it again."

"But you don't think the same thing would happen again?" she asked with a hypnotised air.

"But I don't know, girl, I don't know," Charlie cried desperately. "You might think I'm being unreasonable, but if you went through the same thing with a man that I went through with Polly you'd feel the same. Did Polly ever tell you she thought the mother was putting spells on her?" he added sharply.

"She did."

"And what do you think of it?"

"I don't know what to think, Charlie," said Nora, the dusk having produced its periodical change in her views of the supernatural.

"When I married Polly first," Charlie went on reflectively, "she said: 'Many a better cake didn't rise.' The other night she said: 'That's the hand that'll never rock a cradle for you.'" He looked at Nora to see if she was impressed, but seeing that Nora in her innocent way applied his mother's prophecy to Molly O'Regan she wasn't as impressed as she might have been if she had known it referred to herself. Charlie felt the scene wasn't going right, but he couldn't see where the error lay. "What knowledge would a woman like that have?" he asked.

"I couldn't imagine, Charlie," replied Nora with nothing like the awe he expected.

"So you see the way I am," he went on after a moment. "If I don't marry her—always assuming she'd have me, of course," he interjected tactfully—"I'm cutting my own throat. If I do marry her and the same thing happens again, I'm cutting her throat as well as my own. What can I do?"

"I'm sure I couldn't advise you, Charlie," replied Nora steadily, almost as though she was enjoying his troubles, which in a manner of speaking—seeing that her premises were wrong—she was. "What do you think yourself?"

Charlie didn't quite know what to think. He had come there expecting at least as much sympathy and understanding as he had received from Father Ring. He had felt that even a few tears and kisses wouldn't be out of place.

"If she was a different sort of girl," he said with an infinity of caution, "I'd say to her what I said to Father Ring and ask her to come to Dublin with me for a couple of days."

"But for what, Charlie?" asked Nora with real interest.

"For what?" repeated Charlie in surprise. Charlie was under the illusion most common among his countrymen that his meaning was always crystal-clear. "Nora," he went on with a touch of pathos, "I'll be frank with you. You're the only one I can be frank with. You're the only friend I have in the world. My position is hopeless. Hopeless! Father Ring said it himself. 'Marrying

a girl with doubts like that, what can you expect, Charlie?'
There's only one thing that would break the spell—have the
honeymoon first and the marriage after."

It was dark, but he watched her closely from under the peak
of his cap and saw that he had knocked her flat. No one had ever
discussed such a subject with Nora before.

"But wouldn't it be a terrible sin, Charlie?" she asked with a
quaver in her voice.

"Not if 'twas done with a good object," Charlie said firmly,
answering her out of her own mouth.

"I'm sure she'd do it even without that, Charlie," Nora said
with sudden bitterness.

"If she loved me she would," said Charlie hopefully.

"Love?" cried Nora scornfully, springing from her chair, all
her maiden airs dropping from her and leaving her a mature,
raging, jealous woman. "Don't be deceiving yourself like that,
my dear man. That one doesn't love you."

"What? Who? Who doesn't love me?" asked Charlie in stupefaction.

It was her turn then.

"Weren't you talking about Molly O'Regan?" she asked in
alarm.

"Molly O'Regan?" Charlie cried, raising his face to the ceiling
like a dog about to bay. "What the hell put Molly O'Regan into
your head, woman? Sure, I could have Molly O'Regan in the
morning and the child along with her. Isn't that what I was
saying to you?"

"Oh," said Nora, drawing back from him with a look of
horror, "don't say any more!"

"But my God, girl," moaned Charlie, thinking of his beautiful
scene absolutely wasted and impossible to begin on again, "sure
you must know I don't give a snap of my fingers for Molly
O'Regan! You were the first woman I ever gave a damn about,
only you wouldn't have me. I only married Polly because she
was your shadow. Even Father Ring knew that."

"Oh," she cried as if she were just ready to go into hysterics,
"I couldn't do it! I couldn't!"

"No, no, no, no," said Charlie in alarm as though such an idea had never crossed his mind. "You're taking me up wrong. Whisht, now, whisht, or you'll be heard!"

"You must never, never say such a thing to me again," she said, looking at him as though he were a devil in human shape.

"But my God, woman," he cried indignantly, "I didn't. You're missing the whole point. I never asked you. I said if you were a different sort of woman I might ask you. I was only putting the case the way I put it to Father Ring. Surely you can understand that?"

It seemed she couldn't, not altogether anyhow, and Charlie strode to the door, his hands clasped behind his back and a gloomy look on his face.

"I'm sorry if I upset you," he snapped over his shoulder. " 'Tis your own fault didn't marry me first. You're the only woman I ever cared about and I wanted to explain."

She was staring at him incredulously, brushing back the loose black hair from her forehead with an uncertain hand. She looked childish and beautiful. If Charlie had only known, she was thinking what a very queer way the Holy Ghost had answered her prayer. As Polly had once said the Lord's ways were very peculiar. Charlie waited for some sign of relenting in her but saw none and, heaving a deep sigh, he left. Crossing the bridge when the abbey tower was all black and spiky against the sky and the lights in the back of the little shops were reflected in the river, he was like a man demented. He had done it again! This time he'd done it for good. It would soon be in everyone's mouth that he had tried to seduce a second girl. He knew how it would be interpreted. He saw it already like headlines in a newspaper: WELL-KNOWN SHOPKEEPER'S SHOCKING PROPOSAL OUTRAGED FATHER'S INDIGNATION. The girl who had stood by him when no one else would do it—this was her thanks! And it all came of Romeo and Juliet, the Captain's Daughter and the rest of the nonsense. There was a curse on him. Nora would tell her father and Father Ring; between them they would raise up a host of new enemies against him; no one would do business with him—a foolish, idle, dreamy, impractical man!

XI

He let a week go by before he did anything. In that time he realized the full horror of the scrape he had got himself into, and avoided every contact with people he knew. He spent most of his time in the sitting-room, and only went down to the shop when the girl came up for him and he knew that the visitor was a genuine customer and not an angel of vengeance. Finally, he asked Jim O'Regan in for a drink.

Jim was an ex-soldier, small, gaunt, and asthmatic, dressed in a blue serge suit that was no bluer than his face and with a muffler high about his throat. Johnny Desmond gave them a queer look as they entered, but Charlie, seemingly in the highest spirits, rattled away about everything till it dawned on them both that he had opened negotiations for Molly and the child. Charlie could have gone further but one glance at Jim's mean poker face and he remembered the scene outside the graveyard, and then it was as if Holy Ireland, Romeo and Juliet, and all the romantic dreams of his youth started with a cry from their slumber. It was terrible, but he couldn't help it; he was an unfortunate dreamy man.

Later that morning he had to go to the bank. The whole week he had been putting it off, but he could put it off no longer. He gave a quick glance up the street to see that the coast was clear and then strode briskly out. He hadn't gone a hundred yards when he saw Jerry Lawlor coming down the same pavement. Charlie looked round frantically for some lane or shop he could take refuge in but there was none. "Brass, boys, brass!" he groaned. But to his great surprise Jerry showed no signs of anger, only a slight surprise at Charlie's slinking air.

"Good morrow, Charlie," he said, sticking his thumbs in the armholes of his vest, "as you won't say it yourself," he added jovially.

"Oh, good morrow, good morrow, Jerry," cried Charlie with false heartiness, trying to read the signs on Jerry's battered countenance. "Up to the bank I'm rushing," he said confidentially.

"The bank?" Jerry said slyly. "Not the presbytery?"

"What the hell would I be doing at the presbytery?" Charlie exclaimed with a watchful smile.

"Oh, headquarters, headquarters," replied Jerry. "Who was it was telling me you were thinking of taking the field again? I believe your patrols were out."

"Patrols, Jerry?" Charlie echoed in surprise. "Ah, I'm too old for soldiering."

"I hope not, Charlie," said Jerry. "Begor," he added, squaring his shoulders, "I don't know that I'd mind shouldering the old shotgun again in a good cause. Well, be good!" he ended with a wink and a nod.

He left Charlie open-mouthed on the pavement, looking after him. What the blazes did Jerry Lawlor mean? he wondered, scratching his poll. "Be good"—was that the sort of advice you'd expect from a man whose daughter you had just been trying to seduce? "Be good"—was the man mad or something? He couldn't understand why Jerry, who had the devil's own temper, took his advances to Nora in that spirit. Was it possible that Nora had censored them so much that he hadn't understood? Was it—a wild hope—that she hadn't told him at all? His face fell again. No woman could keep a thing like that to herself. If she hadn't told her father, she'd told someone else, and sooner or later it would get back to him. He heaved a bitter sigh. The sooner he could fix up things with the O'Regans the sooner he would be armed to face the attack.

He went on, but his luck seemed to be dead out that morning. As he went in the door Father Ring came out. Charlie gave him a terrified look, but before he could even think of escape, Father Ring was shaking his hand.

"You're looking well, Charlie."

"I'm not feeling too good, father," said Charlie, thinking how far from the truth it was.

"Tell me," said Father Ring confidentially, "you didn't do any more about that little matter we were discussing?"

"To tell you the truth, father," Charlie said with apparent candour, "I didn't."

"Take your time," Father Ring said with a knowing look.

"There's no hurry. I wouldn't be surprised if something could be done about that kid of yours. Mind! I'm not making any promises, but there's a soft corner there for you all right, and the father wouldn't let her go empty-handed. You know what I mean?"

"I do, father," groaned Charlie, meaning that he hadn't a notion, and as Father Ring went round the corner towards the church he stood on the bank steps with his head in a whirl. It was a spring day, a sunshiny day which made even the main street look cheerful, but Charlie was too confused for external impressions. For a week he had skulked like an assassin from Jerry Lawlor and Father Ring, yet here they treated him like lovers. And Nora went to confession to Father Ring! Admitting that he wouldn't let on what she did tell him, he couldn't conceal what she didn't, and it was quite plain that she hadn't told either of them about Charlie. Now what purpose would a girl have in concealing a thing like that? Modesty? But modesty in Charlie's mind was associated with nothing but hullabaloo. There was another flash of hope like a firework in his head, and then again darkness. "Christ!" he thought despairingly. "I'm going dotty! 'Tis giving up the drink in such a hurry."

"Morra, Charlie," said a farmer going in, but Charlie didn't even acknowledge the salute. His face was screwed up like that of a man who has forgotten what he came for. Then he drew a deep breath, pulled himself erect, and set off at a brisk pace for the Lawlors'.

Nora came out when she heard him banging on the door and gaped at him with horror-stricken eyes. He pushed her rudely back into the kitchen before him.

"Sit down, sit down!" he said shortly.

"What would I sit down for?" she asked in a low voice, and then her knees seemed to give way and she flopped.

"When can you marry me?" asked Charlie, standing over her like a boxer, ready to knock her flat if she rose again.

"Why?" she asked in a dead voice. "Wouldn't Molly O'Regan have you?"

"Ha, ha," laughed Charlie bitterly. "I see the tomtoms were working this morning."

"I suppose you think we don't know that 'tis all arranged?" she asked, throwing back her head to toss aside the stray curl that fell across her face.

"The trouble with you," Charlie said vindictively, "is that you always know other people's business and never know your own. When you met the one man that cared for you you let him slip. That's how much you knew. You're trying to do the same thing now."

"If you cared for me you wouldn't ask me to disrespect myself," she said with mournful accusation.

"If I didn't, I wouldn't ask you at all," snapped Charlie. "Now, I'm asking you properly. Once and for all, will you marry me?"

"But why should you?" she asked in a vague hysterical tone, rising with her hands thrown out and her head well back. "You know now the sort of woman I am. You need never respect me any more."

"What the hell is up with you?" shouted Charlie, almost dancing with fury. Whatever he said to this girl seemed to be wrong.

"There's nothing up with me," she answered in a reasonable tone which was as close to lunacy as anything Charlie had ever heard. "I know what I am now—that's all."

"And what are you?" asked Charlie in alarm.

"You ought to know," she said triumphantly. "I didn't slap your face, did I?"

"You didn't what?" cried Charlie with an agonized look.

"Oh," she cried in a rapture of self-abasement, "I deceived myself nicely all the years. I thought I was a good-living woman but you knew better. You knew what I was; a cheap, vulgar, sensual woman that you could say what you liked to. Or do what you liked to. I suppose it's the just punishment for my pride. Why would you marry me when you can get me for nothing?"

Charlie had another flash of inspiration, this time inspiration mixed with pity and shame. He suddenly saw the girl was fond of him and would do anything for him. Jessica, Juliet, the Captain's Daughter, the whole blooming issue. This was the real thing, the thing he had always been looking for and never found. He nearly swept her off her feet as he grabbed her.

"God forgive me!" he said thickly. "The finest woman in Ire-

land and I tormenting you like that! Your father and the priest
have more sense than me. Put on your things and we'll go down
and see them."

"No, no, no," she cried hysterically like a Christian martyr
offering herself to the lions. "Your mother said I'd never rock
a cradle for you."

"My mother, my mother—she has me as bad as herself. Never
mind what she says."

"But what'll you do if she puts spells on me?" she asked in a
dazed tone, putting her hand to her forehead.

"Roast her over a slow fire," snapped Charlie. He was himself
again, aged seventeen, a roaring revolutionary and rationalist,
ready to take on the British Empire, the Catholic Church, and
the Wise Woman all together. "Now listen to me, girl," he said,
taking her hands. "No one is going to put spells on you. And no
one is going to haunt you, either. That's only all old women's
talk and we had enough of it to last us our lives. We're a match
for anyone and anything. Now, what are you doing?"

"Making the dinner," said Nora, blinking and smiling at anything so prosaic.

"We'll have dinner in town, the four of us," said Charlie. "Now
come on!"

He stood behind her grinning as she put on her hat. She put it
on crooked and her face was blotched beyond anything a powder-
puff could repair, but Charlie didn't mind. He felt grand. At
last he had got what he had always wanted, and he knew the
rest would come. (It did too, and all Mrs. Cashman's spells didn't
delay it an hour.) As for Nora, she had no notion what she had
got, but she had an alarming suspicion that it was the very opposite of what she had always desired.

(Which, for a woman, is usually more or less the same thing.)